THE BRINKMAN

THE
BRINKMAN

by

Desmond Meiring

CONTEMPORARY FICTION
HODDER AND STOUGHTON
London 1965

© DESMOND MEIRING 1964

*This Contemporary Fiction edition was produced in
1965 for sale to its members only by the proprietors,
Readers Union Ltd, at Aldine House, 10–13 Bedford
Street, London W.C.2 and at Letchworth Garden
City, Herts. Full details of membership may be
obtained from our London address. The book is set
in 10 point Plantin type leaded and has been printed
by C. Tinling & Co Ltd, Prescot, Lancs. It was
first published by Hodder & Stoughton Ltd.*

AUTHOR'S NOTE

This novel does not have anything to prove about the ideologies of either of the world's two great power blocs. It is concerned with the man or nation caught between them.

In May 1961 the right-wing Lao Government's expensively-equipped Royal Army ran so fast and far from the left-wing Pathet Lao and from the independent-minded Captain Konglé's paratroopers that the formation of a neutralist Lao government could no longer decently be postponed. Many people who were politically moderate or who were saddened by waste had advocated that solution for years.

This story's action is set before that date. It occurs between November 1959 and December 1960, against a background of things that happened historically. I have thus seen no point in trying to disguise the identity of its main political figures, like the Princes Souvanna Phouma and Souvannouvong and Boun Oum, or General Nosavan, or Captain Konglé, or Quinim Pholsena, who was machine-gunned to death on the steps of his house, and his wife wounded beside him, in April this year.

I have taken some liberties with history* in order to simplify the plot. Perhaps this is pardonable, because the following of the names of the Lao and of their towns and political parties can be a taxing enough exercise on its own for the Westerner. So the best documented allegations about voting irregularities in the April 1960 elections related in fact to South Laos, and not to Vientiane, where the presence of the U.N. permanent representative and Western Embassies would, one hopes, have tended to limit them anyway.

No qualifications are needed about the plot's main characters, like Jean-Philippe, Cuong, Pridie, Short, Dumergue, Xang, Mai, and Jeanette. They are invented.

Caracas.
7th August, 1963.

---

* See "Historical Note" on page 249.

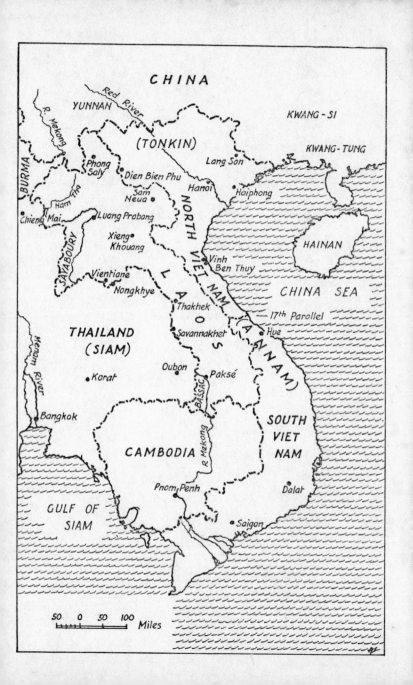

CHAPTER I

"You're sure of Souphan?" said Cuong.

The two men looked down from the first floor window of the house in Vientiane, over the river and the road that ran along it, waiting for the third man who must walk towards them along that road, alone and unsuspecting and damned.

The second man, Xang, sat on his straight wooden chair and watched the road very patiently, like a good pupil. At the interruption, he fanned the fingers of his left hand open on the window-sill in front of him, and studied them quietly. He looked up, and said:

"I thought that his family was in Sam Neua?"

"Yes," said Cuong.

"Yes," said Xang. "Well. They're only a few kilometres from the North Viet Nam border, then. So Souphan will co-operate. He's not a fool."

The two spoke in French.

Xang turned back to the road. It would have been hard to have guessed his age. The profile was high-cheekboned and graceful, remarkably unlined; a Khmer Buddha, but without the sculpted smile of abnegation and tolerance at the corners of the mouth. It was just sure.

"Cuong," he said, without particular irony now, or looking up from the road.

"Yes?"

"Gau will come. Why don't you sit?"

Cuong shrugged and moved his right foot slightly on the seat of his chair and turned his body with it to look back at the river.

It was eight hundred metres across to the Thai bank. The November waters of the Mekong were at their height, swollen by the six months of monsoon rains and the melted snows at their source three thousand kilometres north-west in the peaks of Tibet. The river flowed through the Yunnan, where Xang's Meo had come from two or three hundred years before, and reached and divided Burma and Laos and Thailand. Cuong watched it thrust past from right to left, opaque with silt, ageless and formidable and purposeful and cruel and silent. There were great steps and swirls in the water from the currents, and in places the stripped

9

and twisted branches of uptorn and submerged trees broke its surface. It was like some violent political symbol.

Across it, the Thai village two kilometres upstream was already in shadow. In this region the Thai, ethnically no different, built *pilotis* like the Lao. The front stilts of the village's first bamboo houses drove down over the bank, and the top of the fast smooth waters lapped them. The river rose ten metres between summer and winter, and all summer the Thai threw their refuse diligently down the bank. If you passed then by boat, the village appeared poised delicately upon corruption, drawing its skirts appropriately up against it. The river cleaned the bank and eroded it more every winter.

He looked back to the Lao bank upstream. There were two *pirogues* offshore from the Vientiane customs office. A man squatted in each, still, like a carved part of it, fishing with handlines. In that light the *pirogues* were fantastic on the treacherous waters, long and slim and fragile, artistic constructs more than tools for living. Their bows inclined into the Lao bank. Each would be held to it by a thin steel wire, but he could not see that at this distance. The *pirogues* were static and exactly parallel. This, their lack of any visible anchor, and their improbable angle to the current, strengthened the impression that they had simply been set down there as decoration. The sun fired the low clouds red and gold behind them, and spilled a sheen of silver on the water.

A bullock cart moved past in the road below from right to left, in harmony with the river, under the tall trees which lined it. It threw a thin grotesque shadow forward and across the road in the sunlit intervals between the shadows of the trees. Through the closed window he could hear the creak of the ponderous wooden wheels, carrying the body of the cart high between them. That always looked ludicrously small to Western eyes, a narrow, latticed coffin. He saw the driver's hands, unmoving on his knees above the rumps of the two oxen; the man was certainly asleep. The cart's roof hid his body. The roof sloped up from the back and was curved across like a wimple, so that when he had first seen the cart, coming easily along the road, it had looked like some curiously foreshortened and wheeled Sister of Charity.

The cart moved with the massive lethargy of tradition. The sight of it defeated any idea that it could ever be made to move any faster, even if pursued by *phis* and similar furies. Rapid movement, change, were not the fashion; the cart, the *pirogues*, would not have changed in hundreds of years. He watched it pass, the sun and the gold weight of the day still heavy upon it.

He thought that this could be the real enemy, the sun, the humidity, the great delicate bubble-world which they engendered, sealed and timeless, of languor and grace and subtlety and putrefaction. Perhaps all things, the lush jungles, the people, had fatally to submit themselves to that in the end. If that were true, the Buddha's smile was proof of no elusive metaphysical vision, but of the harshest realism.

Cuong could see nothing else in the road, except a cyclist and a man walking five hundred metres to the right. Both turned in to the *Salle des Fêtes*. There was a CDIN meeting there. The *Comité de la Défense des Intérêts Nationaux,* or Cédin, had recently been formed by ambitious young army officers and administrators. Still only a loose political grouping, not yet a party, it was fiercely critical of the reigning conservative *Rassemblement du Peuple Lao* party under Sananikone, and, even more, of the socialist Peace Party under Quinim Pholsena, and of Prince Souvannouvong's Neo Lao Haksat, which was the extreme left wing parliamentary party that represented the Pathet Lao. The Cédin had already taken on an acute right wing tint. It was obsessed with the idea of action. It had suddenly become very vigorous; somebody was backing it hard with money. The Pathet expected a push from it soon, probably led by the young generals. But its meeting was useful that evening. Almost all the government employees had been volunteered to it. The foreign firms shut at five; at five-fifteen it was still early for the *farangs* to come down for their walk by the river. The road should be clear for another twenty minutes.

To Cuong's right, Xang looked down at his watch, and back to the turning eighty metres to the right which led down from the town's centre. The fingers of Xang's left hand still rested on the window-sill; not at all anxiously; rather, they contrived to look bored. They were long and slender, elegantly violent.

"Well?" said Cuong.

"A few minutes either way," said Xang. "Gau's a man of habit."

Again, he seemed irritatingly detached, professional.

Cuong had come down with him the week before from Xieng Kouang, from the high clean blue hills. In that part on most days the crests were cut out icily from the lighter clear blue of the sky. On others mist or low thin cloud hazed them, and lent them the infinite depth of Chinese painting. The two men had come down by lorry until the track was impossible, then by foot across the sodden uniform green bush, spending each night in a different village. Cuong knew the chalk mountains east of Phontiou better, and the region about Attopoeu to the south, a regular route for Viet Minh through to South Viet Nam. The organiza-

tion and intelligence of the Pathet cells in North Laos had surprised him.

The two had rejoined the road seventy kilometres out of Vientiane at the bridge over the Nam Lik, where it was passable
again. The rest of it, north-north-west to the royal capital of
Luang Prabang, was another miracle of modern engineering. It
had washed out permanently years before, three months after the
Americans had opened it officially with an august Ambassadorial
and Ministerial cavalcade. From the Nam Lik he and Xang had
come separately in to Vientiane.

If he alone had been wanted in Vientiane, Cuong would hardly
have needed that degree of precise secrecy in his travelling. His
papers were in order, as indeed were Xang's. The police were
not notably efficient. But Xang was known in the north, it was
senseless to take unnecessary risks, and Xang had of course to
be in Vientiane to identify Gau. Cuong was too experienced to
rule out altogether that it could also be to report on him.

The trip had had a further official purpose. Xang was to talk
and counsel prudence in each village, to keep the contacts alive,
the morale of the cells high. He impressed in that rôle. It was a
question less of his intelligence, which was obvious, than of his
patience.

Cuong knew that it was no act. The man simply had no doubts.
When Xang talked, indeed, he could even sometimes seem an
ironic miniature of Ho Chi Minh, of Uncle Ho, that totally un-
forgettable man, frail and tireless and undeviating revolutionary
in France and Canton and Moscow and his own country, self-
cultured, ascetic, incorruptible and personally disinterested as a
Saint-Just, whose most enduring trait, allied to his practical
political ruthlessness, was precisely that same frightening politeness and evidently inexhaustible patience.

Cuong would sit with Xang on that voyage until very late at
night, in a ring with the men and sometimes some of the women
of the villages, in some hut or *piloti,* round the central slab of
hard baked clay and the small and almost smokeless fire that
burned upon it. Then, no question seemed too trivial for Xang,
and he answered fully, generally only after due silence and de-
liberation, and always including all who sat in the big main room
in his words. It was as if nothing, not even the execution in
Vientiane, could possibly be so important as the villagers' understanding and acceptance.

When a man leaned forward and threw a handful of hard bamboo on the fire, and the light started up, it would show Xang
seated cross-legged, above the end of one of the many long thin

12

flexible bamboo canes which stemmed out to the men from the huge central jar of rice wine, like the spokes of a wheel. Behind him would be a background of fishing nets or crossbows hung on the walls, and of great tubes of bamboo lined against them, filled with water or rice or salt. Xang would sit unmoving, holding his rice-wine cane lightly, out of courtesy, hardly drinking from it; again Buddhic, his eyes looking into the darkness above the fire, and speaking tranquilly.

But in the long daytime marches between the villages he spoke little. It was clear that he felt that there was nothing to be gained from talking then, and that he kept his mental energies dutifully for his Delphic performances in the evenings. If Cuong had not exactly found him stimulating company, Xang's impersonality had not surprised him unduly. He had known that before, in youths grown up in the Resistance. Simply, a part lacked, because they had not had the time for it.

The last of the sun blazed down gold on the still and empty road outside.

"Something could have delayed him," he said.

"It's possible," said Xang.

"One can't exclude that. He could have heard something. Or a premonition."

Xang glanced down at his fingernails and returned to his concentration on the road.

"There's time," he said.

Xang seemed aptly to demonstrate this theory that a man could be defined exclusively by the political cataclysms of his times, and end virtually without personal nuance. What Cuong knew of his history read like a political tract; the father killed in 1922, just after Xang was born, in the last year of the Meo revolt in Xieng Kouang; the bloody French reprisals; the family which had still kept enough of its opium wealth (that most venerable currency of Old China and the Yunnan and the Meo) to send him to the Lycée Pavie in Vientiane for his baccalauréat; his guerrilla under Faydang, the rebel Meo leader, against the Japanese when they invaded in 1940, and against the French when they returned in force at the end of the war in Europe; his part in the action which critically delayed the columns which the French sent across North Laos to Dien Bien Phu in 1954; his subsequent year's indoctrination in North Viet Nam before he returned to work full time in the Pather's political organization in Laos.

Cuong glanced at his profile. It often surprised him to recall that he and Xang were of the same age. The profile was tranquil, dispassionate, remote. There was a willed simplicity in it, and formidable latent strength. This could be Asia's new face. It was that of the cadres in North Viet Nam, the *Can-bô*, in their ascetic faded-olive uniforms; driving, puritan, selfless. Cuong knew that you could not buy that conviction. What then was the trick? How the devil had Uncle Ho done it? What were the springs of action here? The power released could seem demoniac, enough to make men and women gathered in auto-critique vote themselves reasonably and willingly and literally to death, for real or fancied omissions in their national duty.

It was enough, under the French, to turn a Vietnamese peasant who worked all day in his rice-field under a murderous sun into a Viet Minh at night, shooting off suicidal home-made muskets or gathering intelligence or running messages; or to keep a coolie trotting trance-like seven days up the steep jungle paths to deliver twenty kilos of rice to a fighting-man; or, towards the end, to keep tens of thousands of men and women working day and night primitively as insects to repair the key roads after the French aerial attacks, the bursts of the delayed-action bombs barely interrupting their chanting.

It was the drive for independence after seven centuries of Chinese and French domination, a re-birth, a sustained mass surge of the blood as irreversible once started as the obscure communal movements of flights of birds or shoals of fish. It was really that which had broken the armies of a major world power in an eight-year war, with all its élite paratroop battalions and armour and artillery and aircraft and napalm, and cost it fifty thousand dead and seven Saint-Cyr graduations. It had not been the arms, which characteristically the Russians and Chinese had been slow to supply until the power of Ho's movement was already assured. It had not even been the communism, which was largely secondary; Ho had needed a banner, and the West had refused him theirs. His dynamic came from no text-book ideology, but from a simple idea. (The West had apparently forgotten that an idea could still be decisive.) The Viet Minh mystique had been a literal return to the first principles of Buddhist selflessness. Ho's genius had been to discern that simple magic formula, and add a shrewd nationalistic slant to it, at the right historical time, and with complete inner certainty.

Cuong took his right foot off the chair and eased the cramped muscles behind his knee with his hand and looked past Xang up the empty road. He wondered idly if Xang had a wife, children. But the question was not really pertinent; there was always that curious chastity and touch of death to absolute dedication.

There was a roar of applause from the *Salle des Fêtes*, three

times repeated, and he saw Xang glance up towards it. Cuong said:
"Let's hope that they give the Americans a better return."

"Yes, we don't want to lose them yet. Our best advertisement."

"But the hate against Sananikone puzzles me. Pro-Western, after all."

"Too moderate as a Prime Minister," said Xang. "Becoming a respectable old gentleman. The young *ambitieux* want power quickly, and what goes with it. And the generals. He's in their way. And not ruthless enough against us, they say."

He added:

"After all, one must grease one's palms while one can."

Coung smiled. There was that about the *Présence Française*. It left its mark. You even complimented the French by leading most of the revolt against the West in their precise, impeccable language.

"I wonder just how far this is American-supported?"

"The Cédin?" said Xang. "Well, certain of the Americans wouldn't weep to see Sananikone go."

"No. Not the P.E.O. general and the eighty colonels and majors and captains in plain clothes, who in theory only apply the U.S. military aid budget."

"The Pentagon behind them. The C.I.A. The Dulles men in the Embassy. But for a strong nation they're odd. They seem deliberately to have built in a guarantee of confusion. The P.E.O., C.I.A., and Embassy each report back separately to Washington. So you don't have one American policy, here, but three. It could hardly be more favourable for us."

"Well," said Cuong. "We'll need what help we can get."

Xang looked up at him sharply.

"Meaning?"

Cuong pointed towards the ox-cart. It had stopped seventy metres down the road to the left. The two oxen stood peacefully with their heads down. From the back, the driver was caricatured inside the hoop of the roof. His head was perilously far forward on his chest. As still as his oxen, he was happily stunned like them under the last of the sun.

"*Sovkhozes* or *kolkhozes* here?" said Cuong contemptuously. "Communes here? The discipline of communism here? In this farce of a place?"

"You think that impossible?" said Xang.

"In these countries of soft Hinayana Buddhism? Probably. A work of centuries."

Xang went on observing him speculatively. Xang said:

"So you think that we are wasting our time?"

At his tone, Cuong looked down at him quickly.

"What's it, Xang?" he said. "Oh, deviationism and all that?"

"Something like that," said Xang.

"We're back at school again, are we?"

"Ah, one can dispense with that?"

Cuong jerked one shoulder in irritation.

"All right," said Xang. "If you ask. Yes. I find it a little curious that you should query our aims."

He sounded genuinely troubled. He went on after a moment:

"I know of course that you were at That-Khé and Hoa Binh and Dien Bien Phu and Hanoi."

"But as a soldier, Xang."

"Though surely you wouldn't consider political conformity any less important than your military discipline?"

Cuong examined him again, but Xang's question was rhetorical. He was looking back steadily at the road.

It was the authentic tone of the *Can-bô*, thought Cuong. It was hardly hostile, with no personal enmity in it—certainly with nothing personal in it. Paternalistic, rather; gently admonishing, a little disappointed.

And none the less deadly for that.

There was also no point in deliberately antagonizing him. So he followed Xang's gaze and said:

"All right. Yes. I suppose that the Americans must think now that any change must be better."

There was nothing small about the Americans. In the five years since Dien Bien Phu they had put three hundred million dollars into Laos, to create a shield for Thailand and South Viet Nam. It had corrupted some of their own first men. Its net results had been a rash of Mercedes-Benz and two vigorous night clubs in Vientiane with imported Chinese and Cholon and Bangkok taxi-girls, and some astronomic Lao bank accounts in Switzerland and France.

The men of power in Laos had hailed American aid with surprise, some with delight. There was obviously great good will behind it. Its application seemed startlingly naïve, but the effect might be deceptive. Indeed, the American approach could be read to show an outstandingly subtle diplomatic touch. It fitted only too aptly to a nation almost all of whose men had been in a Buddhist monastery at some time or other as part of their education, and were thus conditioned to getting food and clothes and the other necessities of life from others, with absolutely no effort, and certainly with no loss of prestige. After all, even in Laos you did not look a gift horse in the mouth, except perhaps to see whether it really did have gold teeth.

This intelligent reception meant that not much of the aid had got out into the country itself. It was true that it had produced an amateur army of thirty thousand, (North Viet Nam alone had a highly trained army ten times that size) with only two reasonably good paratroop battalions. But it had added nothing dull like new roads, irrigation or other agricultural developments, local industries, health services, or administration worth the name. Indeed, when Cuong had first seen Laos a year before, it had seemed to him truly remarkable that anyone could have injected quite so much money into quite so small a country in such a way as to leave absolutely no trace of it, except these frivolities. It was a feat which required a rare administrative genius. The towns had absorbed the aid as magically as the jungle swallowed a cut clearing.

The Pathet Lao had found these facts no handicap politically. They had not really needed Mao Tse Tung and Ho Chi Minh dicta to convert the countryside. They would indeed have had a hard time of it if that was all that they had had. For the peasant in Laos in his myriad ethnic varieties was certainly no great shakes yet ideologically. On the contrary, he was a feudal, clannish, unsurprised, and feckless sort of fellow, with an unholy reverence for the King or the nearest chieftain, and for every kind of local spirit or *phi* without discrimination. Still, he got the point about the abysmal gulf between what he had and what the brighter citizens in the towns had, if somebody put it to him forcibly enough. The Pathet put it to him forcibly enough. The Americans obligingly provided symbols. For the peasant, and for many of the less fortunate in the towns, that of the Americans themselves and of the acute right wing governments which they supported became increasingly the ruined face of a certain ex-Prime Minister, with his vast and vivid banking and import-export and night club interests; an astute boxer corrupted and gone to seed.

"The French are supporting this too?" said Cuong.

"The new Cédin right wing revolution?" said Xang. "Not the French. Not now."

"It's an old civilization," said Cuong deliberately. "They'd have seen their mistakes."

His continued sympathy for things French was a bourgeois weakness which he knew particularly irritated Xang. Xang looked at him now. He said curtly:

"They've got Algeria. That keeps them busy enough."

"So, Xang?"

"So it's these American boy scouts who'll move things here. To our advantage. They can't choose men. They think that you can buy anyone."

"That's often enough been true here," said Cuong.

"Generally true, even. But not always all the way. The distinction can be important."

"When? Xang. When do they move things, then? The reports said a month."

"The Cédin push? Yes, a month. It's a guess. About a month."

"Boun Ngong would have known the date within a day or two."

"If anyone could," said Xang. "Yes. It's a pity about Boun Ngong."

Cuong had been watching the figure that had come out of the *Salles des Fêtes* and turned towards them. At five hundred metres, against the blood-red sky, the theatrical molten silver of the river, he could see only that it was a man, in a white open-necked shirt and dark slacks. The sight could signal the end of the meeting, and, disastrously, a crowded road. He saw that Xang was watching him also.

The man expanded tiny and laborious, taking his time, as if deliberately provocative. Cuong could see now that he was European, with black hair. He had not crossed the road to walk by the river. That would have been less dangerous. But at least there was no-one behind him yet in the road.

The man reached the turning eighty metres away, at the American Ambassador's house. He glanced up the side road and crossed it. Almost immediately after him, ten or fifteen paces behind, a second man turned into the road, as though rehearsed. He was small, much smaller than the European. He walked crisply, so that the distance between him and the European did not lengthen. From time to time he glanced cheerfully towards the river.

CHAPTER II

"THE second," said Xang.

"You're certain?"

"The second man is Gau," said Xang.

"The first?" said Cuong. "And the first?"

"An unknown."

"We can do nothing," said Cuong. "We can't do anything now."

"Ah. Why?"

"But this makes it impossible!"

Xang did not seem to have heard him. He was watching the two men, his head on one side. It was as though he were listening to them. He got up abruptly.

"Come on."

Con, thought Cuong. Bloody Hero of the People's Republic.

But Xang was already half across the room. He followed him. They went down the wooden stairs and Xang put on the dark glasses and the blue peaked cap. He wore the blue overalls of a driver or mechanic.

The taxi was next to the house, a small Citroën with a van body. Doors had been cut in the body for the back seat. Souphan started the motor and got out and opened the back door and sat at the far side. From his quick planned movements, Cuong retained a sharp image of the skin tight about Souphan's nose and mouth, very white in the brown face. Cuong walked rapidly to the gate, moderating his pace as he turned right into the road.

The *farang* was still forty metres from him. Cuong was amazed that he was not nearer, was not, with the second man, already past the house. He controlled himself to walk casually, the heavy American Colt in his right pocket banging melodramatically against his hip. If they did not notice that and identify it, he should seem no more than a clerk from some small business. His dress was anonymous, a khaki bush shirt and slacks, open leather sandals.

As he approached the *farang* he heard the taxi draw out into the road and turn up behind him; naturally enough, because a lane led into the road past the house. The European ahead of him walked easily, his face half-turned towards the river. He was tall and slim. Cuong moved to his left to give him space, and the man glanced at him curiously.

It was a strong and mocking face, thirty-five, thirty-eight, already struck for life. Thick black hair brushed straight back, jet black. A high forehead, prominent cheekbones, a thin predatory hooked nose, a sensual mouth. A *conquistador*. But what really identified it was the heaviness of the lines about the mouth and eyes, as if that brandished nose, the cheekbones, had disrupted all the structure, so that the skin could not reasonably fold any other way. French, probably Normand. It tugged at his memory. The black eyes examined him.

" 'Soir."

Probably the fool wanted to stop him, ask him the time, the way. Cuong quickened his pace.

" 'Soir, m'sieu."

He dared not glance back to see if the other had stopped and turned. He could feel the taxi coming up behind him, like an arm. He stood squarely in front of the second man. There was a sharp roar from the *Salle* ahead.

"*Monsieu Gau?*"

The man stopped and looked up at him. He was short, thin, a Cantonese of about sixty, dressed immaculately in a white cotton suit.

"*Te connais pas, jeune homme.* How do you know my name? Let me pass."

Cuong held the man's arm lightly with his left hand and dropped his right into his pocket. He forced himself to smile.

"A friend from the north."

The slate eyes filmed at once.

"And what does that mean, precisely?"

But he made no move to go now. Cuong left his arm and pulled the card from his own top pocket. The Chinese looked at it. His eyes turned to the side to the stopped taxi, and Souphan leaned across in the back seat and opened the door. Gau said:

"This is idiocy. In broad daylight. Whatever it is. Come to my house rather."

"This is safer."

The Chinese looked up the road behind Cuong. It was impossible to judge whether he yet guessed anything, that Cuong held the heavy pistol in his right hand and would certainly kill him with it there if necessary. Perhaps Gau's lizard eyes balanced that probability now, against his chances if he called out to the Frenchman. If *he* was watching, he could probably still see nothing damning. Both Cuong's hands were easily in his pockets, the right holding the pistol, but with the muzzle down, so that it made no bulge, and he stood deliberately a little back from Gau. From behind, they should seem only two friends debating whether to take the convenient taxi.

But he could hear nothing from the Frenchman, no sound of steps going away. As he watched the Chinese endlessly he felt the sweat gather under his armpits, in his crotch, across his back. It was as if they—he, Gau, Xang and Souphan in the car, the Frenchman standing somewhere behind—had all been caught there in that configuration by some trick, outside time, or even sound. In that silence, so intense indeed was Cuong's concentration as he watched Gau, cut out in front of him against the blinding silver river and the blood-red sky, that at one moment the man and the road danced in his eyes, and he thought irritably that he should shoot him and have done. If only Gau would strike out, or shout, or run.

The roars came again suddenly from the *Salle*, but this time not incisive, directed, but continuing, like a long sigh; the end of the meeting. At the top of his vision the people erupted out into the road.

Gau had glanced back. As if reassured at that sight, he shrugged and moved quietly across Cuong to the taxi. Cuong held the door for him and got in slowly after him. As the taxi pulled away Cuong hoisted himself and looked quickly out of the back window. The Frenchman had crossed the road finally and stood now by the river, directly opposite the house, as though uncannily he sensed a connection with it. He was looking absently after the car.

Xang, in front, only blue-overalled shoulders, dark glasses, a driver's cap, turned the car right at the Ambassador's house up the side street from which Gau had come. It was not the plan. The meeting had broken too early. By driving right past the *Salle* they could have kept to the river and missed the town's centre.

"Where is it that we go?" said Gau.

"A little way," said Cuong. "A few minutes."

Gau's hands were delicately on his knees in front of him. He was wedged between the two men in the back. Even if he was armed he was no danger like that. No one could see him from outside; the back windows of the van body were set too high.

"The card again, please."

Cuong gave it to him. Gau studied it carefully, leaning forward a little, the points of his elbows on his knees. He looked several times from the photograph to Cuong before he handed the card back.

"Not so good if the police got you with that, my friend."

Cuong laughed.

"In Laos? There aren't many check-points."

"These two?" said Gau.

"Safe enough."

"I've seen this one about. I didn't know that he was with us."

Because Cuong said nothing, Gau added:

"A taxi-driver, I think."

"Yes."

"The one in front?"

"All right."

"And you?" said Gau. "Why a new man again?"

"Security. The usual abrupt changes."

"Vietnamese?"

"Yes."

"Yes," said Gau. "But not *pur sang*, I think. Half European?"

Cuong did not answer. Gau presumably thought that he paid him a compliment. But, unlike most *métis,* anyway of European fathers, Cuong had no pride in that.

"Hanoi?"

"No," said Cuong. "I'm from the south. Saigon."

The taxi had crossed Setthathirat Street. It turned left at the prison. They had not got Souvannouvong there but in the military barracks outside the town on the road to Tangone. Cuong had once heard him talk, at a Popular Front students' meeting in Paris before the world war. Souvannouvong had graduated as a civil engineer from the *Ecole des Ponts et Chaussées*. At that meeting, he had talked of the work in the docks at Le Havre and Bordeaux which he had then done, then, abruptly, of the contrasts between France and his own country. He talked well, with a kind of metallic passion, strikingly incisive and direct. It was as if he had set out deliberately to show, by his manner of speech, that he was as different as possible from the other men of his class and country who had come to France for their education, or to work, or to visit. They were always incredibly graceful people, their speech musical and gay and charming and circumlocutory, shot exquisitely with courteous ambiguities. In contrast to them, Souvannouvong was like the sharp downwards stroke of a heavy pen. He was a short, compact man, the irises of his eyes so black that they seemed lacquered. He was brusque, exact, closed, always seeming extraordinarily cold; yet redeemed at least by that same cold and furious and controlled intensity, as though automatically assuming stature by the very obviousness and arrogance of his certainty that the old ways and gods of his country were dead.

They passed the *Tribunal* and the power station and crossed the Avenue Lang Xang. Xang meant elephant. Land of a Million Elephants, not forgetting the White Parasol. There were three white elephants, superimposed one over the other, facing outwards, on the red background of the national flag, which hung limply above Sananikone's temporary *Présidence du Conseil* building to the left. Though perhaps you could better see them, thought Cuong, as one elephant looking with agility three ways at once, east to North Viet Nam, west to Thailand, and north and most of all to China. It was no historical time to be a small country.

He glanced through the right window of the car and into the Constellation Bar. This, like the Vieng Rattray night club, was one of the town's true political and commercial and social nerve-centres. (Often, they said, in the gay old days of the currency exchange racket which had lasted up to the year before, the night clubs had been the only places where you could ever reasonably hope to find a government minister.) They said that you could learn most things in the Constellation, the current wholesale price for opium, which Chinese taxi-girl was most co-operative, insights on American policy, whether they would really let Souvan-nouvong escape, or would shoot him in the process. (Either might be quite a bright solution. The popular right wing theory was that he had traitorously got regular Viet Minh units from North Viet Nam to spearhead the fighting against the Royal Government which had broken out again in the two north-eastern provinces in August. But, embarrassingly, the right wing had been unable to produce any sort of proof of this.) The Constellation was a resort of the many visiting foreign correspondents. Ministers and the commercially sound lent it a fleeting respectability. Second-rate French and Corsican adventurers met here, from Hanoi and Saigon and Pnom Penh, at the end of the circuit; happily, there was no extradition from Laos. Genuine professionals sometimes visited it, a killer or two from Saigon, pilots from a small opium-running airline, among the last of the buccaneers—

At once Cuong knew the Frenchman.

Thirteen, fourteen years before, by the massive doors of Reims Cathedral. *That* was the Frenchman: a Free French lieutenant who stood with his arms akimbo, below the Christ crowning the Virgin. It was as if that autocratic blend of power, pity, and cruelty in the statue's features, more apt to a pagan king's, had stamped themselves on the face of the man below who observed them with such evident fascination. There was an affinity between the two faces, in the cheekbones, the heavy lines. But in the man the impression was relieved by a kind of sardonic and explosive buoyancy, a disciplined lightness and elasticity like that of a professional dancer. You half-expected him to leap splendidly a great height into the air, like a coiled steel spring, for no obvious reason, and to return precisely and imperturbably to his former position; indeed, whether from alcohol or from that apparently natural caustic zest, he rocked experimentally on his heels as he stood. There was no awe at all in his face; rather, a critical and delighted mirth, as though he had really known all along that the divinities would finally turn out to look just like that. He swung abruptly, clearly feeling himself watched, and looked at Cuong's *maquisard* insignia and at the slung Schmeisser.

"*Merde, T'es des nôtres?*"

"*De la brigade.*"

"*'Vdemment.* Just as well. The question is in fact pointless. Between ourselves, my holster contains silk stockings only. But

23

I'm a devil with my hands, mind. How's Tonkin?"

"No, no. The South."

"Saigon?"

"Saigon."

"Ah. I've read of it, of course. I propose to go there and make my fortune after the war."

"It's kind. But those days are finished."

"*Remerde*," said the lieutenant. "Truly? No more exploitation?"

"No."

"After all that I've read about the Rue Catinat!"

"The Rue Catinat still exists."

"A patriot, clearly," said the lieutenant.

"Well," said Cuong. "That's a big word."

"Yes," said the lieutenant reasonably. "One mustn't exaggerate these things, you know. But seriously?"

"The exploitation? Not if we can help it."

The Frenchman looked disappointed.

"It's always the same damn story," he said. "One's always born too late. You're a student, inevitably. Paris?"

"Paris. Political science."

"But nobody ever made any money at that!"

"In my country they didn't do so badly," said Cuong.

The Frenchman roared with laughter and eyed him with a new respect.

"Going to limit the competition?"

"You could call it that," said Cuong.

"But what an immense whore of a city!" said the lieutenant. "Saigon?"

"Paris," said the lieutenant, irritated. "A monumental tart. A great expensive cow of a cold-hearted tart of a city. We should drink on it."

Cuong smiled.

"I have to get back. I have another fifteen minutes only."

Above his outrageous nose the Frenchman's eyebrows rose impossibly, but he did not look in the least insulted, as Cuong had expected, only intrigued.

"My God, you ought to be an officer."

"My regrets, sincerely. It would have been a great pleasure."

"Another time," said the Frenchman cheerfully. "In Saigon. In Indo-China."

"Another time," said Cuong. "Somewhere in Indo-China."

When he glanced back across the square, he saw that the lieutenant had taken off his *képi* and was bowing ceremoniously to the statue.

"It's a long way that you take me," said Gau suddenly and un-easily, trapped tiny and fragile beside him, the points of his elbows still set delicately on his knees, his hands locked and motionless.

"It's not far to the end of this road," said Cuong.

CHAPTER III

IN front of them Xang had certainly heard that. It was as if his back listened, its lines deadly, if Gau could have read them. Xang increased his speed fractionally, past the buildings on the right which normally housed the *Présidence du Conseil*, and which Sananikone had lent to the Security Council sub-committee.

The investigators had found no evidence that regular Viet Minh units had invaded the two north-eastern provinces since the fighting erupted there again in August, nor would they find any. The Pathet were not that foolish. Cuong knew that they did not have to be. Their cadres were trained in North Viet Nam, certainly, but Pathet Lao meant about what it said, the Country of Laos, and that was where the revolt came from. Many Pathet militants came from the racial minorities who together made up half Laos' population, and whose existence the right wing governments had tended to ignore except when it came to gathering taxes. The government had produced a few captured weapons to illustrate North Viet Nam's sinister rôle in the revolt. Some were Czech and Chinese. Ironically, as many were American, probably from those which the Viets had taken at Dien Bien Phu, or from the stocks which the American O.S.S. had supplied direct to Ho Chi Minh when they sought him as an ally against the Japanese in 1945.

The taxi reached the burst of Chinese shops before the Evening Market. There was a traffic policeman at the crossroads ahead. This was the main Chinese quarter. The shops held an extraordinary variety, silks from Shantung and Hong Kong and Bangkok. Chengmai cottons, Japanese radios and bicycles and cameras and cigarette-lighters and clocks and watches, cigarettes from America and Britain and Saigon, cheap paperbacked novels from America and France, bronze and gilt Buddhas, trinkets and necklaces of rich yellow Lao gold, Lao belts of silver and gold, Lao swords curved as scimitars, and Thai silver bowls of all sizes from across the river. Every seventh or eighth shop was a restaurant, serving

Shanghai or Pekin or Canton or Vietnamese style. The place was like a child's sumptuous dream, shot vividly with colour and glittering with light, billowing with rich movement.

For at this hour of the late afternoon the people pulsed ceaselessly in and out of the shops and the streets which led back at right angles towards the river, or clustered briefly about the wheeled one-man kitchens of the soup and dried-fish vendors next to the pavements. They could have been following some deep and conscious plan, like ants in intricate yet directed mass manoeuvring.

Cuong saw Lao girls among them, in sleeveless blouses, with heavy gold-embroidered scarves over their left shoulders, and in long Lao skirts to well below their knees, the hems burdened with gold thread. Their hair, black and thick and shining, was drawn directly up off their foreheads, and coiled at the back or side. It left their faces curiously naked and serene, of a passive and frank carnal beauty totally without sense of sin. He saw a few Thai Dam and Meo women, sober in black, the Meo wearing heavy silver earrings and massive silver rings about their throats. The Vietnamese girls moved among them swift and light and delicate as cats. They were oval-faced, their rich black lustrous hair loose to below their shoulders, shod in high-heeled slippers of gold or silver, open to their painted toenails. They were sophisticated and brittle as blown glass figurines, fragile-waisted, in tight high-necked bodices and long ankle-length pantaloons, the bright matching diaphanous outer capes flowing back from their shoulders like foam. There was a powerful impression of animal vigour and fertility to this graceful kalaedeoscopic mass, as though it procreated and multiplied before his eyes.

Almost every shop bore its signs in three languages, some in four, Chinese and French and Lao and sometimes Vietnamese, as if their owners were taking absolutely no chances of missing any trade. The Chinese predominated; logically. The shadows of Mao and Chou and the Marshals and of their six or seven hundred millions fell long and brutal across all this land. The optimists learned Russian, thought Cuong drily, the pessimists Chinese. The Genghis Khan scythe would not leave Reims and Chartres and Racine.

The car stopped suddenly, three back from the policeman. A line of Army jeeps and armoured cars crossed in front of them to the left towards the river, the officers projecting static from the turrets.

"To think that I walked from here," said Gau.

"Your shop, of course."

26

"On the left, near the corner."

A counter, half-glass-fronted, choked with clocks, transistor radios, watches, cheap cameras, china, Thai jewellery. The shop behind was dark, a single compartment. Cuong could see no one in it, though certainly someone sat there silent and alert and watched from the back. If one sought a symbol for the economic might of the Overseas Chinese, this could be it.

Gau leaned across him. The movement was so casual that Cuong did not notice it until the door handle was half open.

"I should tell my wife."

Cuong gripped his wrist lightly.

"You won't be with us long."

In front, the policeman's arm dropped and the two cars ahead moved and the taxi jerked forward. Gau brought his hand back to his lap, and looked ahead quietly. Had he intended to play it like that from the start? But he could only just have seen that chance. It was essential to keep him talking; he could still scream out here, and save himself.

"You didn't go to the meeting?"

"The Cédin meeting?" said Gau. "No. It would perhaps have been reckless. Anyway, unnecessary. I'll have the full reports at my house in an hour. I've already seen the drafts of the speeches."

"Militant?"

"Militant, decidedly."

Gau said again:

"The reports will be at my house."

"Yes," said Cuong. "You said."

"You'll want to see them, of course," said Gau.

"Of course," said Cuong. "We must go and look at them."

"Perhaps even now," said Gau. "Perhaps they have already arrived at my house, even now."

"Yes," said Cuong. "But later. Later will be all right."

They came out on to the main airport road. Only a sudden police or army check could stop them now.

"When will they act?" said Cuong.

"The coup? It must come. Perhaps next month. Nosavan needs to be sure of the older generals. And certain others. The Cédin, there's already no doubt."

"Is their intelligence any better?"

The Chinese looked down at his hands. He had cupped them together. It was as if he looked down at something that he held. He said at last, very carefully, so that, if Cuong had had any doubt before of his guilt, he had none now:

"Boun Ngong, of course. They got him."

"Yes. And the other that someone will dig up by accident one day out of a rice-field or pull out of the river."

Cuong knew at once that he had not kept the hatred and contempt out of his voice. He thought that he had seen Xang's back ahead of him tighten suddenly, as if in warning. But Gau must have seen that too. For the first time, he was looking intently at Xang, from his back to the dark glasses and the visored cap reflected in the driving mirror. Cuong looked quickly out of the car window, but they were travelling at fifty kilometres an hour now and the road ahead was absolutely clear. Even if Gau could get out it would be suicide at this speed.

In the driving mirror, Cuong could see Xang's face tilt upwards slightly for a second and he could sense the eyes behind the dark glasses look back directly at Gau. Xang said:

"Gau."

Cuong felt the man next to him shudder abruptly.

"It's silenced, Gau. He can shoot you now without problems. No one would notice."

Gau dropped his head suddenly. A kind of current seemed to go out of him.

Cuong saw the blur of the shambling airport buildings on his right. There was an Air Laos Stratoliner on the hard standing, fat bellied, its four screws turning silver in the last of the sun. A man in blue uniform ahead of it flagged its motors dead.

Xang held his speed through Wattai village. Past it he turned left at the fork to the Princess. The road ran parallel to the river. They saw no one, except two men walking, an old woman alone. Eight kilometres along, Xang took the car down a rutted track to the left through a thick belt of trees. He stopped at the *piloti*. There were lines of trees a hundred metres either side of it; probably an old rice-field. The river fifty metres in front looked very fast, lines of scum like the froth of beer on it.

"Stay with the car."

Souphan nodded.

The three went up the wooden stairs. The light was already weak inside the room, through the open windows that looked on the river. Xang relocked the door. There was a table and two wooden chairs in the room, at the side, and a kerosene lamp on the table. Xang lit it and pulled the shutters in and latched them. He took a heavy clasp knife from his right pocket. He did not open it. Gau watched him from the centre of the room while Xang walked up to him and hit him across the face. Gau made no sound when he got up from the floor. The closed knife had cut his cheek at the left of his mouth, so that his lips seemed to turn abruptly up in prolongation at the corner. Gau stood with his hands hanging straight at his sides and watched Xang.

"Who else did you talk to?"

Gau did not seem to have heard him. At first the blood from his mouth glanced off the front of his white cotton jacket, but after a while the cloth began to accept it like blotting-paper. Gau glanced down at it and an expression of irritation came on his face and he turned his head slightly so that the blood fell directly on to the floor. The drops made small dark soundless explosions in the thin yellow light.

"Gau!"

But Gau continued to watch him passively. He gave the curious impression of an initiate at a ceremony, willing, but uncertain what to do next.

Xang stepped up to him and jerked suddenly down at the front of his trousers. They fell about Gau's ankles. The front of his shirt projected down from under the jacket, over the thin and hairless legs.

"Give it to me. Take his arms."

Cuong gave him the Colt. Xang took it in his left hand. Cuong stood behind Gau and felt over his coat pockets and under his arms, but Gau carried nothing. Cuong held his arms. He saw Xang put the pistol into his left pocket to free his hands, and he heard the sharp click of the knife blade opening. Xang came forward to the Chinese. Cuong could no longer see Xang's hands, but, through Gau's body, he felt distinctly when Xang laid them on the Chinese; it was like the electric shock of contact when a fish strikes on a line. Gau did not resist, but suddenly he jerked his body forward and screamed like an animal.

"Take it."

Cuong stood away from Gau. Xang took the pistol from his left pocket and gave it back to him.

Gau stood exactly as he had before. He took deep rasping breaths, through his open mouth, like a man numbed by icy water.

"We've got all night, Gau. Tomorrow. The next day. No one comes here."

The blood soaked now through the front of Gau's shirt, but he had begun to breathe more easily.

Cuong recalled suddenly where he had seen this kind of judgment before, made of a man virtually before he had had the chance to speak in his own defence; at the People's Courts during the 1953 Agrarian Reform in northern Viet Nam. An officer

29

in Ho's élite regular army, never a commissar, he had always been able to avoid taking an active part in a Court, though not of attending it when his unit was in a village when one was held. By a wickedly significant symbolism, the landowner to be judged did not even stand on a level with his judges, but below them, in a hole already dug for him.

Gau moved his mouth heavily, as though experimenting with it.

"What am I supposed to have done? Finish it. Get on with it."

The Courts had often been no more than stylized murder, the Agrarian Reform a bloody failure, like the *Cent Fleurs*. But there was no doubt about the justice of *this* judgment. Betrayal of your fellows unto death was the greatest crime, punishable only by the same pain and death. That was a law older than those of any mere political system, old as the blood.

"Thanh too?" said Xang. "Did you sell Thanh too?"

Gau looked round at Cuong, as though noticing him for the first time, as if it were he who had spoken. Cuong looked back at him without expression.

At that moment his mind had in fact jumped back twenty years to something that the visiting Jesuit had said at the school in Saigon, in reply to a question. Be logical, he had said. If the Church's existence itself is threatened there is no law of humanity or morality which should not be broken to preserve it.

"Gau," said Xang. "Your wife's had a message."

Gau looked back at him in quick cunning.

"No," said Xang. "There's no help there." He looked at his watch. "Ten minutes ago. In Chinese. A good copy of your script."

"What did it say?" said Gau.

" 'In Bangkok for four days'. That's all. But enough, isn't it?"

The Chinese went on looking at him.

"The gold that's flown into Vientiane," said Xang. "The two kilos that you sent to Bangkok last week. Somebody could have found out about that. You can fix these things, of course, but it takes time, personal contacts. Who else knew about it, Gau? Only your wife, Praves in Nongkhye. So she won't tell anyone that you've gone, will she?"

"What do I get?" said Gau. "You're going to kill me. You're going to kill me anyway, aren't you?"

"Why should you get anything, Gau?" said Xang. "You don't get anything."

Cuong thought that Gau probably understood that by now.

Xang's voice gave nothing. It was too level, dispassionate, reasonable, patient. It would have been much less deadly if it had been openly hostile.

Gau looked down at the front of his shirt. The bloodstains had spread by now, in odd twists and convolutions, like those of some curious wild textile design. Gau looked up again slowly at Xang.

"What could you give me, after all? What could you give me now, Xang?"

He sounded honestly curious.

"As you like," said Xang. "We've time. There are many possibilities. Your nails, Gau. Like Boun Ngong. The small sack of sand. And another thing altogether. But you're an intelligent man, Gau. You'll have thought of that."

The wick of the kerosene lamp spurted and Cuong saw the shadows of the two men blacken and dance, and he went to the table and adjusted the flame.

"Another thing," said Gau. "No. What do you mean?"

"Your son's fifteen now, isn't he? He comes out of the senior class in the Lycée at twelve tomorrow. Shall I tell you how he goes? Down Lang Xang, left at the Boulevard Circulaire. Then second right and straight down towards the river. There's less traffic after the Boulevard. You recommended that; it's safer. Let's say, usually safer."

About three seconds after Xang had stopped Gau's legs gave way neatly, exactly as though someone had just hit him hard behind the knees. On the floor his legs stuck straight out in front of him, parted, as if in some kind of formal gymnastic. He looked up at Xang and moved his mouth.

"If I tell you—"

"Think a little. With you dead, of what conceivable interest are your wife and children to us?"

"The American," said Gau.

"We know that," said Xang. "But Thanh? You gave him Thanh too?"

Gau was holding his hands down over his genitals now. He did not look down at them. He showed no sign of pain.

"It wasn't always necessary to tell him the truth," he said reflectively. "He pays for anything. If one wanted money, one had only to invent something. Anything would do. Yes, Thanh too. Naturally, sometimes one had to give something of worth."

"Boun Ngong, we know."

"Yes."

"How much?" said Cuong.

Gau looked round at him. He gave him the figure.

"Dollars?"

"Swiss franc equivalent, Zürich."

"Who else are they using now?" said Xang.

Gau turned his palms upwards and examined them and wiped them on the sides of his shirt and gave Xang three names.

"Get them down," said Xang.

Cuong took out paper and a pencil and put the pistol on the table, next to the lamp, and wrote them down. Xang repeated the names, and Gau corrected him once.

"The coup?"

"You know it. That was true. A month."

A long shudder went through Gau's body. Curiously, it made no change to his face, as if he divorced himself from the pain by an effort of will. Xang looked down at him steadily.

"To think of it, Gau. A hero of the Long March. The years in the north. The return."

The contempt in his voice was the first personal comment that Xang had permitted himself. Gau looked up at him with hatred. The violence gave him a fleeting dignity.

"What was that but survival, you fool? You and your theories. All of you. What is any of it for us but survival?"

Against the silence, Cuong said:

"Xang."

"Yes."

"This theatre has some purpose now? He's finished. He's dry."

Xang looked across at him. Cuong could see him considering whether his comment showed a culpable bourgeois sentimentalism or a neat sense of professional economy. In fact, there was probably nothing more that they could learn from Gau. Xang dropped his eyes to the old man.

"Yes. All right. Get up."

Gau put his hands on the floor and levered himself up. Now that he stood again he seemed suddenly diminished in stature. He bent and pulled up his trousers and held them about his waist.

After the shut and kerosene-lit room the night outside had a curious impact, too black, too vibrant with the multiple sounds of its frogs and crickets and insects, as if through some acoustic trick. Gau stumbled once going down the stairs, and Cuong caught him automatically. He saw the white blur of Gau's face as he turned it to him.

"Pardon. My thanks."

"It's nothing."

"It's that I see badly, at night, you understand."

Cuong could make out Souphan standing by the car, but Souphan did not look at them as they went past towards the river.

There was a *pirogue* far across under the Thai bank, a thousand metres away, downstream from them, and going downstream, its existence and movement shown only by the pale light in its bows. Ten metres from the edge of the water Gau began to run towards the *pirogue*, though he must have known that it was much too far away to help him, even for its occupants to hear him if he shouted. It was as if instinctively he was impelled to make some last gesture towards life. It could be no more than that, indeed, because it was clear that he was not seriously trying to escape. He ran without great conviction, holding his trousers tight about his waist, and he did not cry out. The pistol made a dull, flat sound, and Gau stopped at once and stood fully erect, his arms flung out wide; still absolutely and obediently silent, his trousers coiled again ridiculously about his ankles. It was as if he had jerked up mechanically like that at the command of a string, as if one connected him to the silenced snout of the pistol. When Cuong shot him again he stumbled forward and the edge of the current plucked at his trousers. He bent slowly for them and then stayed down and relaxed very quietly into the water, his face downwards. It was like watching a man ease himself slowly down into a bath of hot water.

Cuong could see no bubbles coming from his head when he stood in the water over him.

"We ought to weight him," he said. "We ought to tie something to him."

"Push him out," said Xang. "The bank shelves quickly here."

Cuong saw that Gau's white cotton jacket had opened in the water below him. Its two sides undulated in the current, on each side of his body, like the wings of a drowned insect.

"In the *piloti*," said Cuong.

"There's nothing in the *piloti*."

Xang had come into the water next to him.

"Like this, he'll come up again," said Cuong.

"So he comes up again," said Xang. "Let them see him. Let him come up again."

They pushed him out together. As they bent, the water came tepid up to their elbows, to their shoulders. Gau was suddenly heavy, as if the water had lent his small body substance. The current caught and took him, slackened out and face downwards in it, down and towards the centre of the stream. In a minute they could see only the back of his head, progressing small and steady and dogged, and after that only the water, and the fast thin lines of froth upon it.

CHAPTER IV

"YOU speak English extraordinarily well, Jean-Philippe."

Pompous bastard, thought Jean-Philippe absently, extracting his predatory nose from the tankard. Pridie had asked them to bring their drinks to the table. The Black Velvet, half dry champagne, half Irish Stout, was iced and lethal. Jean-Philippe eyed the last of it with regret, the long dark lines of froth across its surface.

"Thanks," he replied in English. "So do you, really, Pridie."

There was a small startled silence, then a ripple of laughter round the table. Pridie, with a true social expert's subtlety, assessed its weight, accepted it, and bent with it and smiled.

Jean-Philippe watched his reaction with interest, smiling gently too, admiring Pridie's easy control under fire. For Pridie's American accent was unmistakable, studied, perhaps even affected. Pridie used it like a statement of his nationality and Republicanism, like a banner. In all other things he seemed more English than the English; possibly that was an addiction peculiar to New Englanders. Most of his clothes were recognizably Savile Row, and he clearly liked to appear in those that were. That evening, putting most of his guests to shame, he wore a smart tropical-weight London suit in dark blue, a white silk handkerchief discreet at his breast pocket. Jean-Philippe had even seen him in a hacking-jacket three days before, when it had rained steamily. Commenting automatically on the weather, Jean-Philippe had looked down quite unsatirically for the hounds at Pridie's feet.

For Pridie certainly always convinced dramatically. Moreover, the racial ideal which he seemed bent on exhibiting by his appearance remained remarkably consistent, at least until he started to talk. Jean-Philippe had also seen him when the American had got back a week earlier from one of his mysterious trips to Nam Tha, where the north-west tip of Laos bordered Yunnan and the Shan States of Burma. (Dumergue, who sat beside Jean-Philippe that evening, had a cruel and possibly apocryphal theory that these were to deliver crates of Coca-Cola, Chinese editions of *Reader's Digest*, and similar ideological encouragement to the remnants of the Kuomintang troops which the Red Chinese had beaten into that corner years before, and who from then on had led a feckless, marauding existence, remaining nonetheless remarkably well armed and supplied.) Then, Pridie had worn a bush-hat, a bush-shirt, khaki slacks, and short leather mosquito boots. He had looked every inch an East African professional hunter, but still unmistakably an English one.

Pridie was aptly built for his aristocratic myth. He was tall and extremely slim, and when he stood had naturally that casual fluidity, that supple arrogant deference of posture, sometimes set in tall men by the easy assumption of social position, wealth, and power. He was clean-shaven, with wide-set and very light grey eyes, behind rimless glasses as discreet as his breast-pocket handkerchiefs, so that you hardly noticed that he wore them. His hair was black and slightly and elegantly grey at the sides. Despite this cinematic touch Jean-Philippe did not put his age at more than thirty-eight.

The Chinese boy brought the hors d'oeuvres and, at Pridie's sign, poured an iced Chablis.

The room in one section of which they now sat and dined was large, part of a single-storied brick house set on short pillars. It was well appointed. One wall was taken up by book-shelves, heavy polished planks of teak, separated by red bricks. Jean-Philippe had glanced at the titles of the books before dinner, not wishing to miss so obvious and convenient a commentary. They were broadly sociological or cultural, including bound volumes of *France-Asie* for four years back, and the standard French works on Angkor Wat with their magnificent illustrations. Almost a full shelf was filled by political studies on Asia, from Stanford and Cornell universities mainly. The selection was professional. Below it, a little surprisingly, were several thick and severely technical books on psychiatry. A paper-backed rash of the more recent *avant-garde* French plays and novels lent an accent of light relief.

A rattan sofa and several matching armchairs, comfortably upholstered, took up another wall. Two Khâ drums, shaped like the stanchions of great ships, stood between them to serve as side tables. On one, nonchalantly obscene, was the gleaming white skull of what seemed to be a tiger, with all its teeth. It was mounted on dark wood and the cranium had been indented to take a bakelite ashtray. A curved Lao sword hung on the wall behind the sofa between two Shan knives, their scabbards tasselled, each silver-mounted hilt ending in a tiger's tooth; the beasts, Jean-Philippe had thought, were evidently less competent in this region than was popularly supposed. There were alcoves on either side of the entrance to the room, from a short hall. A Chinese ritual

35

bronze vase stood in one; Pridie had told him deprecatingly that it was 12th century B.C. The other held a Buddha head, small and unlined and graceful, which Jean-Philippe guessed to be from Ayutia. But he was not at all impressed by the pair of elephant's tusks which stood under the alcoves, for all that this was the country's royal beast, laboriously used by the King in some of his major processions in Luang Prabang. The tusks were certainly from Laos. Jean-Philippe thought them diminutive, wrenched unfairly from some mere miniature creature, and here at least he judged professionally; some years before he had spent three weeks fruitlessly chasing bull elephants in Somaliland with a photographer for an illustrated paper, and he bitterly recalled the size of these harmless but deceptively agile animals and of their armament.

The room contained no paintings or prints, and only one drawing, half-hidden in the shadow above the bookcase. It was in charcoal, of a woman's face, and must have been done when she was about forty-five. It showed an almost pointed chin, a thin wide mouth, an acquiline nose. The eyes were wide set, and the brow arresting, that of a Greek statue. It was drawn full face. The impact was executive and considerable, so much so that Jean-Philippe, after looking at it, had recalled its subject's sex with surprise.

"And what did the Embassy say about that?" Marivell asked Pridie.

Jean-Philippe glanced at Marivell and round the table. The guests were well assorted. Marivell and his wife were French, old hands in Laos, Dumergue, who sat beside Jean-Philippe, was French too. There was a quiet graceful couple called Justin, Lao, but very francophile. There was a large new American called Wainwright, with a fierce gaunt wife. Finally, there was a dark and vivid girl sitting half-opposite to Pridie, whose name he could not remember.

"I really have no idea," Pridie replied to Marivell. "I go to the Embassy so seldom, you see."

The guests' laughter now supported him appropriately.

Indeed, as cultural attaché, Pridie seemed to have a splendid liberty from set hours of work. In the month that he had been in Vientiane, Jean-Philippe had come across him at original times of the day and night, in the Constellation or other bars or restaurants, generally with Lao Ministry officials or Army or Police officers, and once or twice with cabinet ministers.

"Well," said Marivell. "I heard that it was very well organized, for a political meeting here."

"The Cédin meeting?" said Jean-Philippe. "Yes, it was. I looked in on it for fifteen minutes. Quite a crowd, and highly disciplined. The cheering was very choral. I even felt impelled to nod approvingly myself from time to time."

"In French, was it?" said Marivell.

"I nodded in French, yes."

Marivell smiled at him patiently.

"Sorry," said Jean-Philippe. "No, the speeches were almost entirely in Lao."

"You didn't go?" Marivell said to Pridie.

"No," said Pridie. "Have some wine."

Jean-Philippe saw Marivell glance at his wife, and her smile back, presumably to show that she was following the English successfully. He was surprised that Marivell had known about the Cédin meeting. Marivell was a triumphantly vague man, slim and docile and dedicated and fair-complexioned, who looked much younger than he was. A Unesco counsellor, he worked passionately at the Lao Ministry of Education. Marivell did not like to wear his glasses in company. The absence of this usual shield made him look gallantly naked, slightly defenceless, and wrapped up in his own thoughts, really aware of the presence of only one other person, his wife. Or perhaps that remoteness was a heritage of the war; a member of the underground, he had spent three years in one of the more lethal of the German concentration camps. Jean-Philippe believed that there was a fatality to appearances. You always grew into them sooner or later. It was a thought which sometimes sobered him when he shaved himself in the mornings. Marivell's would always attract the arbitrary cruelties of life. Symptomatically, he and his wife had lost their youngest child from polio some months before, after it had suffered bitterly.

The Chinese produced the snipe cooked in red wine, sauté potatoes, green peas, and served the Châteauneuf du Pape; Jean-Philippe noticed the label, 1953. Pridie was looking quietly round the table.

"You can always run a hotel if they throw you out here, Peter," said the girl half-opposite him.

"That's a nice thought, Jeanette," said Pridie.

"I remember having this once at the Continental in Berne. It wasn't so good."

"No, the management could perhaps be a little more ambitious. I nearly bought that place six or seven years ago, strangely enough. A pity, really. It's a good position."

Now when did I last nearly buy myself a hotel? thought Jean-Philippe.

"That was when you were in Formosa?" the girl said to Pridie.

"Yes," said Pridie. "As I told you, I got across to Switzerland once on leave."

The girl was small and dark and seemed abnormally serious. Pridie had introduced Jean-Philippe to her briefly. He seemed to remember that Pridie had said that she was originally from Lausanne. She had the trim waist and bottom of a model, and, by contrast, startling breasts. He did not think that they owed anything to art. She had told him that she worked as a secretary with the Security Council sub-committee; presumably her fluent English came from the U.N. post in London which she had said that she had had before that.

Jean-Phillipe wondered idly about the strength of Pridie's affair with her, which he read instinctively, or thought he did, by a kind of sexual radar. Pridie looked as though he had sufficient layers of complexity to make the question interesting. He seemed to have a remarkable, even feminine, awareness of people, a sensitivity to atmosphere that made him, among other things, a really excellent host. Indeed, at that moment he glanced across the table at Jean-Philippe, almost as though he had heard the other thinking about him. Jean-Philippe smiled at him cheerfully.

He thought that Pridie's alertness to people seemed notably acute as regards the girl, revealingly so to the keen and critical eye. She had glanced at Jean-Philippe twice during the dinner, and smiled once, and he was certain from the way that Pridie had inclined his head slightly each time that he had not missed that.

Nothing to do with me, thought Jean-Philippe, masticating his snipe with a conscious glow of virtue.

"In fact, how d'you do it?" said Dumergue. "It's just natural?"

Not at all sure what the man beside him meant, Jean-Philippe said safely:

"It's a question of character."

"It always is," said Dumergue. "Your English. If it's not indiscreet?"

"Ah. Not at all. I cheated. I was there at school, partly. At university. My mother was English; we had two homes.

"It's wise," said Dumergue. "English is so useful."

Jean-Philippe glanced at him. Dumergue was looking towards Pridie. Dumergue said:

"After all, the language of the future, in this region."

Catching the undercurrent of bitterness, to balance and mock it, Jean-Philippe said:

"Or Chinese?"

Dumergue looked back at him and laughed.

He was a financial counsellor, part of France's continuing aid to her former Indo-Chinese colonies through the U.N. Jean-Philippe knew that, in Laos at least, these were the men who really carried the administration. In what he had seen in his short time there, he found them no discredit to France. They were generally able, realistic, conscientious, and honest. Above all they knew the local wave-length. They integrated in the country like water. They hunted or fished or photographed or tramped over vast tracts of it. Many spoke Lao well. They ate its food, drank its water and rice-wine, slept colloquially with its women, and occasionally married them. If you needed a bridge between east and west (you did) they were it. They worked, and they were without illusions.

This sense of positive irony was notably marked in Dumergue, whom he had first met in this house that evening. Dumergue was what the French called an ancient of the region, of Hanoi and Saigon and the war. He was one of the few survivors of the notorious and bloody ambush of a French motorized battalion in South Laos in 1954, and thus knew the Viet Minh prison camps; they had that in common. He was a short thick dark vigorous man, with a militant black moustache, and glasses.

"Your wife's not with you?" Jean-Philippe asked him.

Dumergue glinted at him sardonically through his pebble lenses.

"I'm not married. It's more apt here."

"Due to the local circumstances."

"The local circumstances are willing. The Vietnamese women, of course. Venal. The Chinese, a little more difficult. As a point of honour, they require the illusion of emotion first. Brutally, that means several dinners, small presents. It can be costly, and takes time. Yourself?"

"Wifeless, too."

"In that case, we must look at the town."

"Excellent. With pleasure."

"Salad!" said Wainwright, sounding put upon, "I don't think we really should. We've just arrived, you know."

The Chinese had capped the triumph of the snipe with a clean green salad in three large wooden bowls. He had put them, with sets of Italian cut-glass bottles of vinegar and olive oil, democratically down the table.

In the silence, Mrs. Wainwright gave a low poised cough.

"I guess we shouldn't, Peter. Charles is right. I recall that the doctor did say, for newcomers—"

"I can personally assure you—" said Pridie ominously, and stopped.

Mrs. Wainwright looked sharply at the salad bowl in front of her, as though the bowl itself had just used that tone of voice to her. She was a tall flat woman of about forty-nine with extremely blonde hair worn down to her shoulders. This young and gay touch apart, she gave the impression of being stripped for action and knowing her own mind; you knew instinctively that she would fit well on a horse.

"Just as you like, of course," said Pridie, very pleasantly. "We could easily whip you up an omelette. It's been very light."

"Not at all, delicious!" said Wainwright vigorously. It was clear that he was prepared to be quite fair now that he had won his hygienic point about the salad. He smiled round the table, but nobody else was helping. They maintained a resolute and appalling silence, like a hostile union committee. Wainwright fell back finally on his wife.

"Isn't that so, Mary-Anne?"

"Sure," said Mrs. Wainwright like a pistol shot. "Delicious." Mary-Anne, thought Jean-Philippe, delighted.

He knew the husband to be recently arrived in the upper hierarchy of the enormous and shambling United States Operations Mission to Laos. Wainwright was a big man, heavy-shouldered, with iron-grey hair. It was very short, crew-cut, possibly sensibly to align with the remarkable ruddy boyishness of his features.

Pridie had tactfully raised a small separate hum of talk. Jeanette's voice emerged from it.

"I can't really see what else Sananikone could have done. With the strength of the Pathet advance, surely he could only appeal to the Security Council—"

"Wasn't it in fact Khopkhan," said Dumergue suddenly, in his heavy English, "who appealed to the U.N. over Sananikone's head?"

"The Cédin man?" said Jeanette. "The Foreign Minister? Well?"

"Well. Wasn't it just panic, an admission that the Royal Army could never hold more than the main towns? That the government has no support to speak of in the country?"

"What about the Viet Minh battalions?" said Marivell, loyally expressing what was presumably his host's official view.

"Have you seen them?" said Dumergue. "Has anyone? Do they really exist, except of course in North Viet Nam?"

Jean-Philippe saw Wainwright look puzzled and turn to Pridie.

"But these Pathet Laos are *communists*, aren't they? Isn't that right?"

"How's the salad, François?" said Pridie.

40

Dumergue looked back at him and chuckled.

"I don't know when I've liked it so much. So clean."

"Pridie must love you for that," said Jean-Philippe quietly to Dumergue.

"For the political firework?" Dumergue grinned at him cheerfully. "An original man, Pridie. Well, it keeps his parties from going flat. Otherwise indeed I often wonder myself why he invites me. Partly perhaps because he's not sure of me. So he likes to have me around."

"What precisely is his job?"

Dumergue glanced at him with amusement.

"Their Embassy, you know. Our man in Vientiane. Culture, in the practical sense."

That was not brilliantly clear, thought Jean-Philippe, but he said:

"Interesting."

"Interesting as a character, certainly. Yes. As a study, yes. And his evenings are always stimulating. Quite obsessional about his food. Fastidious. A gourmet. A sure touch. So I come with delight. Also, he feels it important to practise his French. Brutally, of course, it is."

"Though tonight we speak English?"

"Exceptional," said Dumergue. "A concession to the USOM magnate. That too is rare, no doubt because he's just arrived. Normally Pridie has no Americans at this type of party. I suspect that he considers that they are not quite up to it. Foreigners, Europeans, well, are different, the old world; odd, but socially acceptable."

"How bad are they?"

"The Americans? They say, don't they, that there are so many opportunities in that country that there is no reason to work outside it if you have talent. Unless you're a foreign service career man. The P.E.O. are that in a way, all regular Pentagon, *en civile*. Very efficient, administratively."

"And their Embassy?"

"Varies," said Dumergue. "Some liberals. A good ambassador. But the men handling their desk in Washington must be encrusted Dulles products. They give the orders. As for USOM—"

"As for USOM?"

"An intelligent acting director, disastrous lower echelons, disastrous procedures; the final triumph of bureaucracy. Isn't it sad that men of good will, but middle-class, amateur, unimaginative, can do infinitely more harm than the professionally vicious? They're the realization of the American mass-circulation maga-

41

zine ideal, healthy, patriotic, scrubbed, decent, generous, domestically fertile. And practically useless, paper and regulations bound, fabulously inefficient."

He added:

"This is not for your paper, mind. Background."

"Accepted," said Jean-Philippe, "unimaginative, bureaucratic. They sound rather like us. Perhaps we were less muscular."

Dumergue looked at him quickly and roared with laughter.

"Touched. Strictly, not so bad, even. We should have known better. After all, we'd been sitting in the damn area for eighty years."

"Curious that one sees so few Americans about. I heard that there were hundreds of them here."

"There are," said Dumergue. "It's not curious. It's fatal. It's their prophylactic phobia. It's spread. It's become mental now as well as physical. The new world of the sealed container, the cellophaned steak. In exactly the same way, they seal themselves off hermetically. The main USOM compound is up behind the National Assembly, well outside the centre of town. It contains offices, houses, flats, a cinema, a recreation hall, garages, workshops, stores, PX's. They can exhaust their entire existence there. They do, antiseptically. All food flown in from Bangkok. At one time, even their drinking water. A separate world of sheer and respectable unreality. If you penetrate it, then Middletown, U.S.A. A fantastically centripetal society, where your objective is constantly to impress your seniors in the internal hierarchy, contacts with the external world being virtually irrelevant. I've met young bachelors among them who couldn't even name three bars in Vientiane, let alone brothels. I think that tragic. But what a demonstration of social controls! Talk about the Russians!"

"And their theory of the Viet Minh battalions?"

"A convenient myth, probably only that. What the government won't admit, and the Americans daren't—or else they just don't know—is exactly how much support the Pathet have. I'd put it at about sixty per cent through the country, twenty-five per cent in the administration itself. Most critically, the Pathet have most of the intellectuals and most of the youth. Time looks as though it's with them. The left wing won fifteen of the twenty-one supplementary Assembly seats contested last year, you know."

"Because the Pathet axe is sharper?"

"Partly," said Dumergue, "better organized, less corrupt. The poor bloody peasant gets it from both sides. The Pathet crucify him if he aids the Royal Army. The Royal Army shoots him if he helps the Pathet. The only difference is that the Pathet always reason with him decently before they shoot him. They tell him very patiently all about their social mission. Their logic impresses the others. Also, the Pathet are generally so much nearer and better informed."

"It's a song that I've heard before," said Jean-Philippe.

"It was like that in Viet Nam, yes. And he who holds the countryside—consider this difference too. A Lao Minister never stirs from the towns if he can help it, with one or two spectacular exceptions. Perhaps once or twice a year he goes where he can reasonably go. There are few good roads in Laos. So he goes to some village near a main road. There's a *Baci*. It's a marvellous day. He's superbly entertained and wined. If he's still able, he sleeps politely with one or two of the young girls. He then gives a most impressive speech. He promises all sorts of things, more roads, less taxes, a better administration, fertilizers, irrigation schemes, a school, a health clinic. He leaves amidst prolonged applause. The next time they see him nothing has changed, except that the young girls are a year older. In time you can get tired of this, even the young girls can. Now the Pathet have two or three thousand cadres in Laos since 1954, trained in North Viet Nam. Professionals. They go to a village, preferably of people of their own ethnic group. They have strict instructions to talk no politics at all in their first year there. Instead, each cadre's mission is to get himself known as the most public-spirited character in the village, the one who will always help mend leaking thatches in the middle of storms and find strayed oxen in the middle of the night and work harder than anyone else in the village's rice-fields and do all sorts of incredibly virtuous things like that. He only starts to talk business after he's been there for a year, when they all know and trust him completely. And one other thing really slays the villagers. The cadres are incorruptible. Not only can't you bribe the bastards, but you don't even have to. Now to a people where bribery is a hallowed form of courtesy, a way of expressing due deference to seniors or officials when you want to get something out of them, this integrity is probably about as effective as a Catholic priest's celibacy once was amongst us. After all, that sort of thing impresses you. The man must be mad, obviously, but you can hardly help respecting him for it. He's abnormal by definition, but he even looks as if he likes it. He must have something. So you tend to listen to what he has to say."

Wainwright's voice broke suddenly and loudly across the table conversation. "No, no. The best I've heard is, The Land of the White Elephant and the Million Parasites."

Evidently now intellectually braced by the evening, Wainwright

43

had delivered this gem with verve. He looked as if he had been holding it back for some time, but he was not waiting for any audience reaction now. He had forestalled them, and was shaking with a rhythmic and contagious inner mirth. He looked like a large champion baby advertising a new soap.

Pridie smiled politely, and Jean-Philippe saw him glance swiftly down the table at Justin, legal counsellor to the government, of a French father and Lao mother. His Lao wife, Annette, sat opposite him. She was dressed traditionally, her hair coiled high on her head, showing her married status. Roger Justin, short and broad and with horn-rimmed glasses, wearing a sober dark blue suit, looked quiet and reflective and moderate. Perhaps the effect came less from the almost complete impassivity of his face than from a quality of repose and balance in his body. He and his wife had been at a school in France, and at university, where they had met, and in speech and manner they seemed intrinsically French. Neither gave any sign of having heard Wainwright's sally. Justin was talking to Jeanette, his wife with Marivell's wife.

"To be accurate, the population is probably nearer two million," Dumergue said to Jean-Philippe, "a million Lao, a million so-called racial minorities."

The Chinese had been expertly replacing their salad plates with dessert helpings of Crêpes Suzette, appeared mysteriously and discreetly flaming from the side hall which led from the separate kitchen.

"We seem to have that splendid genius in this region," said Jean-Philippe reflectively.

Dumergue looked at him enquiringly.

"—Of playing to lose," Jean-Philippe said. "A kind of gallant Russian Roulette. The Americans seem even better at it. We end infallibly on the side of the rigidly conservative, or the corrupt."

"Eating Crêpes Suzette," said Dumergue.

"Eating Crêpes Suzette."

But Jean-Philippe's attention had been distracted by the impact of Jeanette's décolletée as she advanced it upon Justin in deep seriousness, as though she spoke with it. Jean-Philippe did not hear her words, but the noise of Pridie's chair.

"Coffee outside?"

They rose with him.

There were chairs and tables under a tree in the garden. Jean-Philippe found himself next to the girl, through no conscious intent of his own. He held her chair, and moved to his and sat down.

"I believe you're a journalist?" she said.

44

He noticed the slight anxiousness in her face as she put the banal question. Evidently she liked to be accepted.

"*Mademoiselle*. Some are men of action, you know. Some just write."

"Though action isn't really so alien to you, is it?" she said. "In the Free French forces? In Indo-China?"

Now how the devil had she known about that? Jean-Philippe had not broadcast either fact since he had come to Laos.

"You're well informed," he said. "By whom, if I might ask?"

He had smiled, to keep the irritation from his face. As she did not answer, he said:

"Pridie?"

"Well, yes," she said. She was swift to excuse Pridie now. "He's interested in people, you know. He likes to know what they do, where they're from."

"Flattering of him," he said, thinking: interested enough to get his facts very straight too.

"*France-Franche* is a weekly, I believe," she went on, "liberal and independent and rather deep."

"My God, is it?"

She looked at him hurriedly.

"Well, that's what they say," she said defensively, "I don't know it myself, you see."

He relented. She looked charming when she was uncertain. My God, she looked charming anyway.

"Of course it's just a racket," he said confidentially. "It can afford the luxury of being reflective, you see. After all it's got a whole week to publish itself each issue. Not like a daily newspaper. So we've all got enough time to get really complicated about things."

Suddenly bored with his own frivolous social chat, he played his eye in a complimentary manner instead over her bosom. He set himself to judge the moment when, if he continued, she could only lift a hand to cover it decently. At the precise instant that he saw her left hand begin to flutter on her lap he lifted his gaze frankly to her face and said:

"And how many Viet Minh battalions did you discover today, *Mademoiselle*?"

"You mock. You hold that against the Americans, don't you?"

"That view, yes," he said. "Its too simple. And simplicity can be a dangerous quality here, *Mademoiselle*."

"So you blame them conveniently."

"Because true professionals are never really simple people, *Mademoiselle*. Not in this game. But you can't blame the Ameri-

45

cans for the fact of the Viet Minh itself. It didn't do that. That was ready made when they arrived. We were responsible for that. France was responsible for that."

Beloved France, he thought.

And, at that stage, destroyed France, he thought bitterly. Divided France. Corrupt France. Self-mutilating France. Above all, blind France. So blind that we, who fought tens of thousands of kilometres away to restore her shattered tarnished grandeur, were blinded too.

CHAPTER V

JEAN-PHILIPPE sat and looked back over his coffee and his brandy under the tree in the quiet garden, totally and discourteously blind to the attentive and strikingly beautiful girl who sat beside him, and to that explosive yet graceful bust which normally would effortlessly and exclusively and mesmerically have riveted his attention, even against the collapse of empires and the fall of kings.

Blind, he thought.

But how could you have known until the end that you had played a fool's game for eight years? It had certainly seemed a game in Saigon at the start. In the élite paratroop battalions the actions were sometimes surprisingly sharp, though most often when you arrived it was already too late, and there were only the burned or mutilated bodies and the charred villages and the great whispering tree-tops of the jungle (even then subconsciously you always knew that the trees, the jungle, were naturally on the side of the Viet Minh).

When you found the peasants in the rice-fields they were always as patently innocent as their own scimitar-horned and vast-barrelled and enormously powerful water-buffalo, lethargic and domesticated, and known to become violent and charge only against Europeans, whose smell they disliked. The men and women and children, if that was the season, worked in the paddy calf-deep or knee-deep in the water. They moved slowly forward in lines, bending with practised suppleness, their legs straight and apart. The performance could seem religious, for, when the paratroopers were there, they did not talk at all. They did not even look up at them. Clearly they hoped that by ignoring them completely they could dismiss them from existence. When the paratroopers finally hauled some ancient from the lines he invariably knew nothing. Certainly, there had been other soldiers there. Vietnamese, yes, but strangers. Of course they knew that the village's pro-French headman and three of his councillors had been murdered, and their homes burned. It was very sad. In which direction had the Vietnamese soldiers gone? Naturally, they had gone back into the jungle. It was where they had come from, wasn't it?

Often the ancient would smile widely during the interrogation, not at all through bravado, or because he thought the ceremony particularly amusing. It was a nervous tic, a Vietnamese character-istic too often misunderstood by Europeans, to smile hilariously when most terrified. This apart, the man would stand composed, in his great conical shading hat, whose curves were rather like those of the roofs of his temples, of his sculpture, of his writing, impossibly alien.

In your leaves in Saigon you haunted the bars in groups in the Rue Catinat or you gambled or danced in Cholon, or you slept with the pliant and vibrant and murmuring *métisses* or Vietnamese, with their tiny breasts and waists and buttocks, and their lustrous floods of hair, animals groomed for love for a thousand years. It was that kind of war at the start, office hours only. But the warn-ings were already there, the mounting rhythm of assassinations in the city, unceasing and methodical, the acute sense of being out of step with time when some *colon* or older officer, bored in a bar, suggested the diversion of going out again to *casser du Ngac,* to break some peasants.

One morning you woke in some army post in the bush in the centre of an invisible enemy that struck at will, and you knew finally and completely that this was no longer a minor military exercise against a ragged band of communist extremists, which was the official French line right up to the end, but that virtually the entire country and its people were against you. The discovery was permanent and not good for the morale. It reduced you to the splendid isolation of a mercenary in a last outpost, valiantly bran-dishing an outmoded military ethic in the void, heroically defend-ing a distant and divided and largely disinterested government, and consistently beaten by professionals and the facts. You were like some thundering knight in armour facing farcically up to a good shot with a bazooka. The romantic myth could not really be expected to survive after quite so many defeats, the loss of the whole string of garrisons on the north-eastern frontier with China in 1950, the liquidation of the Hoa-Binh pocket over the next two years, the retreat from North Laos in 1953 with the loss of five battalions. All the defeats up to Dien Bien Phu.

There was no myth left after that. Dien Bien Phu suggested

that the Viet Minh, in that terrain, probably had the best infantry in the world, among the best generals, the best logistic support, and the best fifth-column preparation. Who would have guessed that Giap and the other Viet Minh generals would take their model from the Germans under Kesselring in North Italy and the Russians about Stalingrad, and bring their heavy guns down from the heights about Dien Bien Phu and dig them right in, beautifully camouflaged against aviation, in strong points in the saucer plain within easy and lethal range of the French camp? Or that for every fighting-man in Giap's twelve-thousand-man divisions round Dien Bien Phu probably twice as many men and women supplied him in monstrous single unending antlike columns through the jungle tracks, up from the delta, quite invisible from the air? Who could have thought that so everyday and triumphantly respectable a thing as a bicycle could be so militarily decisive?—and of course that was why there had been so fantastically many thefts of bicycles in Hanoi and the main towns before Dien Bien Phu—for a man or woman pushing a bicycle could travel the narrowest path, carrying on it fifty or a hundred kilos of rice or shells or parts of a disassembled howitzer. Or that, a year before Dien Bien Phu, the Viet Minh already controlled at least two-thirds of the whole Red River delta area, which was laughably supposed to be France's secure base area between the battleground and the sea?

Jean-Philippe had always been touched by the mind's autocratic gift of totally ignoring the vast historical importance of such cataclysms when it recalled them afterwards, and instead of identifying them by frivolously minor images. Thus, for him, Dien Bien Phu and the subsequent death marches were symbolized not by the big tragic things, the exhaustion and the casualties and the appalling hunger and the mercilessly impersonal cruelty, but quite simply by a composite image of the farcically tiny Viet Minh. He found that frankly embarrassing. The defeat could not possibly have been quite so humiliating if by comparison the French troops had not seemed such hulking great brutes of men.

On the fifty-fourth day of the fighting Jean-Philippe commanded his battalion, then composed of forty-three men. The last attack came at nine at night, under parachute flares. It was pure surrealism. There was even a grotesque breathless toylike beauty about it. The small, frail, agile men who floated within their overlarge uniforms, swarmed up the last slope again, diligently chanting their *Tien-len, Doc-lap, Tien-len, Doc-lap,* forward to independence, and died in heaps. Three hung like insects, their arms outstretched and fighting it, on the last rolls of barbed wire.

The last bursts from the machine-gun section on Jean-Philippe's right killed them pointlessly, but they jerked sharply and their uniforms flapped again loyally when the Viets slung a bamboo Bangalore torpedo under the wire next to them and exploded it. When the attackers were near enough Jean-Philippe threw his last two grenades and settled back in his slit trench to wait for the sudden and total and ominously final silence.

Again, the key thing to him about the death march of forty days and six hundred kilometres to No. 9 Camp near Lang Son was the sheer visual absurdity of these bloody great bulls of Western Europeans in their soft jungle hats or berets or steel helmets or else bareheaded (and it was another key image that when they walked their heads were always bent, they no longer looked where they were going) in columns which stretched as far as the eye could see, guarded ridiculously by a few tiny patient olive men in flapping olive uniforms who carried American carbines or Skoda sub-machine-guns of almost their own length. The ration for those forty days was fifteen kilos of rice per prisoner. Many were sapped to death by dysentry or the pitiless weight of the monsoon rains or by the bitter cold in the mountains. Yet Jean-Philippe himself found the march curiously supportable physically, perhaps because you passed so quickly to the numbed realm of nightmare.

The final key thing which he remembered about that march was the deadly neutrality of the guards. There were no beatings or obvious cruelty. If a man was caught trying to escape he was shot. That was simple to understand, and accepted. So too, if a man could not keep up with the march, he died at its side. Again that was a rule so primitive that it even grew to seem just. It was as if at base this was all that justice ever really was, simply coherence, simply consistency, whatever the standards of judgment might happen to be. It was as if all that the mind ever really asked for was the chance to predict correctly. In that sense the guards were remarkably just. Their actions were eminently predictable. There were no human errors. They were outrageously fair. Indeed, they frequently advised the prisoners that no less than President Ho himself had ordered that they should be fairly treated, so that they might the more easily see the errors of their past ways; a thousand years of life to President Ho. Even their interminable *Di-di, maû-len, maû-len*, quickly, quickly was said without discernible animosity.

Apart from those who died in that march, three men out of four who reached the Viet Minh prison camps died or disappeared in them. Again, the really memorable discovery was not this, but that human dignity was after all a concept as relative as any other, and that in time you could learn to live with that fact quite comfortably. The Viet Minh taught you this lesson clearly and exhaustively. Over four years, they had painstakingly built up a really formidable system in their prison camps. Its object was to break you psychologically, then to remake you in their own image. For the Viet Minh did not consider you any less an enemy just because they had captured you. They were much too thorough and meticulous for that. The struggle had simply passed to another dimension.

By the time that they left the camps about two out of every five survivors had collaborated with the Viet Minh in one way or another. The Viet Minh had all the weapons. The prisoners did not even keep their corps solidarity. When they arrived at the camps the Viet Minh divided them at once into their racial groupings of Metropolitan French and Algerians and Africans and Germans and Hungarians. Each got its nationally tailored treatment. Prisoners of all groups were required to take part convincingly in sessions of indoctrination and auto-critique, and to sign pompous memoranda to the United Nations expressing their repentance for having supported the corrupt colonialist regime of bankers and plantation owners. If they did not, their rations decreased and their working days lengthened and there was a sudden critical lack of medical supplies. Again, that was perfectly just by the standards of this grey Kafkaesque universe, because completely predictable. Again, there was never any obvious violence about it, but, rather, an odd efficient politeness. At these controlled levels of the under-nourishment and exhaustion, a prisoner's refusal to take part in these sadly serious charades or to add his name to an outrageously bad piece of literature was statistically likely to kill him and his fellows. Heroism was not pertinent here, let alone admired. The survivors grew wise. Of those who did not collaborate some (like Jean-Philippe) succeeded largely because the Geneva Agreements were signed conveniently soon after their capture. The question was decided less by stern moral stances than by calories.

"—France?" said the girl called Jeanette, sitting serious-eyed and watching and lovely, over the empty coffee cups, over her glass of Pridie's excellent brandy, under the tree in the quiet garden. "And why should you blame France?"

"Because, *Mademoiselle*, there was a turning point which needed vision. In 1946 Ho Chi Minh would have come into the French Union as its first member. It would have been worth trying. But for vision you need men who can see. Ours was a congealed Admiral in Saigon. You don't always get two chances. You're from Lausanne, *Mademoiselle*?"

"Yes."

"How is it that so young and attractive a person," said Jean-Philippe, dropping his gaze again rampantly to the exposed part of her bosom, "is not married? *Mademoiselle*?"

Her breasts jumped back slightly and downwards from him, as though she sought suddenly to immerse them further in the unyielding dress.

"Do stop it!" she said. "*Mademoiselle*, I mean. It makes me sound so venerable. My name's Jeanette. I might ask you the same."

"Jean-Philippe Raymond," he said formally.

"No, no, I know that. I meant, married."

Jean-Philippe laughed heartily and offered her a cigarette.

It struck him that as a matter of fact that had been one of his father's last ironic shots in a battle in which there had not really been a victor.

"—frankly, this mania?" his father had said. "Isn't it perhaps time that you settled down? Twenty-seven, Jean, after all. You have that English law degree. You can't say that you haven't amused yourself. And this would then naturally come to you when I died."

His father had put the tips of his fingers together and looked over them at the ceiling, and added:

"No doubt there would be girls from good families—"

"Ibsen? The continuing hierarchy?" Jean-Philippe had replied, leaning forward intelligently in his chair, like a keen undergraduate at a tutorial; quite ready to mock his father in fair return for the half-mockery of his father's deliberate cliché, which the older man was now watching dissipate in the cigarette smoke above his fingertips, with a true artist's satisfaction. It was the more amusing in that he knew that his father was in part deadly serious. He had that obsession with the immortality of his blood sometimes found in men who were born and had built greatly from nothing. It was the only weakness that Jean-Philippe knew of in him.

"Go to hell," said his father amiably. "But what else, Jean? My dear fellow, it would at least be rather less *farfelu* than burying yourself in Indo-China. And consider how unfortunately exact that metaphor might turn out to be. Now, who seriously has ever really heard of the place? And, in passing, just for my information, for what reason, Jean? Adventure? In you I would find that a little—"

"Naïve?"

"Naïve; thank you. Then what else? To expiate some imagined guilt? Come, now. Whose? France's? Mine? My dear fellow, France won't really notice it, you know. Mine? That would be, well, hardly insulting; amusing, rather, except perhaps that I dislike misplaced emotion on principle. But, of course, you must do as you wish. You will, anyway."

The meeting had begun as stylized as one between foreign ministers.

Jean-Philippe had gone to the house by taxi. Pierre had met him at the door. He appeared properly amazed and pleased. He had always been a versatile actor; they would certainly have got his telegram. Pierre had been a strong ally and another idol of his childhood. No doubt he would have been just as strategically faithful to the German major-general who had stayed in the house for a year. Pierre stood now in his usual immaculate white jacket and dark precise trousers, broad and ruddy as a peasant, with his thick blond hair and more than his fair share of a Normand peasant's malignancy and cunning behind the innocuous grey eyes. It was disconcerting how little he had changed. Watching him, Jean-Philippe was struck with the absurd sense of being victim of some trick of time, as though really he stood now in some return of seven years before, in 1939, and all that had passed since, the death and destruction and heroism and betrayal and anguish and humiliation, were only an embarrassing personal delusion. He went up to his room.

The great luxurious empty house was the same. It had always given that odd effect of being on display, like a national monument. If the war had passed lightly by Pierre it had not marked the house at all. Jean-Philippe looked down from his window across the lawn. It was cropped smooth, groomed and permanent beneath all change as one at an Oxford college. At its far broad end the great beech glowed a deep sensual autumn red by the edge of the river, like a tritely reassuring symbol of eternal re-creation. He washed and changed, not surprised that his father was not in the house, and left his single suitcase in the room, and went downstairs.

"The Citroën is of course left for you, M'sieu Jean, at your disposal."

"It's kind. I think a taxi."

The factory was much bigger than he remembered from seven years before; over the last four there would have been urgent extensions. A uniformed guard stopped him when he got out of the taxi at the south entrance, and checked by telephone with his father's office. By the gate masons worked on a shattered building; bombing, or sabotage. One of them, stocky, in rolled shirtsleeves, stood back and rested and watched him with fixed insolence as he passed.

It was now a vast spreading complex, almost a town. You could lose yourself in it. Black and grey defined it, and the heavy submarine pulse of unseen lathes, the sharp tang of burnt cutting oil. There was a high new wing at the north end, architecturally clean, the upper part in frosted glass. This was now the third or fourth of the machine-tool shops in France.

He knew none of the men that he passed. That stressed the interval more than the changes in the buildings. He remembered these intermittently, the shape of a doorway, the slant of a view inside, of men in white inclined like acolytes over the spaced and gleaming and powerful and obedient machines of precision, more silent than silence. It was these that many years before had engraved the contours of his brain, as in another might have done the childhood sights and sounds of a wood or farm or street or river or hill.

The woman in the room before his father's was thirty-five or six and impeccable and blonde as brass, her hair like a casque. She worked expertly at a muted electric typewriter. He sensed no sex in her; the enterprise's hushed efficiencies must have tailored that smoothly from her. She looked up. Not asking his name, she lifted her telephone and spoke and replaced it. He had the feeling that she had identified him from a photograph like a bright policeman.

"Monsieur Raymond will of course see you at once. Please go in."

"*Gentil à lui.*"

She re-examined him, without comment. There was no doubt where her loyalties lay.

His father sat at the heavy dark wooden desk in the far corner of the second room, high windows on either side of him. The thick pastel carpet which deadened his own steps was new, but the tall broad charged bookcase at the left wall was the same and the small Renoir original on its own on the wall to the right.

The man glanced up and took off his glasses and got up slowly.

"You're not in uniform. Good."

He was of middle height, strongly built. There were black hairs on the backs of his hands. The fingers were short and spatulate, grown deft in governing machines and the men who worked them. The face was almost square, on a broad neck, the hair thick and black and scarcely grizzled and cut close. The mouth was thin

53

and wide and straight and almost colourless, and the chin cleft. The eyes were light blue, with heavy pads of flesh under them, hard, like a boxer's. He was a man always in his plant with the first of his shifts, only incidentally to set an example and to drive, much more because of his total self-identification with it; the place was his identity. It seemed less a face than a symbol. It was so obviously open, honest, and resolute that it could have been a heroic statement of the dignity of labour; a left-wing propagandist had indeed once used it recognizably in his idealized poster of a steelworker. On that occasion his father had valued his appearance ironically at a million francs. It was so clearly of them that his men had never really thought to strike against it.

"No longer the militarist then, Father?"

He had withdrawn his hand and his father motioned him to sit and sat himself and laughed without malice. His left hand gestured behind him to the window which looked down on the thrumming hidden machines in the great yard below.

"One is what one needs to be, Jean."

"But *that* is what really matters?"

"What else, child? By the way, a cigarette?"

His father took one himself and lit it and shut the lighter and pushed the box over to his son. Jean-Philippe took one and held it, and after a moment the man opposite pushed the lighter smoothly across the table.

"I'm sorry I couldn't be at the station," said his father. "One has obligations, you understand."

"Of course."

Jean-Philippe got up and crossed to the window on his father's left. A single man walked from a machine shop down in the great concrete yard, carrying a heavy tooled piece of steel in his hands, solitary as a gull in a grey sky.

"You've progressed in these years, Father."

"The occupation? Yes. Fortunately, everyone needs machine-tools."

He was much too big, arrogant, ruthlessly balanced to avoid that issue; rather, he provoked it.

"Essential, for example, for the production of Schmeissers and Spandau and eighty-eight millimetres and Tigers and Panthers?"

His father looked back at him and chuckled, and said:

"Or, for example, for the production of merchant ships and locomotives and cranes and mining and industrial equipment, the sinews of peaceful development? One could argue this indefinitely, Jean. If it would amuse you. You don't think that it's a little outmoded?"

"I hadn't thought that you were ever particularly impressed by fashion."

"Thank you; fashion, no. But you seriously imagine that what one man does today can be decisive, Jean? When one stands at such an infinite distance from the end results of one's actions?"

"It's a convenient theory."

"Convenient, or just correct? My dear fellow, it's simply a social fact. How could it be otherwise? Simply a fact about the world today. Ah, you still have these overprecise concepts of responsibility. The man who dropped the bomb on Hiroshima was personally responsible, he was personally answerable for that? Come now, Jean; you're probably still much more Catholic than you know."

His father looked down a moment at his short spatulate hands, spreading them out on the desk in front of him.

"One man," he said. "Besides, even if that were true—"

"In passing, your aid to the two RAF officers was intelligent."

"You heard of that? Well. Opportune."

"Insurance. You see ahead, Father."

"Naturally; one has to. It was lucky that they came to the house. Did you come here to talk about that?"

Jean-Philippe walked back to his chair and sat down.

"It is what we are talking about."

His father watched him.

"I see," he said. "A partisan's settlement of accounts. Well, I suppose that at least you have my insolence."

He lifted the single pale green telephone at his left.

"Madame?

"Madame, I don't want to be disturbed for—"

He looked at his watch and glanced dispassionately at his son.

"—Let's say, half an hour."

He put the telephone down without sound. He said:

"My dear fellow, you still have something of that glow and dedication of a young Saint-Cyr graduate, don't you know. It's almost audible. Good. It's normal. It encourages the others. I suppose that I glowed with honour too, after three years on the Somme. It's that old correlation between purity and death, of course. I find that I have completely forgotten about that, many years ago."

"One could hardly doubt it."

"Come now, Jean, aren't you just a little too intelligent to be determined by these oversimplifications? D'you really still want to make capital out of what you happened to do in the war? As of your first seduction? Shouldn't one just forget it decently? An initiation? A blooding? A stage of youth?"

"No more than that, indeed. And not the point."

"What precisely is the point then, Jean? To debate the great ideal for which you fought dauntlessly, the fair name of France, freedom, whatever emotional headline you want to select? You can do better than that. And do you *really* believe that you have beaten them now? A nation with so sophisticated a taste for violent romantic myths, whose *mores* are set by Nietzsche and Wagner and Herman Hesse? Come now, blood and buxom flaxen women with great iron breastcups and Valkyrie horns on their helmets? You can't reasonably be expected to beat people who think like that. And of course they have that brilliant sense of organization of the blind. They need to lose one more war and they will rule the world."

"Original, Father?"

The older man looked hard at him, then laughed.

"No. But possibly true. The Russians are intelligent to mistrust them. And, if they are not our enemy next time, then we shall find some other. The Russians. The Chinese. We shall always find our enemy. Christ said, Love your enemy. Really, one might as well. In our civilization one is generally indispensable."

"And your solution?"

"Solution? Who spoke of solutions? I've never tried to teach you that. I have never believed that there were ever any general solutions. Individual compromises."

"Yours?"

The heavy man shrugged.

"Adapt, survive, climb."

"You find that satisfactory?"

His father looked at him curiously.

"I suppose that is a sensible question. Of course."

"For a man who has always fought, whatever your weapons, it sounds incredibly dull."

"Ah," said his father, "you want to be entertained too? A dramatic dimension? But the gods died long ago, Jean."

"Leaving the world to a sage political opportunism?"

The older man observed him with contempt.

"Or to political common sense? What on earth can one get ideologically passionate about today, without being ridiculous? Western democracy? The canonization of mediocrity? A *Deux Chevaux* and a *bidet* and a deep freeze for every home? *This* is the sum result of Prometheus and Pericles and the Song of Roland and Chartres and Racine?"

"Spoken like a man."

"Though as a romantic you'd probably prefer the new Jesuits. They'll make you an even more appalling communal man than the West. All the icy purity you could want. The Russians are still just emerging from the first flush of their puritan revolution. You wouldn't even have to go far, Jean. D'you know how much of the military supplies for Indo-China are sabotaged in France even before they leave?"

"Indo-China? No."

"Often as much as forty per cent. By the P.C.F. So you could even join them here."

"It's amusing that you should mention Indo-China—"

But his father had got up and gone to the window to his left, and was looking down into the great grey concrete yard. Jean-Philippe wondered what scene he was setting now. His father did little without a purpose, conscious or intuitive. He watched him, cut out stocky against the window; solitary, but solid as a tree, curiously intact. He stood there without movement for some while, until Jean-Philippe got up too and walked to the window. His father glanced at him and looked back at the yard.

"One can hear it all the time, you know. It's strange. When I wake up at night in the house, even, I sometimes imagine that I can hear it."

"The house is a long way from here," said Jean-Philippe.

"Of course," said his father. He made an odd gesture of lassitude. "But by all the rules, this should be too deep in your blood too for you to leave it. I always said that you had a turner's wrist."

"That was long ago."

"Still, one can't learn it, one can't really learn it, you know. Look at it, Jean, for a minute. Is it so bad? The third choice, for a few. To govern this, for a time. It goes on, it lasts. To leave a mark, to create durably in your own image. Whether what it makes builds or kills once it leaves these gates. Don't throw it away too lightly, Jean. Look down at it and consider a little."

Jean-Philippe went back to his chair. He said:

"Your mind's still set on that, then."

The heavy man had turned away from the window too, and sat at his desk.

"Naturally. It's my constant regret that your mother died before she produced me another son. If you accept, by the way, I should of course take your decision as unalterable."

"If I decline the invitation?"

"If you refuse, I shall of course marry again."

His father went on after a moment:

"Your taking all of your demobilization leave in Paris, Jean, wasn't that a little excessive, for two months? Your room's always here."

"Perhaps it was. It's not a city that I particularly like."

His father studied him, interpreting his answer exactly.

"Well, then. What do you want, Jean-Philippe? The *Quai*? I can speak to Duclos."

"Thanks, it's kind. The trouble won't be necessary."

"Of course, you have your own money, from your mother."

"In effect."

The heavy man looked down at his desk, and up at his son again.

"What will you do, Jean?"

"Oh, defend the *Deux Chevaux*, defend the *bidets*. For entertainment."

"Meaning?"

"It wasn't demobilization leave. Just leave."

His father watched him.

"I see," he said. "Well."

He went on:

"For my interest, Jean, why did you come back? Just to accuse?"

Behind him, through the grey windows, down in the grey yard, the machines pulsed steadily and ceaselessly, like the unseen engines of a great ship.

"More a kind of nostalgia, perhaps," said Jean-Philippe. "And a verification."

"You found what you thought," said his father. "One does, you know. Well. The A.E.F? Algeria?"

"Indo-China," said Jean-Philippe.

Marivell, sitting across the table from him, next to Dumergue, was saying, "They say that there's some new Chinese talent at the Vieng Rattray."

Marivell was clearly doing his best to sound like one of the boys. Jean-Philippe smiled to himself. Marivell did not really have the build for it. He was probably constitutionally incapable of infidelity.

"Not so very new," said Dumergue. "They're back from Bangkok. They prefer Bangkok, of course, but they can only get three-month Thai visas. So they come back here to renew them."

"It must be an exhausting circuit," said Jean-Philippe. "Perhaps we ought to go and give them some support."

"I think not," Wainwright said to Pridie. "If you'll excuse us."

Justin had also got up with his wife, and, following the Wainwrights, the two were circling the table decorously to say goodnight to the remaining guests.

"How shall we split up?" said Pridie, when they had left. "Jean-Philippe? François?"

"I'm mobile," said Dumergue.

"I have a car," said Jean-Philippe. "An obese beetle of a *Deux Chevaux*."

"Good," said Pridie. "Dominic. Madame Marivell. Perhaps you'd like to go with Jean-Philippe. Dominic, you know the way, don't you?"

"Or I could show Jean-Philippe," said Jeanette. "I know the way."

Before that silence could make its comment, Dumergue said easily :

"I'd be delighted to take the Marivells."

What was this, thought Jean-Philippe, a conspiracy?

Pridie looked at Jeanette for a moment.

"Good," he said heartily, "good."

CHAPTER VI

WHEN Jean-Philippe had seated the girl in his car in the dirt road outside Pridie's house, he was surprised to see that Dumergue's small Renault and Pridie's blue Jeep station-wagon drove off in the direction opposite to that which Jeanette now indicated to him; this was towards the river, which he knew anyway to be away from the Vieng Rattray. She caught his look and laughed.

"Not an abduction. If you don't mind, if we could just pass by my place. I must go back for something."

"Of course," said Jean-Philippe. "You'll show me how to get there?"

"I'll show you how to get there," she said.

Jean-Philippe raised his eyebrows to himself.

As he came down to the river, a brightening lance of silver on the black asphalted road which ran across at right angles ahead of him warned of the approach of another car, and he braked and waited while it swept past in front from right to left; a new cream Citroën saloon, a European alone in it driving, dark-haired, intent, pinned briefly naked in the beam of Jean-Philippe's headlights.

When he eased the car forward again, he noticed that there was a *pirogue* far out in the river, near the Thai bank, eight hundred or a thousand metres away. It was going downstream very slowly, a thin yellow light in its bows.

The girl guided him to the right. He passed the place where the Vietnamese had met his friend late that afternoon, and gone off with him in the taxi. He thought that the Vietnamese had looked rather puzzled when he had greeted him. He wondered why. Because *farangs* did not just greet the locals like that here? But that was unlikely. The social climate had after all changed radically since before the war. The swift Japanese victory in 1940 and the Viet Minh victory in 1954 had seen to that. The comfortable image of the white man's Olympian social exclusivity now definitely creaked. So that could hardly be it.

"It's strange that you've not been to the Vieng Rattray yet."

Jeanette was looking across at him in the car.

"It is?"

No, it was much more as though the Vietnamese half-thought that he knew him. Recalling his face, Jean-Philippe wondered similarly if he had not met the man before. Perhaps somewhere in the town. Or in one of the ministries. It was hardly important.

"Well, most men here seem to know it," said Jeanette.

But that wasn't it. The man had been some kind of official. A policeman? A soldier? And not here. Saigon? Or—

He was abruptly aware that the girl expected some sort of answer from him.

"I beg your pardon?"

"Most men have been to it."

He smiled.

"All right, so have I. But I think that Pridie has a weakness for introducing people to things. A pioneer streak. Why should I spoil his fun?"

He wondered if she would accept this mild mockery of Pridie without protest; it might be a small pointer. After a moment she laughed.

"So my presence isn't really necessary?"

"Always naturally most welcome, Mad—"

"Jeanette."

"Jeanette."

She seemed much more assured now than she had when he had first met her that evening at Pridie's. No doubt that was simply the effect of the spurious intimacy which this short joint voyage in the car through the night had dictated to them. She sat now with her legs crossed and her fingers interlaced over her knees, leaning forward slightly on the seat. She looked as contained as a small animal. He noticed her scent. It surprised him that he had not been aware of it when she had sat with him in the garden. It was as if she could turn it on and off at will.

"You've known him long?" he said conversationally.

"Peter? Not long. About six weeks. That's not so long, really."

Well, thanks, he thought.

"No," he said, "it's not so long. Since you arrived?"

"Yes."

He noticed how splendidly black her hair was when she turned to answer him. It would no doubt stand out most satisfyingly against the white of her body in bed, in a most aesthetic manner. That too would certainly be a sight to see, come to mention it, tapering sharply in from those resounding breasts to the slim model's waist—

He looked severely at the road ahead. It was the first time that she had got him to undress her mentally. He gave her credit for that. He said:

"He's an interesting person."

She hesitated.

"He's been kind to me. I knew no-one when I came. He's helped me to meet many people."

"That shouldn't be too painful for a man, Jeanette. You're something of an advertisement, after all."

She bowed her head towards him satirically.

"I don't think he did it for that."

"He has that capacity, then?" he said deliberately.

"Which?"

"Of kindness. I should have thought him too disciplined, controlled, aware, to have much room left for emotion."

"Ruthlessly controlled," she said, evidently resenting nothing, "In most things. But he can be embarrassingly generous too."

Her sentence hung in the air, as though she puzzled over some flaw in it.

"He'd know many people through his job, of course," he said.

"Yes."

"A curiously impeccable man. Impeccable, I think that's the word. A New Englander, I believe."

He felt her attention focus suddenly.

"Yes. Very much a New Englander."

He glanced at her. She was frowning, her lips slightly apart. He was now certain that she was about to launch into a confidence of some weight, if she could find the words, or he could prompt

61

them. He would not have been notably surprised nor necessarily have misjudged her if she had. Beneath the lacquered surface, something jarred her profoundly in her relationship with Pridie. Clearly she could not stop herself from thinking about it. Perhaps at some time she would have to talk about it. A woman would after all sometimes talk about her lover with startling objectivity, particularly to a stranger. (Didn't part of the appeal of priests lie precisely in their stylized anonymity?) The fact that she did so might seem inevitably to argue the end of the affair. Yet she could return into it totally immediately afterwards, with no apparent sense of contradiction. Of course there had not necessarily been any. The manoeuvre could have been designed simply as an aid to perspective, a mirror.

But on this occasion Jeanette said nothing further, and looked back instead at the road ahead.

They passed the *Salle des Fêtes* and the modern clean building of the Banque de l'Indochine. Some hundreds of metres further on she guided him to the right into a small Lao house which faced directly on to the river. The house stood on short stilts like legs. It appeared constantly about to spring forward into the river, like the small naked brown amphibious Lao boys who lived in the villages along its banks and seemed to spend most of their lives leaping into its waters.

"I'll only be a moment. Would you like to come in?"

He closed the car door behind her. He did not believe particularly in hurrying in the subtle courts of love. Conceivably she was already delicately beckoning him to these, conceivably they were already engaged in the first intricate steps. And conceivably they were not. His interpretation could be completely wrong. The eager gambols of haste were not decorous in such things. Moreover, they were so frequently deflated. The door could shut tartly, mentally blackening the eye, and chastening the spirit. The risks were appalling. And, after all, he had the time to be sure. She had already neatly showed him where she lived.

"Thank you. Perhaps I should get the car turned instead."

When she came out again he drove her back along the river, left at the American Ambassador's house, up to and past the prison, and to the right into the Boulevard Circulaire. The bursts of coloured lights and the muffled sounds of revelry guided him down the steep dip into the Vieng Rattray's courtyard. With a pleasant sense of satire he parked the *Deux Chevaux* between the serried ranks of Mercedes-Benz and the huge new launch-like American saloons. He extracted the girl and walked her to the double-storied building. Pridie's blue Jeep station-wagon was parked near the club door, facing outwards, like a sentinel. He thought that it looked slightly aggrieved.

The night club, on the ground floor, was subtly lit, and from his former visit he knew it to be as expert as any he had seen in Saigon. A long bar curved away immediately on the right of the entrance. There were two Vietnamese serving behind the bar, and, at the cash desk, a superb Vietnamese girl, in a pure white high-collared bodice with long gauzy sleeves, her jet black hair luxuriant down to her slim shoulders, and a considerably more provocative bust than she was ethnically entitled to. Straight ahead was a good wooden dance floor. It was crowded. There were a few Americans, probably Marine guards from the Embassy, or men from the road construction teams that hung hopefully about Vientiane for the elusive USOM tenders. He could also see a few Frenchmen, and many Lao. About two-thirds of the taxi-girls were Chinese, the remainder Vietnamese and Thai. There was a French five-man orchestra on the dais to the right of the dance floor, against the wall. They were pounding out a fast fox-trot with gusto. Pridie and Dumergue and the Marivells would be somewhere in the penumbric gloom to the left of the dance floor or across it.

"Table de Monsieur Pridie?"

The Vietnamese waiter wore a smart white dinner jacket and a black bow tie.

He did not look as though he thought much of Jean-Philippe.

"Pas moyen table. Trop de monde. Devez attendre."

It sounded like a political slogan.

"Doit y en avoir une," said Jeanette firmly. *"Monsieur Pridie. Ambassade Americaine."*

"Ah!" said the Vietnamese brightly. *"Ambassade Americaine. Monsieur Pridie. Par ici."*

He shot a quick pitying look at Jean-Philippe, evidently for not having put the question to him clearly in the first place; in the Vieng Rattray you naturally identified people by their position, not their names. He led them at an astonishingly fast clip round the murk to the left and to a table on the far side of the floor, and disappeared with a marginal bow.

Still unadjusted to the strategic lack of light, it took Jean-Philippe a few moments to realize that the third man at the table was not Pridie, but a short compact Lao.

"Permit me," said Dumergue. "His Excellency Khopkhan. Mademoiselle Resnier. Monsieur Raymond."

"Enchanted."

"Enchanted."

63

The short man had got negligently half up from his chair. By contrast his handshake was fierce.

"Mademoiselle?"

"Excellency?"

"Brandy?"

"Oh. Thank you. Suze-soda."

"Whisky-soda?" said Khopkhan.

"Willingly," said Jean-Philippe.

Khopkhan raised his eyebrows to the others, but there were no takers.

"Suze-soda Whikkie-soda," said the reappeared waiter intelligently.

"*A mon compte*," said Khopkhan.

"*Excellence*," said the waiter.

"Mademoiselle I've had the pleasure of seeing before, I think," said Khopkhan. "Though not of meeting. With Monsieur Pridie?"

"Yes," said Jeanette.

Khopkhan turned to Jean-Philippe.

"More recent, I think, Monsieur Raymond?"

"About a month," said Jean-Philippe.

Lacking the correct khènes, flutes, xylophones, and drums for it, the French orchestra was valiantly producing its best towards a Ram-Vong. Out on the floor the Chinese and Vietnamese taxi-girls were diplomatically assuming the local colour of this dance and gyrating solemnly about their male Lao partners. The few Lao girls, daughters of Ministers or rich Lao merchants, stood out at once. They circled their consorts gravely, never touching them, their arms and their apparently boneless wrists and fingers weaving delicately and constantly, like seaweed curled by currents underwater. Khopkhan followed Jean-Philippe's eyes.

"We're a simple people, Monsieur Raymond. You mustn't expect too much. It's not France."

The French was flawless. Someone had told Jean-Philippe that Khopkhan was Paris-educated. The remark was interesting. Traditional deferential Old Eastern Courtesy, or just possibly the very politest warning? As politely, Jean-Philippe said:

"Or a most complex people?"

Khopkhan looked at him with more interest.

"In what manner?"

"The real frontier of the eternal war between East and West, China and India, Lao Tze and Buddha. More even than Viet Nam or Cambodia or Thailand. The extraordinary ethnic intermixture of Indonesian and Mongolian and Thai and Khmer—"

"You've forgotten the French influence," said Khopkhan gravely. "You shouldn't forget the French."

Jean-Philippe looked at him and laughed. It showed a nice sense of irony. The rumour was that Khopkhan had worked with the Japanese, for the Greater Asian Co-Prosperity Sphere. The French had got him and lined him up to be shot when they came back in 1946. Sommith, deputy for Nam Tha, who had worked with the French, and was related to Khopkhan, had interceded and saved him. It was the way that things were often really done in Laos, through the big family relationships.

"That's true," said Jean-Philippe, "French too can be a subtle language at times."

Khopkhan chuckled.

"Tell me about *France-Franche*," he said.

Jean-Philippe glanced at Dumergue and Marivell, but they shrugged slightly, as if to show that it had not been they who had mentioned that to Khopkhan.

"About what it says," he replied. "Reasonably frank, when it can afford to be. Excellency."

"It's a great moral quality," said Khopkhan wickedly.

"I wonder where Pridie's got to?" said Marivell. He sounded a little anxious. He looked as though he thought that this verbal fencing had gone on about long enough.

"He'll be about somewhere," said Khopkhan, "working, no doubt."

"Working?" said Marivell.

Khopkhan looked at him.

"A very serious man, our Monsieur Pridie."

Jean-Philippe wondered if Marivell had got the faint mockery. Khopkhan turned back towards him.

"Did you understand the Lao, Monsieur Raymond?"

"Excellency?"

"At our little meeting this afternoon."

"Oh. No. I didn't see you there."

"I'm a small man," said Khopkhan modestly. "I stay in the background, you know."

Simple, my foot, thought Jean-Philippe.

"It was well attended," he said. "May I ask you a question?"

"Never refused," said Khopkhan. "Between friends."

"Your own definition of your party's aims?"

"It's not strictly mine," said Khopkhan. "There are quite a few of us. Nor is it strictly a political party. An association, if you like. The aims? Action."

"Against the North Vietnamese battalions?" said Jean-Philippe. "Excellency?"

Khopkhan looked at him sardonically.

"Monsieur Raymond," he said. "You know this region. Seven years, eight years, was it, in Viet Nam? I have the impression that we understand each other. On some grounds, say. You know the Viet Minh. I know the Pathet Lao. I admire their efficiency. And their dedication. They're professionals. And hardly handicapped by scruples. The moral is simple. If we want to survive against them we've got to act as forcefully, by whatever means, before it's too late. And however we happen to present our case to the external world."

"What stops that?" said Jean-Philippe. "What stops the action?"

"You know that," said Khopkhan. "The fatal lethargy of traditionalism. Corruption, which with us has also been a tradition. You don't get dedication to great causes easily in this climate, you know. Let's state our enemy another way. In a word, Buddhism."

"Buddhism?"

"The Buddhist attitude, then, as we have it here. If we do not grow out of that we shall never survive against communism."

Jean-Philippe raised his eyebrows. In a Lao that statement was about as revolutionary as was Galileo's when he insisted that the world was round.

"And what do you put in its place?"

"It's a good question," said Khopkhan, "very good. In passing, as a matter of interest, what are you putting in the place of your Christianity these days?"

Jean-Philippe laughed.

"But if you want publishable information," said Khopkhan, "come and see me. You know the Ministry?"

"Yes."

"Good, Mademoiselle?"

"Excellency?"

"Will you dance?"

The two moved off into the web of dancers. The orchestra had degenerated into a slow fox-trot. It was a rhythm that seemed particularly to suit the Chinese girls on the floor. They moved to it with langorous precision, their skirts slit on the left from knee to thigh, the sheer expensive sensuality of their revealed and silk-sheathed legs emphasized by the contrast of their modest high-throated Shantung bodices, demurely tight across their breasts, and sealed by their two-inch-high collars. The Chinese girls were wearing their favourite expression of immaculate contempt. Indeed, their features seemed set permanently in it, as though their cosmetics had simply frozen on application. Jean-Philippe caught glimpses of Khopkhan through this shifting erotic spectacle, dancing steadily, only fractionally taller than Jeanette.

"Tough little gentleman," he said.

"Regular little man of action," said Dumergue.

"And a very fair share of dignity. Corrupt?"

"Not that I know of," said Dumergue. "A certain integrity, I'd say. The old passionate-nationalist line."

"They say that he worked with the Japanese," said Jean-Philippe.

"I hadn't heard that," said Marivell. He looked shocked.

"So the story goes," said Dumergue. "No one really knows. That part of Lao history is decently obscure."

"He'd like power," said Jean-Philippe.

"Love it," said Dumergue. "And of course the Japanese had the habit of winning their wars at that time. It could have seemed the best bet. Why not? We couldn't have looked so impressive here in our Vichy hat."

Jean-Philippe saw Mme. Marivell glance at her husband. She was clearly not at all interested in all this high-class political comment. Marivell smiled at her at once, and they went on to the floor.

"His market intelligence seems pretty sound too," said Jean-Philippe.

"On you?" said Dumergue. "Yes. You ought to be flattered. I wonder who—"

"I wonder where our friend is?" said Jean-Philippe.

"Pridie? Strode off to the gents. He's been back some time. Busy, by the entrance."

Following Dumergue's eyes, he saw Pridie standing in front of the row of unflagged taxi-girls who were sitting in a row to the right of the main door, waiting patiently for the Madame to signal them to a client's table, where they would earn their percentage on the drinks and on the hundred-Kip-per-hour tickets which the management charged the clients for their company. There were three Chinese and two Vietnamese girls sitting, and Jean-Philippe watched with interest while Pridie went from one to the other of them. Surprisingly, each girl shook her head.

"It doesn't look so much like work to me," said Jean-Philippe.

"I wonder," said Dumergue enigmatically, "you'd say that he was getting a lot of pleasure out of it?"

At the last girl, Pridie shrugged and turned and began to walk round the floor to the table.

"Hullo," he said easily. "Sold her or something?"

"Jeanette?" said Jean-Philippe.

"Jeanette."

"Out on the floor with Khopkhan competing with the Heathen Chinee."

Pridie glanced out to the floor and looked relieved and sat down, on Jean-Philippe's right.

"Pleasant girl," he said, evidently just to show that there were no hard feelings.

"Most attractive," said Jean-Philippe emphatically. He watched Pridie's eyes flick up at him at once. Pridie put his left hand on the face of the table, and reached for his glass with his right.

"Cheers," Pridie said to him.

"Cheers, indeed."

It was the first time that he had noticed Pridie's left hand. Even in that light, because he was immediately next to it, he could see that the top joints of the third and fourth fingers were missing, that all the knuckles were curiously flattened, and that the back of the hand itself was badly scarred. Again, exactly as though he had heard Jean-Philippe think, Pridie lifted his left hand at that moment and put it casually on his knees under the table.

"War?" said Jean-Philippe.

The slow music ended, and the orchestra burst suddenly into several bars of a fast syncopated beat, as though trying to catch up on itself. It stopped abruptly.

Pridie did not seem to have heard him. No doubt the burst of music had masked his words.

"That happened in the war?" he said.

"What?" said Pridie.

"Your left hand," said Jean-Philippe. "That must have been quite a chop."

Even then he could see no harm in having raised the subject. Most men were not exactly loath to talk about their war wounds, if they could be got decently into the conversation.

"A little war," said Pridie shortly.

"You were in France, then? Or Italy?"

Pridie looked round at him then. The light grey eyes behind their discreet rimless glasses were cold and suspicious, and the face shut as a door.

"Nothing so dramatic," said Pridie, and turned away at once, and got up.

Looking up, Jean-Philippe followed him. Jeanette and Marivell and his wife went back to their places.

Modest sort of character, thought Jean-Philippe, glancing at

Pridie, who was exchanging social inanities politely with Khopkhan. Pridie was not letting you in at all to his private world. That was strictly forbidden territory. It was no real loss to Jean-Philippe, though. He could stand it if Pridie could.

Did he let Jeanette in there ever? What was the mystery anyway? What was the big private show? Why was it admission by membership card only?

"My thanks," said Khopkhan. "I must get back to my friends."

He bowed, and as he left the orchestra repeated its rapid syncopated beat, and the lights dimmed further and blacked out, leaving a sharp silver spot on the announcer on the dais. He was a short tubby balding man with dandruff on the lapels of his dinner-jacket like talcum powder, but there was a laudable streak of tenacity in him. Pinned solitary, he waited doggedly for silence. When that was absolute, almost religious, he advised the audience that he had the signal honour to present to them Julie, from Paris.

Julie, from Paris, came on stage from the wings to a positive frenzy of musical adulation from the band. Spare spotlights leapt uneasily about and found her finally and trooped on to the dais after her. She looked arrogant and publicly immaculate as an American drum majorette. The initial applause did not quite live up to her, but a flattering hum of interest arose more appropriately from the audience after it had had time to have a good look at her. On the face of it she was worth it. She was a tall slim girl with elegant breasts, blue eyes, and long blonde hair. She was dressed in pink gauze and high-heeled gold shoes. When the animal hum had dropped again suitably she gave a short imperious lift of her hand, and the band fell over themselves in the background to get back to their instruments. Her blue eyes lost their merciless sniper's focus, her expression softened into one of deep devotion, her lips parted, and her gaze diffused itself into the clouds of cigarette-smoke above the audience. She began to dance lightly about the outer edge of the floor to the band's obedient rhythm of C'est Si Bon, stripping the layers of gauze progressively from her body. They seemed to go on and on, baffling the expectations.

"Original," said Dumergue.

The predominantly Lao male audience did not seem critically so exacting. They were watching the white girl undress herself for them with single-minded intensity, as though bent on helping. Julie stood finally at the edge of the dance floor and took the last gauze from the upper part of her body. Her nipples were fetchingly rouged. They looked a little like decorations stuck on as an afterthought. Daintily and orgasmically, she stepped from her high gold dancing slippers. She fell forward gracefully until she

69

knelt outwards at the edge of the floor, the final gauze still pink about her hips, her expression now frankly ecstatic. The spotlight cut, lit again for a long second, and cut finally, leaving on the mind the sharply-etched image of her kneeling there with her body arched receptively back and her arms and head and hair flung back, as naked and sheer as a statue.

In that last second of full directed light Jean-Philippe had also caught the image of Pridie's iced cold profile; not at all because he had been looking for it, but simply because Pridie was half in his way. Pridie had looked a little like a conscientious soldier about to march hopelessly off at dawn. He did not look very happy. Perhaps the fact that it was now a white girl, not a brown, not an olive, who unveiled herself to a predominantly brown audience, not a white one, distressed him. In fact, as a calendar turned, this change was one between only a few years. But, judged at the infinitely slow pace of changes in culture, this was a leap of centuries. These, not the mere neat replacements of political systems, most truly marked the grave turning-point of history.

Or perhaps more simply Pridie just did not like naked women.

When the diffused lights came up again slowly about the hall, Julie was of course already decently gone. Released from the tension, the audience was now chattering happily to itself, clearly pleased that it had done its bit in the performance. Only the pink gauze scattered around the floor and the two gold slippers at its edge now showed that Julie had ever been there. The two shining slippers stood primly on their heels exactly parallel to each other, facing outwards at the extreme edge of the floor. It looked as if Julie had stepped thoughtfully out of them, preserving the proprieties to the last, before finally diving out in an abandoned manner into the audience. The bespectacled French saxophonist from the band circled the floor and bent in his dinner-jacket and reverently gathered Julie's slippers and her gauzes.

"Will you dance?" said Pridie courteously to Mme. Marivell. His expression was once again set in its usual casual charm. Perhaps Jean-Philippe's sudden sharp view of him had been no more than a trick of the light.

Jean-Philippe glanced at Jeanette. She was looking after Pridie, but she turned and smiled at Jean-Philippe when she felt his eyes.

She was a good and supple dancer. Her pelvis and tummy rumbaed enticingly against him. Slightly distracted, he circumnavigated a Lao-locked Chinese girl, and looked out in a controlled manner above Jeanette's head. He could just make out Khopkhan at a table by the far wall with two other Lao and an expensive spray of taxi-girls. Only too aware of Jeanette's rich black hair just brushing his cheek, of her scent, of her small perfect body moulded in beautifully exact rhythm against his, Jean-Philippe set himself to think safely of Khopkhan instead. Action, Khopkhan had said. Our aims are action. Jean-Philippe began to wonder to himself when the guns would start to go off.

CHAPTER VII

The guns were out in Laos at Christmas 1959, wrote Jean-Philippe. *By chance or design, the new King, Savang Vatthana, was still in Vientiane after the That Luang. This is the annual feast named after the temple which King Setthatirat built in 1566 to confirm this city as capital of his Land of the Million Elephants. Geomanciers fixed the temple's site at Phia Vat, three kilometres to the east, at a small thirteenth-century stupa supposed to hold many treasures, including yet another hair of the Buddha. We are told that heralds announced this decision in the streets, to the sound of cymbals, gongs, flutes, and drums. A pregnant young lady named Sao-Si promptly left home and husband and children and flung herself into the hole dug for the temple's main column, which was then obligingly erected over her like a permanent phallic symbol. Thus she became the new capital's patron spirit.*

The feast can also be a useful time for the King to demonstrate any major change to his policies, for the land's Chaomuong and mandarins and heads of cantons always meet here then to swear fidelity to him, through a Master of Ceremonies who first dips the points of their swords or rifles into a bowl of lustral water.

Modern power politics inevitably jar across this grave background of myth and legend and tradition, like the sound of a whisky bottle dropped in church. This year Dag Hammerskjöld sat imperturbably with the new King in the diplomatic stand at the second day of the That Luang to watch the annual game of Ti-Khi, like a professional swordsman at the school sports. Ti-Khi is inimitably Lao. Reputed to be the ancestor to polo, it is played on a vaguely rectangular field with curved headed sticks and a ball as big as a grapefruit. The aim is simple: to get the ball over the other side's far line. There are no exact boundaries, rules, referees, or limits to the number of players, who stream on and off the field as the partisan loyalty or alcoholic fancy takes them.

The That Luang always starts at full moon, and the nights are as ceremonial. Processions of young men and girls and saffron-robed monks, called canaries by the irreverent French, pattern them. They carry flickering resin torches and walk to the thin sound of gongs, the monks to the many torch-lit temples, the young men and girls to the thriving fair by the That. This is filled with Lao and Chinese and Vietnamese stalls for soups and foods and drinks and sweetmeats and fruits and games of chance of all kinds. Youths and girls, chaperoned by betel-chewing matrons, sit opposite one another on mats at the Courts of Love cross-chanting interminable couplets of flowered words. Rockets soar up above the That and burst into myriad cascading arcs of coloured fire. It is a child's fragile world of immediate sensory delights, and in it this year it was difficult indeed to believe that a civil war really existed. In this sense the Lao are not child-like at all, but most highly civilized. So far here, the wars have always stopped on holidays.

But on December 26, well after Hammarskjöld had gone, the King woke in his Vientiane residence to find three Royal Army armoured cars sitting on his lawns. Happily, their guns were pointing outwards. The reason given for their presence was fashionable: to guard him against an imminent Pathet Lao attack (of which in fact there had been no sign). The shrewd guess is whether the new King was really all that surprised to see them there.

For the ideals of the CDIN or Cédin group (the initials stand impressively for the Comité de la Défense des Intérêts Nationaux) that mounted the coup d'état could not have seemed too alien to King Savang Vatthana, a somewhat autocratically-minded gentleman of middle age who succeeded his late and revered father on November 1. The coup began with intense police and army patrol activity in Vientiane on December 25 and ended by forcing Sananikone's resignation on the last day but one of the year. As the CDIN saw it, Saninikone had two main faults. First, he was a reasonable man. Mid-December he announced publicly that he would follow a policy of reconciliation towards the Pathet Lao, and would consequently call free elections in April 1960. During his visit Hammarskjöld allegedly advised exactly this kind of moderate policy. To some it might seem no more than basic common sense. The Pathet Lao are an established political fact, particularly strong in the countryside. Laos has a thousand kilometres of frontier in common with Yunnan and North Viet Nam. The Chinese and North Vietnamese hold all the strategic and logistic advantages. Outright suppression of the Pathet (a central CDIN

72

aim) could provoke a direct communist invasion and, short of global war, a defeat for the West as certain and humiliating as that which we suffered in this theatre.

Secondly, Sananikone simultaneously purged his cabinet of all CDIN extremists.

The CDIN certainly inspired the coup; it would not be polite to guess who else backed them. Three generals signed the *January 1* army communiqué announcing the coup and the King's acceptance of Sananikine's resignation. One general is the CDIN's president. Four "political counsellors" visited the King straight after the coup, with the generals who effected it. One was Khopkhan, formerly Foreign Minister. All these counsellors were CDIN men.

The French, British, and American ambassadors acted with surprising speed and uniformity. Each saw the King on *January 4* to advise him that their governments no longer necessarily saw coups d'état as the best way of solving political crises. Hammarskjöld sent an irate telegram which improved the impact of their visits. So, for the moment, sanity has returned to Alice-In-Wonderland, and the King has dropped the convenient answer of a right-wing military dictatorship and has instead named a provisional government to organize free elections.

Meanwhile Prince Souvannouvong, head of the Pathet's political party, the Neo Lao Haksat, sits still untried with eight other duly-elected NLH deputies and seven Pathet leaders in an army prison outside Vientiane, and the Pathet in the country stay ominously calm. Probably they calculate that they will certainly win the elections if they are free. If they are not, they will at least be able to look even more righteous than usual when they next attack.

But it would be reckless to think that we have seen the last of the CDIN. They keep the key posts of Foreign Affairs and National Defence in the provisional cabinet. And the present victory for common sense will not please everyone else. Probably not the Pentagon's organization in Laos, euphemistically called the Programme Evaluations Office, and which consists of numerous, muscular, and immediately recognizable active-list officers in civilian clothes; the PEO tend to see the CDIN as clean young men of action after their own heart. Certainly not the special services of one Western power. The better-informed of the small Lao birds say that a member of this service was at a meeting late December in an adjoining capital between that country's leader and the youngest and potentially most powerful of the coup generals, who is also a CDIN leader. The statesman passed the general a sum of U.S. dollars running well into six figures and no doubt

*intended for immediate political needs. The ways of God may be
devious, but Western policy in Laos must sometimes give him
fair competition.*

Jean-Philippe read his article through and folded it. He addressed the Air-Mail envelope to *France-Franche's* Paris box number and marked it Express and put it in the breast pocket of his shirt.

He went out to his balcony. The evening was calm. His flat was at the top of a three-storied building. It was not far from the Constellation, where he sometimes had his meals. He looked down.

It was of course the oldest myth that you ever learnt anything from history, in time. He doubted that they would publish his last paragraph. With the Berlin crisis, official harmony with the Americans was probably too important.

The cloak and dagger experts had evidently acted right on their own, uncontrolled by their ambassador (who was indeed reported to be furious with them). But there was nothing to stop them acting like that again, even if their drive for a solution by force seemed romantic lunacy. In Laos, it was hard to see how the Americans could repeat the British elimination of the communists in Malaya. The facts were against them. The British in Malaya had had a sealed northern border, a trained native administration which was reasonably loyal, good internal land communications, first-rate Commonwealth and Malay armed forces, and fair local support. The Americans in Laos did not have one of these advantages. Probably the only thing to do was to integrate the Pathet as rapidly as possible and so control the bastards, before they got too strong. The drive for a right-wing solution by force would play straight into their hands. First, it would fail. Second, it would bracket the West again delightfully with the reactionary and decayed. For the Pathet would get their external aid all right then. The dangers were not the Russians, but the Stalinist Chinese and Ho Chi Minh, who probably disliked a pro-American military build-up on their borders enough to do something violent about it.

The Chinese and Vietnamese shops opposite the Constellation were still fully lit and active. A peak-capped *samlaw* driver in a blue shirt and shorts stood on the pedals of his machine to brake it in front of the bar, and a man got out of the hooded seat behind and paid him; a big man, a *farang*, in an open-necked sports shirt. A peasant passed along the uneven earth pavement in the street directly under Jean-Philippe. He still wore his conical daytime hat; from above it looked like a large coin. He had a full kerosene tin at each end of his long bamboo carrying-pole, which sprang slowly up and down in rhythm with his paces, as if to encourage him. Jean-Philippe went back into the room and took his jacket over his arm and went down into the street.

The Constellation bar was fraught with foreign correspondents. He saw the stars from *Le Monde* and *Paris-Soir* and a reporter and photographer from *Paris-Match* and the men from the *New York Times* and from *Time* and *Life* and the gentleman from the *Daily Telegraph* sitting aloof at the far end of the bar. Also the French newsreel cameraman who had lost a leg at Dien Bien Phu and had achieved more recent fame. He had spent a few days in Sam Neua town. Finding it excrutiatingly calm, he had enterprisingly organized a mock attack by a Royal Army patrol in the jungle, their machine-guns and mortars and grenades going off in all directions. He had airmailed his film back to Paris with conspicuous success.

Jean-Philippe felt that he had already done his work for the week, so he nodded generally to the correspondents and went straight to the bar instead. Vitry looked over his shoulder and saw him coming and raised his glass.

"Like a Suze, Jean?" said Vitry.

"God forbid," said Jean-Philippe. "No let me."

"All right," said Vitry. "Make it a Suze, then."

"A Suze," Jean-Philippe said to the barman. "And a Ricard. Suze-soda?" he said to Vitry.

"*Suze-sec*," said Vitry with dignity.

"It's an obscene drink," said Jean-Philippe. "It's your homosexual background."

"Even straight?" said Vitry.

"Even straight," said Jean-Philippe.

Vitry observed him affectionately.

"And that to a good father of a family," said Vitry. "Better than *that*, anyway. You know what they say. *Anis* turns you mad. That's bad. Or impotent. That's worse."

Jean-Philippe motioned upwards with his fingers and the Vietnamese barman poured the iced water carefully into the glass. It spiralled into the yellow Ricard, curdling it white immediately. He looked back at Vitry. He said:

"Do those damned machines of yours still fly?"

"Of course," said Vitry. He looked hurt. Flying was sacred to him. It was the only thing that he could do.

"It's a miracle," said Jean-Philippe.

Vitry was pilot of an Air Laos run to Bangkok. Jean-Philippe

75

had known him briefly in Saigon, when Vitry was flying reconnaissance. He was a tall thin angular man with a thatch of prematurely white hair. Jean-Philippe had once shown him exhaustively over the palaces of pleasure in Cholon, and Vitry had always afterwards believed himself indebted to him.

"How's Diane?" said Jean-Philippe.

"Well, thanks."

"And the kids?" said Jean-Philippe.

"The kids are fine," said Vitry.

"That's good," said Jean-Philippe. "Give her my regards."

"Sure," said Vitry. "When are you going to start doing a man's job, Jean?"

"Why pick on me?" said Jean-Philippe. "Anyway, you call driving those things a man's job?"

"Certainly," said Vitry.

"Have a Suze," said Jean-Philippe.

Vitry pushed his glass at the barman.

"Why," said Vitry, "Saurin even got some holes in his Strato the other day."

"That's not surprising," said Jean-Philippe, "it's old age."

"No, no," said Vitry, "he was flying too low."

"A little welcome from the Pathet?" said Jean-Philippe.

"Probably," said Vitry. "It was near Sam Neua."

"D'you get up there often?" said Jean-Philippe.

"We take it in turns," said Vitry. "Business is very brisk. We keep flying Royal Army all over the place. They don't trust their own pilots, you know."

"I met a Security Council man the other day," said Jean-Philippe. "He was up at Sam Neua."

"Oh, we fly them too," said Vitry, "but they never see anything."

"This doesn't bore you?" said Jean-Philippe. He had taken the envelope which contained his article from his pocket and he slid it now across the bar to Vitry. Vitry looked at the address on the envelope.

"Anything for the fatherland," he said. He put the envelope in his pocket and began his new Suze.

"It's just as well that they never read *France-Franche* here," he said. "Or they'd throw you out, Jean."

"They?"

"The Cédin," said Vitry, "with perhaps a little help from the Americans."

Jean-Philippe laughed.

"You still have that obsession about the Americans? Indo-

76

China's finished. Besides, I have influence. You're talking to a personal friend of Pridie's."

Vitry looked at him sharply.

"Pridie?"

"You know him, don't you?" said Jean-Philippe. "Something at their Embassy."

"Yes," said Vitry, "yes, I know Pridie."

But his blond eyebrows raised and his expression lightened suddenly. Turning to where Vitry looked, Jean-Philippe saw Dumergue come into the bar. A slight man was with him, probably about thirty-five, dark, with glasses.

"Meet Joe," said Dumergue.

"Joe Short," said Joe, and shook hands with them.

"Journalist?" said Vitry brightly. "Whisky?"

"Oil," said Joe. "Beer. If I may."

"Ah," said Vitry, making some private leap of the imagination. "American?"

"That's right," said Joe. "You're French?"

Vitry looked startled.

"Certainly!"

Joe bowed very slightly to him.

"Your health," he said.

"Health," said Vitry, after a moment.

Jean-Philippe felt the sharp aniseed bite of the Ricard on his tongue and watched the American over the top of his glass with amusement. The face was pleasant and unremarkable, but the irony and accentless French uncommon.

Dumergue glanced at Jean-Philippe.

"He's really quite civilized," he said. "An *évolué*."

Short looked at him and smiled. He said:

"Those years in France, of course."

"Of course," said Dumergue.

"In the war?" said Vitry.

"I was there for a while," said Short.

"Army?"

"No," said Short. "Air Force. I was a navigator."

Vitry glanced at the glasses which Short wore.

"I'm long-sighted," said Short apologetically, "but not so badly."

"This hero flies aeroplanes too," said Dumergue. "Air Laos Stratos, those fat things that waddle on the ground like ducks. It's all they'll let him fly now."

"And your sister," said Vitry cheerfully. He turned back to Joe. He said: "I used to fly Mosquitoes."

77

"That's a very good aircraft," said Joe, now saying exactly the right thing.

At the table immediately behind them, the Gaumont cameraman said suddenly and so vigorously and loudly that you could not possibly ignore him:

"And why do you make such a thing about the Viet Minh battalions? There are no Viet Minh battalions in Laos. Believe me, friend, you would know all about it if there were."

There was a silence. The voice which replied was very American indeed.

"Our best sources of information lead us to infer," said the man who sat at the table with him, "that there are certainly regular Viet Minh units in Laos. Therefore, what we support now through the United Nations could be looked upon as a sane policy of containment."

It sounded as though he were reading from a text. The tone was pontifical. The American was obviously right. No one in his right mind could possibly contest that. The Gaumont cameraman contested it.

"Ah!" he said nastily. "Containment, is it? And containing myths is a particular American policy?"

There was another silence, this time outraged. In it Jean-Philippe glanced at Short. Short was watching the exchange behind them, without expression. To distract his attention, Jean-Philippe said:

"You're very elegant this evening. And Dumergue. A cocktail? The Vieng Rattray?"

"A funeral," said Dumergue.

"That's nice," said Jean-Philippe.

"The mother of one of my dealers," said Short. "Why don't you two join us?"

Jean-Philippe looked at Dumergue.

"How did you get in on that?" he said.

"Short's dealer is intelligent," said Dumergue. "He got a government loan out of me some months ago, to develop his service stations."

"Enterprising," said Vitry.

"He remembers his friends too," said Dumergue.

"They tell me Lao funerals can be quite gay," said Jean-Philippe. He turned to Vitry. "Well, let's try it. Why not?"

"Sorry," said Vitry. "Diane's waiting for me. Next time, Jean."

"I can't beat that," said Jean-Philippe. "Give her my regards."

"Have a good funeral," said Vitry.

Vitry split off from them when they left the bar, and they

78

walked over to Short's Chevrolet. Short drove them up the Lang Xang, past the National Assembly building, and out on to the road to Tangone. Once they were out of the city, the dark was complete in the empty rice-fields about them.

"What's new on the political front?" said Dumergue.

"You're the expert," said Jean-Philippe.

"No," said Dumergue. "But you know that Souvanna Phouma's back?"

"Only that he was coming," said Jean-Philippe.

"Talking of funerals," said Dumergue. "From Paris, to attend the burial of the King, his father. Officially. Unofficially, also probably to try to get back into power."

"Souvanna Phouma was never in the direct line of succession, was he?" said Jean-Philippe.

"No," said Dumergue, "he wasn't a son of the King's first wife. Though they do say that Savang Vatthana has always been inclined to keep a wary eye on him, presumably as a possible rival."

"He was Lao Ambassador in France," said Jean-Philippe.

"Yes," said Dumergue, "rusticated there since they broke his 1958 government."

"They?" said Jean-Philippe.

Dumergue glanced at Short. The American smiled. He said: "Don't hold me personally responsible for the Dulles line."

"The sin of reconciliation with the Pathet, was it?" said Jean-Philippe.

"Exactly that," said Dumergue, "exactly what Sananikone tried to do last month. And with no better success."

"I used that thing about the Bangkok meeting," said Jean-Philippe casually. "Thanks. But I don't think they'll print it."

Dumergue glanced briefly at Short again. He said:

"No sources named?"

"No names, of course," said Jean-Philippe.

"How good is Souvanna Phouma?" he went on, after a moment.

"Very good," said Dumergue. "Optimistic to a fault. He always believes what people tell him. But probably the only man who could unify this country."

Ahead of them on the right, they could now see broad flames flickering up, back off the road behind a thin line of trees. A rocket went up, miniature in the distance like tracer, and burst high in the black night.

"They must be burning the old lady already," said Short.

They slowed for the turning. Somewhere ahead of them in the dark, on the left of the metalled road, was the military prison which held Souvannouvong. They followed the rutted track to

79

the right towards the flames. There was a break in the line of trees and, just after it, a fenced parking area holding about a hundred cars, mainly new Mercedes-Benz and American saloons; evidently Short's dealer had his connections. They left the car and walked towards the broad orange leaping light.

It was as if a large part of the That Luang had been transplanted neatly. Central to the gathering ahead was the burning bier. It had something of the considerable moral dignity of a Victorian four-poster, which it resembled. Coloured streamers caparisoned it. The wooden coffin was built in about two-thirds of the way down and the fire roared and muttered merrily about it. On the fabric at the sides of this final bed, not yet completely burnt out, were various erotic illustrations, including some, originally dramatized, of the basic male and female sexual organs: evidently, life did not easily lose its prior claims in Laos. From time to time, a bald monk stoked the coffin thoughtfully with a long piece of hardened bamboo.

A rich variety of stalls circled the bier at a respectable distance. There was a well-lit stage on the far side. A play was being acted on it, probably an episode from the Ramayana. About thirty people were watching it, sitting decorously on the ground, or standing with their backs to the bier. The reedy notes of a *khène* struck out across the interval of ground. It punctuated the high wavering notes of some singer hidden in the wings, and cued the slow movements of the actors, a subtle change in the position of a hand, or of the head of the girl dancer, which was charged with an immense crown that spiralled up in silver rings to a slim needle point. To the left of this theatre a film van was showing a sixteen-millimetre documentary to an audience about as big and surprisingly no less absorbed. Jean-Philippe could hear snatches of the French sound-track. From that distance, the commentator's voice seemed absolutely suffused with emotion.

". . . the mission of this vital section of French industry today, to serve the world's ever-increasing needs for ferro-mecous-disulphide compounds . . ."

Merde, thought Jean-Philippe.

". . . And even this. A communal crêche. That really makes the employees feel part of the productive team . . ."

Remerde.

The other stalls were much less static. There were several miniature restaurants serving beer and wine and that lethal Thai brand of whisky which tasted like mellowed turpentine. Lao men and women and youths and girls moved in and out of the stalls, always with that extraordinary natural grace, as though as a race, like the Thai, they found it quite impossible to make any movement at all, however trivial, which could not immediately be construed as part of a slow ballet. Jean-Philippe could also see what appeared to be a raised boxing-ring on the left. About fifteen young Lao couples were solemnly dancing the Ram-Wong in it. No doubt there would be enough lusty conceptions behind the bushes later that night far to outweigh the sad passing of Short's dealer's mother.

Short led them to the right. About thirty shaven-headed monks sat there in three tiers of benches. They gazed impassively at the roaring central fire, scratching episodically under their saffron robes. A young monk at the foot of the tiers lit a large firework shaped like a dinner-plate and loped forward in front of Jean-Philippe, nodding very decently to him in passing, and hurled it hissing up over the stalls to its high point of explosion into multi-coloured stars.

"May I present Monsieur Saovong," said Short. "Monsieur Raymond. Of course you already know Monsieur Dumergue, Monsieur Saovong."

Short had used the Lao greeting, joining his hands in front of his chest as if praying, and bending slightly over them.

"Enchanted," said Jean-Philippe.

"Monsieur Saovong," continued Short.

"Enchanted."

"Monsieur Saovong."

"Enchanted."

"And Monsieur Saovong."

"Enchanted."

The four brothers stood in a descending line next to the tiers of monks. The youngest Saovong, of some sixteen years, also indeed wore the saffron robe and his hair was shaved to the skull. His eyebrows had been removed too. It gave him a constant expression of absolute amazement.

"He enters the monastery for three weeks now, of course," said the senior Saovong. Like his two middle brothers, he was dressed very smartly in a dark lounge suit.

"Of course," said Jean-Philippe. He added:

"I hope it's not an imposition for me to have come?"

"Not at all," said the senior Saovong magnanimously. "Any friend of Monsieur Short's. You can all come."

"It's most kind," said Jean-Philippe. "And my condolences."

M. Saovong's gentle and serene face looked politely puzzled.

"On your loss," said Jean-Philippe.

"Oh, yes," said M. Saovong. He added reasonably: "Well, she was eighty-five."

The coffin roared behind them, and M. Saovong glanced at it, looking mildly pleased. He turned back to his guests.

"If my brothers could help to show you round—"

"Please don't worry," said Short.

The four Saovongs prayed briefly at them.

"Perhaps he just didn't like Mum," said Jean-Philippe as they walked away.

"Not a bit of it," said Short. "He was devoted to the old duck. He's just literal-minded, a good Buddhist. In Laos they call the place where you die the House of Happiness."

The girl in the Ramayana dance on the stage above them, pricked by the sound of the *khène*, inclined forward incredibly on one foot, her knee bent, her other leg raised behind her, and her hands outstretched and weaving. They froze again as static as her heavily-braided body, her delicate beautiful head under its spiralling silver-pointed crown.

"They tend to be a bit passive, though," said Pridie.

Jean-Philippe turned and saw him at his elbow.

"They do?" he said. "Jeanette?"

"You mean, is she with me?" said Pridie. "Oh, yes. Not that she's always with me, you know. But she's about somewhere."

He smiled. It was a London cut again this evening, with the white silk handkerchief precise at the breast pocket.

"You naturally prefer volcanoes of passion?" Dumergue said to him.

"Hullo, François," said Pridie, "don't you? Doesn't one always after all want some kind of—reflection? Or perhaps reaction is a better word?"

Jean-Philippe saw Jeanette then. She was standing four or five people away from Pridie, to the right, gazing up at the girl dancer with her lips parted slightly. She was wearing a high-necked dress of some dark blue silky material, without sleeves. As Jean-Philippe watched her, a background monk hurled another dinner plate firework from somewhere behind them. It whirled high over their heads above the theatre stall, and Jeanette's eyes lifted to follow its burst. When she lowered them she looked round at Jean-Philippe at once, feeling his scrutiny. For a moment her pupils still seemed dilated and unfocused, but she smiled then, and moved towards him.

"Reaction might be better," said Dumergue smoothly. "Peter, you know Joe Short, of course."

There was a hesitation.

"Of course," said Pridie. "Good evening."

"Evening," said Short.

"And Mademoiselle Resnier," said Jean-Philippe. "Jeanette Resnier, Joe Short."

The *khène,* gongs, drums, and xylophones above them rose to a crescendo at the end of the scene and stopped abruptly.

"Good," said Pridie. "Let's have a drink."

He could have been talking to all of them, or to Short in particular.

"Thanks," said Short, "I'm afraid I must be getting back."

"Try some rice-wine," said Pridie, now definitely talking to him. "You'd like it. Strong, but very democratic. Very plebeian, you know."

He was watching Short with the faintest smile. It was hard to decide whether Pridie was busy being obscurely sophisticated, or just deliberately insulting.

"Peter," said Jeanette. "Really. If you have any more you'll fall flat on your face."

Though she said it lightly, it was perhaps not the most brilliantly tactful of remarks. Pridie clearly did not like it at all. He did not even look at Jeanette, but Jean-Philippe could sense his sudden fury at her. Pridie's expression did not change, but he seemed abruptly to have turned extraordinarily icy. For the first time Jean-Philippe realized that Pridie was indeed very drunk.

"Thanks," Short said again. "In fact, I know rice-wine. I've drunk it. It is plebeian, as you say. And I like it. But not just now, thanks."

Pridie looked away from him, and they began to walk slowly towards the entrance. They passed between the tiered monks and the roaring bier. Short glanced at the flames. Perhaps to ease the tension a little, he said:

"Well, night-night, Mum."

Jeanette laughed, but Jean-Philippe felt Pridie beside him break in his stride. Turning, he saw that Pridie was standing still and looking at Short. Short and the others had stopped too.

"Yes?" said Short quietly.

"It's not your country," said Pridie. "Curious taste you sometimes show."

"That's an official comment, is it?" said Short. "Embassy and all that?"

"Peter!" said Jeanette. She was on his left, and she had put her hand on his arm. With a tiny quick jerk he shook it off, not breaking the line of his regard on Short.

Pridie was right on his own now. Whatever curious deep psychological spring had needed to be touched to release this extraordinary antagonism, it had certainly been loosed very com-

pletely. The ferocity of Pridie's emotion seemed to have frozen
him frighteningly sober. He gave an odd impression now, so
strong that it was almost visual, of standing there alone on a kind
of peak, poised for action. He looked absolutely competent, even
deadly, like some silent efficient machine, designed for precise
destruction.

"You could call it official," said Pridie. "Or just personal. As
you like."

Short too was standing dead still.

"Pridie," he said, pleasantly.

"Yes?"

"Go to hell, Pridie. Go and save some other country."

Jean-Philippe was watching with great interest. He wondered
who was going to hit whom first.

"Not at funerals," said Dumergue, "even Buddhist ones. Particularly not at Buddhist funerals, come to think of it."

After a moment Pridie shrugged. He turned abruptly and began to walk back towards the theatre stall. Jeanette stood un-
decided, and Jean-Philippe caught her eye. What was it, appeal
again? But he was strictly neutral. It was her business. She was a
big girl now.

She must have worked that out herself, for she blushed suddenly and nodded to them. She seemed uncertain whether the
atmosphere was right for her to say goodnight to them formally
now, and in the end she said nothing, but turned and followed
Pridie. By this time the distance between the three watching men
and the place into which Pridie had disappeared moodily, a bar
to the right of the theatre stall, seemed indecently long. In the
middle of this space Jeanette looked very much alone, on no one's
side at all. With the gay and graceful and glittering people in
the broad ring of stalls about her, and the flames from the bier
dancing rampantly across her sober blue silk back, she looked a
little like some historic virgin walking slowly but resolutely forward to a rather cheerful pagan sacrifice, possibly of herself.

CHAPTER VIII

WHEN they were in the car again on the way back, with the
burning Nang Saovong behind them to their left, Jean-Philippe
glanced at the intently driving Short and said:

"Pridie's quite a friend of yours, then."

"Quite a friend," said Short grimly. "Quite the American Image Abroad."

"I didn't know that you were such a racialist," said Dumergue.

"I'm not," said Short. "I even like Frenchmen."

"All Frenchmen?" said Dumergue.

"Some Frenchmen," said Short. "Hell, Pridie isn't even particularly American. He bypasses merely national boundaries. Like the United Nations and V.D. Why pick on us? Pridie's a modern phenomenon."

"That's a nice way of getting rid of him," said Jean-Philippe.

"Believe me," said Short. "Pridie doesn't have any particular roots. Pridie doesn't belong to any particular place."

"Nomadic, sort of," said Jean-Philippe. "The Lone Ranger and all. He'd like that."

"I should have hit him, though," said Short, avoiding a pothole like a bomb crater.

"You'd have had to take his glasses off first," said Dumergue. "Jeanette could have held them."

"Maybe she could use them," said Short darkly. "She's been sleeping with him, hasn't she?"

"Forget it," said Dumergue. "Drown it in drink, Joe. Come to the Golden Pavilion with us and drown it in drink."

Short turned to him from above the wheel and laughed.

"I'm a heavily married man, you know. Not the Golden Pavilion."

"You know best," said Dumergue.

When they came into the town again Short dropped them at the start of the Lang Xang Avenue, and they walked across the road and over the hard packed laterite square to the Golden Pavilion. It was a compartment set at ground level in a three-storied concrete building. There were café tables in front of the doorway. The tablecloths were bright Thai silk, gold and light blue and yellow in colour. Gold thread ran richly through the blue and glinted in the light from the Aladdin lamps on the tables. Vietnamese girls sat round the tables with Lao and Philippino men and Americans, a girl per man, very democratically. The light from the lamps threw the high-cheekboned faces of the girls up in relief, shadowing the eyes dramatically. The two men passed between the tables.

They chose a place to the left of the door. There was a short bar at the back of the room. A broad middle-aged Vietnamese woman stood behind it. She looked up and smiled at them. A stairway led upwards from the right of the bar.

The woman behind the bar glanced at three Vietnamese girls

85

who sat at the table nearest to it, and two of them got up and came over to the men.

"My name is Joanne," said the tall girl. "If you would permit me."

She shook hands gravely with each of them. It was as formal as a dinner party.

"Please," she said. "What would you like?"

Dumurgue glanced at Jean-Philippe.

"Whisky-soda, I think," said Jean-Philippe.

"Two whisky-sodas, then."

"My friend is called Marianne," said Joanne, pointedly.

"Enchanted," said Dumergue. "Bring yourselves something too."

The two girls exchanged glances and the tall girl went back to the bar. Marianne sat down delicately in the chair next to Jean-Philippe and crossed her legs. Her feet were miniature, in gold sandals, the toenails painted crimson.

"Saigon?" said Jean-Philippe.

"*Oui. Vous connaître Saigon?*"

"*Moi connaître Saigon*," said Jean-Philippe, at once following her courteously and adopting the pidgin French conventions of Vietnamese tea-houses.

"It's a nice town," said Marianne originally.

"Diem didn't like you?" said Jean-Philippe.

"President Diem doesn't like dancing-girls," said Marianne. "Madame Nhu doesn't like dancing-girls."

"But *we* like dancing-girls," said Dumergue.

"Diem's getting very high class," said Jean-Philippe.

"Oh, it's all the fashion with the new right-wing dictatorships these days," said Dumergue. "You prove how anti-communist you are by the degree to which you hound your ladies of pleasure."

"The march of Western civilization," said Jean-Philippe. "It must impress the visiting Senators no end."

"Like a charm," said Dumergue. "It's just like home."

Joanne came back from the bar with the two whiskies and soda and what looked like two cold teas. She served the whiskies to the men and sat down. Marianne began to suck her cold tea through a straw, remotely, as though doing it a favour. An American walked past them and sat at a table to the right and was quietly joined by the last available Vietnamese girl. Senators or not, he looked delighted.

"Do you get many Americans?" said Jean-Philippe.

Joanne considered the question.

"Many come here, to look. But not so many in a serious manner. More Frenchmen."

"It's an older culture," said Dumergue.

"But some seriously, of course," Joanne went on. "Monsieur Sharkrill. Monsieur Greenklat. Monsieur Wuk. Monsieur Pridie."

"My God," said Jean-Philippe. "There he is again."

Joanne looked at Dumergue. She said:

"You're married, of course?"

"No," said Dumergue. "I lack the necessary terror of solitude."

Joanne looked a little glazed. To aid her, Dumergue said: "You?"

"Of course. My husband is in Savannakhet. With the *Intendance Française*."

"Children?" said Jean-Philippe.

That was fatal. The photographs came out at once, from a pantaloon pocket, in an imitation-leather wallet. Each child looked out with enormous and unsmiling gravity from its compartment, rain-spattered by the protecting celluloid. There was a toy boy of five or six in a precise dark suit with shorts, probably a school uniform, and a girl of about eight in miniature Vietnamese national dress.

"Very handsome," said Dumergue. "They're with your husband?"

"With my sister, also in Savannakhet," said Joanne. "Your friend is not yet married?"

"No," said Jean-Philippe.

"As I thought," said Marianne wisely.

"Marianne can smell a potential husband a mile off," said Dumergue.

"Potential is all," said Jean-Philippe.

"Yet you look a passionate man," said Joanne. "And quite young, really."

"Thank you," said Jean-Philippe. "My friend is also passionate, and quite young."

Joan looked at Dumergue judiciously.

"He appears more settled, mature," she said.

"He is in fact a deeply serious man," said Jean-Philippe. "Devoted to good works and matters of high finance."

"*Merde*," said Dumergue. "Whisky."

The two girls looked at each other. Democratically, Marianne got up this time and removed the empty glasses.

"But no doubt you have had great loves?" said Joanne in a kindly manner.

"Not that I can recall at the moment," said Jean-Philippe.

Joanne looked at him sharply, and he realized at once that he had erred badly. That answer won no prizes at all. It always provoked prostitutes particularly; love was after all their profession. You were supposed to have had at least one great love at some time. It was a social duty. It helped confirm the indispensability of women.

Jean-Philippe had never in fact felt specially urged to challenge this tightest and most universal of trade-unions. It was simply that by nature he was about as nomadic sexually as he was geographically. At an early age he had made the original discovery that all women looked much the same, once horizontal and with their legs well apart. Verifying this fact always pleased him, but never quite enough for him seriously to consider that its particular exponent at the time had been uniquely predestined for him. He had probably read too many books for that.

Jean-Philippe's modesty on this score did not always endear him to women or good husbands. Lauvergne, for one, had appeared to feel that it was a personal insult. Lauvergne had been a fervent Catholic and a passionately faithful man. He wrote fabulously detailed letters to his wife (whom Jean-Philippe had never seen) and children in Antilly twice a week with ruthless regularity, even under the most appalling conditions. When the mail from France was due, before it arrived, his anxiety was visible and (thought Jean-Philippe) slightly humiliating; but presumably Lauvergne thought this a fair price to pay for his security.

Lauvergne had nothing at all in common with Jean-Philippe, but Dien Bien Phu was not concerned with temperamental incompatibilities. One night late in the command post, two days before his throat was neatly removed by shrapnel, Lauvergne had turned abruptly on Jean-Philippe (up till then Lauvergne had been talking at an excruciating length about the virtues of his wife and the education of their children) and said to him, almost in a snarl:

"In some ways I even envy you. You've got nothing to lose. You're an intelligent coward, Raymond, the final solitary and invulnerable hero of our times. You never risk anything more than the loss of your life and your head." Jean-Philippe had almost gone to sleep by this time, lulled by Lauvergne's inventory of his wife, but the snarl woke him up smartly. There was however no more conversation to be had with Lauvergne. He had lapsed into a total and glum silence. Jean-Philippe had thought privately that Lauvergne's tirade was tactless in the extreme and moreover showed no sense of timing at all, for the two of them were only too likely to lose both their loves and their heads at any moment. He had nonetheless (making due allowance for Lauvergne's apparent and sudden and profound conviction that he had really been hoodwinked by fate all along) manfully done his best to look solitary and intelligent, and had passed Lauvergne the third last of his cigarettes, which Lauvergne accepted with alacrity, in as near as he could manage to an invulnerable manner.

By now Marianne had taken Jean-Philippe's left hand possessively and was holding it down lightly in her lap, so that he could feel the curve of her thigh. She had her second cold tea in her left hand and was sipping it demurely as she watched Dumergue talk to Joanne. Marianne was as composed as a duchess in a bath. After a moment she turned her head to Jean-Philippe, and her long jet-black hair rippled attractively back over her slim shoulders. She watched him speculatively. Her face was oval and miniature and delicate as a cat's and now about as impersonally calculating, female and wise and ritualistic, and decently conscious that this had all happened before. She said:

"We finish early this evening, and we go home. You could even come to visit us in our home, if you wished."

"That's truly thoughtful," he said. "Dumergue?"

"It's an old Eastern custom," said Dumergue. "It would be most discourteous not to accept."

Joanne took their money for the drinks to the bar. When she came back the four of them went out and turned to the left down the Lang Xang, and to the left again into a side road, and to the right. Jean-Philippe was with Marianne. Ahead of them, Joanne was walking with Dumergue. She was tall. She walked with a grace that came from a thousand years. Any European woman, even a trained mannequin, would have looked a disaster next to her.

Joanne turned left between two wooden houses which faced on to the road. All their lights were already respectably out. Joanne led them round behind one house, and across a wooden platform which echoed under them. The sound of morally outraged pigs smote them from below their feet. Joanne had already set out ahead like a scout across a long wooden plank, which was set dangerously on piles, two metres above a limitless stretch of water. They followed her. The water was static and luminous below them. The blasphemous croaking of a million unseen frogs rose eerily from it. There was a long low wooden building dimly ahead, also set on piles above the water. The gangplank led up to it like a long tightrope.

"Funerals *and* fornication," said Jean-Philippe with respect. "All in one evening."

"Mind your step," said Dumergue. "This is to weed out the drunkards."

89

No doubt dozens of them already stared glassily up from down in the water.

Marianne turned to the left when they reached the platform of the long low wooden building. She took a bunch of keys from her pantaloons and opened the padlock on one of the wooden doors. They followed her into the darkness. Standing, they waited while she flared a match. Her face appeared ahead of them, warmly lit and absorbed. She adjusted the yellow flame of the kerosene hurricane-lamp.

They sat decorously at the wooden table. There was a low double-bed against the opposite wall. Four wooden poles rose at its corners, and a veiling white mosquito-net fell from their tips. A large technicolour Coca-Cola poster commanded them from the right of the bed. From the poster a ruddy-cheeked and aggressively busted blonde advanced a full bottle upon them like a bludgeon. Lotions and cosmetics and a large mirror stood on the small table under the poster. The room held little else. There was a sinister black thin iron trestle to the right of the door. It cradled a chipped enamelled tin basin as though about to hurl it at them. A china water-jug stood next to the trestle. There was a small dead charcoal brazier and several screw-capped bottles of rice, sugar, and coffee on a low shelf in the right-hand corner.

"Whikkie?" said Marianne.

"Enchanted," said Dumergue.

There was no nonsense about cold tea this time. Marianne poured the Johnnie Walker liberally and the soda and sat down again comfortably next to Jean-Philippe. She sipped her drink and looked about her. She was almost purring.

"It's a nice home," she said.

"Certainly," said Jean-Philippe.

"Joanne lives here with you too, of course?" said Dumergue cunningly.

"No, no," said Marianne. "Further along to the left."

"Indeed," said Dumergue.

"Convenient, too," said Jean-Philippe socially. "It's near to your work."

"Yes," said Joanne.

Marianne was watching Jean-Philippe clinically.

"You would like to make love now," she said, getting up.

"Thank you," said Jean-Philippe. No other answer seemed decently possible, for she had disappeared already behind the mosquito-net, and they could hear the crisp sounds as she removed her clothes.

"Well," said Dumergue. "We must be getting along."

"So you must," said Jean-Philippe.

"I'll wait for you outside," said Dumergue, thoughtfully finishing his whisky.

"Good."

"Don't fall in," said Dumergue ambiguously.

When the door had closed behind them, Marianne reappeared from behind the bed. She wore light blue panties and her gold slippers. Her breasts were minute and her waist and wrists and ankles looked fragile as glass stems. This did not stop her from sitting in his lap in a most mature manner and watching him while he finished his drink. He could see no movement in her at all, but he had the distinct impression that she was undulating her bottom sinuously across his thighs. The sensation was electric.

"*M'sieu.*"

"*Mademoiselle?*"

She was looking pleased, as at a discovery.

"You appear a vigorous man."

"In this position it would be surprising if I did not."

She looked marginally at his empty glass, like a polite hostess.

"All right," said Jean-Philippe.

Feeling mildly like a child murderer, he put his hands round her impossibly small waist and set her down. He got up, and, since this was clearly expected of him, carried her to the bed, brushing aside the mosquito-netting. He undressed and crawled into the bed over her. The mosquito-netting seemed to go on and on. He struck savagely at it with the back of his hand, but it clung resolute about his loins like white samite. He felt faintly mythological. It was as though he had just emerged aptly like that from the sheer lake under the house. He snarled at it hopelessly and left it, and, still sheathed in it, rode her majestically, while beneath him her child's body moved skilled and supple as a dancer's. Her head was turned to one side on the pillow, and she continued to utter small pleased chattering cries for a flattering length of time.

He lay beside her, freed at last from the foaming gauze, and watched the smoke from his cigarette curl up to the white cloth roof of the net above them. The side of her body, small and cat-like and relaxed, had moulded itself easily against him. She would be far too discreet to be watching him directly now; her eyes would also be following the thin course of the cigarette smoke above them.

"Tell me about Pridie," he said idly.

He felt her move. She was looking at him now all right, from the pillow. He raised himself on one elbow and looked round at her. She did not seem at all annoyed by his question, (a European sister of hers in the profession would probably have been outraged) but merely slightly intrigued.

"Well," she said non-committally. "He comes here sometimes."

"He's good to you?"

"Good?"

"Kind then."

This time the question seemed genuinely to puzzle her. She turned her head and relaxed back on the pillow to look up again at the white rectangle of the net's ceiling.

"Not kind," she said. "Not unkind."

"But?"

She shrugged her toy shoulders, and said suddenly:

"A *cérébral*."

He raised his eyebrows and smiled at her. The comment was interesting. It might even be brilliant.

She glanced round at him again, a shadow in her eyes.

"He's not a close friend of yours?"

"No," said Jean-Philippe. "I know him. He's just someone that I know."

CHAPTER IX

"MAI?"

"You don't have to," she said, "I work here, remember."

"I know that," said Cuong.

"What did you expect?" she said. "A waitress? A little secretary?"

Cuong looked across at the orchestra.

"It's a job, isn't it?" she said. "Isn't it?"

He shrugged slightly. He said:

"They pay you for it, don't they?"

"The dignity of labour," she said. "That's right."

After a minute, he said:

"It's not my business."

"No," she said, "that's right too."

"Still," he said doggedly, "we ought to order something."

She looked at his clothes deliberately. He wore a cheap dark blue linen suit, ill-fitting. The jacket particularly looked alien on him. He looked a little like a French peasant at a funeral.

"They can hardly throw you out," she said. "You haven't hit anyone. You haven't broken anything yet."

"As you like," he said abruptly.

She smiled at him brilliantly.

"I drink Martell-soda," she said. "Please, that is. May I have a Martell-soda, please."

He motioned to the waiter. The girl turned her head and looked towards the door. She was small and slight and immaculate. She wore a high-throated Vietnamese bodice in green, and matching pantaloons and cape. Her legs were crossed. One foot in a high-heeled silver dancing slipper tapped up and down. She looked lacquered and expensive.

"You've been well, anyway, Mai?"

She looked back at him.

"Oh, we girls take our precautions, you know."

"I've no doubt," he said.

"All right," she said. "Yes. I've been well. Thanks."

"Friends here, Mai?"

"Men or women, did you mean?" she said.

"Friends. Whatever you like."

"You can see," she said, "there are other girls from Saigon here."

The Vietnamese waiter put the two glasses and the soda down on the table.

"Yes," Cuong said, "I can see that."

He took one of the bottles.

"This far, Mai?"

But she had looked again at the door.

"So early?" he said cruelly.

The foot stopped at once and she looked back at him.

"Who?"

"The American," he said.

Her eyes slid away and came back and focused antagonistically on him.

"I should say probably in half an hour. Forty minutes. Who told you?"

"One hears these things," he said.

"One hears these things," she repeated drily. "Of course."

"Always, Mai?"

"Always, what?" she said.

"He comes always?"

"Most nights," she said.

"Well," he said, "I won't stay long."

"I don't mind if you meet him," she said. "Why should I mind if you meet him?"

"Look," he said patiently, "I came because I wanted to see how you were. That's all."

93

She considered him.

"My boy lover," she said ironically. "How did you find me?"

"A man from Saigon," he said. "Someone I knew before, that I met again in the north."

"And?"

"He had been through here," he said with difficulty. "He had been with you. He did not know that you were my sister. He doesn't know that, you understand. One night, by accident, he talked of a girl in Savannakhet, and he said your name, and he described you."

"What was he called?" she said.

"Nanh."

"I remember no Nanh," she said indifferently.

"It was a year ago," he said.

"Well," she said. "Talk about tenacity. Do they give your prizes for tenacity in the Viet Minh, Cuong?"

"I hadn't heard of it."

"You ought to get a prize, though. I didn't think that I'd see you again."

"I didn't think that I would find you," he said. "You didn't leave much."

"After all, it was my affair. And too long ago. Thirteen years."

"Fourteen, almost."

"So long," she said. "Imagine. And so dull. It has happened too many times. We don't really have to talk about it now, do we?"

"There's no law about it," he said.

"Good," she said, "good."

She drank from her glass and put it down delicately and examined it, turning it slowly round on its base. Bubbles rose brilliantly in the gold liquor, in small obsessional strings. He noticed the big smoke-grey star sapphire, set in gold. It looked too heavy for her hand.

"Why did you come to Savannakhet?" he said.

"Why not, after all? There was always the French base. Then the Americans began to come in, after Dien Bien Phu. Oh, first I went back to Saigon."

"I had thought that," he said, "or Dalat. Or perhaps Pnom-Penh. Or Bangkok."

"Not for long, though," she went on. "I did not stay long in Saigon. Not there."

"Your American's important?" he said.

"You don't know that too?" she said. "A colonel. I'm not supposed to know it, of course."

"Officially he is civilian?"

"It is their favourite myth that we still all really think that," she said.

"Kind, Mai?"

She shrugged.

"In his way. Serious. Generous. A little stupid."

"He'll take you out of here?"

She looked at him and laughed, really delighted.

"So that it should all end well, Cuong? He's stupid. But not that stupid."

He said nothing.

"All right," she said soberly. "It was to be that way at first. It always is, of course. But then it turned out that he had a wife and children. Just imagine."

"Here?"

"In his own country," she said.

There were three couples on the dance-floor which began five yards behind her. Two of the men were Lao, one French, and the girls Vietnamese. The band had reduced itself to a drummer and the pianist. They had relaxed into a slow and almost inaudible fox-trot, and the dancers wore remote and faintly disillusioned expressions, like professionals practising. There were a few other couples at the tables. It was still early, and the noises from the street outside were still strong, not quite muted by the door and the heavy dark red curtains which masked it. Cuong could hear the jagged cries of street vendors, the sounds of passing cars, fragments of the speech of people who walked. The great river ran straight past the town three blocks away, brutal and certain and ageless, surly and low now in March, sudden small islands and murderous reefs of rock protruding from it.

"How are they, Cuong?" she said, more gently.

"They?"

"In Saigon. Mother and Father."

"He's dead," he said. "She's gone back to Dalat. You knew that."

"No, she said, "no."

"I thought that you knew that."

"No," she said.

"I'm sorry," he said.

He did not think that she had heard him, for she was still looking at him, without reaction. She said suddenly:

"It doesn't matter. When?"

"Five years ago. Six."

She shook her head.

"Well," she said. "Well. So he is dead. An accident. Or was

he shot? But he wasn't political. Nobody could say that. A grenade? Grenades were popular."

"Nothing like that," he said. "He was sick, and died."

"Like his life," she said. "So unoriginal. Like his whole life." She looked down at the table for a long time.

"You understand," she said, "I didn't see them when I went back. I should have gone to see them. But it would have been difficult, you understand."

He did not answer her.

"Humiliating, even," she said.

"I didn't see them again either," he said at last, as though to help her.

She looked at him and laughed.

"Always the Christian, Cuong. No, you had an excuse. An honourable excuse."

"Honourable?" he said.

"One would say that, though, wouldn't one? Patriotism. Love for your country. Really *your* country, Cuong?"

"I don't know," he said. "Yes. Viet Nam is my country. Yes, I see it like that."

"Men have excuses, you see," she said thoughtfully. "Are you still Viet Minh, Cuong?"

"No," he said, not liking the half-truth.

"But?"

"As I said, I'm in Vientiane. The *Bic*."

He would be well away before the American colonel could check that, if Mai told him, and if he were suspicious.

His answer seemed to amuse her. She seemed now quite to have forgotten about their father's death.

"A clerk, Cuong?" she said maliciously. "Like in Saigon? After all?

"Like in Saigon," he said.

That had been a defeat, a capitulation, made more terrible by the image of his father. But the times and his blood were not favourable to Cuong when he came back from France early in 1946. The French already deeply mistrusted the Vietnamese. His recent militant past in France was no passport. The French military in Saigon were regulars, the first to return after the British had made the breach for them. They were inclined to be sensitive. They had to live down the Japanese humiliation of their Vichy representatives in Viet Nam in 1945 and the German defeat of themselves in France in 1941. Professionally they did not have much time for members of the French maquis in general, and less for those not of their own race. It was as if they considered

96

that the maquis was the sort of bizarre and melodramatic history
that was only just tolerable within the strict bounds of your own
family. Cuong's resistance record and his mixed blood excluded
him as summarily from the company of the young Vietnamese
whom he had known before in Saigon, in most of whom the lust
of independence from France already burned with all the ferocity
of a new fashion in dress or a new religion.

The discovery saddened Cuong but did not greatly surprise him.
A balance is generally struck at some point in a person's history
which defines him for life. In this sense Cuong was a professional
outsider. The trait was set in him early; not cataclysmically,
but suavely, over time. His father had been a devout Catholic.
At some financial sacrifice, he had sent the boy to an excellent
Christian Brothers school in Saigon. These good and dedicated
men would never have countenanced racial discrimination, but
they could hardly be expected similarly to militate against the
more subtle and entrenched distinctions accorded by wealth and
power. These were decisive at the school, and moreover accepted
as quite natural by the boys themselves. They were between the
sons of the French administrators and officers and executives and
of the wealthy Vietnamese landed aristocrats and merchants on
the one hand, and of the sons of the poor and the *métis* on the
other. Cuong learned his social lessons young. He stayed out of
trouble. In return, the Brothers gave him a severe and thorough
groundwork for the French Government scholarship to Paris
which he won in 1937 at the age of seventeen.

The racially mixed status of Cuong's family, and the restrictions imposed by his father's salary, fixed their home with nice
precision on the borders of a French residential area, and at the
start of the pulsating and much more colourful areas of the Vietnamese. Their flat was on the fourth floor of a great block.
This block had a careful but secretly volatile character, like a
shrewd old man with cheerful minor vices. It, like those beside
it, presented a sober front to the street, but was frankly explosive
viewed from behind. Women, like cliff dwellers, talked intermin-
ably to one another from the small balconies, upon which laundry
hung vividly out to dry, ranging from the bleak black trousers of
the elder women and the provocative white silk of the younger,
through the modern intimacies of panties and brassières, to
the smug and sexless pomposity of the men's shirts. Vertically
below, small olive children played diligently in the jealously
demarcated quadrangles, like miniature troops.

Their friends in this building and their visitors from outside
it were nearly all men like his father, small *commis* from the bank

or from *Dragages* or other of the French trading and construction companies then strong throughout Indo-China, or from the head offices of the great plantation syndicates. Many had married Vietnamese or lived with them. They were a seedy, industrious, likeable, and faintly doomed lot. It would probably be impossible ever to repatriate them successfully to France. It was as if only the hard international shell of power and success could preserve the European intact here, against the heat and the humidity, the *anis* and the opium, and the easy ubiquitous fertile sensuality. These did not so much rot the weak and the underprivileged, as claim them irrevocably over time.

Cuong's father had made two original and possibly brave actions in his life; first, when, from an obscure Breton family, he had answered a Bank of Indo-China advertisement for a clerk's post in Saigon, and had gone optimistically out to the country in which he would die. The second was when he had married a Vietnamese.

But this last action was really probably more realistic than courageous. The chance that he could ever have married a French girl in Saigon, one of the luxurious, mannered, and scarce daughters of the powerful, was about as completely excluded as it would have been in France. That given, his marriage was even a success. His wife was respectable, the daughter of a small penurious landowner near Dalat. He had met her at a Catholic youth club in Saigon. She was plain, despite the passing glow imposed by youth and good health, and in character pleasant, stubborn, honest, and formidably virginal. This last virtue had impressed him particularly at the time; a few nights before he had lost his own virginity in Cholon at the incredulous and hilarious insistence of his companions at the bank. It was the only illicit sexual excursion of his life, and to make up for it he married his wife very thoroughly indeed, both civilly before the mayor, and ecclesiastically in church.

In turn she found this some achievement. The social climate suggested a decent concubinage as the normal relationship between Vietnamese girls of her class and Frenchmen. She not only married into this master race but set her conditions for doing so. Among these was her requirement that their children's first names should be Vietnamese, (since their surnames were his, and thus inevitably French) that they should spend a fair part of their time at her home near Dalat, and that any daughters should keep the Vietnamese national dress. (No one in his right mind could really object to this; it was so infinitely more graceful than the European.)

Cuong's attachment to his country probably came mainly

from his visits to this home of his mother's near Dalat. It was old, wooden, rambling, dangerous, and crowded. Its lands and their production were small. But there was a formal charm and dignity to the place. It belonged.

Cuong's mother was technically more Catholic that the rest of the family; she was convent-educated. This did not stop her at all from being on the most friendly terms with those of her many aunts and uncles who were Caodaist. Perhaps indeed it was precisely the celestial internationalism of this sect, whose gods ranged broadly from Christ through Victor Hugo to Sun Yat Sen, which had so liberalized the family's attitude to religion. Everyone went seriously to mass in Dalat on Sundays and Holidays of Obligation, as people duly prepared to take all reasonable precautions. The aunts and uncles went once a year to the annual Caodaist festival at Tanyin. Everyone gathered each evening to burn their candle to their ancestors at the small altar which stood in its special place in the house.

This benign eclecticism, and the farm's archaic amenities and precarious solvency, did not exactly seduce the neat book-keeper's mind of Cuong's father. He was known to have visited the farm only once. Probably what most appalled him was the way his wife at once assumed its character when she was there, and returned to being pure Vietnamese. He could not have liked that. A deal was a deal. It was the francophile and Catholic image of her that he had married in Saigon, and to which indeed he remained remarkably faithful, if only through a kind of imaginative impotence, and cost what it might.

It could not in fact have cost him much. The French in Indo-China hardly considered a racially mixed marriage indispensable for a Frenchman's progress, though they were generally much too sophisticated to oppose one openly. But Cuong's father could never have risen meteorically in his career anyway. His class, education, and character conspired against it. When he married, after ten years at the bank, he was third cashier. After twenty-five years he might head that section. Anything more would have disrupted natural order. Cuong's father had himself an enormous respect for that, an awe of authority that was depressing. He was a short man, rather too white, as though (as was the case) he instinctively avoided the sun. He inclined already to bulk and baldness in his early thirties. He had the broad, shrewd, and strategically amicable face of a French village grocer.

As a child, Cuong had often been sent on errands to his father at the bank. He had not liked that duty. His abiding image was of a middle-aged man trapped in curious ballet with two others, behind bars and high glass, nimbly serving money to exacting and visibly more important men outside, or counting it with impressive speed, Marie-Theresa silver dollars or piastres or banknotes, checking and rechecking it, as though in some difficult race against time, and dancing briskly subservient under the vigilant eyes of passing bank executives.

The fruits of this marriage were improbable. The boy was intelligent and ambitious, and the girl exotic. She was born three years after her brother. From the age of two she had had that disturbing beauty sometimes found in children of mixed blood. She grew slight, olive-complexioned, and black-haired. She had a precision of limb and feature which could not be traced to either of her parents, a controlled vivacity, a kind of luminosity. By this flagrant physical perfection she seemed to have gone out of her way to mock all established doctrines of class and breeding. From an early age, she appeared completely aware of herself. She seemed docile.

Though she was probably the only person that he had ever really loved, Cuong was wary of that impression. His parents often required him to look after her. She took this in good part, as a convention, but he had no illusions that he could ever teach her much. She was a wise little girl, beyond his range. He had, however, some sense of the more vivid traits of her character. Games of chance attracted her remarkably. They could have been a language that she had known from birth. When she was away from the flat too long, on some small mission, Cuong would almost always know where to find her. She would be in one of the small courtyards behind old twisted buildings, where poor men squatted over gaily-painted cloths or watched the crisp merciless run of dice. She would be standing, as professionally absorbed as they, the vegetables or spices or bottle of kerosene forgotten beside her. She came to no harm, even amongst the most violent of such company. Once, when she was thirteen, he found her only after an hour, in the upstairs room of a select Tea House off the Rue Catinat. It was a Sunday morning and she was still in her best clothes after mass. It was at once apparent, not so much that the girls had adopted her, as that she had adopted them. There was an affinity between this small perfect creature and these silken and fine-limbed and manicured and scented women, their fingers slim and swift and jewelled and rapt over the clicking cascading pieces of mah-jong. It was as if, by a rare precosity, she could step forward when she chose, already as completely formed and finished and exquisite as they, and claim her place beside them, without dissonance.

She had too a knowledge of the more sophisticated obscenities of the Chinese and Vietnamese languages which seemed intuitive, but which in fact came no doubt from such places. She never expressed these in their parent's presence, only in his. On her small red petulant lips, beneath her frank and childlike gaze, they had an exciting and suspect innocence, like that of lush exotic fruits hanging untouched in some green glade.

He spent much of his free time with her, particularly in his last year in Saigon, at the flat, in the streets, at the farm at Dalat. She did not seem to have close friends at the convent whose claims could have prevented this. He grew bored quickly without her. She was a wise listener, and could gauge his interests and desires uncannily. She had a swift and mordant intelligence which, in conflict, she would always retract quietly before his. He was often aware of her beauty; at fourteen this was already almost fully developed. He saw no dangers in his feelings for her; close access to her seemed one of the few natural rights of his blood. She seemed content to give him this company generously, in her decorous and controlled way. It was as if she found the manner of behaviour which she so formed with him a useful qualification.

One curious incident happened. A year after he had first found her in the Tea House off the Rue Catinat, and two days before he left on his scholarship to Paris, he took her to the evening show at a cinema not far from their flat. This was at her request, and, naturally, with their parents' accord. No sooner had they placed themselves in the armless seats of the (again at her request) back row than she turned and kissed him passionately on the mouth. She forced his lips open and darted her tongue between them. She pressed her hard small breasts against him and ran her hands swiftly over his back and loins. This sinewed and expert assault, from a creature hitherto so discreet, so porcelain, unnerved him totally.

She leant back, her head on one side, and watched him speculatively, then she took his hand and placed it strongly between the warm division of her thighs, and closed them over it. She was afterwards quite still. She seemed both grave and gracious, studying his reactions with interest. It was a demonstration and a lesson, and also a private test of him in which evidently he failed dismally, for when he gasped finally and pulled away he continued to watch him for some time, her slim body shaking with pure ripples of laughter. In the two days following, before he left for Paris, she was quietly affectionate, as befitted the occasion, and, just before he went up the gangway on to the ship, she kissed him like a sister and cried appropriately. He had the impression that she had enjoyed the whole performance enormously. The experimental brothels of his student days in Paris and the easy immoralities of the war finally dulled his carnal and heroic fantasies about her.

CHAPTER X

WHEN Cuong returned to Saigon in June 1946 one of the first things which he learned was that Mai had been living with a French lieutenant since 1941, and had borne him a daughter, Chantal, now three years old.

Cuong met the three of them on a family visit with his parents two days after his return. The three lived in a flat in a similar block of apartments, but sited just within the French residential area; it was as if, adding the lieutenant's, they now had just enough European blood to qualify mathematically for this social advance. The man, Coutin, was of the *Intendance*. He was a great bull of a figure, blond as a Viking, blue-eyed, with a heavy cavalry moustache. He smiled readily. In his flat, with Chantal on his knees, and Mai sitting submissively nearby, he looked like a 1914 *père-de-famille* photographed just before he went gallantly off to the Front. But, however suspect this analogy might be, there was no doubt that Coutin worshipped the child. This was understandable, for at three Chantal already had all the former dangerous magic of her mother, that air of miniature and mature and knowing perfection, as if she had simply been born like that, ready-made, completely accomplished; as if her mother had simply passed that nymph-like dynamism umbilically and totally to her. By his manner Coutin nonetheless contrived himself to assume exclusive rights to this perfection. He gave it out pontifically, yet without a word, that he was fully responsible for the child's construction. Perhaps because the contrast was a little too sharp between this patriarchal spectacle and Coutin's resolutely unmarried status, between his heroically militant dimensions and his severely sedentary career, Cuong recognized him at once. He was a born collaborator, a born grocer like Cuong's father.

Coutin must at least have been sufficiently astute to have felt his thoughts. He made a serious bid to gain Cuong's sympathy that night, and after it. Conceivably he was impressed because Cuong had fought professionally for years in a bitter underground war, while he had stayed in the comfortable Vichy vacuum of Saigon. But this interpretation was doubtful; Coutin was obviously not particularly prone to social guilt. More probably he was just sensibly wary of Cuong's caustic intelligence, with its puritanical overtones. Coutin did not fail for want of trying. Magnanimously, he talked freely to Cuong, as to a friend of his own race. He spoke, exploratively, of the New France and the New Viet Nam. Cuong watched him politely and ruthlessly and gave him no leads. He knew that the slightest such would at once provoke Coutin's vehement support for anything at all, capitalism or communism, colonialism or nationalism, De Gaulle or Pétain, Blum or Laval.

On this return Cuong found that it was Mai who had apparently changed most profoundly. His father (except professionally; he was now second cashier) was completely static, only marginally fatter and balder. His mother was abruptly old, but that too had been predictable. It was the way of the women of her race. At a given time old age came down upon them as mercilessly as the Vietnamese night, without dusk.

In Mai the change seemed more basic. The old fires seemed quite gone, and all her energies directed now to love for a child and service to a man. It was worthy, and a little disappointing. He did not think that it really suited her. When he watched her in the flat, he was reminded of the way that all the colour went out of an iguana when you killed it. Now, she was as dull as a bank. She had even followed the best traditions of womanhood and proved her loyalty to her man. She had suffered considerable pains and some danger on Coutin's account. The Japanese *coup-de-force* of the ninth of August 1945 had taken the Vichy French in Viet Nam quite by surprise. The Japanese had extracted them from their apparent civilized security and herded them ignominiously into concentration camps. Mai had at once left the child with her parents and followed the astounded Coutin. She took her small savings and worked as a servant to the Japanese in the camp in which Coutin was placed, to smuggle vital food and medicines in to him. Her unlimited fidelity to this large blond man seemed indeed to prove some strange new human law; that exceptional beauty, vitality, and grace in one sex was irrevocably attracted to the most banal and spurious in the other, by some single fatal flaw of taste.

One point puzzled Cuong for some time; why his father, that fanatical Catholic, that entrenched conservative, should so long have continued to tolerate that his only daughter live unmarried with Coutin. Cuong understood that when the two first cohabited Coutin's explanation had seemed acceptable, even rather edifying. It was in 1941, and the Germans had already occupied

France, so that Coutin could not communicate with his family. As a good son, he had naturally wished their prior blessing to a step so permanent as marriage. But this theory had rather less force in 1946. Cuong believed that he had found the true reason in his father's attitude to Coutin. This was always more than deferential. It was even grateful. Evidently in his father's Breton-peasant scale of values the laws of man were at times much more pertinent than those of God. A French Officer was anyway by definition already on the sides of the gods, even if he was only of the *Intendance*. If he supported and copulated regularly with your daughter, so efficiently indeed that he had even produced a child by her, and if moreover he had even expressed the firm intention of marrying her (though for high reasons connected with international politics he had so far unfortunately not been able actually to do so) then it was still after all really something of an honour. You had arrived.

Two things important in Cuong's life happened early in July of that year. First, he exhausted his limited money, and understood completely that his Parisian political science degree was no advantage at all to his finding work with the administration or with any of the French commercial houses, but on the contrary the greatest possible obstacle. Rather than accept his family's charity, he was glad to take the job of a ledger clerk cautiously offered him by the Bank of Indo-China, on his father's recommendation, and solely because of his father's unblemished record. Second, Coutin was transferred abruptly to Hanoi. Mai and Chantal went with him.

Mai's next communication was dramatic. It was a telegram dated the third of August, asking Cuong to come urgently. It gave no explanation. He added what he could borrow from his parents to his first salary to meet the costs of the voyage, but he could not arrive in Hanoi before dawn of the ninth. It took him time to find Mai's address. There was no-one in their room. He found an old black-toothed Tonkinoise in the yard. She laughed heartily when he asked her where they were, showing (though Cuong did not know it then) a truly masculine sense of humour. He shook her until she was frightened, and talked.

He ran out and found a *cyclo-pousse*, bribing the man for speed. This was only a romantic gesture, for the streets were choked with ox-carts and ancient lethal Chinese buses, and French armoured cars and troops, and French civilians, their confidence restored, in cars and taxis and on foot. When he got to the citadel the scene was deplorable. It was the war again. It was the start of a load of Jews for the camps. It was a dismally successful version of the Inferno. There was the same air of ritual about it, of mercilessly disciplined misery, justified by some obscure and nightmare greater plan.

There was a column of G.M.C. trucks in the yard, surrounded by soldiers and civilians. Other soldiers were erecting barbed-wire barriers, and expelling the civilians. They were almost all Vietnamese women. Cuong stood outside the wire. Two soldiers pushed a woman through a gap in the barriers. She screamed and stumbled, and Cuong caught her; Mai. He looked up at the trucks. Coutin stood by the tail of one of them, waving cheerfully at him. He had the air of a practised but modest traveller, properly flattered that his friend had been able to come and see him off after all. Coutin had Chantal on his shoulder. Emulating him, the child was waving happily.

Mai told him afterwards that she had discovered the trick the week before. She had fought it alone and without hope. There were two hundred French officers and men in the convoy. They had been in Indo-China since 1939 or 1940. Many had found Vietnamese mistresses and had had children by them. By an unbeatable military logic, a laborious blend of humanity and middle-class morality, the French Army had decided that it ought to repatriate these men with their children, but hardly with their mistresses. According to Mai, Coutin must have known of that decision for months.

When the motors started, the men took their children from the arms of the women who still remained inside the barriers, and climbed into the lorries. The reactions of the women varied sharply. Some tried hysterically to throw themselves under the trucks' wheels, or clung on to their sides or backs. Others seemed to have their minds set exclusively on the welfare of their children. They ran after the trucks, holding up baskets of fruits and eggs, like ambitious street-sellers. One bearded soldier, a son of about five in his arms, jumped from a moving lorry and ran back to a woman and put the child down and embraced her and stayed with her. There seemed no risk of any similarly gymnastic display by Coutin. As soon as it moved, he had disappeared smartly with Chantal into the depths of the third lorry, bound for the Bay of Haiphong and France, his past with Mai neatly erased. Mai herself had made no move or sound since the trucks started. Cuong looked at her with concern. The pain and hatred had heightened her colour vividly. It had sharpened her beauty. It seemed to have rejuvenated her. She looked exactly as she had when he had known her before; the interval of nine years might never have existed. Or her years with Coutin, their creation of the child, had simply been some kind of training, a temporary deviation, an excursion. Now she was herself again, as she had really been destined. A section of French soldiers cleared the yard.

The incident was decisive for Cuong too. It was even convenient. It gave him justification and a direction. By now war with France was almost inevitable. Hanoi saw that more clearly than did Saigon. And, unlike Saigon, Hanoi had nothing against a man with a French resistance record. On the contrary, Ho Chi Minh and Giap saw any man with a professional knowledge of arms and fighting as worth his weight in gold, for the *Chu-luc*, the regular army units which Giap would forge during the next eight years, tempering them patiently with action, until he judged them ready to deliver the final blow to the French forces in Dien Bien Phu in 1954.

Mai disappeared from Hanoi the day that her brother joined the Viet Minh, eight days after Coutin had gone. Until this night, Cuong had not seen her again.

"My brother. Mr. Bender," said Mai, without enthusiasm.

"Brother?" said the large hovering man.

"He came today," said Mai. She might have been commenting on a distant natural calamity.

"Enchanted," said Cuong. He had got up. He had the impression that the big man might dance buoyantly off at any moment, like froth, still eyeing him accusingly. Presumably courtesans did not have brothers in Bender's world, or at any rate not ones that you could be called upon to meet socially and without the slightest warning. But Bender shook his hand vigorously and sat down.

"What's that?" he said.

"Enchanted, I said," said Cuong.

"Ah," said Bender. "Enchanted."

He examined Cuong keenly. Bender had nice frank blue eyes, frank and clear as Coutin's had been. Perhaps here, thought Cuong, lay the attraction for Mai.

"You really her brother?" said Bender.

"Yes, Mr. Bender."

"Fred," said Bender. He added conversationally: "The family send you along, sort of?"

"Nothing like that. Just a brotherly visit, Mr. Bender."

"Fred," said Bender automatically, looking happier. "Fred. Really?"

Bender was then absolutely still for some time, frowning down at the table in front of him. Probably he had just run out of small talk. Or perhaps it was indigestion, or a yoga exercise. Bender had a large square functional face like a truck, short cropped black hair, and a thick neck. He looked like a *Time* front cover. His French was atrocious.

"She's a fine young girl," he said suddenly, looking up again, and leaning across the table in a man-to-man fashion, absenting Mai as completely as if she had just gone off to the Ladies. He had the air now of having thought it all out. The situation was hardly original after all. French literature was full of this kind of thing.

"Your sister," he said, getting it quite straight. "You're up from Saigon?"

"Vientiane," said Cuong.

"Quite a surprise," said Bender gaily, looking massively round to Mai and back to Cuong, hauling her back now physically into the conversation. "Well, I think I can say that the young lady's in good hands. I hope I can say, in very good hands."

He laid his hands down helpfully on the table, palms upwards; he was evidently a man who liked to make his points quite clear to foreigners. He examined his hands thoughtfully, then clapped them together and looked over his shoulder for the waiter.

"Calls for a drink. You're in the government, Mr. Chang? That administration is certainly doing great work up there—"

"Cuong. Just Cuong."

"You even have that young general up there who speaks good English," Bender went on undeflectably. "I consider that remarkable. Truly remarkable. Nosavan, isn't it?"

"Nosavan, yes."

"Giant problems, of course."

Giving the giant problems their due weight, Bender did his breath-holding exercise again. After some seconds he said:

"Well, I can say that we know a little about *them*."

"The giant problems?" said Cuong.

Bender assumed a deeply responsible air. He could have been posing for an official photograph.

"Yup."

"You're in the economics aid mission, Mr. Bender?"

Bender looked at him craftily.

"Economics?" he said. "Well, you can say that. In the broad sense. It sure costs money. You can certainly say that. We do our best to help, you know. We do our best."

"I'm sure that the people are most grateful," said Cuong.

"They should be," said Bender feelingly, "if I do say so. Sixty million dollars a year. Christ. *Sixty* million. Not that we resent that, of course."

"You've always been a generous people, Mr. Bender."

Bender observed him moodily.

"We have our responsibilities, Kwung. We've got to keep on our toes."

"Indeed."

"You know anything about these commies?" said Bender. "You've got to watch them. What ministry did you say?"

"No," said Cuong. "A bank."

"He was in a bank in Saigon too," said Mai neutrally.

"Well," said Bender respectfully. "Finance. That's enterprising. I expect you hold a fairly senior position?"

"A ledger clerk, Mr. Bender."

Bender looked disappointed for a moment.

"We all have to start young," he said reasonably. "Your health. Let's hope that you get on fast in that bank."

Cuong raised his glass.

"Let's hope that, Mr. Bender."

"Give you any time for politics? How are the elections going up in Vientiane?"

"You mean, how will they go, Mr. Bender?"

"Let's put it like that."

"I'd say that it would depend on three main things, Mr. Bender. What the people think. That not so much yet, here; they're hardly fully articulate politically yet. How strong the Army control is. That's more important. How much money is put at the disposal of the major parties. That's the most important of all."

"You don't talk like a clerk," said Bender.

"It's my education," said Cuong. "I have too much of it."

"Oh," said Bender. "In Saigon?"

"In Saigon," said Cuong, "also, in Paris."

"Really," said Bender. "Education. I can't agree with you there, sir. You can't have too much of that. Not of Education."

He had given it a full capital and canonized it, so that it was like Hygiene or the Rotary or Universal Plumbing, things whose fundamental importance to civilization you could not possibly contest. He was in full flight now. He went on:

"And Paris, you say. That's a great city. Think of all those museums."

"It's got a lot of brothels too," said Cuong.

"—Art Galleries," said Bender. "Hell, even all those little shops on the Left Bank. I'd be the last to belittle what the French have done here either, for that matter. Culturally speaking, that is."

"Kind of you to say so, sir," said Cuong.

His tone had registered on Bender that time, and Bender looked at him sharply. Cuong met his eyes innocently. Bender opened his mouth at him again, and changed his mind and looked round at Mai instead.

"And how are we tonight, Madame?"

"I would like to dance," said Mai. "Also, I need money."

"But only on Wednesday—" said Bender. He stopped and smiled back gallantly at Cuong. Even in that light his teeth were brilliant.

"You'll excuse us while we dance?"

"Please," said Cuong. "But I must go."

Bender looked enormously relieved.

"Is that so? What a great pity. I had hoped that you could have dinner with Madame and myself."

"Thank you, but I can get a lorry back as far as Thakhek if I go now."

"Well," said Bender. "Well. Another time."

They got up. Cuong embraced Mai lightly.

"Good-bye, sister."

"Good-bye," she said, adjusting a fold of her bodice.

"Stay well, Mai."

"Yes," she said. Now that he had demonstrated that he was no particular threat to her, it was clear that she had already really forgotten him; she had never been a person to waste her energies.

"Come on," she said to Bender.

As they walked from the table, Bender hung back a little with Cuong.

"About this," said Bender, "you know how it is."

Cuong glanced at him. Bender's candid blue eyes blinked painfully. He looked like a big embarrassed boy scout. For a moment Cuong thought that Bender was going to tip him.

"I know how it is, Mr. Bender."

"Well," said Bender briskly. "Anything I can do to help, Kwock, or whatever your name is. Any time. Give me a call next time you're down."

"I'll do that, Mr. Bender."

Bender looked religious for a moment and hit him violently on the back.

"Got to win those elections," he said.

When Cuong looked back from the heavy dark red curtains of the door, Bender was towering above Mai on the dance floor, but holding her carefully a little away from his body, as if afraid that she might break. Bender seemed to have gone off into one of his trances again. There was a pleased and rested expression on his face and his eyes were half closed. Though Cuong waited at the door for a moment, Mai did not look towards him.

CHAPTER XI

EARLY on April 24 Jean-Philippe sat by a voting bureau in his dilapidated *Deux Chevaux* with Dumergue. The bureau was canvas. An Army lieutenant and two men checked the voters' electoral cards and gave them their voting slips just inside the entrance. Each voter passed then into an *isoloir*. He sealed the slip for his chosen candidate in an envelope and put it into a ballot box. When he came out he threw his unused slips into a second and larger box.

The electoral law passed in February split the country into fifty-nine constituencies each of about thirty thousand people. Voting age was twenty-one for both sexes. Everything seemed very democratic.

At second sight it looked a little less so. While not departing from strict legality, the provisional government had militated against the left wing where they could. The constituencies had been re-drawn to break up left-wing concentrations. Voting bureaux were located only where the army and police could control them. Deposits required from candidates were doubled. For the first time, candidates had to have a certified minimum of education; this particularly handicapped Prince Souvannouvong's Neo Lao Haksat, most of whose leaders were unschooled.

The provisional government's direction did not stop there. A left-wing deputy had given Jean-Philippe a photostat of a highly secret telegram of the sixth from the interim Interior Minister to all Provincial Governors. It instructed them under pain of sanctions to give all necessary financial, material, and moral support to named candidates. These were all right-wing *Rassemblement du People Lao* men, led by the deposed Sananikone, or from the extreme-right-wing *Front National* party which the CDIN had just formed, or known sympathizers who called themselves Independents.

Startling things seemed to be happening to the voting lists too. That for one Vientiane constituency closed at 15,500 mid-March. By mid-April it had jumped 5,500, of which 5,000 were military. The left wing wailed that these military had already been in the mid-March list. This accusation was never answered. Other lists expanded right up to the voting date, although the new law ruled that they should have closed at least fifteen days before it.

The voting lists were never published. Thus, only the army and police who controlled the bureaux knew their contents. You could argue that there was nothing odd about this aura of mystery. Laos was the land of the Mobile Fact, the auditor's nightmare. In Laos you never really knew anything for certain. There was never anything decently occidental about Laotian facts and figures. They were ruthlessly dynamic. They could always prance off and turn themselves inside out and upside down the moment your back was turned. And other more prosaic reasons could be adduced to help explain the bizarre mathematics of these elections. Jean-Philippe's reports from the South were that the going rate for a vote for the right wing was holding steady at 1,200 Kip, or fifteen U.S. dollars, in cases where the army or police could not make a voter's mind up for him.

The two great power blocs were watching the elections closely, which was logical; they were more their trial than Laos's. Pekin and Hanoi radios were gloomy. Quinim Pholsena's socialist Peace Party, which had won seven Assembly seats in the 1958 supplementary elections, was free to campaign, but the communists' real favourite, Prince Souvannouvong's Neo Lao Haksat, was practically hamstrung. The Prince and his eight political leaders still brooded untried in their Vientiane military prison. At the end of March the Provisional Government had very sportingly decided to accept nine other Neo Lao Haksat candidates, for the nine N.L.H. Assembly seats now unoccupied; but this gave the N.L.H. almost no time to campaign, and their alternative candidates were mainly nonentities.

"*Isoloir!*" said Dumergue caustically.

There did not in fact seem to be much isolated about it. Jean-Philippe and Dumergue could just see into the *isoloir's* entrance. A policeman had followed a voter into it and was apparently helpfully showing him what to do. The policeman had a rifle and the young Lao voter eyed it respectfully. Finally, he chose a slip and sealed it and stuck it into the ballot box. He and the policeman beamed happily at each other.

A Renault drew up at the booth and four young Lao got out of it. They were dressed as civilians, but they walked in step, and Jean-Philippe would not have been surprised to hear them burst out into a marching song. They went into the bureau and showed cards to the lieutenant. The lieutenant smiled at them. They went correctly one by one into the *isoloir*, without escort, voted, and went back to their car. They looked serious, willing, and busy.

"Why don't we follow them?" said Dumergue.

"Back to the Chinaimo barracks?" said Jean-Philippe.

"I don't think so," said Dumergue. "Let's see."

They drove after the Renault at a diplomatic distance. It stopped at a second bureau. Jean-Philippe drew up thirty metres behind it and he and Dumergue got out. The four men ahead went again smartly into the booth, showed cards, voted, and went back to the Renault. As they drove off one of them waved cheerfully at Dumergue and Jean-Philippe.

"Friendly sort of chap," said Jean-Philippe.

"He thinks we're in the act too," said Dumergue.

By the exit, they could see easily into the bureau. A soldier with a rifle sat next to the voting slip reject box. As each voter came past him after emerging from the isoloir, the soldier looked at him and into the box at his rejected slips, then wrote on a pad on his knee.

Jean-Philippe picked up a crumpled envelope. There was a voting slip in it. The envelope was almost completely transparent. If you stood next to a voter, you ought to be able to see whom he had voted for, even if the envelope was sealed. Jean-Philippe passed the envelope to Dumergue.

Dumergue looked at it closely.

"What did I say?" he said. He looked righteously outraged. He looked like a schoolmaster.

"You simply have a suspicious mind," said Jean-Philippe.

Dumergue opened and closed his mouth several times.

"What?" he said. "What? Suspicious?"

"Suspicious," said Jean-Philippe. "Malevolent."

"What do you want me to do?" said Dumergue. "Beat this into your head with a brick?"

The soldier with the rifle liked them. He was smiling and pointing vigorously at the bureau's entrance. They could vote too if they liked. They could help democracy along too. The soldier liked his job. He was eager to help.

"After you," said Jean-Philippe.

Dumergue had deflated himself by now and was glinting again at him more normally.

"What a bastard," he said, with admiration.

"Thank you."

"Malevolent, merde," said Dumergue. "You colonist lacquey."

"Atheistic inconoclast. Assassin."

"Ha," said Dumergue. "Imperialist stooge."

"Stooge," said Jean-Philippe reflectively. He knew when he

was beat. He wished he had thought of that first. He had always wanted to have the opportunity to use it.

"Stooge," he said. "All right. You win."

"I'm tired," said Dumergue. "How much more of this farce do you want me to show you?"

"Certainly no more in this heat."

"Then I would suggest a good moral democratic *anis*," said Dumergue.

"To take the taste from the mouth?"

"That," said Dumergue. "And because any excuse for an *anis* is worth consideration."

The Constellation bar was crowded.

"*Anis*," said Dumergue.

"And," said Jean-Philippe.

"This drink," said Dumergue. "Has a fine straight lethal bite."

"Yes."

"It's a most honest drink," said Dumergue.

Jean-Philippe did not reply. He had adopted a fatherly air. He turned his glass of *anis* round slowly and deliberately. His brows were bent and his eyes fathomless. Here, obviously, even from a hundred metres off, was a thoroughly mature, balanced, and impartial man, absolutely fraught with decency. He said gently:

"One must, of course, try to see these incidents within the larger scheme of things."

"Ah."

"François. (May I call you that?) You see, if I might presume to say so, I have been here many years, in this region—"

"*Merde.*"

"These little—dishonesties, shall we say? Expediencies? Expediencies is better; after all, we must not forget that this is a severely practical world. One must, I think, François, see these little things in the context of the greater good."

Dumergue looked at him and made a loud vulgar noise with his tongue.

"In the long run," said Jean-Philippe.

Dumergue repeated his noise.

"Now, now," said Jean-Philippe patiently and paternally, sticking to his act. He was nauseatingly good at it. He was practically convincing himself. "It's not your country, now, is it?"

Dumergue observed him deeply. Then he nodded slowly and seriously.

"You're right. It's not my country."

Jean-Philippe levelled his brows at him.

"So, then you're nothing but an acute idealist, Dumergue. An arrested anal-erotic. A perfectionist."

"My," said Dumergue. "*Merde* yet again. Sir."

"No sense of world strategy, Dumergue. Be realistic, man. Think big."

"Though for the sake of accuracy might I venture to point out, sir, that it was you in the first place who doubted that it would happen like this."

"Touched, but without importance. I agree that I made an error in that. Of aesthetic judgment, you might say. I had not imagined that any—fixing, ha, ha, could be quite so blatant. A child's error."

"Sir."

"You'll note, however, Dumergue, that I'm large enough to admit my mistakes."

"Again, sir."

"This is indeed so violently exaggerated that it has a distinct lunatic charm."

"But no finesse."

"Ah, Dumergue, you and your overcivilized inbred European lust for subtleties! Be direct, man. Forceful. Even dominating. No nonsense. You have to show these orientals exactly what you mean."

Dumergue shrank theatrically. With an evident giant effort, he re-erected himself. He was clearly stricken in his most cherished illusions, yet too fair to deny the truth. He clicked his heels.

"The American Way of Life!" he said reverently.

"The American Way of Life."

They drank.

A man leapt to the bar next to Dumergue and jogged his elbow. Dumergue looked round at him savagely and back at his own trousers.

"Christ!" he said.

"No," said the man. "Auvergne. My apologies. Barman, another *anis*. That makes two *anis*. No," he said, looking at Jean-Philippe's glass, "three."

"Prepotente," said Dumergue.

"A question of economics, Dumergue," said Auvergne. "I'd buy you another pair of trousers too, but I haven't the money."

"Forget it," said Dumergue. "What are trousers, when liberty is at stake?"

"To liberty," said Auvergne.

"Oh, well," said Dumergue, "to liberty."

"Come on," said Jean-Philippe. "Sound a bit more pleased about it, can't you?"

"Who is this man?" said Auvergne.

"Oh," said Dumergue, "I present Jean-Philippe Raymond. This moron's called Auvergne. Philippe too, but *sans* Jean."

"Poor fellow," said Jean-Philippe.

"Don't mind him," said Auvergne. "He's always doing it. Enchanted. I've read your vitriolic articles, of course. You'll certainly be declared *persona non grata*. Quite right too. How strange that we haven't met before."

"It's a big city," said Jean-Philippe modestly.

"His interest in your articles is purely professional jealousy," said Dumergue.

"Ah?"

"Certainly. He's a resident correspondent too." He named Auvergne's agency.

"What will you say?" said Jean-Philippe.

"The elections?" said Avergne. His small eyes gleamed wickedly. "That the West has triumphed yet again, of course. What else? That, inescapably, the people's will always manifests itself correctly in the end, for the things that really matter."

"Christ, all that?" said Jean-Philippe.

"Certainly," said Auvergne. "With padding, a good two columns, double-column headline, syndicated."

"You're that sure of the results already?" said Jean-Philippe.

Auvergne looked at him scathingly.

"Wait and see," he said.

"Right is after all on our side," said Dumergue impressively. They both turned and looked at him.

"What?" said Auvergne.

"Right," said Dumergue. He spoke gravely, his gaze lost in the infinite distances of the bar wall. Jean-Philippe was not the only one who could put on theatre. Dumergue could play too. Jean-Philippe recognized him at once. Dumergue was busy being the solitary hero now, dedicated as anything, hopelessly lost and outnumbered in some dismal underground war, tragic but undaunted, morally victorious if practically inefficient, about to be led smartly off to the firing wall; a familiar and spuriously comforting cinema symbol of our times.

"Oh, yes," said Auvergne. "Right."

"Remember Chiang Kai-shek," said Dumergue.

Auvergne looked at him respectfully.

"Remember Syngman Rhee," he said.

"Ah," said Dumergue, "Ngo Dhi Diem."

"Remember Dien Bien Phu," said Jean-Philippe.

The three raised their *anis* glasses to one another and to their lips, with the courteous formalism of fencers.

"Complete betrayal," said a fourth voice.

Jean-Philippe turned with the others; Laclos, an Algerian-born a *pieds noirs*, whom he had met once or twice before in the Constellation.

"My God," said Auvergne, "you're right. Sorry—"

"This character," said Laclos to the other two, "is sitting talking earnestly to me. Like a gentleman, he says, I must get us more drinks. He disappears."

"It's their fault," said Auvergne. "These two. They trapped me into a deep political discussion. You know them, of course?"

"Oh, yes," said Laclos. "But deep political discussions at a bar?"

"It's a point," said Auvergne. "*Anis?*"

"Ricard," said Laclos. "Like I said. Please."

"Auvergne thinks we've won again gloriously," said Jean-Philippe.

"We?" said Laclos.

"They, if you like," said Jean-Philippe. "The right wing."

"What do you think?" said Laclos.

"It's very possible. The control of the voting. That's very thorough. Here, thorough organization costs good money. And there was good money. The army intimidation in the country. In the South, for example—"

"It's not possible," said Laclos. "It's certain. For the short run."

"And for the long?" said Jean-Philippe.

Laclos's left hand went up and the fingers ran slowly over the livid V-shaped scar on his left cheek. He said:

"In the long term, I think the answer is as we have known it here before, Jean."

Though he was Algerian-born, it was Indo-China and its long bitter war which had most truly determined the contours of this man, as, deeply enough, it had done for both Dumergue and Jean-Philippe; as for Auvergne, Jean-Philippe did not yet know enough of his past. But Laclos was certainly a fledged member of this dour society, which had been forged by one of the saddest and most significant wars of this century. An anthropologist, he had come out to Hanoi just after the world war with the *Ecole Française d'Extrême Orient*. He had gone then to Saigon. This other war had claimed him there. A soldier, he had survived the death marches, his cheek suppurating unattended from a shrapnel wound; in the camps the amateur Viet doctors, no better than former medical orderlies under the French, had sewn it crudely, but he whirled and twisted still in a long wild fever when the Geneva peace evacuated him. Afterwards, cured at least visibly, he had come to Laos for the *Ecole*. But he had lost that position years before, and lived now precariously by teaching. The wound and the march and the camps had left more than a snarling scar upon his cheek. They had set a germ subtly and more deeply in him. Now, the place rotted him. He had married a Chinese girl in his early days in Hanoi, an intellectual, from the people, without particular beauty. Her love and his obligation to recognize that still gave him some slim meaning, and the malice and intelligence in his quick dark eyes still shielded him savagely from pity.

"And a pox on politics," said Auvergne, turning with the Ricard for Laclos. "My wife's story gives it true perspective. My wife is Lao, you understand."

"Congratulations," said Jean-Philippe.

"No, no," said Auvergne. "This is a funny story."

"Go on," said Laclos.

"Well, my wife presented herself to vote at her bureau this morning like a good citizen. There was a Lao just ahead. She was surprised to see that he had a whole sheaf of electoral cards. The police lieutenant behind the table asked his name and consulted his list and looked just as surprised.

" 'But you've already voted!' he said 'It says so here. Pheng Pan Oulavan.'

" 'That's me' said the Lao. 'But I haven't voted yet. Anyone can tell you that. Who says I've voted? I've just left home. I can produce witnesses. Any number of witnesses.'

" 'You can?' said the lieutenant. He was clearly impressed. He frowned deeply and looked at his list again. Then his face cleared like a child's.

" 'Ah!' he said. 'But you're Ouvet's cousin, aren't you? Why didn't you say so at first?'

" 'You mean it doesn't matter if someone's voted for me before?' said the Lao craftily.

" 'Not if you're Ouvet's cousin,' said the Lao. 'Well, not so much, anyway. That's exceptional.'

" 'Even if I've got twenty cards?' said the Lao.

"The lieutenant looked startled. He said:

" 'Twenty?' "

" 'That's what they sent me,' said the Lao. 'I had nothing to do with it.'

" 'Oh, well,' said the lieutenant. 'All right. Just this once.'

"He counted twenty sets of voting slips carefully and passed them to the Lao.

" 'For Ouvet, of course?' he added, as an afterthought.

"The Lao looked at him.

" 'Ouvet?' he said. 'Not bloody likely. I'm voting left wing. I never did like the bastard.' "

There was an awed silence.

"Seriously?" said Jean-Philippe.

"She swears on it," said Auvergne.

"He got away with it?" said Laclos.

"Oh, yes. They were so surprised that they even forgot to note down who she voted for."

"There's hope for virtue yet," said Dumergue.

CHAPTER XII

THERE might still be hope for virtue, but there was not much left for the left wing by four that afternoon. Twenty-four of the Assembly's fifty-nine seats had already been decided. The Provisional Government's *Lao Presse* and radio announced the results with gusto. All twenty-four were right-wing *Rassemblement du Peuple Lao* or CDIN *Front National* or known sympathizers. They eclipsed the Neo Lao Haksat and the socialist Peace Party in six constituencies. In these, the imagination boggled at the percentage of votes recorded for the right wing. They ranged from ninety to ninety-nine-point-nine. The N.L.H. or Peace Party had won these seats decisively in 1958. This was no mere landslide victory for the right wing. It was a roaring avalanche.

Jean-Philippe had once met the Peace Party leader socially, and banked on that fact to call on him that evening. As the *Lao Presse* had it, the CDIN candidate had whipped Quinim Pholsena in his Paksone constituency in the south by seventeen thousand to seven hundred.

Quinim ran a bookshop in the same street as Jean-Philippe's flat, across from it, and about forty metres west. The shop door was open, and the lights on. Jean-Philippe went in. There was a long glass-topped counter on the right. A young Lao girl was sorting books into the wall shelves behind it.

"May I see Monsieur Quinim?"

The girl turned and put her books down on the counter and looked at him steadily. She wore a loose-sleeved white blouse and a long Lao skirt to below her knees, of dark blue cotton with lines of gold thread running intricately through it. The thick shining black hair was drawn directly up off her forehead. Always these young Lao girls' faces were like that, cool, tranquil, soft, carnal, guiltless, aware.

"And you are, m'sieu?"

"Raymond. I've met him once before."

He gave her a card. She went through the open door at the back of the shop. He looked at the newspapers on the counter; *Figaro*, *Paris-Soir*, *Le Monde*, a few others, all a week or ten days old. There was no sign of *Humanité*. Quinim was too shrewd to display it, or not that far left. Jean-Philippe saw a small headline: *Laos, Echo du Passé*. He looked away abruptly, and walked to the shelves on the wall opposite the counter.

One learnt nothing from echoes, he thought drily, one learnt no lessons from history.

The books in the shelves in front of him now were all cheap school editions of the French classics, Alexandre Dumas, Victor Hugo, Balzac, du Maupassant, Flaubert, a collected Beaudelaire, three Zola.

Eugénie Grandet, Les Fleurs du Mal, La Bête Humaine, Bovary, La Tentation de Saint Antoine.

That was probably all that you could ever leave, this view of man finally aware of the pattern of his own fatalities. It was the only durable monument. Not cities or political systems or love or loyalty or courage.

"Monsieur Raymond?"

Quinim was barefoot and dressed only in a sarong. He was quite broad, the flesh of his chest and stomach smooth, but without much fat. The face was high-cheekboned and completely composed. He could have been thirty or fifty years old.

"Monsieur Quinin. Could you be so kind as to give me five minutes?"

Quinim considered him. The girl had gone back behind her counter to her books.

"If you would prefer," said Jean-Philippe, "I could come back tomorrow."

"Would you like to come upstairs?" said Quinim.

There was a stairway at the end of the shop, to the left of the door, leading up left. The naked feet padded up behind him. The room upstairs was choked with sofas and armchairs. There was a dark malevolent hatstand with a vast mirror just to the left of the entrance from the stairs. Jean-Philippe saw a series of framed photographs on the walls. They were of Quinim, suave in a suit, with (presumably) the members of his family. No doubt they had been taken at various anniversaries or key ceremonies. Everyone in them, from the youngest to Quinim, bore the same adult, direct, and unwinking inscrutability, as though they had all been holding their breath, or as if it were some salient and ineradicable family feature, like a hooked nose. This far, the room was unrockably middle-class and respectable. It could have been the drawing-room of a socially ambitious clerk in Britain. It was a statement to the public rather than a room for living.

Above the scheming hatstand, an exotically tinted print showed the tubby upper half of the late King Sisavang Vong, in his stiff high-collared and heavily braided white tunic, bejowled with age. The old gentleman had won immortal fame early in 1953 when the Viet Minh invaded and their columns reached towards his capital of Luang Prabang. While others fled, the old gentleman remained. Perhaps it was less bravery than inside knowledge. He had after all taken expert opinion on the probabilities. The Bonzes, consulted, had carried out their tests, and advised that the Viet Minh would not invade the city. Incredibly, they did not, but flowed past it, then recoiled. In the subtle tangled world of Laos, the lie of a bird's entrails could still determine a major political decision.

There was a heavy teak sideboard behind the chair to which Quinim guided him, covered by a glass door. He saw the usual Thai and Lao silver bowls in it, and a small surprisingly cheerful Buddha in gold-lacquered wood.

"Whisky-soda, Monsieur Raymond?"

"Thank you."

Quinim opened a cabinet to the right of the sideboard and poured the drink.

"Please don't wait. And excuse me three minutes. I'll make myself respectable."

"Please don't worry," said Jean-Philippe. "This is your home and your time."

Quinim smiled.

"One should always keep up appearances. Even in adversity."

When Quinim had gone down the stairs Jean-Philippe took his glass and walked to the window and drew the curtains and looked down into the street. He caught the blur of two faces looking up from the other side; soldiers or police. He raised his glass courteously to them and turned away from the window.

Quinim reappeared progressively upwards into the room from the stairway like a noiseless mechanical device. He had put on a khaki shirt, brown slacks, and sandals. He said:

"Got their eyes on you, Monsieur Raymond?"

Jean-Philippe smiled.

"Perhaps just passers-by."

"I doubt it, Monsieur Raymond. It's a compliment which they've been paying me for some time, on and off."

Quinim poured himself a whisky and sat down on the sofa near Jean-Philippe's chair, so that he faced at right angles to him, no doubt so that his toes could not point at him by accident. For a Lao, to point your feet at anyone was to insult him diabolically.

"I admire your calm, Monsieur Quinim, in that case."

Quinim laughed.

"Again, one has to satisfy the appearances, you know," he said. "We're all trapped by our own myths. Our well-known oriental impassivity. Your health, Monsieur Raymond."

"Your health."

"You're also thinking that we seem to take our defeats very lightly," said Quinim.

"We've got our popular myths too, Monsieur Quinim. Our reverence for the good loser."

"For a man who is interested in results," said Quinim, "a good loser is a contradiction in terms. I'm a very bad loser. You've heard the results, of course?"

"Yes. It was really a defeat?"

Quinim looked at the opposite wall with amusement.

"Seventeen thousand, against seven hundred," he said. "I'd call that a defeat."

"Yet in 1958 you won your seat easily?"

"As did the other deputies from my party," said Quinim. "Let's say that the conditions were a little different then."

"Meaning, no armed control of the voting bureaux, no bribery?"

"Isn't it just a question of degree, Monsieur Raymond?" said Quinim patiently. "I was thinking of my four years in Paris, as a student. Now, can you say that your elections are ever completely free from this kind of thing? It's much less obvious, of course, than here. I'm not criticising, you understand."

"Well—"

"Well, let's just say that this time the right-wing preparations were extremely thorough. Here, that implies money, Monsieur Raymond. They used a great deal of that; one knows who supplied it, of course. And some force, including that applied by the eight-battalion sweep of the South which you described in (I think it was?) the last of your articles."

"I didn't think that *France-Franche* reached here."

"One shouldn't be too modest, perhaps, Monsieur Raymond."
Jean-Philippe laughed. He said:
"It's never really been one of my faults."

"Good," said Quinim, "modesty is stupid. Your paper has weight, Monsieur Raymond. So your views are certainly known here."

Jean-Philippe raised his eyebrows.

"Not that that should matter at all," said Quinim. "Anyway not with us. We consider you a fair man in what you say."

"Thank you," said Jean-Philippe. "We, Monsieur Quinim?"

Quinim looked sharply at him. After a moment he said:
"I, Monsieur Raymond. A few people who think as I do."

Jean-Philippe smiled. You struck steel early here. Strength, ambition, ruthlessness. Quinim would tell him exactly as much as he wanted to, no more.

"Fairness," said Quinim. "Objectivity. It's quite rare, you know. Even among friends. Sometimes, of course, one has to be a little careful about one's friends, these days. Unhappily."

Jean-Philippe looked at him, but Quinim was simply holding his glass easily, his profile as placid and cheerful as his wooden Buddha's. Whatever that message, Quinim would certainly not elaborate it, or would deny that he had given him one, if Jean-Philippe questioned him further about it.

"What will you do, Monsieur Quinim?"

Quinim glanced round at him.

"I have my business here, you know. And in Paksé. Wait. I shall wait."

"You think that things will improve?"

Quinim shrugged delicately.

"Consider, after all, that seven hundred and twenty-one men and women voted for me, Monsieur Raymond. Shouldn't I be fairly hopeful? Who would have believed that seven hundred and twenty-one people would be prepared to die for me? Or, rather, for what I think?"

"Assassination?" said Jean-Philippe. "The right wing would really go that far?"

"No," said Quinim. "But my supporters must have feared that when they voted. They had every reason to fear that, believe me. Isn't that the point?"

"It's hard to read the capacity for violence into your people."

"We can all learn," said Quinim. "Violence? Oh, yes. Think of Somsat, my deputy. They killed him with a grenade in his house in Paksé; what is it now? A few months ago. We can all learn, Monsieur Raymond."

"So your Peace Party will withdraw and regroup and turn further left?"

"Communist, you mean?" said Quinim. "No, Monsieur Raymond. You think that we really care so much for all these ideologies? Even Souvannouvong? We're a very small country, Monsieur Raymond. A nothing. Our only hope for survival is through neutralism. That's not a question of ideologies, but common sense. My party wants this small country to survive. That's all. It's most unoriginal. And develop. So we should take aid from anyone who will give it to us freely."

"Including North Viet Nam, China, Russia?"

"Why not, Monsieur Raymond? Provided that their aid doesn't become an excuse for implanting another para-military force here. After all, have we really gained so greatly by depending exclusively on the West for aid so far?"

"All right," said Jean-Philippe. "Corruption. Mismanagement. Disastrous mistakes. But the Marshall Plan saved Europe, Monsieur Quinim. Have the intentions all been bad? It's not a police state. They haven't done that."

"They, Monsieur Raymond?"

"The Americans."

"Not we, Monsieur Raymond?"

"We, the French? Hardly. We're the death's head at this feast, surely? With the experience. Without the power."

"These good intentions, Monsieur Raymond. At this late stage we can still afford the luxury of considering the importance of a few men having good intentions?"

"All right. Probably not."

"You were saying too that it's not a police state. I think that's true. Nothing professional like, say, Hitler's Germany, or Diem's South Viet Nam."

"No."

"No. Though perhaps the way that these elections are being held is indicative of the future here. And, in passing, when are they going to try Souvannouvong, Monsieur Raymond?"

Jean-Philippe smiled.

"Shouldn't I ask you that? Wasn't it you who defended him at the preliminary hearing?"

"A whisky-soda, Monsieur Raymond?"

"With pleasure."

Quinim bent over the cabinet.

"They won't try him, Monsieur Raymond. They have no case at all. But they'll keep him locked up. Well, he should be used to that. He spent most of last August under house arrest, when the fighting broke out again in the north. As did I."

"On suspicion of having ordered the revolt?"

"That. Oh, and of having connived at an invasion by regular Viet Minh army units, that favourite and convenient fiction of theirs. Well, frightened people are always suspicious, Monsieur Raymond. They're still deeply suspicious of me. The cabinet even required a special oath of loyalty from me last September. I duly swore that I would support the government without reserve against any attack on Laos proved to have come from another country. Perhaps that was a little unkind. Nobody really believes in that theory about the North Vietnamese invasion, not even the cabinet. But they've alleged it too often officially. They daren't admit that the revolt comes from within Laos itself. So, with me, they were caught in their own trap. They had to let me go."

Jean-Philippe got up and took the re-filled glass from him.

"And perhaps they're not the only frightened people," said Quinim. "Tell me, Monseiur Raymond, a small thing that has always puzzled me, is neutralism a dirty word?"

"Not in my vocabulary."

"To us, it had often seemed to be that for the Americans. He who is not with me is against me. Isn't that, forgive me, the statement of a fanatical and frightened man?"

"Of a simple man, perhaps."

"Simplicity can be so dangerous, Monsieur Raymond. As dangerous as innocence. But are they really so uncertain of the values of their system that they don't even dare to discuss it? Even to admit the bare possibility that some other political philosophy might be right too, in its particular context? Are they always doomed to fight first?"

Jean-Philippe smiled.

"Which Americans, Monsieur Quinim?"

"Well," said Quinim, "yes. Which Americans."

"I'm hardly a member of the C.I.A., Monsieur Quinim."

"Forgive me," said Quinim. "I'm being most discourteous. You'll see now that I am in fact much less impassive than my appearance."

"What will the Prince do?"

"Prince Souvanna Phouma? Well, I think that the *Rassemblement du People Lao* will be beaten badly. Moderation's no longer the fashion. You'll know that they made the Prince Honorary President of the R.P.L. some months ago. He was politically wrong to accept it; the R.P.L.'s a sinking ship. He'll wait now, I think, like me."

"You can afford that?"

124

"He can. I too, I think. The communists have some striking aphorisms, Monsieur Raymond. Don't push the point that I quote them too far. He who holds the countryside, Mao Tse Tung said. Well, I believe that we hold them here. The people are frightened now, but I think that we still hold them."

"Time, then, Monsieur Quinim?"

"A question of time. Perhaps not so very long. I hope that you'll be here to see it, Monsieur Raymond."

"I should be interested to be here to see it."

CHAPTER XIII

"THIRTY-TWO, I think," said Pridie politely. He did not sound enormously interested. The high night-life whine of the Constellation Bar made a nice pseudo-sophisticated background to his voice.

"All right wing?" said Jeanette.

Pridie put his glass down quietly.

"Well," he said, "let's say, no communists, no socialists, that we know of."

He did not sound as though he liked communists or socialists very much.

"Some of the voting percentages seem quite remarkable," said Jean-Philippe.

The light grey eyes behind their wafer-thin rimless glasses fixed him for a moment. It was a depthless and neutral regard, like a cat's. Pridie looked as though he was busy thinking about something totally different.

"You find that strange?" said Pridie.

"I think some of the figures a little—far-fetched," said Jean-Philippe.

"Such as?" said Pridie gently.

"Quinim's," said Jean-Philippe, "for example."

"That fellow-traveller!" said Pridie. The violence was surprising.

"Is he?" said Jean-Philippe. "Is he, now? I saw him this afternoon. I thought that he might just be an honest man."

That comment was not popular. The flat grey eyes set hard on him again an instant, but Pridie did not answer. There was a burst of laughter from the next table, and Jean-Philippe glanced over at it; several American correspondents. Foreign correspondents always seemed to clot together by race like that in a strange country, as if from a sense of duty. Cavalstan, the Constellation manager, walked delicately past and caught his eye and smiled; a man brilliantly aware of the latest trends in the opium market, the gold traffic, the girls; a man who had the gift of survival. Which way had he betted on the elections? thought Jean-Philippe.

". . . knelt first," said one of the men at the next table. "Stark naked. Then she did a complicated obeisance."

"A what?"

"Obeisance."

"Obeisance," said the man opposite him, impressed. "Say, that's straight Pulitzer."

"After that there was no stopping her," said the first man.

"But how did the Buddha get in on this?"

"Well, he wasn't in the bed itself. In the wall. In an alcove, sort of."

"Brinkmanship," said the second man.

"Sure. He damn near fell on us, in fact, once or twice."

"And how do you suppose the commies would have handled it?" said a third voice. "So a fix is a fix is a fix."

"Maybe it's some kind of local custom," said the second man thoughtfully. "Maybe they do that too before they—"

"You've got to act from a position of strength," said the third man. "Look, that's basic politics. That's all they respect, isn't it?"

The fourth journalist at the next table nodded back at him seriously. So far he had not said a word. He had probably not had the chance.

"No, they use the left hand," said the first man. "I have that on good authority."

The second man laughed heartily.

"So anyway," said the first man, encouraged, "you can forget all this oriental passivity crap. Strictly for the birds. You work them right, and they romp around like rattlesnakes."

"Like rattlesnakes?"

"Like rattlesnakes."

Jean-Philippe glanced back at Pridie. Pridie had taken the discreet white handkerchief from his breast pocket and was dabbing his lips with it. He looked a little pained. The next table was nothing to do with him. He was busy disassociating himself from it. They were not exactly the sort of people that he would have asked to one of his dinner parties. Jean-Philippe said:

"How's culture these days, Pridie?"

The white silk handkerchief stopped abruptly.

"It's so strange that they have so few other good bars in Vientiane," said Jeanette.

She wasn't missing a thing, thought Jean-Philippe. She wasn't allowing anyone to bait Pridie tonight.

"Isn't it?" he said back to her.

"And the food's very good here too," she said.

Why did she bother to protect Pridie? he wondered. Wasn't Pridie big enough to look after himself? She loved him, or she was afraid of him, or both. But why did a girl so obviously beautiful and sexually attractive need to be frightened?

"All right," he said to her. "It's the French influence. The only place where you dine better is Pridie's."

She glanced at him gratefully. Pridie too looked at him. Pridie said:

"It's just a matter of knowing how to choose your cooks, you know."

He was talking with the deprecating note of one who was secretly thoroughly pleased with himself. He had forgotten all about the embarrassing Americans at the next table. He was re-established. Jean-Philippe looked at him amazed. Could you win him over so easily, this veiled, complicated, intelligent character, by nothing more astute than flattery?

"Of course we have to go it alone," said the third man at the next table. "You think these limeys would ever really back us up anyway?"

"Hell, they still have commercial relations with Red China, don't they?" said the fourth man. He had got in at last.

"And who was it who armed the French in their Indo-Chinese war, tell me that?"

"Sure," said the fourth man, bitterly. "Sure. Good old Uncle Sam."

The third man looked morose. He was feeling things deeply now. He was going to write policy at any moment.

"Not that it did them any damn good," he said. "But hell, the French!"

"You've heard about Marivell?" said Dumergue.

Jean-Philippe looked up quickly. Dumergue had materialized suddenly next to the table like a rotund fate, his short black militant moustache and his thick orbed glasses set on them as if in accusation. There was something not so funny here. Jean-Philippe said:

"Sit down, Françoise."

Dumergue looked surprised at the idea, but he sat down slowly. He glanced at each af them in turn.

"A nice night," he said. "A full day, really, with the elections and all. Full of surprises."

"What kind of surprises?" said Pridie.

Dumergue looked at him.

"You remember Marivell?"

"Marivell?" said Pridie. "From *Education*? Of course."

"Marivell went through quite a lot, really," said Dumergue reflectively. "A German concentration camp, for example. That kid with polio. But a nice, willing, harmless sort of fellow wouldn't you say?"

Pridie looked at him impatiently.

"Look," he said. "Of course I know Marivell. He was with us at dinner at my place that night, remember? With his wife."

"With his wife," said Dumergue obscurely. "That's quite a point too."

"Come on, François," said Jean-Philippe. "What's the mystery?"

Dumergue looked at him absently.

"'*Soir, Jean*."

He sounded very correct.

"'*Soir*. What is it?"

"Oh. He was knifed to death, you see," said Dumergue. "Two nights ago. At Bat-Keun."

"Knifed?" said Jeanette.

"To be exact," said Dumergue, "knifed first, then later finished with rifle-butts; I understand in the presence of the children."

"At Bat-Keun?" said Pridie.

"Who was it?" said Jean-Philippe.

"The Pathet," said Dumergue.

"Did you say Bat-Keun?" said Pridie. He was looking quietly at Dumergue. Dumergue glanced back at him with irritation.

"Yes. Yes, I said Bat-Keun. Why?"

"Nothing," said Pridie.

"Where's Bat-Keun?" said Jeanette.

"About eighty kilometres away," said Dumergue. "In the hills. A small holiday resort. A small hotel, a clinic, a few villas."

"Why Marivell?" said Jean-Philippe. "Why did they kill him?"

Dumergue glanced marginally at Pridie again.

"They seemed to think that he was American."

Pridie did not say anything.

"How did it happen?" said Jeanette.

"The wife and the two kids were up there on holiday for a few days," said Dumergue. "Two days ago Marivell had the afternoon off. So he drove up from Vientiane in his station wagon, to spend the afternoon and night with them. In the middle

of the night a band of men broke into the hotel and went straight
to their bedroom. Marivell resisted, and they knifed him at once."

"The children were there?" said Jean-Philippe.

"Yes. Two of the men stayed in the room with them and Marivell's body. The others took his wife. Oh, and one of the French
women who ran the hotel. She spoke English. Apparently they
wanted someone to translate from French into English for them.
They took the two women to a man in the forest. He seemed to
be their leader."

"They were in uniform?" said Jean-Philippe.

"No," said Dumergue. "Not from what she said. But they were
well armed, with rifles and machine-pistols. The man went into
a long speech as soon as he saw them, in French. That the land
was for the people. That the Americans sought only to dominate
it for their own political ends. That the Americans had brought
it nothing but corruption and decay, nothing for the people. That
they were worse than nothing. They were worse than the way
things were before. They were like a new plague. That the Lao
sought only peace and their own rights. Well, the usual line.
Then he asked the woman from the hotel to translate it all into
English.

"'Why?' said the woman from the hotel. "She understood
everything you said. Why shouldn't she? She's French."

"She said that the man looked deeply puzzled when she said
that. He was a young man, she said, probably a student. She
said that he looked much too young for his gun. He didn't say
a thing for a while. She had apparently killed his nice long
political speech stone dead.

"'What d'you mean, French?' he said at last. 'French. She's
supposed to be American.'

"'French,' said the woman from the hotel.

"'Well,' said the young man reasonably, 'her husband's American anyway.'

"'Her husband's French,' said the woman. 'Marivell. A United Nations counsellor. Marivell. That's a French name, isn't
it? Isn't it French enough for you?'

"The young man looked down at the ground for a long time.
Then he looked up at Madame Marivell. He said:

"'Madame, your husband's American, isn't he?'

"He sounded as though he were pleading with her. Madame
Marivell said to him:

"'You have killed my husband. My husband is French.'

"The young man looked from one woman to the other, without
speaking. Then he turned to his men and gave them instructions

I   129

in Lao, rapidly. They took the women back through the forest. It was a long way, and it was almost light when they reached the hotel."

"Marivell?" said Jean-Philippe.

"By then Marivell was very dead," said Dumergue. "Apparently they had not killed him outright with the knives. Later, when the two women were already in the forest, they say that he groaned and began to move on the floor."

"They?" said Jean-Philippe.

"The children," said Dumergue. "It is as they told it afterwards."

"And?" said Jeanette.

Dumergue looked away from her.

"The two men killed him then with their rifle-butts, on the floor."

In the silence Jean-Philippe said:

"You've seen Madame Marivell?"

Dumergue looked at him like a blind man.

"Just now, Jean. I come from them now. They brought her and the woman from the hotel to Vientiane. And the children. You see, I'm the Marivells' friend. I've known him, and her, for a long time."

Jean-Philippe looked up and saw that a man was standing between his chair and Pridie's. He was a young Philippino.

"Yes?" said Pridie.

"Please, sir," said the Philippino.

"At the Embassy, is it?"

"Sir. They would like you to come now."

Pridie looked round the people at the table.

"I'm sorry," he said. "I'm sorry."

"It's not your fault," said Jean-Philippe.

Pridie looked at him for a moment.

"No," he said, "no, it's not my fault. Would you take Jeanette back home?"

"Of course," said Jean-Philippe. He watched Pridie leave with the Philippino.

"Of course they like it too," said the first man at the next table, coming back uncannily on wavelength with a fine sense of timing.

The second man was still sceptical.

"I won't buy that," he said. "They could be reading newspapers over your shoulder."

"That doesn't mean a thing," said the first man earnestly. "It's just that their facial muscles are kind of atrophied."

Jean-Philippe looked back at Jeanette. He said:
"Would you like to go now?"
"Yes," she said, "please."

Again, she had that curiously fragile look, as if the sudden absence of Pridie and the sharp vicious facts of Marivell's murder had stripped and struck her unfairly.

"You don't mind if we go?" he said to Dumergue.

"What?" said Dumergue.

"If I take Jeanette," said Jean-Philippe, "if we leave you."

"No," said Dumergue, "no. You see, I have to get back to see Marivell's wife again soon. In twenty minutes, say. We're getting them ready to go back to France, you know."

Jean-Philippe looked back from the door. Dumergue was sitting stock still, with no drink in front of him. He was staring moodily at the Americans at the next table. It was unlikely that he was hearing a word that they said.

Jeanette said nothing as he guided her to his car, and he drove her in silence down past the Lido night-club and the Ministère des Travaux Publics and to the great low broad river. He turned to the right and drove along next to it. There was no moon. Across the river, higher upstream, there were just the soft small yellow lights of the Thai village. He could also see two *pirogues*, far out in the river, drifting down, with frail yellow lanterns in their bows. A great rectangular shape was moving very slowly down the river too, in the centre, where the current was strongest. There was a small square superstructure on it, bathed in pale light. It would be one of the giant rafts of bamboo logs which the Lao sailed down from Nam Tha or Phong Saly or Luang Prabang, to Vientiane or Thakhek or Savannakhet. The Lao lived on them, adapting themselves to the slow pace of the river, moving patiently down with it to the point where they delivered the logs and sold them.

Sampans were moored in a line near the customs house. They were big enough to carry petroleum fuels and oils and general merchandise up and down the river. He saw a woman in one of the deckhouses. She was at its window, not moving, looking out as they passed. Light from some kerosene lamp inside the cabin fell half across her face. It was very old and dispassionate, the hair shot with grey and cropped short. Age had lined it and drained the sex from it. She could have been watching birth or death or God or nothing.

Jeanette had not spoken. He turned the car right, into her short drive.

She looked at him.

"Will you come in?" she said.

He had stopped the car.

"Well," he said.

"I would like it."

He considered her a moment, in the darkness of the car, and she looked back at him, without movement.

"Then, with pleasure," he said.

She went into the house and the front room ahead of him, and turned on the lights. There were two, low, one at each far corner. He would have known this room. She turned.

"Will you give me a minute?"

"Of course."

There were many books, in two long bookshelves, along two walls. Simone de Beauvoir and Sartre and Camus and Gary. Bound sets of *Réalité*. Malraux and Saint-Exupéry and Koestler. Bernanos and Mauriac. Ignazio Silone and Carlos Levi and Malaparte and Moravia. Some English. Many Graham Greene, including his *Quiet American*. Evelyn Waugh. Conrad and Charles Morgan (some odd blind spot of sentimentality in the cool lacquered French mind drew them to him quite infallibly.) Faulkner and Truman Capote and Fitzgerald and Hemingway. Mann and Rilke and Hesse. Lorca and Lope de Vega.

The prints on the walls were not far from what he had expected either. Degas, Manet, Pisarro, Van Gogh. Too much Van Gogh.

It was quite a display. It was a lot to live up to. He had seen it before and he would perhaps have preferred something more original.

He was glancing dutifully at the books when she came back. She carried two glasses, a whisky-soda and what looked like a Dubonnet.

"I hope this is right?" she said.

"Perfect."

"You were drinking it earlier this evening. And at Peter's, I remember."

There he was again.

She had gone to the sofa. He went to a chair near it and sat down. The point was strategic. From it, he could be decently sympathetic, or rampant, or possibly both. It would depend on what tone she set; she was the host. He could hear nothing from outside the room, no sound from the town, none from the great river.

Jeanette sat demurely, her legs together, the light coral-coloured cotton dress down to her knees. The splendid sculptural breasts rose and fell gently. She balanced her Dubonnet on her right thigh and looked at him.

"How will it turn out?"

He did not find this question notably brilliant. She had heard about the right wing's mathematically outrageous victory in the first thirty-two seats to have been decided, hadn't she? She had heard about Marivell's murder, hadn't she?

"It really interests you?" he said.

She looked hurt.

"Of course it interests me."

"All right," he said, "I think that it will end badly."

"You're a Frenchman, Jean-Philippe. You don't say that just because it proves you to have been right in the end?"

He looked at her in irritation.

"As simple as that?" he said. "You don't think that we are over our hurt pride yet? Anyway, we didn't exactly prove that we were right in Viet Nam, did we, against Ho Chi Minh? No, I don't say it for that reason at all. I say it simply because I believe, without sentiment, that the extreme right wing's days are numbered. In Laos, or anywhere. History's just gone too fast for them. The world has changed. Well, that wouldn't matter if it simply left them as harmless anachronisms. It doesn't; they have power. That makes for an explosive mixture. People tend to get hurt."

She looked past him. She said:

"I find it a little like watching a complicated game, not knowing the rules. They're always so polite."

"Here?" he said. "The Lao? They're a very polite people."

"So that the violence is the more shocking."

He shrugged impatiently.

"As I said, it's an explosive mixture."

"And your left wing are so much better, Jean-Philippe?"

"Here? From what one can make out, more dedicated, more professional, less prone to personal corruption. Perhaps these are just the qualities of youth. Perhaps that sense of purpose comes just from an arrogant certainty that time is on their side."

"And the professionals will win?"

"The professionals generally win, Jeanette."

"Your professionals killed Marivell," she said.

He looked at her.

"Many Marivells have been killed in Indo-China," he said. "Some deserved it. Many did not. Some on purpose. Some by accident. And no one side has had the monopoly of killing them. If there is one moral, it's this: Today, if you're a Marivell, you're a poor survival risk. There's no pay-off today to being the nice human guy in the middle."

She was quiet; he had spoken with too much bitterness. He said more gently:

"What does your friend Peter think of it?"

She looked up at him quickly.

"After these elections, that the West will certainly hold Laos."

"The Americans will hold Laos," he said.

"All right," she said, "that the Americans will hold Laos. If they go on being really strong, making no compromises. The firm stand, you know. Peter's a great believer in the firm stand."

"Yes?" He could not be sure if she was mocking a little.

"Yes. He considers that this is the true modern crusade, against them."

"Christ," he said. "He said that? In those words?"

"Oh, yes," said Jeanette. "It's one of the things in which he's completely sincere. I've no doubt that he'd die happily for it."

"Tell me," he said, "his crusade is against the communists only? Or also against the socialists? and the liberals? and the neutralists? Against anyone in fact who would not fully satisfy the exigencies of the Un-American Activities Committee?"

She looked at him for a long while.

"You really hate him, don't you?" she said.

He looked at her in surprise.

"Pridie?" he said. "Intelligent, interesting, amusing, sophisticated. Even if his political views are as oversimplified as you say. He's not an activist, is he, after all? So why on earth should I hate him? Do you?"

She looked down suddenly.

"I don't know," she said. "I don't know."

"Good God," he said. "I thought that there was even some talk of your marrying him."

"There was," she said.

"Well?"

"She didn't approve," said Jeanette.

"She?"

"His mother," said Jeanette. "You remember, she came out to see him, for a week or so, a month ago.'

Jean-Philippe had indeed met the lady once, marginally, at some cocktail party. He recalled her as a tall woman, gaunt, striking, impeccable, the contours of her New England breeding as precisely defined and legible as the light and elegant structure of her bones. It struck him now that he had of course seen her once even before that. The point had been puzzling him subconsciously. Of course, it was she who was the subject of the solitary charcoal drawing which hung above the bookcase in Pridie's home.

"Why shouldn't she approve?" he said. "The two of you fought?"

"Not at all," said Jeanette. "We got on rather well. And at that time I think that I would still have married Peter, if he had asked me. And he would have asked me."

"Would have, Jeanette?"

"Would have, yes," she said. "There'll be nothing now. Her visit was to screen me, of course. I didn't particularly like it, but I suppose that I thought it fair enough. Besides, she seemed to like me. I think that she did in fact too, but of course that wouldn't really be the point, for her. Oh, and I learned afterwards that she had also checked discreetly on my time in London, before I came here, through friends of hers at the Embassy there. But, again, I don't think that that revealed anything really sinister about me."

"Well?"

"Oh, well," said Jeanette, "on her last day here she had a heart-to-heart talk with me. It was still all very friendly. She told me of her ambitions for him. She had set her sights very high, but I supported her warmly. She was completely frank, and rather impressive. I think your word describes her best: dedicated. She told me that she couldn't quite see how I could fit into that picture."

"And you told her, as politely, to go to hell?"

Jeanette looked embarrassed.

"She hadn't really left me room for that," she said. "She hadn't left much room for emotion. She'd done it all awfully well. The tone of the meeting forbade it. She had made it quite clear that she was talking from the facts as she saw them. She seemed to imply that there wasn't much appeal from the facts."

"Look," said Jean-Philippe, "this is nineteenth-century stuff. You accepted it? What about Pridie? He's grown up now. He accepted that?"

"He accepted it," she said, after a moment, looking down quietly at the floor beside her feet. In that manner, her perfect delicate dark profile was towards him, a little flushed, with the lips parted slightly, and her breasts rising and falling faster now with her quickened breathing. She did not look humiliated by her admission—her frankness had preserved her from that— only rather vulnerable. It was an effective posture. He put his hands instinctively out towards her. His sense of reality caught up with him just in time, and he stopped himself smartly.

"Pridie's not a weak man," he said. "I'd say that Pridie generally gets what he wants."

"That would fit," she said. "He could always keep me on as a mistress, you see. I think his mother rather approved of that idea. She's no petty moralist. She even added a stamp of respectability to it, you might say."

"If you see it that clearly," he said. "Then it's your choice, isn't it?"

"My choice," she said doubtfully. "Yes. Yes, I know that's true."

"You look well enough on it too," he said cruelly. "You like being his mistress, don't you?"

She inclined her head a little further away from him.

"It's a strange country," she said obliquely. "I don't much like being on my own, you see."

"Then it's a fair enough bargain, isn't it?" he said. "You could always have dropped him, you know. You can always still do so."

She looked back at him swiftly.

"Could I?" she said. "Could I? D'you imagine that I didn't think of that? And I was hardly prompted by a young virgin's conventional fury at seeing her marriage broken. There was no wasted organdie and lace in this case. I'm not that young and I wasn't that innocent. It was the insult of it that made me want to break. Because her decision was so damned executive."

Jeanette was watching the ground by her feet again. Her curt honesty had surprised Jean-Philippe. It had even rather impressed him. He put his glass down on the table. A solitary car drove past the house at dangerous speed. Its sound receded, then cut off abruptly. Perhaps it had fallen into the river. Jeanette said:

"But have you ever seen a person that you have admired shatter suddenly, Jean-Philippe, then hold you by an even more tenacious weakness, compassion?"

He did not answer her, and she looked over at him.

"How I envy you, Jean-Philippe. I don't think that you'd ever commit yourself fully to any one person."

Jean-Philippe sighed to himself. There was something about the bracing primitive ballet of sex that obliged people to this sort of thing, to these moments of truth; an irresistible impulse to make incisive statements about the world, or love, or life, or oneself, or other people. He could do it too.

"It's your compassion," he said. "One can spend one's emotions as one wishes. But it's your decision. The world would even back you up if you cut Peter off. The world's conservative in these things. It likes them simple. It likes lovers to marry. It's so much tidier. You'd get sympathy all right. And, after all, there are other men."

She did not look at him, but set her glass down slowly on the small table, not far from his.

Now what the hell am I talking myself into? thought Jean-Philippe.

But in a way he was quite pleased. Sex was a resting place along the way. There was a reassuring certainty about it. It was there to stay. Nobody could know beforehand the subtleties and ironies in any particular episode of love, but in general it was certainly known territory. This could after all be light relief to the real tragedy, which was that of this country.

He thought that she had really set her scene quite well, seeking that same transitory exhilaration of sex, and, perhaps, more profoundly, also that transitory warmth of humanity which could sometimes accompany it. Sitting there gravely in her beauty, she was quite confident now. He thought that, in uncertainty and stress, she probably always moved frankly to this level if she could. It was wise; it was here that she was strongest. It was the same characteristic that he had observed in her that first night, after Pridie's party, when she had sat beside him in that first short joint voyage through the dark.

And here now, she was not only assured, but also knowing. He was now sufficiently impressed by her maturity to be certain that she had set her scene quite deliberately, that she would know that he knew it, and that she would know that he would even rather appreciate her skill in having done so. It was as if implicitly she complimented him, in her nice frank way, on his own fluent knowledge of this subtle and important and silent idiom. Jean-Philippe found it all rather graceful and civilized.

She crossed her legs now quietly as he watched her, and leaned back easily on the sofa on one elbow, relaxed, and not looking at him particularly. By that light movement her skirt had moved very delicately back over her knee, and he could now see the start of one thigh, sketched in lightly under the low and shadowed light. Jean-Philippe had a reasonably developed sense of timing, and he got up quietly. She watched him walk over to her, her face tilting upwards as he came. She returned his kiss with passion.

"Jean-Philippe. Does one always say all of that?"

"Or Jean."

"Jean is better. Jean. And Jeanette."

"It's neat, isn't it?" he said.

"I was afraid of you when I first met you, Jean. You know that."

It was clear that no such emotion handicapped her now. She had put up her hand to his cheek, and she looked at him levelly. She said:

"It would be good if it would last."

"An orgasm lasts twelve seconds, Jeanette."

She looked at him shocked, then she laughed, still watching him.

"All right," she said. "Like that, then. If that's your way."

"Isn't it yours too, in this case?" he said gently.

She looked down. She did not seem at all insulted, only troubled, considering his words.

"That I use you now only as a scalpel?" she said. "No. Or that, only in part. You thought that that was all of it? No, Jean."

He knew at once that he had set some part of her former uncertainty back in her now; complete honesty as such a time was foolishness. He was a little ashamed; in part at least she wanted no more than warmth. She watched him still seriously, without accusation, and without guile now, and he bent and kissed her again, more gently. He felt her shiver.

He undid the catch at the back of her throat, and slid the dress down to her waist, and loosed the hooks of her brassière and let it drop. Her breasts were vividly white against the bikini brown above and below them. The nipples sat meekly in their broad delicate pink circles of skin. He caressed them, and she glanced down once remotely, with an expression of slight surprise, as though it were the first time that she had noticed them there. He slipped the dress down over her thighs, and put his hand down under the light gauze fabric below and over her animal fur. The sudden warm moist yielding familiar contact fired his blood appropriately, and she held him violently in return.

But then all her body tightened abruptly, as though in shock, rejecting him. He knew it certainly. He knew as certainly that he would be stupid to contest this answer at this moment, or to blame her. The answer was too physical and too decisive.

He lay back slowly from her on the sofa, and she said nothing, only staring up at the ceiling above them. He had left his hand over hers; he did not lift it away. He was sure that hers was no previously calculated tactic. It had none of the hallmarks of that. From the tension which he sensed now in her, that decision of her body seemed to him again exactly that, one made against her conscious will and direction, struck instead at a deep level in her blood. Perhaps the clamouring imperative which forced it stemmed from an instinctive hatred of betrayal, even the betrayal of a known or suspected enemy. It was exactly as if some third person, who bound her to him by some real or pretended rights to her loyalty, (perhaps indeed the agile spirit of the absent Pridie himself) had at that moment just leaned over and touched her lightly on the shoulder.

CHAPTER XIV

SOMEONE touched Short lightly on the shoulder and he turned into the blaze of light. He had been standing by the American Ambassador's swimming-pool, looking down into the clear water, the cocktail party's lunatic bursts of chatter and movement lapping about his back. The pool was vividly tiled and kidney-shaped. The French knew it as the Blue Bidet.

"Hi, Joe," said the man happily. He was brandishing a Scotch on the Rocks like a maracas player in a South American band.

He was a large and willing-looking man who leaked slightly under the arms and across the chest into his smart dark-blue party suit. His face was heavy and lined and ruddy, set on a short neck, and his hair thick, close-cropped, and grizzled. He looked like a civil engineer, old and tough and efficient. The facts, thought Short ruthlessly, had so far confirmed only the first of these adjectives.

"Hullo, Frazer," he said. "Letting any more contracts these days?"

Frazer was a procurements officer at the United States Operations Mission. He deflated at once.

"Look, Joe," he said.

"I'm looking."

"Well, we can all make mistakes."

"Sure," said Joe, "but it gets to be such a habit."

Frazer looked down accusingly at the swimming pool. Somebody laughed heartily somewhere behind them.

What the hell, thought Short. After all, it was a party.

"Tom," he said.

"Yes?"

"Forget it."

Frazer looked back at him cheerfully.

"It's the country," said Short.

"It's the country, Joe," said Frazer. He changed the subject expertly. "How's Patricia?"

"Fine," said Short. "Kathleen?"

The simple question had a curious effect on Frazer. He crouched slightly and looked back over his shoulder.

"Jeeze," said Frazer. "She said two."

"She did?"

"I did see her somewhere," said Frazer. "Two. As a maximum. Imagine!"

"Imagine, indeed," said Short.

"Five!" said Frazer, looking reverently at his glass.

"I see," said Short patiently. "You mean drinks. You've had five, have you? My."

"Two, she said. Christ. I can take it, can't I, Joe?"

"Like a sponge," said Short.

"Sponge," said Frazer, nodding, evidently pleased with the word. He looked back at Short keenly. He said:

"Your wife ever do that to you, Joe?"

"What?"

"You know. Make rules and things. Control you, kinda."

"No," said Short.

"What, never?" said Frazer.

"Not that I can think of."

Frazer compressed his lips.

"They got to do it to you, Joe," he said.

It was impossible to keep up with him. He changed moods uncannily. Now he was disappointed with Patricia. He glanced back at the crowd vaguely.

"She says we must get together some time," he said. "Fine little woman."

"Splendid," said Short. "Who?"

Frazer looked at him impatiently.

"Kathleen," he said. "Bridge or something. Dinner one evening."

Frazer raised his glass to him very formally and turned and escorted it back to the depths of the party, watching it carefully. It could have been an old lady. Frazer was taking no chances with it. After awhile Short strolled after him.

The main concentration of the ambassador's three hundred guests were standing within striking distance of the long white-linen covered tables which were set out across the lawns, and charged with an ambitious variety of sandwiches and snacks. The ambassador had taken a gamble holding his party outside; there could be rain in August. But so far the night was clear.

As Short advanced upon this smart assembly he was struck once again by its natural hierarchical groupings. He had the impression that if you dropped all these people from a large aero-plane they would certainly all have arranged themselves in the right groups by the time that they hit the ground. The British, French, and American ambassadors, with similar inevitability, were talking together now, with the disguised general in charge of the American P.E.O. A brace of first secretaries and several veiled colonels and majors attended them. Near them Prince Souvanna Phouma was talking to Zellstern, a tall slim Swiss, who had been Hammarskjöld's permanent U.N. representative in Laos since the previous September. The Prince was one of the few Lao present. Sommith, the CDIN cabinet's new premier, Khop-khan, the Foreign Minister, Nosavan, the Defence Minister, and most of the rest of the cabinet had flown up to Luang Prabang that day to hear what the new King had to say about the ceremo-nial for cremating the old King (the old gentleman was still around, embalmed to the eyebrows since his death nine months before) and to give the new King an account of their stewardship in government. Prince Souvanna Phouma was naturally not in-vited; he was not a cabinet member. He had in fact got right out of party politics after the CDIN had eclipsed the moderate *Rassemblement du Peuple Lao* in the May elections. In that month the Prince had successfully proposed himself as President of the National Assembly, a non-party rôle roughly like that of a House of Commons Speaker.

The USOM acting director stood in another group with Wain-wright and two of his other department heads. Their party was lightened by a spray of sunken wives, transfixed into place in the soft lawns by their stiletto heels. There were a few Lao women; generally only the most emancipated attended such Western cere-monies. Squads of white-tunicked Vietnamese and Chinese wait-ers wove through the guests like experienced football players carry-ing trays of whisky and soda and Martell and dry Martinis and Pernod and Dubonnet and soft drinks.

Short removed a passing whisky and soda and joined the nearest group; Ward and his wife, and Raten, the Indian Ambassador. Ward was something of middling seniority in the United States Information Service. He was a long broad shambling horn-rimmed man with hands like spades and startlingly blond hair.

"It's the seventh," said Mrs. Ward firmly. She was a large dark woman with a slipped figure.

"The eighth," said Ward.

"It's the seventh today, honey."

"Aw, drop dead," said Ward. "The eighth. Hey, Joe?"

"It's the eighth of August, yes," said Short. "Sorry, Mrs. Ward."

Ward glared at her maritally and returned to the Indian Ambassador.

"So it's six weeks ago now. Now how could he do a thing like that?"

Someone had let Ward down. There was no doubt about it.

"Hum," said Raten.

"He couldn't have done that on his own," said Ward. "Or just with external help. It was an inside job."

Raten raised his eyebrows at him. Raten was a tall springy man, normally a fact-snapper, a pouncer, a define-your-sources man. But tonight he was doing a Cambridge on Ward. He eyed him now with a sort of distinguished suspension of belief, as though he were a beast in the salad in a good restaurant. Raten said:

"What do you think, Mr. Short?"

"It's the Souvannouvong jail-break, is it?"

"Yes," said Raten.

"Well," said Short, "it's remarkable that he got out with all fifteen of the other Pathet leaders. And that they took all their guards with them."

"It's amusing. He's clearly nothing if not thorough."

"Amusing!" said Ward pungently.

Raten looked at him quizzically. Short had always wanted to see someone do that.

"Force," said Ward, "bribery."

"Perhaps he just reasoned with them, Mr. Ward," said Raten.

"*Reasoned* with them?" said Ward.

"Well, you're a professional in media of propaganda, Mr. Ward," said Raten. "Surely it could be done?"

"Yeah?" said Ward.

"Yeah," said Raten. "You know, conviction, dedication, patience, that kind of thing. I must say that I always found Souvannouvong a very convincing speaker. That was before you—before they locked him up, of course."

"Information," said Ward.

"Pardon?" said Raten.

"In USIS we call them media of information," said Ward.

"Ah, information, is it?" said Raten.

Ward eyed his glass nastily.

"We'll see trouble," he said. "What's your view, Jackie?"

"Back in Hanoi planning the next wave of insurrection," said Mrs. Ward promptly and all in one breath.

"Well done," said Raten. "You don't think Souvannouvong might still be in Laos, then? Sam Neua, say, or Xieng Khouang or Phong Saly. They do say that he has many friends here."

Raten was now busy looking eager for knowledge, for expert opinion, but Ward no longer appeared much of a bet for satisfying him. Ward was taking a long remote pull at his drink instead.

"Honey," said Mrs. Ward.

"Yup," said Ward morosely.

"Teddy, honey," said Mrs. Ward. "Over there. He's signalling."

"Uh," said Ward, "so he is."

"He must want to talk to us or something," said Mrs. Ward subtly.

"Sure," said Ward, clicking almost audibly. He smiled heavily at Raten. Ward had hoisted himself back into his official rôle. After all, an ambassador was an ambassador. He said:

"Certainly glad to have met with you, Mister Ambassador."

"Mrs. Ward," said Raten graciously, "Mr. Ward."

Raten watched them go with an expression of polite amazement. He looked back again. He said:

"You're a dedicated man too, Mr. Short?"

"Like Ward?"

"That kind of thing," said Raten.

"I can't afford it," said Short. "You see, I have to work for my living."

Raten looked at him and barked suddenly and clapped him on the shoulder and steered him off forcibly to the right.

"I'm sorry?"

"No, the Prince," said Raten cryptically.

When they reached Souvanna Phouma's elbow he was saying: "Perhaps three things. Two connected with a trip I made four years ago."

"*Altesse*," said Raten.

Souvanna Phouma smiled round at them. He was still standing with Zellstern.

"Mr. Raten," said Souvanna. "Delighted."

"You know Mr. Short, of course."

"Mr. Short," said Souvanna. "Yes."

Zellstern nodded briefly at them.

"We're interrupting, *Altesse*," said Raten. "The three things?"

"Not at all, Mr. Raten," said Souvanna amiably. "Hanoi and Pekin's congenital mistrust of us; why? An intriguing question. Not that I have illusions, you understand. I have few illusions. But, for us, China and North Viet Nam are big tigers. Now, should one provoke tigers unnecessarily?"

Souvanna was of middle height, thickly built; a Paris-trained engineer like his revolutionary half-brother Souvannouvong. His French was elegant, precise, mocking.

"Well. When I headed my government in 1956—you know, I wanted to re-integrate the Pathet in the nation, to end this stupid civil war—one of the first things I did was to visit Pekin and Hanoi, to assure them that we should be genuinely neutral as between the two big power blocs. When they had heard me, Hanoi asked me a pertinent question. Then, my precedessors had already exchanged legations with South Viet Nam. So Hanoi asked if we would give them equal diplomatic recognition. I satisfied them finally by promising that we should never raise the South Vietnamese legation to an embassy. Pekin too wanted me to prove my words by admitting them at least a legation in Vientane. I blocked that, on the grounds that we should admit none from Formosa. Well, when the right wing broke my government in 1958, they promptly accepted a legation from Formosa and raised the South Vietnamese legation to embassy status."

"Embarrassing," said Raten.

"For me, more than a little," said the Prince. "You understand, they considered mine a lasting undertaking. What happened must have been a great loss of face for them."

"And the third thing, *Altesse*?" said Zellstern. He looked bent on the facts, a little irritated that the other two men had interrupted.

"More recent," said Souvanna. "Last year's accord which the Americans got out of the French to supply a hundred American military instructors to the Lao Army. The Geneva Agreements of course explicitly forbid anything more than a fixed number of French instructors. The Chinese and North Vietnamese, as you know, are quite psychotic about the Pentagon—rightly or wrongly, and saving your grace, Mr. Short. They see that as the thin edge of a dangerous wedge."

The British Ambassador had drifted over. He was a muscular bachelor in his early forties, recognizable as an English public schools product at a hundred yards. With the genius for improbabilities of his race, he was both an acknowledged expert on Ming pottery (he had formerly been chargé d'affaires for some years at Pekin) and a fanatical tennis player. It was rumoured that he constantly outraged visiting generals and foreign office officials by breaking off pregnant discussions of the political situation at exactly four p.m. for his daily game.

"*Altesse.*"

"*Monsieur l'Ambassadeur,*" said Souvanna.

Short moved away quietly. He wondered where Patricia was. It was their agreed practice to separate at cocktail parties immediately they arrived, and to join up again only to leave. In this way they could jointly net more of Vientiane's quaintly-coloured fish.

He saw her then by a sandwich table with Frazer and Frazer's wife, a small birdlike fertile woman who dominated Frazer effortlessly. Frazer was leaning at Patricia, swaying in perilous slow motion. He looked like an old teak monument in a high wind. They were almost certainly fixing the bridge evening. It would be awful. Frazer, chided prettily by his wife, played a truly disastrous game, mainly because he would keep reminiscing about the Seabees during the war in the Pacific, a fine body of men which he had adorned in some violent capacity but, probably happily for the final course of the hostilities, only briefly. God knows where they dig them up, thought Short.

He recalled that he still had to finish his report on the bitumen that evening after the party and to try to get it off with the Air Laos flight to Bangkok early next morning; with luck, he would know the pilot. The regular mail was excruciatingly slow. He eyed Frazer balefully.

Also looking fairly monumental that evening (Short was pleased to see) was Mary-Frances, a blonde as slim as a girl but in all other respects more lethal, whose married name he could never remember. The husband worked in some remote department of the ubiquitous prolific USOM, perhaps trying to calculate just where it would break out next. He was a small diligent man with a face like a hat. Mary-Frances was dressed in glinting gold Thai silk that evening, and wore a large white orchid on her bosom. She liked men, and Short knew that she had had her sharp pelvis lined up on him for some time. (There were bachelors at USOM, but they had been selected for their integrity.) But it was clear that Mary-Frances' mind was set now on other things. She was standing along with her scenic breast heaving and her legs apart and her eyes fixed relentlessly in one direction. She looked like Boadicea blazing her gaze upon the invader. As Short passed she held him fiercely as a swimmer.

"Joe," she said, without turning her head, and evidently identifying him through some kind of sexual sixth sense.

"Mary-Frances."

"Can you beat it, Joe. In here. A roaring Negress."

Short followed her eye. The sight was indeed mesmeric. Some yards off a large black woman in a shapeless orange dress and sensible low-heeled shoes was bounding about with a thin-stemmed glass of champagne, laughing her head off at two small white men and a small reflective Negro in a dinner-jacket; her husband, head of yet another USOM department; America's concession to the winds of change and the United Nations. The lady was not so much square as cubic.

"She's just happy," said Short. "Probably because she chose the right kind of shoes for these lawns."

"Why did I ever leave home, Joe?'

"Old pioneering stock, Mary-Frances."

"Crap. You're just another damned liberal, Joe. It's all this man William Faulkner. It's his fault. I'm going. Where's my husband?"

"I did see him by the Blue Bidet a moment ago with a high yaller Lao princess."

"Thataway?"

"Thataway."

"You're nice, Joe. Come and make love some time."

"Next week, Mary-Frances."

"Next week."

She dismissed him abruptly, still fascinated by her target. Short moved over to the nearest table and picked up a caviar sandwich. It was extremely good. There was nothing small about the Americans.

He glanced up and saw Pridie. Pridie was standing at the other end of the table, talking to the aged and improbably decorated Lao Chief of Staff. As usual Pridie looked like an Esquire illustration, his temples flecked with grey, his grey suit immaculate, the white silk handkerchief at his breast pocket as precise as if it had been painted on, and his supple length bent in subtle court to the general. Short turned his back on him.

Ten yards ahead where (he now recalled noticing) Pridie had once glanced casually, Short saw the tall Frenchman whom he had met somewhere before, with the very attractive dark girl who Short had understood was Pridie's particular friend. Her face was turned up towards the Frenchman's and she was laughing. The sight was refreshing in the stylized atmosphere of the party; Short could not remember having seen her laugh with such pleasure before. In that light, from the myriad coloured electric bulbs looped between the trees, the Frenchman's face had fleetingly the values of a tragic mask, shadowed and savagely lined; but the vast comic hawk nose, flung suddenly out upon the vision like a third hand as he turned his head back to the girl, reduced it comfortably to absurdity. Short walked over to them.

"Of course you've got to win," she was saying. "Who was it who said that he who is the aggressor in these things forsakes an advantage?"

"So," the Frenchman said banteringly. "Because I don't aggress here, I shall win your heart, Jeanette? But I don't think that's true. I wish it were, of course."

"But why so much modesty, Jean-Philippe?"

The tall beaked man shrugged.

"Once one has gone certain routes with a woman without success, Jeanette, it can sometimes be impossible to retrace them."

The dark girl looked frankly disappointed. She said:

"Oh. Why?"

"One's done it before already then, you see. One already knows it, almost. Except for the final cachet, of course. But that can be almost irrelevant."

"So intellectual, Jean-Philippe?"

"No, Jeanette; just calculating. But what can one really do in the end against true virtue? And Mr. Joe Short."

"I'm sorry," said Short. "I'm intruding."

"Not at all," said the Frenchman. "We're just having a deep discussion on virtue. Jeanette is for virtue.

"I thought we all were, in principle," said Short. "Even the Pathet."

"Look at that for loyalty to you, Jeanette," said the Frenchman. "Well, I suppose that's fair. I'll bet he doesn't even remember my name."

Jeanette's breasts had risen slightly at the Frenchman's light reference to her. They contrived to look pleased. The Frenchman was definitely on her side, and she knew it. Short saw that he was indeed intruding.

"Rayard," he said.

"Raymond," said the Frenchman.

"Jean-Philippe," said Short.

"Ah, but you cheated there," said the Frenchman. "You heard Jeanette call me that."

They did not seem to resent his presence. Perhaps instinctively they wanted to test him out, as an ally.

He felt someone come up beside him and looked round; Patricia.

"Joe," said Patricia.

"Patricia."

"Joe, they're starting to break up. Don't you think we should move?"

"Oh, yes. You know Jean-Philippe and Jeanette? Patricia."

Patricia smiled at Jean-Philippe.

"We talked earlier this evening."

She shook hands with Jeanette.

"I should go too," said Jean-Philippe. Jeanette glanced up at

147

him, then looked away over Short's shoulder. She seemed suddenly withdrawn, almost wary of them. She said:

"We too, I suppose."

Joe took Patricia out past the ambassador and his wife. While not yet exactly stationed at the exit, they were conveniently near it; their joint presence there was like the politest of coughs to remind their guests that they had already overshot the last line on their invitation cards by a good forty minutes. Short and his wife shook their hands and thanked them appropriately. They went on to the car. It was parked, one of a long line, in the road along the river. A Lao policeman materialized magically beside it, looking dedicated and optimistic. The effect, totally spurious, was that he had been there all night beating off thieves and the Pathet Lao from that particular car. Short inserted his wife and passed the policeman a fifty Kip note without protest. He drove quietly up past the *Salle des Fêtes*. He could see nothing to his left out on the river. Under the stars, it could have been some vast steel silent road, secret and never used.

"Joe," said his wife.

"Pat."

"Who was that girl, Joe?"

"Which girl?"

"Which girl. You know. The dark one with breasts."

"Pat."

"Yes?"

"They all have breasts."

"As if you didn't know. The one just now."

"Oh, *that* one."

"That one, he says. I thought rape was a capital offence?"

"Not in Laos, Pat. Five thousand Kip for a princess. A descending scale thereafter, according to rank. It's all very carefully computed."

"You were distinctly leering at her."

"Not at all. She's merely the friend of a friend."

"Oh, yes. Whose?"

"Now that," said Short. "Is quite a point."

"Come on."

"Well, I'd thought Pridie's."

"God's gift to women," said Patricia. "But?"

"I don't know,' said Short, "now I'm not so sure."

Patricia had put on her canasta face. She had small bright features, with fawn eyes and short straight blonde hair. When she concentrated, small twin vertical lines came down from between her eyebrows and at each side of the bridge of her nose.

"That Mary-Frances woman is attractive too," she said carefully.

Short glanced sideways at her.

"Isn't she just?"

"In her way," said Patricia.

They left the Banque de l'Indochine building behind them on their right.

"Dresses well, too," he added. "I thought she looked particularly smart this evening."

That was the tactic, to lay it on with a trowel, with ingenuous honesty. In that way, by the obscure syllogisms of feminine logic, she would finally be absolutely convinced that he had no interest in Mary-Frances whatsoever.

"It's fixed for Thursday night," said Patricia severely.

"What is?"

"Bridge," said Patricia. "The Frazers."

"God," said Short. "Our house or theirs?"

"Theirs, but we could bring a bottle of wine if we liked. Eightish."

"God again," said Short. "Guam and three no trumps."

"Oh," said Patricia, "and I thought that that Frenchman was nice."

"Which Frenchman, Patricia? The place is stiff with Frenchmen."

"You know, the one just now. With that girl. A face like an old apple with black hair and a beak on it."

"Jean-Philippe Raymond. I'm sure he'd be enchanted with that description."

"Jean-Philippe Raymond?" said Patricia. "Are you sure?"

"Sure I'm sure."

"That's funny," said Patricia. "He said his name was Clappique, Baron Clappique, a well-known anthropologist. He even seemed a little insulted that I didn't know that he was in Vientiane."

"Anthropologist? Jean-Philippe?"

"Yes," said Patricia. "Oh, and he seems particularly well up on African ants."

The bastard, thought Short, taking the slight curve past the customs' office.

"Joe," said Patricia, "You find Mary-Frances *really* attractive, Joe?"

"Certainly," said Short, "I should say so. The kind that absolutely dilates men's nostrils."

"You pig."

"Patricia."

"I'm not talking."

"She's probably not so good in bed, though."

"No?" said Patricia.

"No," said Short, pontifically and inaccurately. "Men can tell these things."

"Joe."

"Pat?"

Short turned the car to the right, leaving the river.

"Am I really all right?" said Patricia.

"Ah," said Short. "In bed, you mean?"

"Oh, I'm drunk," said Patricia. "But it stands to reason that there's a limit to the number of things you can do. In spite of all they say about all those different positions. So how can you tell?"

"Well," said Short judiciously, "you jump about a lot, you know, and you squeak. You generally sound quite pleased. That's the main thing, really."

He could sense her blushing ferociously beside him. She was always furious with herself when he could get her to do that. It disrupted her ideal image of herself as an uninhibited modern.

She was not really that. A Northern Rhodesian, she had come to Paris on a post-graduate scholarship after getting a degree at some South African university. Short had met her during his two years at the Sorbonne. Patricia was racially liberal and somewhat incompetent at running her own life. It gave her a certain charm. It invited marriage. She was a blend of sophistication and innocence, of startlingly frank carnal hungers and sudden unchartable islands of chastity and reserve; in fact, a fair enough compromise between the nymphomaniac and the Virgin Mary to form an almost ideal middle-class wife, durable and reasonably intriguing. Short was bound to have married someone more or less like her sooner or later. It had been she rather than another largely because at a time of his life when his sap ran strong, he had finally become bored of needing to leave her Parisian bed at three in the morning to skirt a particularly insomniac concierge.

Patricia said:

"And I saw the general. He says everything's fine."

"Mister Rolfe to you," said Short. "Remember the instructions."

"Mister Rolfe of the P.E.O., then. Everyone likes us really."

"He says," said Short. "Us?"

"You. The Americans. He says that the elections proved it. The Pathet Lao are just a myth, no more than a shaking of tree-tops in the jungle."

"That's lyrical," said Short. "I didn't know that Rolfe had it in him. But it's a pretty tenacious sort of myth."

He stopped at the iron gates and the night-watchman opened them with a flourish. The night-watchman was a very old Lao with a face like God. He carried a heavy wooden stick. He put that down and joined his hands and prayed at them as they drove in.

"Sam bai di, Khun."

"Sam bai di le drap, kop chai le," said Short, exhausting his Laotian and raising his own hands dangerously from the wheel a moment to pray correctly back at him.

The office building was to the left, and the house ahead. The house was two storied. French windows opened out on to its wide raised front terrace. The roof looked like a festival hat. It was tiled in gay pink, and had Siamese upward-curving eaves. The company had built it magnificently from three years' profits at a time when restrictions on repatriating capital had prevented them from doing anything else. Long separate quarters rambled feudally back behind it, for the cook and assistant and gardener and driver and servants and their multiple wives and children. Here at times a mad marital or face quarrel shocked the quiet Buddhic air. A small lithe trousered Vietnamese lady chased her husband round the back garden with a large knife, or the cook and assistant cook violently disputed the division of labour for a dinner for important guests. These events were relatively rare, but always reassuring, proving at once the common bonds of humanity.

Short garaged the car and went upstairs with his wife. Ti-hai, Number Two, was sitting on the landing outside the children's room. She was in fact head servant, but the Vietnamese were superstitious about using the number one in their titles. Number Two was a thin brisk Saigonnaise, fast as a flyweight boxer on her feet, with a quick tongue and hand for discipline. It was she who sped about the garden at times after her husband, an amiable, feckless man with diffuse sexual interests, hurling curses at him, but her dignity still marvellously intact. She recovered herself effortlessly after these exhibitions, only panting healthily, as if they were simply an occasional and normal form of exercise. She was a great friend of Patricia's. Though quite flat in front she was very feminine and (said Patricia) would recount her husband's sexual abilities, quirks, and failings to her in striking detail on the slightest provocation. Ti-hai was reading the comic strip from an outdated Saigon paper when Short and his wife reached the landing. Short said:

"And the Viet-Cong? More attacks?"

151

She looked up. She said unbeatably:

"You must never believe what you read in the papers."

"How are the children?" said Patricia.

Ti-hai got up and opened the door quietly. The light from the landing fell across the two cots. Miranda, two years old, was sleeping on her back, frowning, perhaps against the fall of the light. It made her look as though she was working very hard at her sleep. Christopher, thirty months older, was on his side, one arm and leg flung out in front of him, as if he hurled himself timelessly forward in some dream. Patricia went in and covered them.

When Patricia came out and closed the door gently, Ti-hai ducked her head at them, her mission accomplished, her charges re-delivered.

"Goodnight, M'sieu, 'Dame."

"And thanks," said Short. "Sleep well."

Number Two disappeared at speed down the stairs, her newspaper rolled like a marshal's baton.

"Joe," said Patricia.

"Yes?"

"Come to bed."

She was clearly maddened by the drink. Her twin canasta lines were concentrating on him.

"My God, child," he said. "You can't go on manufacturing them. Think of our budget."

"No?" said Patricia.

"Definitely not."

"Oh, well," said Patricia. "Just practising is still acceptable."

"Not tonight," said Short, "I still have to finish that damned report."

Patricia put her head on one side and examined him. She said:

"I knew it was that dark one all the time."

"Not brunettes, dear," said Short. "Bitumen."

"Balls to your bitumen," said Patricia.

CHAPTER XV

HEAR, hear, thought Short, balls to my bitumen indeed.

He let himself out of the house and walked across the yard to his office door and unlocked it and put on the light. He sat down at his desk and opened his drawer for the file and thought savagely about Frazer.

In spite of what he had diplomatically said to Frazer at the party, it had certainly not been the country's fault this time.

For years USOM had planned to resurface the nineteen kilometres of bitumenized road between Vientiane and Thadua, which was the main port of entry to Vientiane on the Mekong River. The railway from Bangkok came up to Nongkhye, and motorized ferries (for which USOM had paid about three times their market value) brought the goods across the river to Thadua. The road between Thadua and Vientiane was originally a dirt track which closely followed the anarchic course of the Mekong. Years before, the French economic mission, which produced rather more concrete results with its million dollars a year than did the Americans with a budget sixty times that size, had plotted a road only ten kilometres long straight between the river port and the city. The thought of being beaten to it by the French stimulated the Americans into asphalting the existing dirt track along the river at fiendish speed. They did the job during the rains. Their new road fell smartly to pieces. Driving along it was perilous, unless you knew it really intimately. You could easily fall clean off it into the rice-fields, or see the entire front of your car drop magically and backbreakingly out of sight into profound potholes. One section was magnificently switchbacked, like the frozen profile of a heavy swell at sea, or as though the former humble dirt track had reared itself successively in sheer horror at the amateur way in which this ribbon of boiling pitch had been slapped down upon it.

Since accomplishing this feat the Americans had repeatedly budgeted to hold it together. The year before they had at last decided to call tenders to resurface it completely. They should have done this in time to be able to decide the tender by October, so that the contractor could begin work at the start of the five months' dry season in November. But by now something about the road inhibited USOM seriously. *Phis* and hoodoos dogged it. Craftily, they flew road experts out from the States to re-survey it. Consequently, they did not call and decide the tenders until the following April, when the rains were due to start again. The choice was then to wait until the next dry season, and lose another year, or to require the job to be done at once, when it would probably again be a failure. USOM chose the second course.

Short had attended the public bid opening, to forestall his American and British competitors and offer petroleum supplies and bitumen to the successful contractor on the spot. Frazer then suggested that Short should get the two hundred tons of bitumen needed up from Bangkok at once. A month later USOM apologetically advised all bidders that it had underestimated the job's costs in terms of USOM's disposable budget, and must therefore cancel the tender until the year following. By then the contractor selected already had some of his machinery in Laos and Short had all of the two hundred tons of bitumen sitting forlorn and unsaleable in his Vientiane depot.

As Frazer had said at the party, everyone could make a mistake. But the story had a familiar ring. It was a little like that of the famous all-weather road from Vientiane south to Savannakhet. In this case, for once, the American and French aid missions had agreed to co-operate. The French would build the bridges, and the Americans the new road, which, sensibly, would depart in many places from the course of the existing dirt track. For two years now, some twenty really excellent steel bridges had sat in splendid isolation in the jungle, hundreds of metres to one side or the other of the existing track. The Americans never built their road. The French steel bridges, rapidly festooned with creepers, remained like some monumental and pointless statement of a remarkable ancient culture, a kind of mechanized Angkor Wat.

Short finished his report at about two-thirty a.m. In it, he noted that USOM had declined to pay for the bitumen. He suggested that this was hardly ethical. USOM was, however, a most important client, and the client was always right. Short admitted, with disarming frankness, his own error in importing the bitumen before he had got a written order for it from USOM. He also tactfully pointed out that he had been the only oil company representative to attend the public bid opening, and had thus secured the chosen contractor's petroleum supplies business at once. Thereafter, he had simply acted rapidly and in good faith. The loss might perhaps be some indication of USOM's business ethics and efficiency, but hardly, he suggested, of the company's.

He read it over with an artist's satisfaction. It was a nicely balanced document. It fairly hummed with frankness, business realism, initiative, and the desire to serve. It exactly reflected the mores of the ideal decent modern American executive. The only thing that ruined it was the results, but it would be a hard man indeed who could think of that after he had read it. Short was sure that he would get away with it. It had taken him years to learn that style.

Short sealed the envelope and locked the office behind him. As he walked back to the house he heard the shooting. He stopped and listened. It seemed to be from somewhere off beyond the

National Assembly, on the way to Tangone. The single explosions were too heavy for rifle shots; mortars, perhaps. There were bursts of machine-gun fire between them.

He went on. Shooting at night was not uncommon. For a mere myth, the Pathet kept the Royal Army remarkably alert, especially in the dark.

He went into the bedroom without switching on the light and undressed and lit a match selflessly to set the alarm for six. As he got into his side of the double bed, Patricia snarled mildly at him in her sleep.

The alarm blasted him out of bed. It was an old French machine as big as a side plate, with fierce black Roman numerals, a bell on top, and three prim chromium legs. When it went off it always danced sideways across the table like an enraged crab. He shut it up and got out of bed and shaved and dressed quickly.

It was a clear and still morning. The sun just touched the tops of the trees, in a static and molten and brilliant sky. He wished that he had had another five minutes, to drive down past the river. At this hour it had the sky's quality of beauty and cruelty, the *pirogues* and sampans set delicately upon it, their wakes spreading endlessly out behind them, the ripples like slow silver beats of time.

He took the car out along the road next to the house, towards the airport, and parallel to the main road to it. He saw no one. That was strange. Normally, the little old women were already by the side of the road at this time, half-kneeling, as ceremonial as statues, with plates of rice and dried fish and meat and fruit. The bonzes came along this road in a single line each morning, men of all ages, in loose orange robes, shaven-headed and barefoot. They would stop silently next to each woman and hold their wooden bowls out to the side, not turning at all or looking down or thanking the women; it was the women, not they, who achieved merit by this donation.

Short saw a soldier at the end of the road, where it turned right at right angles to intersect with the main road to the airport. The soldier was a stocky man in a paratrooper's smock, armed with a sten gun. He stood in the middle of the road and beamed at Short like an old friend. Short beamed politely back at him. Short said:

"*A la droit? Aeroport?*"

Short pointed vigorously to the right as he spoke; the soldier probably did not understand French.

The paratrooper looked obligingly up the road and back at

Short. He held his palm flat up towards him and shook his head. Now he looked rather sad. Nothing could have been clearer, even to a *farang*. There had been an accident to some military vehicle, or they were digging up the road again. Short backed and turned and took the earlier sidestreet up to the main road, and swung left into it. There were cars and trucks stopped ahead of him, where the other sidestreet came out. He stopped by them. There were oil drums across the road, and seven or eight paratroopers; probably a routine security check. Short pulled out his passport and looked at his watch. It was six-thirty. The Air Laos Strato for Bangkok took off at seven and the pilot generally got aboard about ten minutes before that.

He stuck his passport out of the side window. He said in French:

"I must get past quickly. Air Laos, you know."

The nearest two paratroopers looked at each other and back at him. They shook their heads slowly from side to side, in unison. It was like a music-hall act. They would break into a dance step at any moment.

A second lieutenant walked up to the car. There was a sub-machine gun slung over his right shoulder, muzzle down. Short got out and pushed his passport at him.

"Air Laos," he said. "If your men could let me through. I must see the pilot."

"I'm sorry," said the lieutenant. "Nobody passes."

The lieutenant did not look at all impressed by Short's nice American passport. Indeed, on seeing it his expression seemed to have hardened slightly.

"Get back in your car, please," said the lieutenant.

"But the Strato takes off at seven!"

The lieutenant did not seem interested in take-off times. He examined Short in a bored manner. He looked as though he had been through all this before that morning. He lined his sub-machine-gun up thoughtfully on Short's navel.

"There's no Air Laos this morning," he said. "That simplifies things, doesn't it? Get back in your car."

"You're right," said Short, getting promptly back into his car, his eyes on the gun. The man with the gun was always right.

"Why?" he said, as he put the car into reverse and accelerated the motor to show a proper spirit of co-operation.

The lieutenant re-examined him. He looked as if he thought this a fair question, all things considered. He had dropped the muzzle of his gun again.

"Ah," he said, "you see, we've taken over the city."

"Thank you," said Short. "We?"

"The Second Paratroop Battalion," said the lieutenant.

"I see," said Short. "Why?"

The lieutenant sighed. He had obviously been a fool to have gone this far. He ought to have known better. This was rapidly developing into a debate. In Laos, everyone loved a debate. Indeed, two or three of his soldiers were already looking interested and beginning to move over to the car to join in.

"Later, if you don't mind," he said. "It will be announced."

He patted the stock of his sub-machine-gun and nodded at Short conclusively.

Short turned his car and drove back to the centre of the town. The Lao were going quietly about their early morning affairs, opening their shops, and thronging to the morning market. Evidently it took more than a coup d'état to disrupt their habits. They had after all established those over many centuries, so that now they were some slight protection against the cataclysms of war and politics. They were even a sobering comment on them. The habits remained unchanged, the cataclysms passed. They said that the Chinese in Hankow had continued to act like that, with crushing normality, even when the Japanese had taken their city. Second Battalion paratroopers were everywhere. Most were patrolling in jeeps, four to the jeep, individually armed, and with a Bren gun mounted on the bonnet. The paratroopers looked remote and professional. The Lao in the streets hardly glanced at them. They could have been carrying out a routine demonstration of strength, or they could indeed have been men from an invading race.

A further roadblock stopped Short from getting through to the U.S. Embassy. On his way back to the house he went into Saovong's service station. The old man was in his sales room. He looked up and smiled and came out.

"*Monsieur Short.*"

"*Monsieur Saovong. Des emmerdements.*"

A Chevrolet drove in next to the pump island and a horn-rimmed man got out and motioned to the attendant and came over to them; Ward. Short said to him:

"I'm glad to see you're buying the right brand of gasoline."

"A full tank too," said Ward bleakly. "I may need it."

"What's it all about, Monsieur Saovong?" said Short.

"They want a neutralist government," said Saovong.

"It sounds harmless," said Short. Ward looked at him.

"Why?" said Ward to Saovong.

"They say they're tired of killing other Lao," said Saovong.

"It's a point of view," said Short. Ward looked at him again and said nothing.

"Why this group?" said Short. "And why the sudden action?"

"We've only really got two good battalions, you see," said Saovong. "The First Paratroop, north of Savannakhet, and the Second, here. So they've always been the units most used in actions against the Pathet Lao."

"Those bastards again," said Ward. His amazing blond hair sparkled in the sun like a knight-errant's sword.

Saovong glanced at him and looked back at Short.

"And perhaps not so very sudden, Monsieur Short. They chose their time. I understand that they were issued full munitions yesterday, for another sweep against the Pathet Lao, near Bat-Keun. They were fully armed, and most of the cabinet was away. So they took the city at three in the morning."

"Communist-inspired," said Ward, like a radio communique. Saovong looked at him politely.

"It may be, Monsieur Ward. There's no evidence of that yet. But I'm not a political man, of course. Konglé says they're just interested in peace."

"Konglé?" said Short.

"I'm sorry," said Saovong. "The Second Battalion commander."

"They'll have been getting at him," said Ward darkly. "Or he's just scared."

Saovong did not say anything.

"French-trained, no doubt," said Ward.

"Yes," said Saovong. "Both our paratroop battalions are French-trained. Very highly trained, I believe. Though I believe Konglé himself also got part of his training in the Philippines, under the Americans."

Ward looked disgusted and walked to his car and kicked the nearside tyre as though it were Konglé. He glanced back and laughed abruptly.

"You know Sounlet?" he said.

It was the name of the venerable and bemedalled Lao Chief of Staff whom Short had seen with Pridie at the ambassador's cocktail the evening before. He said:

"Sounlet, yes."

"Poor old gentleman," said Ward. "They shot him out of bed at three a.m. He wouldn't leave his house. Either he was too brave or he just wanted his sleep. So they put some Bazooka bombs in to fetch him out."

"I forgot to tell you that," said Saovong. "They've arrested the five generals."

"Any casualties?" said Short.

"Three soldiers," said Saovong.

Aircraft flew across the city that morning, dropping tracts. They said about what Saovong had forecast. Konglé wanted peace. He saw no point to Lao going on killing Lao. Concentrating on that, he maintained, had done nothing visibly to develop the country. A neutralist government seemed the only solution. The government elected in May would certainly change nothing.

To Short, these statements looked remarkably like straight common sense.

Konglé carefully disavowed any personal political or military ambitions in his tracts and in his subsequent radio announcements. Similarly, he did not explicitly accuse the Americans for their heavy backing of the CDIN. But his message was clear enough. Short did not think that the brinkmen in the C.I.A. and Pentagon and State Department would like it. Nor would Sarit and his extreme right wing military dictatorship in Thailand.

The Second Battalion had evidently executed their coup very efficiently. At three a.m. they had taken every key point, the Ministry of Defence, the Police Headquarters, the power station, the airport, all the city's key entrances and exits. They had even given a dinner for their French military advisers at seven that evening. It had ended early. The French had suspected nothing.

The following days were calm. There was no interference with *farangs* or their property. Konglé applied a curfew strictly from seven p.m. to six a.m. Its only casualty was an elderly Chinese who was shot in the leg without having the faintest idea what it was all about.

Jean-Philippe came to see Short on the fifteenth of August. Short was busy deciphering a harassed telegram from his General Manager in Bangkok, who, no doubt under similar pressure from New York, appeared to be holding him personally responsible for the coup.

"Any communication with the South?" said Jean-Philippe.

"All cut," said Short. "I've no idea what's happening to my offices in Savannakhet, Thakhek or Paksé."

"They'll probably be all right," said Jean-Philippe. "The right wing needs fuel too. It'll look after them. And what news of the Nongkhye blockade?"

"It's a hundred per cent effective. There have been no oil products across since yesterday. Or rice or anything else."

"What stocks d'you have here, Joe?"

"About two months' gas oil and diesel fuel for the power station and industries. Rather less motor gasoline. Curiously, the Thai are still letting Air Laos fly through to Bangkok. They can refuel there. So there's no aviation gasoline problem for the moment."

"The Thai will stop Air Laos too when it suits them," said Jean-Philippe. "There's no other way of getting your oil products through to Vientiane, except Nongkhye?"

"None," said Short.

"How well off are your competitors?" said Jean-Philippe.

"Rather worse than we are," said Short. "They don't have as much tankage."

"And the Army here, Joe?"

"They've got no bulk tankage at all. Stocks in drums only, in that big depot near the airport. I'd say that they'd have about two months' supplies of gasoline for their tanks and transport, and rather less aviation gasoline."

"That Thai blockade of Nongkhye starts to make sense," said Jean-Philippe. "To cripple the power station and industries by stopping the fuel. And Konglé's tanks and transport. And to starve us into submission by stopping the food."

"What do you know about the South?" said Short.

"There's a very strong right wing build-up going on," said Jean-Philippe. "You know that Sommith and Nosavan and the rest of the CDIN cabinet didn't fly back to Vientiane as planned the morning after the coup. Somebody filled them in very thoroughly on the situation here, while they were still in Luang Prabang. They overflew to Savannakhet."

"You've seen Konglé, Jean-Philippe?"

"Yes."

"And?"

Jean-Philippe shrugged. He said:

"Sincere enough. Even garrulous. He's probably a good soldier. And he could be dangerous; a man with a mission. He's the factor that the extreme right wing didn't allow for when they fixed the elections—a spontaneous and effective reaction against them from the people. He'll almost certainly ask Souvanna Phouma to form a neutralist government; that's on the cards."

"How neutralist is neutralist, for him?" said Short.

"Complete. No military alignment with either power bloc. Aid without strings from either side. Diplomatic recognition to one and all. The American P.E.O. out. Live and let live, sort of thing. It might work. It might even be the best solution. Maybe the only one."

"I wonder if the Pathet backed him?" said Short.

"I'm certain they didn't," said Jean-Philippe. "They're probably as surprised as anyone else. Favourably, of course. Konglé nearly hit me when I asked him the same question. No, I don't think he likes competition. He wants to be the saviour, nobody else."

Short picked up the ruler on his desk and bent it thoughtfully and put it down. He said:

"How do you see it now, Jean-Philippe?"

The half-tragic half-comic mask looked at him steadily, then relaxed and smiled.

"As a Frenchman, Joe?"

"As a Frenchman," said Short. "Hell, any way you like."

"All right," said Jean-Philippe, "I'll be a Frenchman. We and the British would probably recognise a Souvanna Phouma neutralist government at once. Why? Probably simply because we've stopped being romantics. It's less trouble. On the reasoning that you've got to be very good, and ruthless, and lucky, and powerful, and persevering, to beat what people think they want, in the long run. Whether they're right or wrong. If you can't beat them, live with them. Let them find out for themselves. If you can do that without having your throat cut. It's certainly good practical sense. It might even be good political morality too. India, Joe. Indo-China."

"This is of *that* order of importance?"

"No," said Jean-Philippe, "not in size. It's miniature. But it's classic enough. We, you, have let ourselves be manoeuvred once again on to the side of the past and the reactionary. It's too late for that luxury, Joe. The world thinks too fast today. The world judges you very fast today, Joe."

"And the people judge us here, Jean-Philippe?"

"All right," said Jean-Philippe. "One always overintellectualises about them. I know. The blunt mass. They're not at all articulate here yet. Marx, Lenin, Borodin, Paine, Jefferson? They've never even heard of them. They'll follow the first magic formula that has enough general appeal. The Pathet probably have the monopoly of that. I don't think you're too long on magic these days, Joe."

"But Souvanna Phouma is?" said Short.

"He probably has enough," said Jean-Philippe. "Princely enough to satisfy their feudal awes. Probably statesman enough to keep them afloat in the modern world. A neutralist by conviction, by common sense, but a Western European by education and sentiment. Probably the best solution that we and his country dare hope for."

"All right," said Short, after a while. "I might buy it."

"Put it another way," said Jean-Philippe. "The Pathet are probably there to stay, Joe. You're stuck with them unless you kill the lot of them. And, if I'm right, time is on their side, not ours. So for God's sake integrate them in the country and in the government before it's too late. Now, and not later. Under Souvanna Phouma. There's your chance of control. If your people blitz Vientiane and Souvanna and the neutralists you may never get another chance. You won't hurt the Pathet. They can wait. They get stronger as they wait. Then when they do finally make their big drive they'll take the whole damned country. Remember, Joe, and this is me talking as a Frenchman, we didn't get two chances in Viet Nam."

Short could hear his Vietnamese secretary typing away in the next room, busily and ostentatiously, as if to assure them that she was not really trying to listen.

"All right, all right," he said. "So I'll sack Dulles. I must have a word with the ambassador. And how are your African ants these days, Jean-Philippe?"

Jean-Philippe looked at him and the shadow left his face and he laughed.

"Patricia told you about that, of course," he said. "Well, you've got good taste in wives, Joe. Mind you, my African ant is a fair symbol. He's a tenacious little bastard."

"He is?"

"Certainly," said Jean-Philippe. "Take the red soldier ant, for example. When he makes up his mind to go somewhere, he just goes. Even to his death. And in a straight line, whatever you put in his way. He simply eats his way through it. He's got lots of time. You can't really hope to win all your political discussions with a red ant."

"I knew this was going to get political again," said Short.

"So you come to terms with him," said Jean-Philippe. "All right, you kill him if you really have to. But otherwise you learn to live with him. The world's generally big enough for that. And you certainly don't try to talk him into being a nice well-behaved Western lap-dog."

"I never did like lap-dogs much," said Short. "Give me a good red-blooded ant any time."

Jean-Philippe looked at him again and laughed and got up.

"My regards to Patricia, Joe."

"Thanks," said Short, getting up too. "I won't forget."

He walked out to the Deux Chevaux with the Frenchman. Jean-Philippe got into it and his beaked lined face looked up from over the driving-wheel.

"Come to think of it," he said, apropos of nothing, "I haven't seen our friend Pridie about for the last few days."

"He'll be around somewhere," said Short.

"Curious man," said Jean-Philippe. "Curious how much he seems to get about for his culture."

Short looked down at him.

"You could always try Savannakhet," he said.

CHAPTER XVI

"THE build-up at Savannakhet continues," said Xang.

From across the table, Cuong watched Xang's controlled and tranquil profile, poised at its head like some smooth efficient piece of machinery which had never failed. As usual, Xang was effortlessly in command of the meeting.

The Regional Committee's six men and one woman sat about the table at wooden chairs. The room was long and rectangular and correctly spartan. It was normally the school. There was a blackboard against the wall behind Xang, and a wall-map of the north-eastern provinces of Laos to its right. The map was printed in Hanoi, and emphasised the network of roads leading east to that city from the town of Sam Neua, and the road due east from Xieng Khouang to the North Vietnamese port of Ben Thuy on the China Sea. Similarly, by the absence of roads, it stressed the north-eastern provinces' isolation from the rest of Laos. The inference was clear: these provinces, with their opium riches, belonged logistically as much as ethnically to North Viet Nam. That claim was centuries-old, and neither communist nor anti-communist, but simply nationalistic. From well before the mid-nineteenth century, Laos had been a protectorate of the Annamese court. The French, by their occupation of Indo-China, had stopped that, and thus, ironically, the disappearance of Laos as a separate entity.

"What about the Savannakhet Revolutionary Committee's finances?" said Keng.

The committee's vice-chairman, he was a *métis* about sixty years old, half-Tonkinese and half-Khâ, with the shrewd small quick eyes of a monkey; a veteran of Komadome's Khâ revolt against the French. Including him, thought Cuong, the room was probably fairly representative of Laos' various revolutionary movements, which so often had been simply local and tribal and

163

amateur until Souvannouvang had helped form the Lao Issara, and developed his Pathet Lao from it. Phammasone, opposite him, was a plains Lao who had once been an administrator under the French; he had taken part in Chao Pha Pachay's revolt in San Neua Province. Kham, on Cuong's left, was a young Meo from Si Thon's movement based on Phong Saly.

"This month the Americans have passed Nosavan personally thirty-five million Kip for expenses," said Xang. "And twenty-six million more for the funds of his so-called Revolutionary Committee. So it's certain enough that Savannakhet will get all the money they want. And arms."

"Boun Oum is with them?" said Keng.

"There's no doubt of that," said Xang. "Their figurehead."

Boun Oum, hereditary prince of Champassac, or the South of Laos, was a large chubby jovial gentleman who still had great influence. As though it were not already confused enough, Laos had formerly been three Kingdoms, Luang Prabang, Vientiane, and Champassac. The French had laudably tried to unify them under Luang Prabang, and had silenced Boun Oum's claims by making him Inspector-General of the new Kingdom. Boun Oum took this in good part. Nobody knew what he had to do, but the uniform and salary were impressive. But Boun Oum was no mere decoration. He had even fought valiantly against the invading Japanese as a guerilla. Basically he was a splendid old-time warlord, without the remotest notion of modern politics. The Americans loved him. He looked just right for Laos.

"What do we know about their arms?" said Khamphet. She was a Lao from Vientiane, a Paris-trained doctor.

"The air bridge is intensive," said Xang. "The Americans are mainly using a private American company. They're flying C46's in from Bangkok to the French air base at Seno, thirty kilometres from Savannakhet. Nosavan even tried to expropriate the base this month. The French general resisted. But the point's academic; in practice Nosavan can use the base all he likes. Correct?"

Xang had turned to Cuong; security information was his province. Cuong watched Khamphet across the table as he spoke. She had a striking face, broad, with a high forehead and wide-set eyes, and a very level regard.

"Yes," said Cuong. "Savannakhet's supposed to be on war footing, under martial law. They're training all civilians in the use of arms. Part of the American P.E.O. has already left Vientiane via Thailand to re-establish itself in Savannakhet. But none of this is too serious yet. The Savannakhet forces' morale is still low. They haven't forgotten Ba Ca Dinh."

Earlier that month Nosovan had tried his first armed thrust up the road which followed the left bank of the Mekong from Savannakhet up through Thakhek to Vientiane. Men from Konglé's Second Paratroop Battalion had met them at the Ca Dinh river, seventy kilometres east of Vientiane, and beaten them badly. They had fled broken, many crossing the river in boats or rafts to the sanctuary of Thailand. The Pathet forces had stayed on the fringes of this action. They had not been fully committed.

"What is more serious," said Cuong, "are the reports that the First Paratroop Battalion will now follow Nosavan. I understand that the officers who refused, so as not to fight against their sister battalion, have been shot or imprisoned. Second, that Sarit is ready to send regular Thai troops across to help take Vientiane. Third, that Savannakhet now has artillery, a regiment of American 105 millimetre field pieces. Fourth, that Nosavan's gunners and certain paratroops and infantry units are in Thailand under intensive training by American and Thai instructors."

The Committee members were silent. Cuong looked to his side and out of the wooden flap that ran along part of the outside long wall of the room. A thin track came past the school. Beyond it, the ground fell almost vertically for four hundred metres, into a rocky ravine in which a small stream flowed fast. There were terraced fields on the far side. Higher, the fields ended abruptly at the thick belt of the jungle, which seemed poised dangerously above them, on the point of flowing back over them. Above, steep blue-black peaks closed in the valley, against an ice-blue sky.

There were temporary shelters in the fields. The troops were working in the fields with the peasants on the crops. Many of the soldiers were in uniform. It made the scene faintly suspect, as if it had been mounted specially for one of Hanoi's worthy propaganda films, or just for the benefit of the Regional Committee's meeting. But Cuong knew it to be normal enough; most of the troops probably did not have any other clothes anyway. It was nonetheless one of the sights that easily seduced, that of an army integrated in a people. That image was valid too. It pointed up a main reason for the Pathet Lao's tenacious survival and growth.

As this was the Regional Committee's centre, the Pathet had been at some pains to push their policies with the local populace, who had accepted them with amazement. This was one of the last Khâ villages, north-east of Xieng Khouang. Higher in the blue mountains there were only the Meo. Khâ meant slave; traditionally, the plains Lao or the Thai had always exploited them cheerfully. Only the French had ever really bothered about them. Indeed, before Dien Bien Phu finally deflated them, the French had been toying with a most ambitious scheme of creating autonomous states based on minority ethnic groupings such as that of the Khâ, across the north-eastern provinces of Laos and into northern Viet Nam. The Pathet went one better. Formerly, a Khâ in the valley might have to give up as much as a hundred days a year of his time to working the lands of the *tasseng*. The Pathet broke the *tasseng*, and redistributed all the valley's arable land. They reduced the taxes to almost nothing. (After all, it was not their government in Vientiane.) They injected trained instructors in all directions. These serious young men and women had produced an irrigation scheme, a school, a clinic, and even a semi-elective village committee which had rapidly achieved a really startling international political maturity, and had already sent off memoranda condemning (in succession) Eisenhower, Foster Dulles, Macmillan, Syngman Rhee, Diem, Sarit, Pandit Nehru, and Strydom.

Cuong could see a man fishing with a throwing net down in the stream which lay sharply below him. The man was balanced on the rocks above a still pool. He would certainly be from one of the village's ten Lao families, bound to the land's rivers by the links of centuries. The Lao's back was towards him. There was a thin loincloth like a T round his waist and between his buttocks. Foreshortened by the height, his arms curved forward with the folds of his net, he was like a slim brown predatory insect, tense in posture of attack. The weighted rim of the net broke a sudden ragged circle on the polished water immediately in front of him, and Cuong watched the pattern break as the man jumped in upon it.

"Why did Souvanna Phouma permit the arms build-up in the South?" said Phammasome, from across the table. "Couldn't he have tried to stop it?"

Cuong looked back into the room and shivered; in mid-November the mountain air was still sharp at that hour.

Xang had looked across at Phammasome. Xang said:

"Because Souvanna Phouma is an incurable optimist. The rumours are—it would be logical enough—that he asked for and got from the American Ambassador an assurance that the American arms for Nosavan in the South would never be used against the city of Vientiane. And that he believed him."

"Why should he have believed him?" said Phammasome, as though that was not normally a sensible thing to do with American ambassadors.

"Because he wanted to, presumably," said Xang. "The Southern build-up could provide him with a useful counterweight, so long as he could come to terms with Nosavan."

"Counterweight against whom?" said Phammasome.

Xang looked back at him with some contempt.

"Against us," he said. "Against Konglé."

Souvanna Phouma had formed his neutralist cabinet in August after Konglé's coup, at Konglé's request. A majority of the National Assembly in Vientiane had approved it. The King had ratified it. The British recognized it at once, the French shortly after, and Pekin, Moscow, and Hanoi. The Americans did not. The Thai had recognized Nosavan's Revolutionary Committee in Savannakhet as the country's legitimate government as soon as Nosavan formed it.

Souvanna Phouma had done all he could to negotiate a peace. His half-brother Souvannouvong had sent a team to Vientiane weeks before for this purpose. But their stiff terms, and above all the rigid opposition of Nosavan, the Americans, and the Thai had blocked a rapid countrywide solution. Nosavan had refused to talk unless Souvanna broke completely with the Pathet and reversed the whole orientation of his neutralist government.

Souvanna had other problems in Vientiane. Konglé had remained almost a law to himself. Against Souvanna's desire to maintain order at all costs, Konglé had given out fifteen thousand small arms to the city's people, mainly to the students. He had also outraged Souvanna's developed sense of protocol by arranging himself to be the first to meet Abramov, the Russian Ambassador to Cambodia, who had also been accredited to the Vientiane government at Souvanna's request. Konglé had raised the Russian's eyebrows by organising a series of hair-raising jumps by his paratroopers to welcome Abramov at Wattai airport on this occasion.

But the Thai's continued economic blockade of Vientiane remained the Prince's most crippling handicap. He had appealed to the Security Council to stop it in terms of the conventions of international trade. The grapevine had it that the British had forced a joint secret note in the U.N. in New York by which they, the French, and the Americans engaged themselves to get Sarit to lift the blockade at once. If it ever in fact existed, the note had no effect. Sarit, who was one of the Americans' few blue-eyed boys left in the Far East, had a patented way of making himself clear to them in such cases anyway. He would simply invite the Russian Ambassador in Bangkok to call to discuss a further exchange of cultural missions or extension of trade. The system had never been known to fail. The Americans got the point at once. So the stocks of oil fuels for Vientiane and its army and of rice for its people went on dropping perilously. Oil products had been severely rationed for two months, and rice was scarce and already five times its normal price. With Souvanna's capital city so crippled, the loyalty of the other centres like Luang Prabang which still remained loyal to him was wavering.

"Nosavan will certainly drive again from the south to try to take Vientiane," said Cuong. "This time with artillery, probably also with American 'advisers' to the battery commanders and observation officers. He may also have tanks, and some Thai regulars."

Xang and the others were watching him. Xang's usual aloofness seemed even more pronounced.

"Well?" said Xang.

Cuong glanced round the table, and looked back at Xang. Cuong said:

"In my opinion we should defend the city."

There was again silence. All the others, except Khamphet, were looking carefully at Xang to gauge his reaction before they committed themselves. Cuong knew at once that he could not gain them on his own. And, even if he could force a vote and win it, Xang, as the Central Executive representative, could always over-rule him. It was Xang who was the key man here.

From the heightened tension in the room, Cuong knew that the others understood too that this was going to be something more than a difference of opinion on a point of political strategy. It would also be a fight between Xang and himself at a more personal and basic and probably fatal level.

Xang did not look directly at him. He tapped gently with the point of his pencil on the pad in front of him.

"I have always known you to be an intelligent man," said Xang. "You would not make that recommendation without reasons. Would you tell us those reasons?"

"I have four," said Cuong. "First, it could be argued that there would be an even chance of success. Konglé won decisively at Ba Ca Dinh, against much better armed and numerically superior forces. It's true that next time Nosavan will have artillery, and probably American field advisers and Thai support. But couldn't we counter that by committing our forces fully? If that provoked large-scale Thai intervention, wouldn't that in turn justify full entry by North Viet Nam, perhaps China too?"

"And secondly?" said Xang.

"Secondly, surely the longer that we can maintain Souvanna Phouma and Vientiane, the more certainly we shall gain the sympathy, not just of the communist nations, but also of the Bandung Conference neutrals, not to speak of powerful sections of opinion in Britain and France—France has already stated that she will not take part in any action against Vientiane, in SEATO or any other guise. Thirdly, we simply cannot afford to lose Vientiane. If we do, we shall also lose every other main centre."

"Your fourth reason?" said Xang.

Cuong felt the silence build up on him. He looked slowly round the table, and back at Xang. He had a quick vivid image of Gau, the Cantonese that he and Xang had killed, from the back, at the moment that Gau flung out his arms to his sides under the impact of the bullet, so that his body had made a brief frail cross, before it fell slowly forward into the dark and swift and silent river. He looked directly at Xang and said:

"On their own they have no chance. We can hardly just leave these men to their defeat and death."

Xang put his pencil down on the table, exactly parallel to the edge of the pad. He did not say anything.

"It's true that there are Khâ in the Second Battalion," said Keng. "That's true."

Perhaps there was some support there; Cuong looked round the faces of the others. Phammasone met his eyes and looked away at once at Xang. Phammasone said:

"Perhaps if there were really some reasonable possibility of success—"

There was nothing there. Xang could use that argument as profitably as could Cuong.

No one else spoke. Only Keng, then, and not with any strength. Indeed, Keng himself had obviously realized that. Keng's sharp black eyes looked at him, and back to the head of the table.

"Presumably one requires something better than a reasonable possibility," he said.

That half-support was gone too, then.

"How can you possibly ask for complete certainty of success in this?" said Cuong. "Look, men will die in it."

Keng looked back at him with his flat eyes. They made no comment. Keng was sure now that he had been right to change sides.

"And they will not be doing that on the basis of statistics," said Cuong.

Xang had picked up his pencil again at the head of the table. He leant the point of it on his pad. He was holding the pencil very lightly, and quite still. If he was pleased with his results, he was not showing it yet.

"Every minute, hundreds of thousands of men die throughout the world," Xang said, looking a little above Cuong's head. "The life or death of a hundred human beings, a thousand, tens of thousands, even if they be our compatriots, is of little importance. Cuong, you know who said that, of course?"

"Chou," said Cuong, "Borodin."

"A Vietnamese," said Xang, "like you. Giap. Your famous general, Giap. You *do* consider yourself Vietnamese, don't you?"

Cuong's eyes narrowed on him. Xang was missing no trick. It was the fate of any *métis*; either side of your blood could mock you.

"Yes," said Cuong. "However diluted my blood, I consider myself Vietnamese."

"Well, seriously," said Xang paternally, "we can afford this sentimentalism?"

"I think that one can argue full commitment of our forces at Vientiane on grounds totally other than those of sentimentalism," said Cuong. "By not doing so we could lose the people's sympathy for years. How many years' support did Moscow lose by failing to back the Chinese communists in Hankow and against Chiang Kai-shek in Shanghai in 1927?"

"Nonetheless you wouldn't deny that China is now securely communist," said Xang. "What are a few years? Konglé? We have no obligation to Konglé. He would totally refuse our control. Even Souvanna Phouma can't manage him. And intervention? It's really in our interests to provoke another Korea? When time is with us as it is, in precisely this situation of localized civil war? As for external sympathy, we already *have* the Bandung neutrals' sympathy and that of much of Western Europe. We shall not lose by losing Vientiane. The reverse is probably true. What better way is there of highlighting American interference in Laos than by gallantly losing Ventiane to their protégés, in a shroud of military and civilian casualties?"

"Such dramatic external sympathy is of any practical use to us at all," said Cuong. "If we lose the confidence of our own people here?"

Xang tapped gently with his pencil. He said:

"How many years was it that you were with Giap's regulars, Cuong? Seven?"

"Seven."

"Another quotation for you, then. Aim always at the destruction of the enemy, rather than at the taking of urban centres and other fixed points. Before fighting, be sure of sufficient superiority to be able to destroy the enemy completely. Avoid battles where the issue is not certain."

"Giap, Truong Chinh, did not ever seek to apply all of Mao Tse Tung's maxims literally in Viet Nam."

"But these particular ones they did, Cuong. Giap did not even undertake Dien Bien Phu until you had marked superiority strategically, in fire power, and logistically. Defend Vientiane? What do you want, Cuong, a repetition of Giap's one great military error, when he threw your best divisions too early against De Lattre's tanks and artillery in the Red River Delta in 1950? De Lattre cut you to pieces. Or Souvannouvong's error in 1946, when he based the resistance movement too much on urban centres, and the French almost bombed and machine-gunned him out of existence in Thakhek? To commit our forces fully to Vientiane would be to invite exactly that sort of débacle."

The dice were already thrown and fully stopped and legible, Cuong thought. His own moment was already well past in that room. Perhaps outside it also. He thought again of Gau, the back of the small black head drawing away from them, caught finally in the black certain river. He said:

"It is decided then to let the city starve and fall?"

"Without histrionics," said Xang. "It probably won't starve. The Russians have promised Souvanna an air lift of food and oil products from Hanoi."

"They won't hold Nosavan off this time with rice," said Cuong, "or drums of diesel fuel."

"No," said Xang reasonably, "probably with arms too. Some arms, say. Two or three batteries of 105 millimetres with North Vietnamese gunlayers. To even the odds a little."

Xang was ahead of him there. Cuong had not heard that. He said:

"We wait and watch, then. Only that."

"Until Nosavan and Konglé exhaust themselves," said Xang. "After he takes Vientiane, Nosavan must try to drive north after what Konglé forces are left. That's Konglé's natural line of retreat. Nosavan must follow him. American and Thai opinion will force him to it. Then Nosavan loses all his advantages. In the jungles and mountains of North Laos. *That* is our logical battleground."

It was betrayal of the city and the neutralist government, of the civilians and the Second Battalion and the students' movements. Konglé had armed the students with rifles, but they would be suicidally weak against regular troops with tanks and artillery.

Militarily and politically, it was also the right decision. Cuong knew it. It was all simply a question of perspective.

Xang said:

"You can of course always put it to the vote."

Xang had chosen his moment for that nicely. Cuong looked round the table. None of the others would meet his eyes, except

Khamphet. She was looking at him steadily. Though she had not spoken for him before, he knew suddenly that she would support him now. But she would be alone. He turned back to Xang.

"No."

"Good," said Xang.

There was a discreet knock and the door opened and a man in khaki drill uniform walked to the head of the table. Xang took the folded paper and opened and read it.

"Well. There is no reply."

The people round the table watched him. When the door shut he looked up at them. He said:

"Luang Prabang has defected to the Savannakhet Revolutionary Committee."

It was the next inevitable step. Now all focus would be on Vientiane.

"It changes nothing," said Xang.

CHAPTER XVII

"You were of course wrong," said Khamphet.

"Yes," said Cuong. "Why then would you have supported me? Because I think that you would have supported me."

She shifted her body a little. She said:

"Yes, I would have supported you. Why? Perhaps I too sufficiently dislike the idea of people dying without great hope, even if it is politically expedient. And Vientiane's my city. I was born there, you understand. Also—"

"Also?" he said.

"You were alone. And Xang doesn't readily tolerate challenge to his authority."

She lay on her back beside him, naked, her body strong and relaxed, that of a peasant, with its strong thighs and calves and shoulders, without subtlety, and with the features of her broad face softened and unbound, as if touched by sleep. It was less that she had permitted him to make love to her than that she had almost bidden him to do so, in a manner nearly masculine, medical, as though she had simply been administering a needed drug. But her action could equally have been more feminine than it seemed; her instinctive return to sex, in the presence of danger and death. Perhaps she already felt that death obscurely in him.

What she had done had even required a certain courage. So

small a village would know at once that she had let Cuong sleep with her that night. The Pathet Lao mystique did not admit promiscuity, any more than did that of the Viet Minh upon which it was based. Each had that curious imperative common to most modern left-wing political revolutions, to make puritanism the central spring of its sexual morality, the drive which in the Chinese communes rationed the times when a man could copulate officially with his wife, and which in Hanoi made the authorities frown on women who went on wearing the bright gay colours of the old days, instead of the sombre ascetic shades of the new régime. Here that same sober drive had even ironed the sex from Khamphet's working clothes, which were a shapeless leather jacket, or one of the khaki drill, and khaki slacks or a khaki skirt.

"Xang," he said with contempt, "and the others of his stamp. These cold rulers."

"The people are not cold," she said.

"But these new rulers," he said, "these new patricians. Their decisions a power-play of mathematics. As cold as their own cold myths. Is that all that we end with, these cold myths?"

She did not answer him at once. She found his question alien. Temperamentally she had never felt any need to justify herself intellectually. In her student days in Paris the powerful and brilliant left wing students' movements had not attracted her. Their exhaustive analytical lucidity and obsessive self-examination had seemed to her a trait of adolescence, a kind of intellectual masturbation. By contrast, the mandate of medicine seemed to her embarrassingly clear and simple. Daughter of a rich and enlightened family of landowners in Vientiane, she had never known poverty or illness. These privileges of her birth had seemed to set a duty on her.

When she had qualified in Paris, she returned to work in Vientiane's Hôpital Pavie. She would have continued there happily with the French doctors, whom she admired, but her feelings changed when the administrative control began to pass from French hands. The French had begun to work on the true medical problems of the country. Here the enemies were ignorance and superstition, and the remedies preventive medicine and basic education in hygiene, for the Lao themselves and, above all, for the racial minorities in the provinces. There was no high-class cinematic drama about these problems, no epic last-minute surgery in shining operating theatres, but their solution was nonetheless essential if Laos were ever to change from being simply a charming and dilapidated backwater.

In Laos, over the centuries, the soft and graceful Hinayana

Buddhism had entrenched the power of the *médicastres*, the magicians, and the sorcerers, and of the *Mo Sado*, the midwives.

Traditionally, a *Mo Sado* used an unsterilized bamboo blade to cut the umbilical cord. If a child's arm emerged first in a birth, the *Mo Sado* would fill the hand with rice and salt and push it back; if a foot, she would beat it back gently with an old shoe. She would continue in this richly symbolic and septicaemic way until the baffled infant's head finally emerged first in the proper manner. The *Mo Sado* was as brisk with the mothers themselves. Her main post-natal care for them was to seat them smartly on a pan of alcohol or raw salt. Khamphet admitted that the replacement of these and similar exotic practices by the aseptic disciplines of modern medicine would rob the place of some fascinating local colour, but she also felt that it might reduce deformities and infant mortality rates and save a few adult lives.

"Haven't your cold myths given us something after all?" she said.

Lying next to her, he was staring up at the ceiling. The small bamboo fire on its hard clay slab in the centre of the room flickered its pale yellow light across him.

"Of course," he said. "But also how many blunders, cruelties, so-called political necessities? The Agrarian Reform in North Viet Nam. The *Cent Fleurs*. Here, Vientiane."

"You cannot say that you would prefer the old ways again," she said. "You made a country in North Viet Nam. Even here, isn't it better? Only a little so far, perhaps, but it's better. Surely it's *that* which you must judge? Not the failures. We should have got nothing at all with the others."

She had no doubt of that herself. The pattern of small clinics in the north-eastern provinces had been her idea, and the people's acceptance of them. however painfully slow that had been, was her justification. For that satisfaction she was prepared to pay whatever lip service was needed to the principles of the only political group progressive enough to back her plan.

"You can't go back," he said.

"No."

"In time," he said, "or to a belief that you have lost."

He went on with difficulty.

"It can take one long to see that," he said. "It is as one can love a person. One day you can know that you are nothing to her. And you can't go back, because the thing is dead."

"It can be like that," she said.

"It can be like that in these things too," he said. "As when love is finished, you can go back in your mind to search the mistake that you might have made, and there may be no mistake that you can see. Yet the thing is dead."

"One should not expect too greatly," she said, "of people, or of things."

"Perhaps that is true," he said, politely, and with no conviction.

She understood abruptly that he had nothing like her tolerance. He would probably always be obsessed by the exceptions. He would probably always discard his beliefs the moment that he could no longer apply them literally. He lacked the usual convenient capacity for temporary blindness. He was more perfectionist than she had thought; it was an immaturity that could be fatal. Or perhaps he was simply too human.

She understood too, sadly, that there was not really anything that she could do for him. He was alone, like all men finally.

"Your concern for Vientiane," said Xang.

Cuong stood and looked down at him. Xang had not asked him to sit; he was maintaining the distances. Xang himself sat behind the cheap desk in the Lao *piloti* which he had been using as his office and his home during these months. The stream ran past the *piloti*. Above it was the sharp cliff, the track, and the school in which the Regional Committee had sat seven days before. Cuong could hear the thin voices of children from out in the sunlight by the clear stream.

"Yes?" he said.

"We have been reconsidering your opinion," said Xang.

Presumably that meant the Central Executive Committee. Xang had been to Sam Neua since the Regional Committee had met. He had returned in the night.

"We are to commit our forces at Vientiane?" said Cuong.

"No," said Xang. "There is no change to that decision."

"Well, then?"

"But we agreed," said Xang, "that it would be useful to have an experienced observer in Vientiane during the fighting."

That was the way they had framed it then, thought Cuong. The objective was transparently unnecessary. The Pathet had trained agents in Vientiane. They could have reported accurately enough on the fighting afterwards.

"I see," he said.

"Of course, there may in fact be no fighting," said Xang. "Souvanna Phouma may be prepared to negotiate the city's surrender. Konglé, I doubt it. With him it's a question of prestige. Souvanna Phouma, of course, just does not like destruction."

175

Xang sounded a little like an experienced parent warning his child that an anticipated party might not take place after all.

"From the intelligence the attack seems certain enough," said Cuong. "Nosavan's battalions have left Savannakhet. Konglé will probably try to meet them again at Ba Ca Dinh. But you'll have heard that in Sam Neua."

Xang had listened to him politely.

"Yes," he said, "I had known that."

Cuong said:

"It's not desired that I organize any Pathet units in the city, then?"

"No."

"Or irregulars; the students, say?"

Xang shrugged up at him. Xang said:

"You can put yourself at Konglé's disposal. Officially you're there simply as an observer. Naturally, nothing could prevent you from fighting as a private citizen if you so wished."

The pointlessness of the mission, the absence of specific tasks, and the suggestion that he might fight as a civilian cemented Cuong's suspicion that the Central Committee, under the influence of Xang's reports on him, now mistrusted his loyalty enough to wish to see him liquidated. If that were so, the means they had selected were both discreet and fairly sure to work. If Nosavan had to fight hard to take the city there was some probability that he would afterwards shoot any of Konglé's officers that he captured. It was almost certain that he would execute any *franc tireurs* that he took.

"When should I go?" he said.

"Tomorrow."

Xang was looking up at him steadily, his high-cheekboned face precise and disinterested. Cuong had the disturbing impression that Xang did not really see him at all. He could already have been thinking of someone or something totally different, or just looking up at him out of courtesy while listening for something else much more important. Xang had always had the habit of looking like that at a committee member who had contradicted him. It was the look of someone who was always really rather surer of the facts.

Xang put his left hand down on the table in front of him, palm down, and fanned the tips of his fingers open delicately. He looked down at them a moment and up again at Cuong.

"One other thing," he said.

"Yes?"

"There is a man whom we should like you to eliminate. After the fighting, when the city is taken, or after it is surrendered, if there is no fighting."

"Who is the man?" said Cuong.

"It's essential that this should be done *after* the city is taken," said Xang. "As it was so much more effective that Souvannouvong and the others should escape with all their guards in Vientiane *after* the right wing had won their rigged elections so conclusively. So that we can demonstrate that we still have our power *after* the right wing think themselves most secure, you understand."

"It's ingenious," said Cuong. "Who's the man?"

Xang glanced down at his fingers again, turned and curled them so that the nails were upward, stretched them out again, and dropped his hand gently on his lap. He looked up.

"The American," he said.

"There are a number."

Xang smiled at the irony.

"So there are," he said. "The one to whom Gau sold Thanh and Boun Ngong."

"I see," said Cuong. "Why? He's really so efficient?"

"It's not that," said Xang reasonably. "They'll replace him anyway. They can always replace their men, after all. Just as we can. No one's indispensable."

He held his silence for a moment, like a good artist, no doubt to let the meaning of his last remark sink in exactly. He went on:

"You understand, it was a decision that required some delicacy of judgment."

"Indeed?" said Cuong.

"Put it like this," said Xang, "an ambassador, a first secretary, the head of a mission—that would be too extreme. There would be so much publicity that the Americans would feel bound to act drastically."

He sounded rather disappointed.

"Why should we really risk that, after all?" he said. "This will be of about the right weight. A man of their special services. They'll get the message."

"Xang," said Cuong.

"Yes."

"A question."

"Of course," said Xang. "Yes?"

"We have agents in Vientiane. Why not use one of them?"

Xang looked straight up at him. He said, without discernible irony:

"We have every confidence in you."

He seemed to be looking now just past Cuong's shoulder. It

was as if somebody had come quietly into the room. Cuong turned automatically, but he saw no one.

"I can select my own way to do that?" said Cuong.

"Of course," said Xang. "But it must be clear that it was an execution. It must not look like an accident."

Cuong looked down at him with hatred. But, professionally, he was admiring Xang's thoroughness. If he, Cuong, survived the fighting but had to stay on in Vientiane after it for this murder, he would also have to escape the security police's witch-hunt of the left wing that would certainly follow as soon as Nosovan controlled the city.

"I'll leave tomorrow," he said.

Xang looked up at him and smiled again.

"You and the American," he said. "Thanh, Boun Ngong, Gau. There's even a certain dramatic irony to it."

Now he sounded definitely pleased.

A child's laugh, and the shrill following voice of a woman, cut across Cuong's mind from out in the hard sunlight by the stream.

"You should appreciate that, really," said Xang.

"I should?"

"With your feeling for French culture," said Xang.

CHAPTER XVIII

A DELIGHTED squeal cut across Jean-Philippe's attention, and he looked up over his dry martini and away from Ward, who was talking heavily at him about the communist menace in the United States. A slim girl with sultry eyes was standing by the side-table which was being loaded with the buffet supper. She was blushing sociably at MacNaughton, the Acting Director of USOM, whose party it was, and extracting a small teaspoon from the cleft of her marginal bosom. Jean-Philippe thought with relief that it was going to be that sort of party after all.

"You can say what you like about the John Birch Society," said Ward.

Jean-Philippe sighed and looked back at him.

"You can indeed," he said.

"Yeah," said Ward. "But there's a lot to what he says."

"I thought he was dead," said Jean-Philippe.

"Who?" said Ward.

"Birch."

"So Birch is dead. No, this captain."

"Oh, this captain," said Jean-Philippe.

Ward looked at him. Ward's heavy horn-rimmed glasses gave him a highly concentrated and lethally earnest air. His startlingly blond hair glittered. Jean-Philippe had always wondered if he dyed it.

"In the States," said Ward patiently, "lecturing, like I said."

"Oh, yes. About Korea. Yes."

"About the guys who defected," said Ward in a hushed voice, looking raped at the thought.

"It's a big word."

"This psychiatry angle," said Ward. "Hell, says this captain, what do you excuse next? He thinks we're going soft."

"Well?" said Jean-Philippe companionably.

"It's too easy, see?" said Ward. "Doesn't it just show a degeneration in our values, like he says?"

"My," said Jean-Philippe. "He said all that?"

Ward eyed him suspiciously. Whenever he talked politics intensely, Ward always tended to look like that, as though about to break into a lope at any moment and make his point succintly by physical assault. But this time Ward glanced down at his side instead, perhaps for his wife. Not finding her, he looked back at Jean-Philippe.

"He got a good press in the States too," he said tangentially.

"That's good," said Jean-Philippe.

"Sure," said Ward, "he was in Korea himself, of course."

"And a prisoner there too?" said Jean-Philippe.

"Certainly not," said Ward.

"No," said Jean-Philippe, "I suppose he wouldn't have been."

"Look," said Ward, at last pricked by the satire in Jean-Philippe's voice, "what d'you find so odd about it? It's basic, isn't it?"

"Basic," said Jean-Philippe, nodding absently. He was watching the girl again. She was laughing up at MacNaughton, using all her eyes, and holding a large bowl of white rice down in front of her at the full stretch of her arms. She looked richly symbolic.

"You've got to make a firm stand on these sort of basic values sooner or later," said Ward.

"Ah, yes," said Jean-Philippe. "A firm stand."

He was glad to see that the girl was there. She was a USOM secretary, one of the few American women who had stayed in Vientiane. After Konglé's coup in August, the American Ambassador had ordered the evacuation of all American wives and non-essential personnel. MacNaughton, a highly competent man with a satiric turn of mind, had promptly evacuated about three hundred or ninety-five per cent of his staff, and swore privately that he got much better results out of the fifteen or so that he kept. A few wives had refused the order, through loyalty to their husbands, a high regard for the competitive abilities of the secretaries and local women, or because they were damned if they were going to be relegated to a relatively celibate existence in Bangkok for an indeterminate period anyway. Short's and Wainwright's wives and Mary-Frances were among these. The exodus was nevertheless imposing. Long convoys of limousines and pickups and lorries, flagged and numbered and marshalled like the general staff of the army corps, and fraught with linen and suitcases and light furniture and pictures and portable radios and wailing children and Coca-Cola, had transferred this vast human tail across the town to the airport at Wattai, where aircraft waited to fly it to Udorn and ultimately to a sympathetic Bangkok.

"It's not that I have anything against psychiatry as such, you understand," said Ward. "I certainly respect the advances made by modern medicine. Don't get me wrong, now."

"Good God, MacNaughton," said Jean-Philippe. "I must have a word with him."

"MacNaughton," said Ward intelligently.

Jean-Philippe smiled brilliantly at him and turned and left him hanging on his charged unspoken words, like a shot soldier on barbed wire, and walked over to MacNaughton and the girl. He noticed with approval that the rice contained raisins and nuts and spices; the girl had finally put the bowl down on the table, which now also held two crisped brown turkeys and a strikingly naked pink cooked ham, surrounded by red half-circles of orange, and a great variety of salads, vegetables and sauces. Fortunately, the economic blockade had evidently not affected the PX's stocks.

"*T'as l'air affamé, Jean.*"

MacNaughton's brisk narrow face bore upon him like a hatchet. MacNaughton had been educated in Lyons; he did not mind if you remembered it. A few years before this posting, he had also been an Information Officer in Paris.

"Like a wolf," said Jean-Philippe in English, smiling politely at the girl.

"I meant the food," said MacNaughton.

"Oh," said Jean-Philippe. "That too, of course."

"You know Susan, my secretary. Like Felicia, my daughter."

"Enchanted," said Jean-Philippe. "Jean-Philippe Raymond."

He half-bent and brought the girl's hand negligently near to his lips. People still seemed to expect this sort of stunt out of French-men these days.

"It sounds like an incantation," said Susan, examining him frankly with her large liquid black eyes, removing his underpants and replacing them with a slight professional nod.

"Another damn intellectual Frenchman, Sue," said MacNaughton.

"Yes, you can tell that from his glittering eye."

"I knew his paper, you know," said MacNaughton. "It's very cerebral. He thinks we're all wrong here. Well," he glanced about him histrionically. "*We* think we're all wrong here."

"Shush," said Susan.

"What do I care?" said MacNaughton. "They can't do any-thing to me. I've got shares in American Motors."

"I don't think he's too intellectual," said Susan. "An Iron Man, I'd say. Dry Martinis for the first hour!"

She had a pleasant husky bedroom voice that suited her eyes.

"I propose now to pass the whisky and soda," said Jean-Philippe.

"It's wiser," said Susan. "We don't want to lose you, you know. There's a long way to go."

Indeed, the party had started at seven, and had inevitably to go on until at least six the next morning. You were liable to get shot if you were outside between these curfew hours. It was no parties, or parties all night.

"You're married?" said Susan to Jean-Philippe.

"An elfin, subtle child," said MacNaughton.

"No," said Jean-Philippe.

"Good," said Susan. "I find that wives do clog so, at parties."

"It's upstairs on the left," said MacNaughton obscurely. "Do knock first, though."

"Sorry?" said Jean-Philippe.

"Basic geography," said MacNaughton maliciously.

"Ha, ha," said Susan. "Dear John!"

Jointly they watched his retreating back; he had gone off like a good host to check on his guest's drinks. Jean-Philippe looked down mystified at the girl.

"That bit about upstairs on the left?" he said.

She looked up at him happily.

"No, no," she said, "not the toilet. The bedrooms."

"What a kindly thought," said Jean-Philippe.

"What a mess," said Susan abruptly.

"The party?" said Jean-Philippe. "Is it? Why?"

"No, no," she said. "Things."

"Oh, that," he said. "I thought they were to be a forbidden subject this evening?"

"Oh, all right," said Susan. "But one does feel so beleaguered."

He smiled.

"No doubt we'll survive. Pridie, for example, will certainly survive."

Jean-Philippe gestured with the last of his dry martini towards the ten or twelve people in the centre of the room. Indeed, Western civilization looked as though it was still good for some years yet. Pridie was standing with Mary-Frances, drooped elegantly over her; he could have been giving her expert advice on the set of her brassière. Jean-Philippe glanced automatically to the far end of the room; Jeanette was there as he had expected, talking to Short and his wife. There was a bigger group near them; Wainwright and his wife, with the Justins, who were the only Lao present that evening. On their fringes Dumergue was talking with two girls, probably also USOM secretaries. It struck Jean-Philippe that, coincidentally, all the people whom Pridie had had at that first dinner-party at his house by the river almost exactly a year before were there that night; except, of course, for the Marivells.

"He looks as though he's going to give her a prize," said Susan.

"Who?" said Jean-Philippe.

"Pridie," said Susan. "To Mary-Frances. Friend Pridie. Our New Englander."

"You sound quite sad," said Jean-Philippe.

"It's sheer envy, really," said Susan. "But she really is remarkably equipped. Nearly as well as Jeanette. You know how men are about these things."

"Men are such fools," said Jean-Philippe soothingly.

"Actually," said Susan, "I hardly know him at all."

"Pridie? He's really so mysterious?"

"A little cold and closed, isn't he?" said Susan. "We hardly see him, you know, with all his secret voyages and all. He has his—friends, of course; Jeanette."

"We, Susan?"

"The American community. Our famous American community. Oh, I don't mean just in work. In USOM, except at the top, we don't really have all that much daily contact with the Embassy anyway. But, socially, we never really see him."

"Tell me about these intriguing secret voyages of his," he said.

"Oh, you know. Savannakhet, Paksé, Luang Prabang."

"Recently too?" said Jean-Philippe.

"Of course."

She looked up at him, as if surprised that he had not known.

"Women and children first," said MacNaughton, steering Mary-Frances past them to the side-table like a ship in full sail. Susan smiled at Jean-Philippe and shrugged and followed them obediently. Jean-Philippe stood for a moment, then drifted over to Dumergue, at the far side of the room.

"*Vieux,*" he said.

"*Salaud,*" said Dumergue.

"How goes it?"

Dumergue glinted at him through his thick lenses. He said: "Inside or outside?"

"Outside," said Jean-Philippe. "I could see that you were well enough accommodated in here. Say at the Nam Ca Dinh."

"It warms up," said Dumergue. "Brutally, it should be very warm. Nosavan must have attacked by now. With artillery. Konglé's men have never been under a barrage. Ten to one it will break them. Then say a week to Vientiane."

"How's the Administration here?" said Jean-Philippe.

"Frightened," said Dumergue. "They thought that something would come out of Souvanna Phouma's last radio appeals to Savannakhet, after he met Souvannouvong on the twentieth. You know, a coalition government, neutralist, with both Pathet Lao and Savannakhet Revolutionary Committee representation, but excluding Nosavan and Boun Oum. No reaction; Nosavan's much too confident now."

"It's as I thought," said Jean-Philippe. "With the Americans still trying to force Souvanna to break unconditionally with the Pathet and go over to Nosavan, or else to get out and leave the field to him entirely."

"About that," said Dumergue.

"They won't change that line now," said Jean-Philippe. "They'll probably support the attack on Vientiane at all costs, now that the Ilyushin 14's have started to arrive."

"You've seen them?"

"With binoculars, yes," said Jean-Philippe. "From the second floor of the new terminal which the French economic mission are building at Wattai airport. They're like D.C.3's, but with square-cut fins, and big hydraulically-operated cargo ports at the sides."

Dumergue put his hand up to his small black militant moustache. He said:

"Thank God it was the Russians, anyway. Thank God they got in first."

"And not the Chinese or North Vietnamese? It's a point."

"Quite an important point," said Dumergue. "If it were the

Chinese or North Vietnamese, we'd probably already be back carrying guns again by now, Jean."

"Not Raymond," said Jean-Philippe. "I wouldn't fight this time. Not for this."

Dumergue considered him seriously.

"No," he said, after a while. "No, I think that one would certainly not fight this time."

"Our friends started it," said Jean-Philippe. "And our friends are wrong. Let them finish it."

"If you saw the Ilyushins," said Dumergue. "It's true that so far they've brought only oil and rice?"

"So far as one can tell. They've certainly brought oil; Short's seen the drums. Diesel fuel, Baku markings. They could have brought arms too. They unload on the far airstrip, you see, under tight security, then take the stuff in closed trucks to the army depot by the airport."

"It builds up," said Dumergue.

"How's the army loyalty here?" said Jean-Philippe. "How are the non-Konglé units?"

"Doubtful," said Dumergue. "Kuprasith at the Kilometre Four camp at Chinaimo would probably go over to Nosavan if he could. But there are still too many Konglé men in the city. Plus the armed Youth Movement. Souvanna may try negotiating to the end. But the others will fight."

"It's just as well that we have nice strong stone houses," said Jean-Philippe.

"Yes," said Dumergue soberly. "Brutally, it will not be amusing for the Lao civilians in their *pilotis*."

"It's sex again, is it? said Short. They had not noticed him come up to them.

"Sex, certainly," said Jean-Philippe. "How's Patricia?"

"That's a nice quick mental association," said Short. "In fact, we husbands hardly ever think of sex, you know. It's one of our privileges. Actually, she's eating."

He nodded towards the french windows. They opened out on to the terrace and lawn, upon which small square tables were set, each with four places. The women had finished serving themselves, and the men had just started. Wainwright and a USOM secretary were sitting at one of the tables. Pridie was holding Patricia's chair for her at one of the remaining two places at it.

"Chap has nice manners," said Dumergue.

Short looked at him quickly.

"Oh, charming," he said.

"Why the low snarl?" said Jean-Philippe.

"Snarl?" said Short.

"Come off it," said Jean-Philippe. "You hate his guts. I've always wondered why."

Short examined him. He said:

"So have I, really, I suppose."

"Passes at Patricia and dull things like that?" said Jean-Philippe. Short laughed at him.

"Not Pridie," he said. "He has his love-life well subordinated, I should have thought."

"Hum," said Dumergue. Short glanced at him. He said:

"All right. Well, nothing that would hurt his career, anyway. Nothing so crude as assaults on American wives, certainly. That could cause quite a drama, even here."

"Then?" said Jean-Philippe. "Of course, you could always tell me to mind my own damned business."

"So I could," said Short.

"Don't do that," said Dumergue. "We have such a long night to get through."

"Why not?" said Short. "All right. Let's just say that I don't much like people who take short cuts all the time. Not the way he does."

"Short cuts?" said Jean-Philippe.

"The cry of the born underdog," said Short.

"It's too subtle for me," said Jean-Philippe. "Anyway, I can't recall having seen Friend Pridie cutting any corners particularly."

"You haven't?" said Short. "That really surprises me. Isn't his kind of politics always that?"

"Hell," said Jean-Philippe, "he's only the cultural attaché, isn't he? That's harmless enough, isn't it?"

"What a sense of humour you do have," said Short. "Pridie's a breaker."

"Pridie likes to break things?"

"You know that," said Short. "The original white avenging angel. A regular little missionary. The kind of character that always has to have a mission in life. Even if it busts him. Or you."

"Modern crusader," said Jean-Philippe. He looked thoughtful.

"Come again?" said Short.

"A modern crusader," said Jean-Philippe. "It's not original. Jeanette said that to me about him recently."

"Well, well," said Short. "That's not bad. Maybe Jeanette's growing up at last."

Jean-Philippe did not say anything, and Short lit himself a cigarette. Short reflected that there were still a few people about whom he would rather not see broken. Jeanette for one, for that matter, but she ought to be able to look after herself. Some of the Lao. Khamling, for example. He wondered if they would break Khamling.

Short had last seen Khamling a week earlier, before the Ilyushins had started to fly oil in from Hanoi. At that time Vientiane's situation was desperate. Sarit's economic blockade had not let up at all for three months. Short had told Khamling that his diesel fuel stocks would be finished in four days. Khamling managed the archaic power station. He was a Paris-trained mechanical engineer, young and immensely conscientious and likeable, toy-like in build, with an equally tiny quiet wife who constantly produced him small perfect children as calmly as she did his breakfast. At that interview Khamling had finally raised his head decorously and said, quite without rancour, simply stating a fact: Mr. Short, you force us now into the arms of the communists. You will then destroy our city. Short had had no answer. He had reflected obliquely that it would be Christmas in three weeks. Season of peace to all men of goodwill, he had thought savagely.

"My," said Jean-Philippe. "White avenging angel. I say, Joe—"

"Yes?"

"You write novels, do you?"

Short eyed him fiercely.

"We have no lakes around here," he said, "but you could always go and jump in the river."

"Take some ham and turkey with you," said Dumergue. "Mac-Naughton's making signals at us."

Jean-Philippe took a tall crystal glass of iced white wine, Lieb-fraumilsch from the taste of it, and charged his plate liberally with turkey, ham, mince pies, roast potatoes, rice, and mixed salads, and went out to the terrace. Short and Dumergue had preceded him, but he stopped nonetheless with the air of one who still had many alternatives to choose from in front of the only remaining cover, to the right of Jeanette, opposite MacNaughton, and to Mary-Frances' left.

"May I?"

"Of course."

He sat and parked his vast plate and his wine in front of him and looked round the table. Jeanette met his eyes. She was wearing a dress of pure white, of gleaming Shantung silk, and shoulder-less. It cut straight round modestly above her breasts, and inclined tight in to her waist. She wore stiletto-heeled and sharply pointed evening shoes; the toe of one was visible, hooked under a leg of her chair. Her jet black hair was coiled high. Crystal ear-rings, shaped like the blades of old Roman swords, danced and twinkled brittly as she turned to him. She said:

"For so long, Jean-Philippe. I haven't seen you this evening. Or indeed since that cocktail party, on the night of the coup."

"Always in my thoughts, Jeanette."

She laughed frankly at him, the black hair and etched eyebrows, the glancing flash of silver at her ears, the full red lips and the white skin addressing him.

"*P'tit son de cloche, Jean*. But what a loss to the diplomatic corps!"

"Regrettably not," said Jean-Philippe. "I'm not really complicated enough sexually."

The bright remark had an odd effect on her, almost as though it touched her personally. She looked down quickly at her glass, and toyed with its stem, turning it so that the rim of the gold liquid spun and wavered.

"He always dresses so well," said Mary-Frances. "I always find him amusing. He's a cultured man. Intelligent."

MacNaughton eyed her sardonically.

"Peter's certainly intelligent," he said.

"How's Maud, John?" said Mary-Frances.

"Bored, I understand," said MacNaughton. "Loaded with the children, you know. And apparently the Bangkok wats have palled."

Jeanette stilled her glass and lifted it to Jean-Philippe.

"All right, then," she said, "to simplicity."

"Sorry?" said Jean-Philippe.

"To sexual simplicity," said Jeanette.

"Oh," said Jean-Philippe, "yes. By all means."

She put her glass down and began to eat. Jean-Philippe followed her lead with rather more vigour. He had had no lunch; Quinim, now Souvanna's deputy and Minister of Information, and head of the Souvanna delegation negotiating with the Pathet Lao team, had been able to see him only at two. It had been a depressing interview. It was the first time that he had seen Quinim admit the possibility of defeat.

"The turkey's very good," he said originally.

"Fiddles," said Mary-Frances.

"Pardon?"

"You know," said Mary-Frances. "Nero and Rome and all that."

Lending some depth indeed to this exciting theory of orgies in the shadow of the sword was the low throbbing dance music which came from a huge chromium-plated radio like a juke-box which stood in one corner of the main room which they had just left, where MacNaughton had thoughtfully switched the lights to a strategic low. Couples were already interrupting their meal to go and dance. Jean-Philippe could see Dumergue circling heroically in the gloom, the dehydrated Mrs. Wainwright towering over him, but still holding him carefully at arms' length, as though she feared that he might yet impregnate her even from that distance. Jean-Philippe raised his eyebrows to Jeanette and she smiled and got up with him.

Deliberately he held her lightly, but she came naturally close against him. It was a slow fox-trot, so slow indeed that the couples in the darkened room (he could not see Pridie among them) were practically stationary, only swaying slightly, their expressions rapt. It was like some submarine ritual of the elegantly drowned, stroked subtly by the underwater currents.

He became more conscious of Jeanette's body against him, the pelvis, the gently shifting thighs, the stomach and soft breasts. Her face was sideways against his chest; in height she came to just above his shoulder. He glanced down at the top of her head. The parting in her black hair was exactly in the centre. It ran back ten centimetres before it was covered by the coiled weight of her braids. The flesh which it revealed seemed extraordinarily white and clearly defined. There was a small impact to this sight. It was as though, in miniature, he already looked upon the naked beauty of her body. Her scent was the same as she had used in the car that first night, and in her home. It, and the soft rhythmic pressure of her body, quickened his blood suddenly. Down, Fritz, down now, down there boy, he snarled to himself, then smiled and nodded courteously, catching the eye of Ward a few metres from him, ambling unco-ordinated forward at him at twice the beat and totally enveloping a small USOM secretary, leaning on her resolute as a cripple. This small distraction and that of getting safely out of Ward's way returned Jean-Philippe his control, and he danced more easily on.

At Quinim's interview with him that afternoon Quinim had said that as he saw it the Pathet would never commit their forces to aid Konglé at the Nam Ca Ding. In that case they would as certainly not commit them to defend Vientiane. That was bad. It showed how exactly the Pathet assessed the outcome. And sad, for the city. It was also the kind of disciplined thinking that won wars.

Outside this room, in the early night, he knew that the city would already be as deserted as though some sudden final plague had struck it, its streets as blank and empty and atavistic as the black secret river. Only the crisp echoing sounds of the patrols would sometimes break that silence. Outside the brief bubble statement of Western culture which this room now made, gay and stylized and subtle and isolated and totally alien here, the city would be lying sober and expectant, a great grey quiet beast, crouched by its river, gathering itself stoically against the coming attack.

CHAPTER XIX

DANCING close up against this tall Frenchman, as completely conscious of him physically as if his flesh already joined hers, Jeanette was at that moment not at all concerned about the political situation. Here I am practically taking my pants off to the man, she thought, and he hives off independent as a bird, no doubt trying to solve some vastly unimportant male problem. Damn the race of them, she added, glancing up at him, observing the curved arrogant outrageous nose, the deep grooves about the eyes and mouth (of pain or mockery or both?), the wide carnal lips, and the shock of black hair. What was he finally, clown or robber, success or failure (he had no discernible ambition for position or power), capped fool, sad wandering Jew, or simply astute and rootless adventurer, entertained sufficiently by his own sense of irony?

Anyway he was dark thrusting male, and intact; he would serve. Her proof of that lay in the filigreed web of her own blood, which bound her now intricately to him. The slow surge of his easy riding body, guiding her effortlessly with his shoulders and thighs, beckoned the fragile silver pinpoint of light from its infinitely far end of the long corridor. If he so willed, he could summon that to full flooding tides with the power of his arched rippling back and beating thighs, and leave her stripped and purged and shaken at their ebb. Her first lover had had that gift, and Jean-Philippe would have it. Pridie had had no trace of that. She could not reasonably have expected it. The winds keened too fierce at that dreadful height of the intellect, the frosts over the waste doomed lands were too sharp for that warm silver—

She shivered suddenly, so that Jean-Philippe looked down at her, puzzled, and, recovering, she smiled up at him.

How finally trapped you were, she thought, in what it pleased you to call your values. In this the face of God and the Devil were certainly one. Almost always they could as accurately be called your weakness.

Her compassion, and her curious secret timidity with people, had bound her to Pridie with links of tempered steel. Pridie could so easily lend her an unquestioned secondary identity in the shadow of his own. It had given her a kind of security. But there was no health and no dynamic to it. It could go nowhere. Pridie wanted in her both the mother and the skilled harlot. That was not notably original; many men wanted that. But in Pridie these desires hummed with the high tension of insanity. They seemed completely polarized; he could appear two quite separate persons, joined arbitrarily by the accident of his body.

She had been able to discover no key to this cyclic sway in him, though indeed his spells of impotence, as now, often pointed like some sad shattered spear to appalling pressures in his work. Appropriately too, they had hovered like a blank white sheet over the period that his mother had visited him, and over the month that followed. She could not bear to remember him visually when he was like that. At such times he was a child crying, with the tragic knowledge of a man.

The transformation to his other personality was truly fantastic, a Merlin's trick. It still did not make him particularly gay. On the contrary, his remarkable potency at such times seemed curiously weightless, fragile, and insecure. He was much too lucid. He watched himself profoundly, as in a mirror, as if marvelling at his powers. Yet he could never really hide that he was haunted already with the certainty of their impermanence. He was like a surgeon, struck fatally by the same disease that he studied, and given no secure time in which to complete his work.

That analogy was really quite apt, for indeed she felt herself to be rather like that then, a subject of surgery, manipulated. She could have been some animal of no particular sentimental importance to humanity; a rabbit, say, a monkey, something about which you could not fashionably be expected to feel too much sympathy, the needs of science being what they were. Like that, she too could have been splayed out and pegged down by wrists and ankles on some sheer sterilized white table, beneath blazing white lights. For his attention to her body then was dedicated and indecent. She sensed that he feared even to close his eyes, as though he felt that by doing so he might forever lose all chance of learning the secret; as though some frail lie or fold of her skin or some quiver of it or some subtle change in her expression when she called out might suddenly and perfectly deliver to him the tangled way out of the labyrinth.

He sought that way out desperately at such times, and, from her, a dark peace which she was now sure that no woman could ever give him. For the true monster was imprisoned within this man himself, immortal and terrible beyond any which his schoolboy's farcical world of action could produce. (What on earth after all was the mere taking or loss of a city? He could not even free his own locked inner citadels.) Yet his monster was decorous enough in public. (Pridie came after all from a very good family.) It even permitted him, by the bitterest irony, a prince's easy bearing.

Even now, it was hard for her intellectually to grasp that she would leave this half-man, half-child, with his scarred and broken left hand. (As if even that were really an accident. Fate was generally mercilessly apt in the symbols it selected.) But who else would help him? Would not the next simply cry his shame out on the winds?

But the question was nicely academic only. Her blood had already decided it fiercely, her body had taken over. It was that which flaunted itself now upon this other and convenient male, whose rearing plunging force she would make cleanse and pleasure her, in the conventional and approved and slightly comic but generally satisfactory manner, if it killed her, even if she had to seduce him at high noon on the steps of the National Assembly.

She saw Justin dancing with his wife. The city said (it was after all a very small city) that Mme. Justin had just taken the first steps to divorce him. The city said that, after ten years of marriage, he had started to go back to the supple charms of the Vieng Rattray; she, emancipated, would not accept this hallowed privilege of his sex and caste. The news had upset Jeanette. It clashed too much with the grave gracious timelessness of Laos. It smacked too much of the stale methodical courts of law of the great modern cities of the world. She thought of the beaked blithe face above her. At least he would be safe from her in that respect. She knew that she would never try too hard now to hold any man to marriage, to so long and sullen a covenant. Probably no one was ever really built for it. It was asking too much. She reflected that there was at least that one good thing about perversion, or intimate contact with it. It sharpened your view of reality.

"Your ham," said Jean-Philippe unromantically.

She looked up at him, startled, and realized that the stack of records had come to an end. MacNaughton had got up to reverse it.

"Of course," she said.

Jean-Philippe held her chair for her, and she sat, conscious, without meeting them, of Pridie's eyes from the next table turning to and away from her.

"We thought we'd lost you for good," said Mary-Frances.

Jean-Philippe looked down at her and smiled.

"The dark," he said. "You lose your sense of time, you know."

"Your timing was fine," said Mary-Frances. "You two made rather a pretty picture, in fact. Peter nearly fell off his chair watching it."

"Fancy," said Jean-Philippe, hoping that Pridie had not heard that. He did not think that Pridie would take kindly to being mocked about Jeanette, however lightly.

"Have some wine, Mary-Frances," said Jeanette, in a suspiciously dulcet tone.

Mary-Frances looked at her sharply.

"And stop being provocative," said MacNaughton, returned from his records. "Come and dance instead."

When McNaughton and Mary-Frances had left, Jean-Philippe said:

"That's an old Southern custom, Jeanette?"

"What?"

"Mary-Frances," said Jean-Philippe. "Taking the mickey out of people."

"Oh, Mary-Frances is all right," said Jeanette. "I don't mind anyway."

"Good," said Jean-Philippe. "How are you, Jeanette?"

"Tingling," said Jeanette. "Just waking up, thanks."

"It must be the wine."

Jeanette looked at him and smiled.

"Of course," she said.

"Get you some more?"

"Why not?" said Jeanette. "Please."

"Splendid," said Jean-Philippe. "And a mousse? Say a small mousse?"

"I've always felt a deep interest in small mousses," said Jeanette.

He took their plates and presented the plates to the Chinese behind the side-table and filled the glass. The Chinese watched him impassively. He would have looked the same if Jean-Philippe had walked up to him balancing the glass on his nose like a seal. He said economically:

"Mousse?"

"Two mousse," said Jean-Philippe.

The Chinese served him with two ochre mounds, and capped them swiftly with whipped cream from a large silver ladle, with a skilful backhand flip of his wrist. He was clearly good at that. He knew it. The ochre mounds looked slightly obscene. Jean-Philippe balanced them and Jeanette's glass and turned and nearly fell over Pridie, himself arrived with a clatter of ravaged plates and knives and forks, presumably his own and Susan's.

"Hullo, Pridie," said Jean-Philippe. "So sorry."

"Evening," said Pridie, after a moment. He was standing with a plate in each hand. He looked like a statue of justice.

"How are things?" said Jean-Philippe.

Pridie went on looking at him. After a while he said:

"Fine."

Scintillating, thought Jean-Philippe as he gave Jeanette her glass and her mousse, and put down his own. If Pridie was going to get frigid, he might as well give him cause for it. Jean-Philippe ate his mousse moodily.

"Jeanette."

"Jean-Philippe?"

"Perhaps after all I should aggress just a little."

She looked at him and considered him gravely for some moments, holding her spoon quite still, above her empty plate. She put the spoon down gently. He heard the sound when it met the plate. It was tiny and exact and very clear.

"Perhaps you should, Jean," she said, "even on your own terms."

"Good," he said, after a moment. "In that case, it would be pleasant to dance again."

"Yes."

"And to hell with the coffee."

"We can afford to be devils about the coffee," she said.

She could sense the change in him at once, when he took her on the floor this time. There was nothing mentally absent about him now. Not at all.

"All right," he said, above her. "Why?"

She laughed up at him.

"Why this?" she said. 'It's your Gallic charm, Jean."

"Ha, ha."

"All right," she said, more soberly. "Because it suits me. Because I want to.'

"It's a good reason," he said, still probing. "There's always a good reason."

"Yes, of course."

"Interesting, though," he said.

"Fascinating."

He looked down at her and laughed, admitting the truce to questions, and, glancing up again, saw Pridie in the gloom ahead,

dancing as closely as he was, but with the dark and lissom Susan.
Pridie looked very much at his ease.

"Nice-looking girl," said Jeanette, astutely, having presumably
seen them too as she turned with Jean-Philippe.

"Yes, isn't she?"

"Well, the king is dead, long live the king," she said. "It's very
healthy."

She sounded very cheerful about it. She had certainly got her
thumbs down conclusively on Pridie. Well, it was making a
woman out of her. There was nothing like a little good red-blooded
hatred to give a person stature.

When the reverse side of the batch of records ended, Jean-
Philippe watched Pridie guide Susan over to the sofa and armchairs at the far end of the room. He glanced at Jeanette.

"Join them?"

She looked back at him mockingly.

"Why not?" she said.

They reached the corner, and Jean-Philippe said:

"Room for us, Peter?"

"Of course," said Pridie, getting up elegantly.

Jean-Philippe waited until Jeanette had sat in one of the armchairs, then moved to one beside her. Susan said, from the sofa:

"Lots of room here, you know."

"I'm sure he'll be happier where he is," said Pridie.

Susan laughed, and Jean-Philippe looked at Pridie quickly.
Pridie was leaning back comfortably in his armchair. Jean-Philippe
said:

"Very busy these days, Pridie?"

"So-so," said Pridie.

"A lot of trips recently, I believe," said Jean-Philippe. "You
know, Savannakhet, Luang Prabang and so on."

Pridie sat completely still. Then he took off his light rimless
glasses and cleaned them meticulously with the white silk handkerchief from his breast pocket. It was the first time that Jean-
Philippe had seen him take it out. So it was not painted on after
all.

Pridie put his glasses on again and his flat light-grey eyes looked
at Jean-Philippe and flicked over to Jeanette.

"Of course some people will talk," said Pridie.

"You mean me, Peter?" said Jeanette. "No. Finally, I'm not
really so interested, you know."

"Liqueur?" said Jean-Philippe.

The Chinese was standing by his elbow, with a tray. He was
again loyally supporting his national myth of inscrutability. He

already looked like a permanent fixture. The glasses pinged in a nice faint friendly manner as he set them down on the table. Jean-Philippe saw the rich amber of the brandies, the oiled clear brilliant white of the Cointreau.

"It doesn't matter," said Pridie.

"I thought that your work always mattered to you all too much," said Jeanette.

Pridie examined her flatly again. He looked as though he could happily have throttled her. He said to her:

"You find that curious?"

"Psychologically, no," said Jeanette.

"My God, all these big words again," said Pridie. "You can always reduce it to just that?"

"It's sometimes very revealing when you do," said Jeanette.

"Cheers," said Jean-Philippe.

But that cheery manly greeting seemed to have quite the wrong effect. Pridie looked at him for some seconds before he appeared able to focus properly. Pridie was having one of his icy spells again. Jean-Philippe recalled the night that Saovong had cremated his old mum, when Pridie had looked at Short like that.

"You two would probably get on rather well after all," said Pridie deliberately. "Your friend Raymond's a good clean liberal too. Somebody else who thinks you get your sums right these days just by being nice and moderate and understanding."

"Do I, now?" said Jean-Philippe.

"Why all the blood?" said Susan. "Would somebody mind telling me what it's all about?" Her lovely eyes were moving from one to the other of them. She looked neglected.

"Don't you, Raymond?" said Pridie. "Isn't that what you're always writing? Isn't it?"

"I'm flattered," said Jean-Philippe. "I didn't know that you read what I wrote."

"Oh," said Pridie, "I read it. I read it all right."

"Couldn't we just play party games instead?" said Susan.

"God help you all," said Pridie. He was really getting into his stride now. "You and your goddamned sense of social justice. What the hell is that? It doesn't exist. It never did. Just an abstraction for long-haired academics. For introverted neurotic professors of moral philosophy to play with."

"Introverted is good," said Jeanette. She was looking straight at Pridie. "Neurotic is good."

But Pridie was not to be deflected. It was Jean-Philippe that he was gunning for, at the moment.

"That famous so-called French spirit," he went on thoughtfully.

"Anarchy and pure egotism. Dressed up in a psuedo-liberal realism. The French gift of intellectual clarity, Christ. It didn't really do you so much good in Indo-China, did it?"

"Pridie," said Jean-Philippe patiently. "Look, no one really minds if you want to be bastards, you know. Just so long as you're reasonably successful ones. You do want to win, don't you? So be as big a sod as you like, if you think that that will help. But let's just go on the probabilities a moment. You really think that you can win here with absolutely no support in the country, Pridie? Because you've got none. Why should you have any? What have you ever done for the damned place except sow corruption in its cities and entrench a bunch of old-time war-lords in power just because they said fervently that they were anti-communist? (My God, and how they are, but for all the wrong reasons.) And bowed their heads appropriately when you played the Star-Spangled Banner at them? If the people see you like that, Pridie, do you *really* think that you can sort this out permanently now by your famous rugged solutions by force? Like a lot of boy scouts with dollars in one hand and guns in the other?"

"*Why* are they getting so excited?" said Susan.

"It's Peter's sex-life really," said Jeanette.

"Really?" said Susan, looking much more interested.

Pridie did not seem to have heard them at all. He was still concentrating on Jean-Philippe.

"You honestly think that?" he said incredulously, and with complete contempt. "You honestly think that there is really ever any other kind of solution, anywhere?"

Jean-Philippe looked at him in silence for some time.

"My God," he said at last, with a kind of awe. "You really are like that, aren't you, Pridie? Force is the only truly permanent solution ever, in anything, anywhere?"

"Do you even have to discuss it?" said Pridie quietly. "Isn't that obviously true? Always. Not just in this."

At that moment, you could no longer just laugh Pridie out of court. He was, even, curiously impressive. Perhaps it was because he had not raised his voice at all. Yet his quiet statement had all the impact of a lost cry in the dark. For he sounded completely alone. He had spoken finally, not just with absolute conviction, but even with resignation. It was as if this were his final human truth, simply what he most deeply knew, what he had lived. And, despite his casual contempt, he did not sound as though he really had much hope of convincing them of what he said. Nonetheless, he had put his scarred left hand on the table in front of him, broken and misshapen and humiliating. It was as if he were decently trying to show these people the best concrete evidence he could find of this final and desolate truth. He looked down and saw what he had done, and he brought his hand back quickly to his side.

He thought bitterly that the Chinese major had known all that there was to know about that kind of truth.

CHAPTER XX

AT that time, four years before, Pridie's job was to organize a network of agents in a part of the Yunnan. The Chinese communists had completely proved their military power in Korea. From then, a thrust by them from the Yunnan could not be excluded, south into Thailand to take the whole great rice-growing bowl of South East Asia, and to cut off the Malay peninsula and Singapore and Diem's South Viet Nam. High-altitude aerial reconnaissance, and a screen of agents in the Yunnan, seemed among the few means by which the West could get some prior warning of such an attack.

The need to get an efficient screen of agents into place had become more apparent since the Americans had discovered, finally, that the Chiang Kai-shek remnant battalions, who had been cut off into North Burma by the Red Chinese victories in South-West China, were no more than a costly farce. The polite theory, vigorously promoted by Chiang and the China Lobby, had been that this excellent body of some seven thousand men provided a guerrilla force which could raid into the soft under-belly of China with telling effect, and serve as an unbeatable source of intelligence. The Americans had therefore continued generously to parachute them arms and money for years. They finally found that the majority of these heroes regularly sold the arms to the Chinese communists, and used their swelled funds further to develop the extensive opium plantations which they owned on the lands from which they had ejected the Burmese.

Pridie had thus little enough to start with. The operation was highly dangerous from the outset. It was a crash programme. The mathematicians at Foggy Bottom and Langley had no doubt done their post-mortem on it afterwards with relish. Almost all the usual iron rules had necessarily to be broken, including that which determined that no one operative should even know more than any one other, his contact. Pridie himself was by no means the ideal choice. He was simply the best then available. His time with Western Enterprises in Formosa had helped him to learn some Mandarin, and six ruthless months in the cinema and headphones rooms at Langley had made him fairly fluent over the most common two thousand five hundred characters.

His identity too was just the best that could be fabricated under the circumstances. It creaked. No one could ever have passed him off as pure Chinese. He was, thus, the son of a British Shanghai banker, long dead, and a Pekin woman. He worked in Pekin as a minor official in agricultural planning, and had specialized in local irrigation. (The brilliantly detailed course which they had given him in Langley had really made him quite professional in this.) They had selected the centre of his operations in the Yunnan as meticulously. It was a mountain village, still virtually feudal, where the central communist organization had not yet really penetrated; it did not even have a village committee.

But, still, too many things could go wrong, and probably only a lunatic or a very brave man would have accepted the mission in the first place. So Pridie was content to play his hand very slowly. He was careful to infringe no entrenched rights in the village, and to show himself as useful as possible in promoting the irrigation development for which ostensibly he was there. His caution paid off. The villagers were not abnormally suspicious, and accepted him without comment within two months. He had given it out, tactfully, and shown by his actions, that he was more interested in his profession than in politics.

Pridie had gone into the Yunnan with three other agents, two Formosans, and a renegade Cantonese. It was one of the Formosans who betrayed him. So, like almost anything else that his agency did anywhere, there was that final accent of the sordid to it. It was somehow always that which capped the spurious glamour of the adventure, the melodrama, the bad theatre. Even his capture was ignominious. They took him in the middle of the night, when he was in bed. They effectively denied him his standard exit. One of them covered him with a machine-pistol, and another went straight to his table, and unscrewed the false top of his fountain pen for the poison pellets.

The initial interrogation was rather long-winded. Indeed, his captors gave the impression that they had all the time in the world, or that really they already knew all the answers, and were simply going through the motions for the sake of good Chinese form. From another angle, this confidence and lack of urgency were frightening.

Pridie did not see the major at all in the first fourteen days, except once, in the first hour. Even then, the major had only sat at the back of the room, behind a small wooden table. He had said nothing. Most of the time he had not even looked at Pridie, but out of the window, which gave on to the small town's main street. He had looked frankly bored. He was, however, clearly the leader. Pridie knew that at once. Subtly, the manners of the others in the room confirmed it. The major was of a different stamp. Probably he had been sent down specially from Pekin.

The major was an extraordinarily good-looking man. He had fine features, perhaps a little effeminate, and the slim manicured fingers of a girl. There was a small black mole on the left of his chin. Short black hairs grew from it. It obsessed him, perhaps as the only flaw to his beauty. He touched it sometimes, lightly, with the tips of his fingers. He could have been thirty-four or thirty-five.

Pridie found their first techniques trite. He would have suffered them as a criminal suspect in the States. At night, they beamed blinding spotlights on him and, unseen themselves, shot sudden questions in upon him, with the patient merciless precision of hunters, fanned finally about some cornered beast, normally popularly supposed to be dangerous, now winded and stilled for execution. He knew these skilled hunters from the daytime; a captain, a lieutenant, a civilian. He never knew whether the major was sometimes there with them too, behind their sharp lights at night.

But they were more original in the way in which they timed these sessions, and, sometimes, changed their tone totally. A few minutes could pass between the sessions, or hours. The first time that one followed closely on another, early on, it caught him unprepared, over-relaxed, and vulnerable. In it, it seemed to him that they put exactly the same questions as they had asked twenty minutes before. He tried to give the same answers, word for word. His interrogators made no comment. It was a mad parody, seriously played, deeply disturbing. It was the first of the many times that they made him doubt his sanity.

In general the interrogations were coldly analytic, about his work, his agents, his organization's structure in South East Asia. But sometimes, when he went in, the tone was startlingly different. They offered him coffee and cigarettes. If it was at night, they would have shaded their murderous lights. They asked him then about things apparently quite divorced from his work; his childhood, his student days, his interests, his authors, what he thought of the American system of government, of Britain, of France, of Germany, of Russia's part in the Second World War. At first, wary of traps, he would not talk even in these sessions.

He could never discover any pattern to their timing of the sessions, or to their complete changes in tone; their genius was to keep him uncertain, unable to predict. Nor could he really sleep, even when the sessions stopped for eight or ten hours, or, once, for almost a full day. He had two jailers, a tall, broad, and bald Yunnanese, and a squat Manchurian with narrow eyes and the forearms of a blacksmith. One of these men would come into his cell about every half-hour (he could only estimate it; they had taken his watch from him, when they took his belt and the laces from his boots) and make him stand and say his name. The ritual amused him at first, but in time he saw its effectiveness. Within six days, he spoke only an inane echo of himself into a void. The hard contours of his personality already seemed to have begun to blur. James Peter MacDonald Pridie became no more than a name from a book, or someone he had once known years before, or a face half-recalled from a dream.

The cell's one light was not conducive to sleep anyway. It was always on. He could not reach it, and he had nothing he could throw to break it; besides, they could always have replaced it. Its beat was painfully like that of the lights in the investigating room. The Great Leap Forward had evidently overshot this town by some distance, for its electricity plant must have been primitive. It produced its light in tiny throbbing waves, as inevitable as water controlled to drop on some wretched victim's anchored forehead. He could not escape it in the cell even by day. There was little else to look at, except the privy, a hole in the stone corner, of no marked scenic value. The one barred window was too high to reach. He had, once, leapt with a great effort to see out of it. He saw a great rectangular concrete yard, closed by a high brick wall. There were two heavy closed wooden crates in the far right corner. He could not see out over the high wall.

They controlled his food as ruthlessly, in a definite trend to starvation levels. Nevertheless, there were short-term exceptions to this, again completely unpredictable. A total absence of bread or rice or fish could quite well follow a very civilized session in the investigating room. As inscrutably, a good meal could follow the most vicious interrogation. This lack of coherence had an alarmingly disproportionate effect on him. He felt morally outraged, almost hysterical. It took him time to see what they were doing. They sought a neat Pavlovian destruction of the patterns in him. You lived by patterns. You could support almost anything if you could predict it, a superior's sadism, a guard's cruelty, a lover's coldness, perhaps even physical torture and death. You positively insisted that villains be evil and saints good. Disruption of that law sent the mind wailing into lunacy and helplessness. It was the unexpected that could shatter the bravest man.

By the eleventh day Pridie was talking freely about himself, always scrupulously avoiding anything to do with his work. He found it a great relief to do so, after the psychological pressures they had put upon him. He could see no harm in it. Privately he thought them fools for listening so attentively. It even strengthened him. He felt that by talking he at least maintained a slight bond of humanity with his captors. More important, it seemed a way by which he could entrench his identity against their constant threat to disintegrate it.

He talked of the great house in Boston. He supposed that it had been rather a gaunt place, always incredibly neat and clean and disciplined. It was set in a wide avenue lined by trees. His mother and his great-aunt were its main characters. Pridie had not known his father. The colonel had died before Pridie was born, killed by some disgrace which (or so Pridie inferred from the women's rare reference to it) he had richly deserved. The house censured this unfortunate man as strictly. No picture of him hung from its walls. He was faceless, erased so efficiently that the child could fairly have thought himself the product of yet another immaculate conception.

Visitors were rare in Pridie's first years. His mother's family had always been army, and this had directed all their social life. His father's fall had evidently been resounding enough to exclude his widow totally from that society, and so from any. At least the disaster did not affect them much economically, for his mother's family had money. With it, the two women had canalized their energies into a drive to regain their just place in the world, which was now that part of Boston society which excluded the military. It was a fair reply to them, or to fate. The women's patient and ruthless zeal had begun to reap its rewards in the boy's seventh year.

So these two women and their curious dedication dominated his extreme youth. The old lady was slight, aristocratic, and inviolably virginal. She seemed ageless. You could not imagine her as a little girl. She must have emerged just like that from the womb, her rimless glasses with their thin gold bridge already precise upon her, and the delicate skin of her face already set in its final fine parchment. Benign though this face appeared, it covered formidable forces. Passion must always have fallen back at once from it, as if knowing instinctively when it was beat. He could never recall her by any kind of scent or smell. Obsessionally clean, she restricted her toilet accessories to talcum powder and eau de cologne. She made no statement of her sex.

But she seemed to like to talk to him. During the evenings, she could relate effortlessly to him the names of the men in her family, and his mother's, who had passed from military academy to acceptable appointments, and the dates when they had been promoted to high rank, and the intricacies of his geneology, which she traced back to the family in Perthshire with whose descendents she still corresponded regularly. Her views on the importance of race and blood were uncompromising. She had a lethal way of saying the words nigger and Jew, always prefacing them with a kind of double sniff. She stressed constantly to him the high ideals and duties which she considered that his birth had set upon him. Yet she was always embarrassingly generous to him with gifts, as if here at least she did not feel that she needed to limit her humanity.

The imprint of this powerful old lady on his mother was clear, though sophisticated by the latter's greater first-hand knowledge of the world and its societies, which she had gained during her travels with her husband. His disgrace and death had probably not changed her much. She was a tall woman, physically elegant, and highly ambitious, for herself and, if no longer for her husband, then for her son. She taught him to read, and, herself an adequate pianist, to play the piano. Severe, never spontaneous, she was however surprisingly tolerant of the normal fears and frailties of his childhood; indeed, even until he was eight, and began his official schooling, she would still sometimes recognize his one great terror, that of being alone in the dark, and accept him into her room and bed at night.

Pridie did not find a great deal else to say about his childhood and early youth, beyond give shorthand sketches of these two salient characters. He had progressed well enough through school and university to the minor post in the State Department that his Mother's influence had obtained for him in Washington late in the World War. He supposed that he had learned to depend on himself early, under the grey matriarchical disciplines of the house, almost cut off from the world. Certainly, he already read very widely from the age of seven, and could already perform competently on the piano in the interludes when his mother would present him during the afternoon teas which she began to give that year for the ladies of some of the city's older families.

His reward for giving his questioners an edited version of this (he supposed) rather normal and dull picture of himself as a child and young man was prompt. They began the physical torture on the thirteenth day. He still had enough mental energy to feel some contempt for their lack of originality. They started with the old trick of the long bamboo slivers under the fingernails. He was able to hold himself steady and watch the slivers burn down to the end. That night his guards' repeated entry into his cell, the repetitive need to stand and state his name idiotically, was no particular hardship, and the call back to the examination room early in the morning almost a relief.

They were more enterprising this time. It was the hallmark of the little major. It was he who supervised the application of the apparatus to Pridie's left hand. The apparatus was a melodramatic thing of black metal, with handscrews at the sides. Perhaps it was Chinese, or perhaps the major had picked it up from some obscene antiquary in Europe on his travels. It was mounted on a heavy chest, about ten inches from one edge. Two thick buckled straps ran across the chest, between the appliance and the end. When a man knelt by the chest, as Pridie was required to do, the straps fitted neatly over his wrist and forearm. The two levels of black metal fitted above and below his fingers, across their second joints. A small man in an olive uniform tightened the screws. The major sat in a wooden chair near the chest, his legs crossed. He had sent the other men away. A single spotlight was focused on Pridie's strapped left hand. He heard the bones break. The hand, nakedly white in the strong light, writhed like a trapped animal, like something that lived independently.

The major must then have made some sign to the small man in the olive uniform, or else the next step had been arranged before. The man bent under the light and loosened the screws and reset them higher, across the knuckles and across the first joint of Pridie's thumb. So far Pridie had not heard the major say anything. This time Pridie fainted when he heard the bones break. They must have thrown cold water over him then, because it was dripping from his face when he opened his eyes, and some of it had splashed irritatingly across the left lens of his glasses. He found that he was looking directly on to his broken hand. From so near, it seemed enormous and alien and crouching. His head must have fallen forward on to the chest just beside it. He lifted his head and tried to kneel up straight again. They had turned on another light. Besides that which still beamed solitary on his hand, the new light fell equally on his own face and the major's. The major's face was delicate, beautiful, and reposed. When Pridie closed his right eye, experimenting automatically with his glasses, the blurred left lense distorted the major's face strangely.

"Tell me," said the major pleasantly. "Just when was it that you discovered your sexual—weakness?"

He was touching the mole on his chin very lightly.

Pridie stared back at him incredulously. The major glanced at him and took out a cigarette case and opened it. He seemed quite prepared to give Pridie time, to make due allowances for his condition.

"Your—ambivalence, should we say?" he said finally. "Or, frankly, would one not call it something a little stronger than that?"

The major tapped the cigarette precisely on his case and examined its end and looked back at Pridie and added reasonably:

"To be clear, I don't myself have the slightest feeling against homosexuals, you know."

"Homosexuals?" said Pridie.

It was the first word that he had spoken, and he realized that it sounded remarkably hollow. But the man must be mad, he thought. He licked his lips and said patiently:

"I have never been a homosexual."

That was most certainly true. But, even as Pridie said that, it struck him suddenly, with a hideous personal immediacy, that the man's face was indeed extraordinarily beautiful, with the high graceful structure of its bones, the delicate precision of the lines, the thin clear mouth. The experience seemed to Pridie a shocking, terrifying insight into himself. He was aware of this man's beauty in his loins, with a restless, physical pain. The major looked directly at him at exactly that moment, and met his eyes and smiled. Pridie had never before seen any face which seemed to have so final and complete and damning a knowledge of him.

"Naturally not," said the major. "Not overtly, that is. Otherwise, if you were reconciled to it, I think that you would hardly be mixed up in this sort of sordid and spurious heroics."

How could he answer the utter certainty in that voice? As the major said it, it was not even an accusation. It was a statement of fact. Here, truth was a thing that this man made.

Pridie heard himself begin to talk desperately about his work. Now he was being really splendidly co-operative. The major could not possibly have asked for anything better. Pridie was getting it all out most diligently. In the appalling lucidity of that room, it seemed to him that only by talking honestly and exhaustively about his work could he disprove this other lurking monstrous thing, or at least cover the suspicion of it decently again, the terrible rift which this gentle, smiling, and devilish man had so skilfully set (or was it simply discerned?) in him.

He realized that the major, by some sign to the small man in the olive uniform, had called back to the others, and that they sat now somewhere at tables beyond the rim of light, writing and recording. Pridie was not particularly interested in that. He was too busy destroying his work, the clever and intricate organization which they had built, and upon whose success the fate of so many could depend. For how could that possibly be important any longer in this blinding room of judgment? How could *they* ever know of his struggle here, his mortal fight with his angel, or dare to assess it if they did? He was already sure that his questioners would kill him when they had squeezed him dry. It was standard procedure. One thing alone seemed essential to him now; that he should be able to die in some way intact, as a human being, with dignity, as a man, with that at least regained.

But, most cruelly, they did not kill him afterwards. It was the final unforgiveable insult. They allowed him no sleep or rest, no doubt so that he should appear the more completely broken, but took him back at once by forced marches to the first of the Shan villages over the border into Burma, one which before had been favourable to him. At its outskirts, they tied his wrists in front of him, so that his hands would be the first thing that anyone would see, and they hung a small bell about his throat, and pushed him forward on the road.

There was the theory, he knew, that the Turks had done just that to Lawrence when they took him, with his tragic puritan half-hidden terror of his own homosexuality. They had held him down in a cell, and a man had raped his anus. Then they had let him go free. There was no way in which they could more brutally and conclusively have shown that they did not think that they could possibly have anything more to fear from him.

"Powder my nose," said Susan, and got up with an air of outraged finality.

Pridie barely noticed her go. He was looking at Jean-Philippe with hatred; not of the man himself, but of what he thought. Indeed, he knew that he would have liked the other to accept him. So it seemed to him the more vital that the Frenchman should understand him. Without thinking, Pridie was massaging his own left hand with his right as he watched him.

"Isn't it always that in the end?" he said patiently. "Force, or the threat of force? Isn't that the final discovery, the one basic truth that doesn't change? However much graciousness you can graft on top of it? Look at the sanctions of our society, or of yours in France. We're of the same civilization, Jean-Philippe. You know the others as well as I do. The communists. My God, they're not amateurs in this, are they? It's dog eat dog. They have no mercy. And hasn't it always been like that, really? Isn't this the only really strange thing, that one can take so long to discover it?"

His voice had changed subtly as he talked. Towards the end, under the hard short matter-of-fact sentences, there was, again, the high thin faint note of desolation.

"That's the final discovery, is it?" said Jean-Philippe. "That's your final discovery, is it?"

"For God's sake!" said Pridie, with a burst of anger. "And you seem to think *us* naïve! What on earth else do you really expect from the world?"

But the Frenchman did not answer. He was looking down at Pridie's hands. Pridie looked down too, and saw what he had been doing with them, and pulled them back abruptly out of sight, down to the chair, beside his thighs. With them bunched beside him there, it looked for a moment as if he were preparing suddenly to launch himself tremendously upwards and outwards. Jean-Philippe looked away at once, quickly, too quickly.

"Well?" said Pridie. "Well?"

The Frenchman opposite him looked at Jeanette; not, Pridie thought, obviously to try to gather her in as an ally against him; probably Jean-Philippe too had hardly even noticed that the girl was still there. Pridie followed his eyes. Jeanette was looking fixedly at Jean-Philippe, and in that instant Pridie knew certainly and with a sharp shocking pain that he had lost her completely and for all time.

"Pridie," said Jean-Philippe.

He looked back at the Frenchman.

"Yes?"

"You poor sod," said Jean-Philippe. "You play to lose, don't you?"

"That's out of some second-rate French film, is it, Raymond?"

"You have to lose," said Jean-Philippe. "You see, that's what you really want."

Pridie looked back at him, now hating him utterly. He found that he needed to make a great effort to control his voice.

"God damn you," he said at last, very softly, making it sound almost like a benediction. "We shan't lose. I shall not lose."

CHAPTER XXI

THE day following MacNaughton's party Jean-Philippe got up at two p.m. and had some lunch at the Constellation. He had left

MacNaughton's house at six that morning, when the curfew lifted, and gone straight home to sleep. When he finished his lunch he walked across to Quinim's house, but, though it was a Sunday, Quinim was not there; they said that he had been at the Ministry of Information since early that morning. Jean-Philippe found him there. Quinim saw him almost at once. Nosavan's artillery had broken Konglé at the Nam Ca Dinh, and the Second Battalion was already retreating on Vientiane. The Pathet had not committed their forces. Conciliation with Nosavan was now obviously impossible, and Quinim judged that Nosavan's troops would be at the city within a few days. Jean-Philippe went back to his room and wrote his cables and walked down to the Post Office and mailed them.

As he was coming back, and turned into Samsènethai Road, he bumped into a man coming from the opposite direction. His file with the copies of his cables fell to the pavement, and the man stooped at once and picked them up.

"My apologies," said the man.

He was short and slight, dressed simply in a khaki bush shirt and slacks and open leather sandals. He could have been a *commis* from a bank or someone who worked for one of the ministries. He was bareheaded and good-looking, with very regular features, and rather light-complexioned; perhaps a *métis*.

"It was my fault," said Jean-Philippe. His mind caught at something suddenly.

"But I know you, of course," he said.

"I don't think so, m'sieu," said the man. "I don't think that I've had the pleasure—"

But he looked slightly disconcerted. His French was perfect.

"Perhaps very briefly somewhere," he added, as if doing his best to help.

"I'm sure of it," said Jean-Philippe. "In some city somewhere."

The man had recovered himself. Now, he could have been a little amused about something. He smiled.

"Perhaps in some crowd somewhere, m'sieu. In some city, as you say. Some other city."

"Hanoi?" said Jean-Philippe. "You're Vietnamese?"

"Yes," said the man. "But not Hanoi. That's a cold city, you know, hard as a whore. Perhaps it was Saigon."

"Well," said Jean-Philippe, frowning in recollection. "Well. Somehow I thought that it was some other, I'll remember it. But the Constellation is just there. Come and have a drink while I try."

The man smiled again.

"My regrets, sincerely," he said, "but I have only a few minutes."

"You're working?"

"Yes," said the man.

"My God," said Jean-Philippe. "It's Sunday. Even at week-ends?"

"Even at week-ends, m'sieu."

"Well," said Jean-Philippe cheerfully, "another time, perhaps. In some other place."

"Another time," said the man, "with great pleasure."

Jean-Philippe looked after him for awhile, puzzled, but the man did not look back. Jean-Philippe shrugged and went on and into the Constellation and ordered a Pernis. With luck it would clear his head; it was still heavy from the all-night party. He poured a little water into the Pernis and watched it explode in slow motion in the yellow liquid like an inverted white atomic bomb.

The night before, he had not danced much with Jeanette after his battle of wits with Pridie; once only, for the sake of the record. What was between the girl and him could wait. He had thought that further provocation of Pridie at the party would probably have ended physically, to the detriment of MacNaughtons furniture. Violence, which ironically seemed Pridie's final answer to everything, was indeed probably the only issue left to any further relations with him. So Jean-Philippe had spent the rest of the night talking with Dumergue and MacNaughton, or dancing with the supple and yielding Susan.

Jean-Philippe turned his back to the bar and hooked himself on it with his elbows and surveyed the tables and the drinkers. Laclos, with the livid V-shaped scar on his cheek, whom he had not seen since the first day of the elections, here in this bar, was sitting at a table talking to a man whom Jean-Philippe did not know. At that moment the unknown got up and patted Laclos on the shoulder and left, and Laclos looked up and met Jean-Philippe's eyes. He smiled and beckoned, and Jean-Philippe took his Pernis and went over to him.

"That drink looks low, Jean," said Laclos.

"It'll last me, thanks," said Jean-Philippe. "I was at an all-night party."

As Jean-Philippe sat down Laclos snapped his fingers for a waiter.

"*Aut' Ricard.*"

"You're salting it away, Paul," said Jean-Philippe. "You're celebrating?"

"The city, friend," said Laclos. "I drink to the city."

"Perhaps that's no bad thing, while we can."

"How long do you give it?" said Laclos.

"A week," said Jean-Philippe, "ten days."

Laclos considered his Ricard and permitted the waiter to add an equal amount of water to it. He raised his finger to stop him. He looked very serious about it.

"A week or ten days," he said, "about that. Much of the big Chinese money is getting out now, you know. They're intelligent, Jean. They generally make a much more accurate political barometer than your experts."

"Thank you," said Jean-Philippe. "Why didn't they get out earlier?"

"Ah, because they look on the taking of Vientiane as the really decisive thing. They have the most to fear from the pro-communists, naturally."

"Though it's the pro-Americans who'll take the city?"

"Precisely," said Laclos. "That's what dooms the Americans. If they or the Thai come in too obviously, so will the Viets. The Chinese like to gamble, you know, but not that much. They know damned well who would win then, short of a full-blown nuclear war. Take the only other alternative. Suppose the Viets don't come in, even. The Pathet will then simply draw Nosavan north into the mountains and slaughter him. In that case too the left wing will come back heavily into power."

"I'll buy that, Paul," said Jean-Philippe. "But the Americans won't."

"Ah, our friends, our allies."

"You love them all equally, Paul?"

"You can't blame their Embassy too much, you know," said Laclos. "Harmless onlookers, most of the time. Of course one blames them for letting just that happen. But the C.I.A., friend. They rule. They make this policy. That given, the rest is inevitable. When you're as extreme right wing as that, you put your shirt on anyone else who looks reasonably like you, however destructive they are."

"Why don't you get your wife out?" said Jean-Philippe.

Laclos looked at him sadly and shrugged.

"She's Chinese, remember. Where would she go? And I don't have the money, you know. Besides, we have the kids."

"Let's get these filled," said Jean-Philippe.

"Another thing," said Laclos, "she doesn't much like to be on her own, you know."

The Vietnamese came over with the two bottles and filled their glasses.

"Perhaps it won't be all that rough," said Jean-Philippe.

Laclos looked at him and laughed. He said:

"Tell me about your party, Jean."

"Not much to tell," said Jean-Philippe. "It was all night, of course, with the curfew. Let's see who you'd know. MacNaughton. Dumergue. Short and his wife. And Pridie."

"Ah, yes," said Laclos. "Friend Pridie."

Jean-Philippe laughed.

"I had a long argument with him," he said. "Very high class. All about ideals and values and that."

"I'm not so surprised," said Laclos seriously.

"No?"

"No," said Laclos. "Jean, after Nosavan and Boun Oum and company get in, don't count on staying in Laos too long."

"Pridie, is it?" said Jean-Philippe.

"Pridie," said Laclos. "And others."

Jean-Philippe looked at him without smiling. He knew that Laclos was generally amazingly well informed, through his wife's wide contacts with all shades of Chinese opinion, and through the influential Lao whose children he taught.

"What you were just saying, Paul," he said. "He's C.I.A?"

"Of course."

"It's funny how long it's taken me to get used to that idea," said Jean-Philippe. "Friend Pridie. Dear old Friend Pridie."

"Their cashier, really," said Laclos. "Their bribes man, you know. Not so very high up, but apparently he made some mistake or other in the past. He pays off all the informers, among other things, many of them Chinese. And he's one of their contact men with the ministers and army and police. One of the few men they've got who speaks an almost understandable French, of course."

"It's a job," said Jean-Philippe. "I suppose it's just another job."

Laclos studied his new Ricard and smiled.

"Your health," he said. "Yes, it's just a job. Like all jobs, it can sometimes look a little dirty on the ground."

"For instance?" said Jean-Philippe.

"For example," said Laclos, "Marivell."

"Marivell?" said Jean-Philippe, his stomach tightening. "What about Marivell?"

Laclos looked at him with amusement.

"Look," he said. "What kind of car does Pridie drive?"

"A Jeep station-wagon," said Jean-Philippe. "You know that. Blue."

"Yes," said Laclos, "I know that. And you remember what Marivell drove?"

"No," said Jean-Philippe, thinking back on the rare times that he had seen Marivell in his car. "Wait a minute. It was a station—"

"That's right," said Laclos. "A Jeep station wagon. Green. You could make a mistake about that. Somebody did."

"Come on," said Jean-Philippe.

Laclos looked at him.

"Marivell drove up in the evening to Ban-Keun in his station wagon," he said. "Remember? And the Pathet killed him that night, in front of his wife and kids."

"I know that," said Jean-Philippe.

"Then add this," said Laclos. "Pridie was up in Ban Keun too, the day before, also in his station wagon. He was there to buy votes with C.I.A. money for the Cédin candidates. The Pathet got a little annoyed about it. But they killed the wrong man."

Jean-Philippe sat back and said nothing. He was certain that Laclos was not lying. He had no particular reason to. Besides, Jean-Philippe was remembering Pridie's reactions, when Dumergue had come in that night and told them about Marivell's death, at exactly this table in exactly this bar.

"Never mind," said Laclos. "Perhaps they won't make the same mistake twice. Perhaps friend Pridie won't be with us for so very much longer either."

Jean-Philippe looked at him quickly.

"Just something I heard from a little bird," said Laclos.

"Chinese?"

"It could have been Chinese," said Laclos.

Laclos put down his glass quietly. He seemed suddenly to have sobered up.

"Also," he said, "it could have been nothing at all. Maybe I heard nothing at all."

"No?" said Jean-Philippe.

"Forget it," said Laclos. "Just now, I didn't say a word."

Jean-Philippe looked down at the table. He supposed that you could not really blame Pridie for Marivell's death. It was just one of these things. It had just happened on the side. Pridie hadn't caused it consciously. Marivell's death and the agony of his wife and children were just the kind of things that tended to happen on the side, if you did that kind of job. There would always be innocent bystanders.

But, if you could fairly argue that Pridie was guiltless in that, in his dedication, you could also perhaps argue by the same logic that you had no call to reach into his privileged isolation to help him with a warning, if he was in danger. If you did not warn him, it might legally make you party to a murder. Or, perhaps, just to a simple act of hygiene.

It was an interesting little moral puzzle.

He looked up at Laclos.

"I didn't hear you say anything," he said.

As Jean-Philippe walked back to his flat it struck him that there was really only one apt political comment which he could make under the circumstances, in reply to this knowledge about Pridie and about the true manner of Marivell's death. He looked at his watch; four o'clock. There was still time.

He took his car and drove down quietly to the river and turned to the right along it. It would be Konglé's men who would be floating in the river now, their bodies slackened out in their death, moving gently in the currents, a hundred kilometres south-east by Ba Ca Dinh.

There was only her small Renault in Jeanette's drive, under the open garage at the side of her *piloti*. He left his Deux Chevaux deliberately in the drive, where anyone passing would see it.

She opened the door almost at once. She looked very smart. She wore a light blue dress, of cocktail length, but sleeveless, and with a Vee in front to just between her breasts. He saw the blue satin sandals. Her face was made up, but her black hair was loose down to about her shoulders. She said:

"Do come in, Jean."

He could have been a guest expected for family tea.

She stood back from him. When the door shut behind him, she watched him gravely for awhile, as he stood still in front of her, then she put her hands up gently on his shoulders.

"I have waited for you so long," she said.

This time no jealous ghost of an absent lord stepped between them. It would have had to move fairly briskly, for their passion took them like an explosion. It had left no margin at all for decent prior hesitations. He could not afterwards recall either of them having said a single further word before they reached her bed. They had gone there with docility, absorbed and splendidly single-minded and diligent. The act of love was immediate, fierce, rich, and consuming. There was a nice arbitrary quality about it. At the same time, it was intact in its own right. It had made its own rules. You did not have to do a thing about it, fill in any of the details. All you had to do was like it. It was as complete in itself, and as deeply satisfying, as the chance glimpse of a woman's face perfect in the abrupt mushrooming glow of a lamp, masked then by warm darkness. Like that, its pleasure lapped on and on in the blood, long after the action was over. This act of love, then, had far outraced their conscious direction of it, and reached far into these primitive areas of awe. Fired at that particular moment by nothing more worthy than Jean-Philippe's final disgust with Pridie, and his sense of irony, it yet now appeared inevitable. It was all things; at once violent and peaceful, grave, and seeded and bubbling with laughter. It was a brief improbable pagan excursion, into which they had stumbled by accident, or conceivably by deep design, but certainly for most of the wrong motives; and it was outrageously successful.

He saw her body gold-brown beside him, her breasts and loins sharply white from where her bikini had covered her against the sun. It was as if she had just before thoughtfully painted on these new narrow clear provocative strips especially for this ceremony. Neither he nor she had thought to switch off the small shaded side lamp next to her bed. In its light her body looked clean and washed. It looked far too tranquil to have possibly had anything to do with their recent fused violence.

She said, perhaps really to herself:

"I wonder now how it could ever really have been different."

She sounded as if she were still slightly astonished.

"It can be simple, in the end," he said.

"In the end, yes," she said. "But you didn't exactly rush back into my arms, Jean."

"Well," he said. "We've all the time we want now."

She looked round at him doubtfully.

"All?" she said.

He thought that her mind had gone back to the coming attack.

"One shouldn't exaggerate it," he said, irritated at this intrusion of the world. "It'll pass."

She looked puzzled.

"Ah, that," she said, and smiled.

She was leaning up on one elbow to look round at him now. Her loosed jet black hair fell beautifully half across her throat, like a garment of modesty. The smile had smoothed out her features, like a hand. The love had anyway suffused them discreetly, putting a million pinpoints of light under the skin. It seemed too to have washed her eyes, which were now extraordinarily clear, the irises and pupils brilliantly defined. He felt, at that moment, a faint deferential shock of surprise that it was he who was object of this fluid rich intimacy, not another, an unknown. The feeling passed quickly.

"Why didn't you leave, Jeanette?" he said. "You could have gone, with the others."

"No," she said.

"No one would have blamed you, you know."

"I couldn't have left then," she said. "I could go now."

"Thank you."

She laughed.

"With you, Jean. I should take you."

"You got that in just in time."

But she seemed disturbed at what she had said.

"I wouldn't bind you, Jean. I wouldn't try to hold you. It would be for as long as it lasted."

"It's a fair proposition," he said gravely, mocking her. But she went on seriously:

"One can't have obligations in these things. It doesn't work. There shouldn't be any obligations."

He knew that she talked now of Pridie.

"It could go well, Jeanette," he said, as though to comfort her. "It could be very good."

She smiled suddenly, accepting the distraction. She said:

"Where would you take me, Jean?"

"There are many places," he said. "The places don't matter so much."

He did not want to talk too much, not about the future; that talking could kill things. But there were places he could show her, indeed, many places. Normandy itself. The sharp clean black-white mountains of the Val d'Isère, where he had climbed and skied. Chartres and Rouen and Reims. The parts of Paris that the outsiders did not see.

She had lain back on the bed. A car went past in the road outside. The side of its headlights spilled into the room and the light and shadow fled across her body and she did not move, and the car was gone. She smiled to herself.

"Well?"

"I thought that you'd never come back, Jean. It was a grey thought."

"Well. You won't keep me away now. You'd better put in an extra bed."

"Ah, you don't like my bed?"

"Your bed's fine. But brutally narrow. I'm ruthless when I sleep."

"Jean."

"Yes?"

"I could make you a good lover, you know."

"You already show marked talent."

"No; but I've been cold for so long. I've forgotten. Jean."

"Jeanette?"

"You must tell me things, you know. What you want."

"You don't learn these things. You don't need to learn anything."

"You understand; it's simple, Jean. I love you. There. Just like that. You thought it was just Peter, to block him out. No."

"Good."

"And without claims. It wasn't just Peter, Jean, I swear it. Isn't it strange? I don't want anything. You see, I just have this feeling now for your mad thin body and your thin quick muscles and the fact that you have no fat on you and for your preoccupied mad lined face. Jean."

"Sir?"

"You're a mad sad old crow, very wise, perched gloomily on your stripped winter bough—"

"Thank you. And, like all crows, I have secretly a heart of gold."

"I was coming to that."

"Also, between ourselves, a sharp beady eye for the main chance, at all times."

"It's logical. And I have just registered for the crows' political party. I'll do great things for you, Jean."

"It's a proud mission."

"No; but it's a spring with me, you see. I didn't expect it. I'd forgotten it could exist. So I do have an obligation. I owe you, Jean."

"You'll find me limitlessly receptive."

"However long it lasts. But there's a condition, Jean."

"That's bad."

"You must come and see me. I can't do that."

"I'll come and see you, Jeanette."

"Until they come. Anyway until they come."

"That's nothing," he said. "That'll pass."

"When will they come, Jean?"

"It could be a week," he said, "ten days. You just have to wait. But it's nothing. These things are nothing when they happen."

"I know," she said wisely, "it's the waiting. One waits so much."

CHAPTER XXII

TUESDAY, December 13, 1960.

"Why hasn't it started?"

Cuong glanced at him. The waiting was always the most difficult. Tay had said that almost under his breath, as if to himself.

"They can't talk all day," said Phouvong. He looked east along the street.

He was the more mature. Otherwise the two were nearly identical. They were seventeen or eighteen years old, students from the School of Administration in Vientiane. Each was slight, with the quick smooth muscles of youth. Their faces were high-cheekboned and immobile, so without expression indeed that they could have been those of statues, or asleep, or absorbed in contemplation, already in the presence of death.

There was a pile of grenades between them under the window. The room was on the second floor. The building was brick and concrete, towards the east end of the Rue Setthatirat. There were shops at street level, compartments, most of them closed now by iron grills, and padlocked. The compartment below them had been empty for days, and this living quarter above it. Cuong and the two students had protected it as well as they could. They had dragged the heavy charged bookcases against the wall which gave on to the street, and stacked mattresses on their sides against the other walls, to trap any bullets or shrapnel flying within the room. They had bolted one of the iron shutters closed over the only window. It left them an opening of half a metre wide by a metre high on to the street.

Cuong got up from his chair and went to the right side of the window. He could not see the river. It ran parallel to the street, seventy or a hundred metres from it. Irregular lines of houses and *pilotis* hid it from him. There were still people down in the street. They stood in small groups and talked and looked up it to the east. The river made a great loop past Vientiane, so that Thadua and the Thai port of Nongkhye were to its east. The attack would come from there. The sun shone down clear and vertical into the street, printing the shadows of the trees black and static on it and upon the pavements.

The city's fate had been decided for a week, since Nosavan's artillery had broken Konglé's men at Ba Ca Dinh. From then Souvanna Phouma had fought to have Vientiane declared an open city, by contacts with the American Ambassador and by radio contacts with the enemy in Savannakhet. He had finally admitted his failure on the ninth and left the city by air for Pnom Penh, with some of his ministers, leaving the civil and military powers to General Sounlet, the Lao Chief of Staff. This was academic only. Quinim had stayed and kept the civil powers; the British had at once recognized him in practice as the head of the government. Sounlet was no match for him or for Konglé. Konglé had again shown who held the real military power in Vientiane just before Souvanna had left. On the seventh Kuprasith, the colonel commanding the Chinaimo army camp at Kilometre Four on the road to Thadua, had tried to jump on the pro-American bandwagon by staging a coup of his own in anticipation of Nosavan's arrival. His men occupied Vientiane for one day. They wore white scarves. It was the start of a colour symbolism that would be fatally known within the week. The pro-Americans wore scarves or bands of white, that dubious colour of purity, and the Konglé men red. Some such identification was needed, for with few exceptions each side had exactly the same American arms and uniforms.

By the eighth the red was back in the city. Konglé had simply returned in the night. No one was killed. The whites simply trooped back obediently to Chinaimo. The front line became an oil barrel in the centre of the road at Kilometre Three. Soldiers wearing red scarves and soldiers wearing white scarves chatted amicably across it. Representatives from all three factions, Nosavan's, Kuprasith's, and Konglé's, talked truces in a riverside bar next to them. Meanwhile arms flowed in to the reds and whites. The Ilyushins flew arms in from Hanoi to Wattai airport at the west of the city, some Russian and Czech, mostly American 105's probably captured in Indo-China or Korea. The Thai sent American tanks and field-pieces over the river to Thadua from Nongkhye. From the tenth, Nosavan dropped parachutists by day in the white territory between Thadau and Kilometre Three. The people in Vientiane could see them clearly, drifting beautifully down from the skies.

Cuong heard the first shell, fired from Chinaimo or somewhere beyond it. He glanced at his watch; one-twenty. The shell sounded like a misfire. It seemed to be turning over and over in the air. It would land somewhere high in the north of the city. The civilians in the street below had not made that interpretation. They scattered at once, and the doors of their compartments banged shut. Two jeeps filled with red soldiers came up the street, fast, going towards Chinaimo.

The artillery fire had suddenly become very heavy from the east, and the machine-guns were going constantly. Shells were landing in the city. Some of the fire seemed to be concentrating on the headquarter building of the Chief of Staff about three hundred metres north of them, where Konglé had his command.

"Tanks?" said Tay.

Cuong stood by him and listened. There were certainly heavy vehicle movements to the east, but he could not hear tanks. He glanced at Tay and walked back to his chair and sat down. He said:

"What are the instructions?"

Tay looked at him and dropped his eyes. He was holding his carbine tightly.

"To let them pass," he said.

"Well," said Cuong, "tanks are nothing. Leave them to Konglé. He has tanks."

Murderously few, he thought.

"Our job's the infantry," he added.

"Yes," said Tay.

"Tay," said Cuong, "what about the rice?"

"Now?" said Tay.

"It's not a bad thing to eat," said Cuong.

"What if they come?" said Tay.

"We'll call you," said Phouvong. "We'll call you if they come."

When Tay had gone out Phouvong said, still looking down at the street:

"A tank shell could of course easily penetrate this wall."

It sounded like a statement from a gunnery officer's lecture.

"Of course," said Cuong. "But why should the tank know we're here? The tanks can hardly shoot up all the houses in the city. Even in this street."

"No," said Phouvong. He glanced round at Cuong.

"I'm not concerned, you understand," he said. "Tay is concerned."

His French was very formal.

"It's natural," said Cuong.

"You understand," said Phouvong. "We don't know tanks."

Shells had begun to drop higher in the street. They cut branches off the trees. The branches sprawled awkwardly across the pavements. They looked curiously animate. Something was burning fiercely to the east, by the river; a house, a store. The machine-gun and mortar fire was much nearer.

Tay came in with a tray. There were bowls on it; meat soup, rice with dried fish, rolls of bread, a bottle of cheap Macon. The three men sat on the floor in the centre of the room and ate and drank. Sometimes they looked up at the firing.

As Cuong sipped his Macon he was thinking about the Frenchman. He was sorry that he had not gone to drink in the Constellation with him, when the Frenchman had asked him, after Cuong had knocked the file from his hands, and picked it up, and given it back to him. It would have been amusing to have talked more with him. It would probably have been safe enough. He did not think that the Frenchman would ever remember the incident outside Reims cathedral now, in that other war, so long ago, when they had both been on the same side. He thought it curious how their lives had crossed; then, and then a year before, on the day that he, Cuong, had killed Gau. And, again, ten days before, when he had again just arrived in this city for an execution. Perhaps he would see him again one day, and this time it would be he who offered the drink to the Frenchman. It it was safe, if all this was finished then, he might even tell him where and when they had met before. It would probably amuse the Frenchman considerably.

About four in the afternoon the first of the red soldiers came back up the street. They came in trucks and jeeps and on foot. The men on foot ran, looking back, keeping to the walls of the houses, and diffusing up the side streets like water. The machine-gun fire whipped straight up the street now, from the east, richocheting off the buildings. Firing broke out very heavily by the river ahead and to the right and went on for about thirty minutes; probably an attempted landing by the whites. Just before five the firing stopped and the street was deserted.

"Tank," said Tay.

He sounded almost satisfied. He sounded as though he had known all along that he was bound to be right in the end.

Cuong took Tay's place at the right of the window and looked up the street. The tank was about a hundred and fifty metres away, advancing very slowly. It halted at each side road, as though gathering its courage, then accelerated across it. It was taking no chances. The hatches were down. As it came closer Cuong saw the fantail of infantry behind it. There were seven or eight, with white scarves. He could see no other vehicles or men behind them in support.

"Keep down," he said.

He stayed at the window, his eyes just above the rim. The tank's forward machine-gunner was sending a burst now and then up the street, on principle, but he was not spraying the windows of the houses. The first of the infantrymen was about fifteen

metres behind the tank. Cuong could still see nothing behind the
man and his six companions. Cuong dropped down below the
window. He said:

"It might be possible. The infantry are too far behind the tank.
Keep your grenades ready. First, give me twenty seconds."

"Too far behind the tank," said Tay doubtfully. Phouvong had
already put his hand down to the grenades.

Cuong moved slightly to his left and raised his eyes again above
the sill. He was behind the iron blind. From outside, he would
be invisible through its slats. The tank was just abreast of him.
Behind it, the infantry were looking from side to side at the
doors and windows of the houses.

A side road led down to the river, fifteen metres higher up
the street. As the tank hesitated before it, then poked its nose
out into it, fire broke out sharply from down the side road; a
Konglé heavy machine-gun post, dug in. The fire from it bounced
noisily and harmlessly off the tank. The tank stopped dead. It
looked absolutely outraged. It spurted forward suddenly, spinning
on its left track, and churning up a long slice of asphalt from
the street. It faced directly down the side road. Its cannon shot
twice and its forward machine-gun began to hammer.

The infantry had gone straight to the far side of the street in a
very nice text-book manoeuvre and were crouching down behind
the low wall there, facing towards the machine-gun nest. But the
seven men were bunched much too close together for their own
good. They were directly opposite the house. Cuong moved to the
right so that he was in the open and kept his finger down on the
trigger. The Thompson jumped in his hands. He aimed low and
moved the barrel from left to right. Only two of the men spun
round towards him, but the first fell as he did so, and he hit the
other with the last two shots in his magazine as the man started
to run bent double across the street towards the house.

Cuong dropped back into the room.

"The grenades," he said. "The far side."

They pulled the pins and threw the grenades. Cuong could hear
the screams of the men. When they had thrown six grenades he
stopped them and looked out. He could see no movement in the
men.

The heavy machine-gun down the side road had stopped firing.
The tank must have hit it. The tank reversed back into the street.
Cuong watched it through the iron slats. He thought that he could
see the turret-periscope swivel; the tank commander checking up
on his escort. The tank stopped abruptly. It looked extraordinarily
still, even perplexed. He could almost hear it think. Its cannon

swung round to the compartment next to Cuong's, hesitated, then turned to the compartment opposite. The tank looked like some nightmare insect, blinded, feeling its way in a hostile medium. It accelerated forward to the entrance to the side road and turned on its tracks and rolled back fast past the compartment, carefully avoiding the dead man lying in his blood in the street, back to the east, its cannon still swinging suspiciously from side side to side on to the compartments. The infantryman in the street and the six at its side lay still in the last of the sunlight.

"Tanks," said Cuong. "What did I tell you?"

"The next may investigate more thoroughly," said Tay.

Phouvong looked at him. He said:

"There's nothing to show that we killed them from here."

"Still," said Tay, "that tank crew will talk."

"The tank crew didn't know where it came from," said Phouvong.

Cuong had changed his magazine. He said:

"The way out is at the back. If they search, we go at once. As we planned."

"We understand that," said Phouvong.

But the next groups of whites did not stop. The tanks and armoured cars came through, followed by jeeps and infantry on foot. They moved precisely, clearly under orders to get through to some definite objective past the street, perhaps the airport. Behind his iron blind Cuong watched the infantrymen glance down at the dead men, avoiding them. All of the vehicles pulled scrupulously to one side to miss the man in the street.

Later, a group of infantry came through on foot, more slowly. They set up a machine-gun at the corner of the side road. Dusk was falling. Their officer went over to the dead men and looked down at them. The officer was a slim man in a beret, with a white scarf tucked inside the throat of a dark paratrooper smock. He crossed to the man lying in the street, and he spoke to his men and two of them took the dead man by his heels and dragged him to the side of the street. His cap came off and his arms came forward above his head. His rifle had got caught under his stomach and it made a harsh rasping sound on the street as they pulled him. The cap sat on its own in the blood in the street and the officer looked down at it absently. He moved it with the toe of his boot, and turned and looked up across the street straight at the window. Behind the slats Cuong could feel his eyes fixed uncannily on him, though he knew that the officer could not possibly see him. Cuong did not move. The officer spoke again, rapidly, and the nearest of two men sat down on their bottoms in the street and lined their carbines up on the window. Three others ran across the street to the compartment. The officer walked to the middle of the street under the window and pulled a grenade from his belt. As the officer looked down for the pin Cuong dropped flat to the floor.

"Get down!"

Phouvong was already flat behind him. Cuong looked up swiftly. Tay was still standing at the other side of the window, holding his carbine, looking down at him. Tay said:

"Down? Why don't we—"

In the blinding white flash Cuong saw Tay's features collapse and the intelligence go from them. He heaved at Phouvong's shoulder behind him and the two ran doubled up across the room. The grenade's blast had blown the door open and the two men flattened themselves against the wall outside as the second and third grenades exploded in the room.

"The back," said Cuong. "Leave your carbine."

"You?" said Phouvong.

"I'll cover you."

"I could stay. Or together."

"It's better alone," said Cuong. "Go."

Phouvong put down his carbine and went ahead through to the landing. Here one flight of stone steps led down to the shop. The landing continued on past the kitchen and past another room. An iron flight of steps led down to the garden. There was a solid wooden fence about fifteen metres away, two metres high. The garden was deserted. They could hear the soldiers at the front of the compartment shooting off the padlocks. Phouvong ran down the iron steps and across the garden. Cuong sat on the top step with the machine-gun in his hands. He saw Phouvong pull himself over the wooden wall and drop. At once, he heard a short chopping burst of machine-gun fire from the other side.

Cuong could hear the men pulling open the steel trellis in front of the shop now. He ran back along the landing and down the stone steps directly towards the sound. The compartment was dark. He visualized it quickly; a long L-shaped counter, certainly with deep cubby-holes in it behind; wooden stands against the wall at the back. Normally they would have been charged with Thai silver bowls and Thai and Lao belts of silver and gold, Buddha heads, and the counter with a wealth of cheap jewellery, watches, clocks. They were empty now; the Chinese shopkeeper had stripped everything when he left. Cuong felt his way round the edge of the counter and slid open the first cubby-hole door behind it at ground level. The Thompson handicapped him, but he dared not leave it outside. He pulled the cubby-hole door half shut behind him and crouched in the restricted space. The soldiers were three metres from him, sliding open the shop's second set of doors.

Through the half open door of the cubby-hole he could see the glare of the torch on the floor inside the counter.

"Not there, you fool. What the devil would they be doing downstairs?"

"Perhaps the grenades didn't get them."

"Then they'd have gone out of the back. Khamleck says that they got one going over the fence."

"A Konglé man?"

"A student."

Cuong heard them going along the outside of the counter behind their torch and up the stone steps and into the rooms over his head. Then their boots retraced his and Phouvong's path to the end of the landing. They came back down into the compartment.

"Two men, two carbines. What did I say?"

"It would have been good to have taken one of them alive."

"Forget it; others have been taken alive."

Cuong judged them to be three; two soldiers, the third probably the officer in the beret. He guessed that from the authority in the voice. He was certain also from the accent that the officer was Thai.

"Still, perhaps we should look more thoroughly. Say in the compartments on either side."

"We're fighting a war, had you noticed?" said the officer. "But since it concerns you so much, you can stand guard until the security police arrive. Then you can play searches with them."

The second soldier laughed. The first said:

"Afterwards, sir?"

"Join us where you can. We're going on."

"And the machine-gun at the corner?"

"Will come with us. There's nothing here."

Cuong grimaced with relief. He had been worrying about the machine-gun crew. He had to make his break from the front; the back might still be covered. But in front the machine-gunners would almost certainly have seen him if they stayed.

He heard the officer and the two soldiers go out into the street and draw the steel grill half shut behind them. His muscles were already badly cramped, but he could not yet think of moving. He could hear the officer and the rest of his men moving up the street now, in the direction of the airport, but he had not yet localized the guard. Then he heard him cough, by the entrance to the shop, and begin to pace up and down outside. Cuong began to pull the cubby-hole door open by fractions.

He found that he needed time to be able to stand up straight. He put the Thompson down very carefully on the floor behind the counter and took off his sandals. Sooner or later the guard would probably get bored enough or interested enough in a little loot to come back inside. Cuong went round the edge of the counter on his bare feet and stood at the left of the metre-wide opening in the shop's door. He had no knife, but the Colt was in the right pocket of his khaki jacket. He took it out and reversed it in his hand and held it by the bulky silencer. He lifted it and rested the butt on his left shoulder, his forearm across his chest, so that he could strike at once.

The soldier went on pacing slowly outside the shop, and twice Cuong lowered his right arm to rest it. The soldier was muttering to himself as he walked, probably in resentment at the officer's sarcasm. Once several vehicles, probably lorries, went at a walking pace past in the street, going west towards the airport. They must have been driving blind, for Cuong could see no reflection of lights from them through the shop door. The night was now ominously quiet; all firing had stopped.

The dark grey of the shop's opening filled abruptly, and the guard leant forward into it. He was supporting himself idly by his hands on either side of the door so that his head projected inwards. His carbine was slung over his left shoulder. He wore a khaki cloth cap with a short peak. He was short and stocky, probably a Khâ. He looked young.

The soldier began to whistle softly, and looked slowly to his left. As his face turned back Cuong hit him savagely with the butt of the pistol under his right ear. The man sighed thoughtfully and Cuong stepped forward as he fell and caught him and pulled him fully into the shop and eased him on to the floor. He hit him again with the pistol in the same place. The soldier had made no further sound; Cuong thought that the first blow had probably killed him.

Cuong took him under the shoulders and dragged him round the edge of the counter and put him on the floor beside it, so that he could not be seen from the door. He left the Thompson on the ground next to him. He put on his sandals and slipped the Colt back into his right pocket and went naturally out of the shop and turned right into the street, and began to walk towards the west.

It was a clear night, and he could already see the stars. The branches lay chopped across the street like animals. At the first corner he saw the body of a young girl on the pavement. She was lying on her back with one leg drawn up so that her thighs were uncovered. He could see no mark on her.

CHAPTER XXIII

Wednesday, December 14, 1960.

Jean-Philippe looked down from his balcony into Samsènethai Road. Things looked fantastically normal. The previous day's fighting could have been a dream. There was no shooting. Both sides had evidently decided to break for breakfast in a civilized manner.

The townspeople were walking about happily in the road in the early morning air. They grouped together a little more than usual but that was all. There were few signs of destruction yet. Some of the compartments were scarred, and the Constellation had been hit in the roof by mortars, fifty metres down the road from him. He could not see Konglé's command buildings, some hundred metres north-east as the crow or the shell flew. They had already been badly hit.

When Jean-Philippe had first looked out that dawn he had seen a dead soldier in the street below, lying on his stomach, with his arms bent forward above his head, and his face down. He could have been praying, or a Thai Boxer making his histrionic obeisances in the ring before he fought. Jean-Philippe had not even been able to see whether he was red or white. Perhaps he was both; many were changing colours with the swell and ebb of the fighting. When Jean-Philippe came out on his balcony the next time somebody had already tactfully removed the dead soldier.

After the whites' first thrust along the main arteries of the city the afternoon before, the reds had counter-attacked from about nine that night and driven them out, carrying the fighting heavily to the east again, so that Konglé's men held this road again, and the main Setthatirat Street, and the road along the river. The whites seemed to have held on to the north of the city, including Radio Vientiane, which had been silent all night.

It had probably been the only radio station within several thou sand kilometres that was. Jean-Philippe had listened to his radio most of the night. The King had dismissed Souvanna Phouma's government promptly, on the grounds that Souvanna had deserted the country. Savannakhet Radio had read out with gusto the King's decree of December 12 which appointed the Savannakhet Revolutionary Committee as the new government. The United States had recognized it with what could only appear indecent haste. The Thai followed them closely. Radio Pathet Lao, Pekin, Hanoi, and Moscow went on supporting Souvanna volubly. Without moving a muscle of its face the Voice of America had denounced Russia for sending arms in to Laos. The Thai Radio had noted piously that the Thai had been remarkably patient under severe provocation, including that provided by several bullets which had arrived over the river on to Thai soil. Radio Pathet Lao observed that, not only had America and Thailand armed and trained Nosavan's troops, but America, Thailand, South Viet Nam, and Formosa had also contributed officers to lead them.

For all Radio Pathet Lao's tone of moral outrage, Jean-Philippe had seen no sign of Pathet troops in the fighting. As he had thought they must have pulled out the moment it got really intense. It would not have been through cowardice: that theory was unfortunately much too convenient. They were just going strictly by Mao's and Giap's text-books. They would strike when they judged the time and place right, not before. That meant that the entire red side was the three or four hundred paratroopers who remained to Konglé. Aided admittedly by the Youth Movement's *franctireurs*, they were fighting against twenty or thirty times as many trained white troops.

He wondered again how Jeanette was down at the river. He still cursed himself that he had not had the sense to get down to her in one of the lulls, or, better, to have brought her back to his flat. It was stone-walled, with a good roof, and was probably safe from anything short of a direct hit by a 105. It struck him that it would still be worth trying to get down for her before the troops finished their breakfast, but at that moment the machine-guns began again suddenly, from all the street corners, together, as if at a prearranged signal, and with great ferocity, as though bent on making up for lost time. The white artillery and mortars had also opened up at once. Jean-Philippe laid himself down smartly on the floor of his balcony.

He could hear Konglé's headquarters taking another beating. But then he heard Konglé's guns too, from somewhere near the airport, firing over the town, probably on a counter-battery task. It sounded like a nice disciplined shoot. He doubted that Konglé's layers were amateurs. The civilians in the road below had once more disappeared like magic. There was sense to that. The shrapnel had begun to come into the road, whining as it cut the air, and spattering across the roofs like hail.

226

He heard heavy house-to-house fighting ahead of him in Sett-hatirat Street, the short tearing runs of sub-machine-guns, and the muffled bursts of grenades, probably exploding inside rooms. An ambulance went up the road fast under him, going west. Parts of the town burned. The smoke rose straight and slow in the still air, against the perfect light blue of the sky. The white 105's and heavy mortars began another fire task on Konglé's command buildings, and Jean-Philippe edged himself back on his stomach into his room and lay against the wall by his radio.

When he looked out again at about ten he could see to his right, a kilometre off towards Wattai, that the whole line of corrugated-iron living quarters and *pilotis* by the evening market was burning fiercely. Poor devils would be busy dying in there, men and women and children, burning to death inside that tin and match-wood or in shallow panic trenches under it, or cut down by the shrapnel that sang in the street if they ran out into it.

Thursday, December 15, 1960.

Short dived briskly back into the trench with the bottle of Mar-tell. He might have known that the lull was just too good to last. The early morning had once more been quiet, but now, just after nine, the whole damned thing had broken out again all over the city. Something had whacked very hard into the roof of his office thirty metres away as he had left the house with the Martell. It had probably been a mortar bomb; some eagle-eyed bastard of a white forward observation officer must have seen him mov-ing.

"Do you think we really should?" said Patricia, looking at the bottle.

"I can't think why on earth not."

"Well, so early," said Patricia, looking at the children.

Christopher looked delighted at the idea. He looked delighted about everything. He had never before been allowed to be so con-sistently filthy for anything like as long. His sister Miranda, as befitted her sex and more tender age, had grizzled most of the night, but now she slept quietly.

They had spent the night in the trench. After the first day, when the reds had surged back at night to retake the centre of the town, Short had realized that the fighting might go on for weeks. Almost all of his office staff, mainly Vietnamese, had stayed in the office compound; the house and servants' quarters were much safer than their flimsy homes in the city. Short had not wanted to shelter them in the house; the mass of glass in its windows made it perilous. Instead, the morning before he had set them all, with the cook and assistant cook and gardener, to dig a trench. It had seemed a good idea to start with. He had scratched its outline on the ground between the house and servants' quarters, in a professional and military series of zig-zags. Digging it was somewhat harder. It had to hold twenty assorted men, women, and children, and the ground was brutally stony. His own palms were raw from the garden hoes and spades. They had dug all day and finished the trench that evening, falling into it in a cinematic manner each time that the machine-gun bullets and shrapnel whistled over their heads. They roofed it with slats of corrugated iron and loose earth. They could sit upright in it. It was really quite luxurious.

"Don't hog it now," said Short.

"Oh," said Patricia. "Of course."

She passed the bottle to Ti-Hai. Ti-Hai refused it with dignity. She was sitting bolt upright in the trench next to Patricia and the children, maintaining her just place in the hierarchy. She had been correctly imperturbable during the shelling, merely snarling slightly when a shell or mortar bomb fell particularly near, as though she looked upon it as a personal insult. She passed the bottle along to Cheun. Cheun took it and turned and smiled and nodded formally at Short and poured some Martell into his tin cup. He was a slim wiry unrockable Chinese, quite tall, and Short's office manager in times of peace. Short had constantly to stop him from hiving off from the trench at all hours to wander round the compound and see who was winning. Cheun took this discipline tolerantly. He had the air of having seen this sort of war before, much worse. As a former citizen of Hanoi, he probably had.

Cheun's wife sat next to him in the trench. Squads of incredibly neat and totally silent children blocked off the next turn. They looked like large dolls stacked precisely on a shelf. Not only were Cheun and the Vietnamese in Short's staff inclined to rove around through shot and shell to watch the fighting, but they also seemed to have completely unquenchable appetites. The men slid regularly off to the kitchen every two hours to cook rice. Short had never eaten so much of the stuff in his life.

Cheun and his band had also struck up a ready rapport with the Konglé mortar crew over the road. The mortar crew were an engaging lot, always ready to give a sporting commentary on the progress of the fighting. Short had gone across early that day to say good morning to them, and they had prayed and grinned very cheerfully at him; Cheun must have given him a good character.

They seemed not the only ones on their side who were taking their war lightly, if efficiently. Before he had got the Martell, Short had gone up out of curiosity to the attic. He could just make out a tank flying a white pennant at the end of Setthatirat Street, by Saovong's service station. Its cannon was trained belligerently down the street towards the airport. There was an abrupt chatter of machine-gun fire from Short's left. Turning, he saw a jeep manned with four red soldiers swing into the main street from the side road that cut down to the river a little way behind his house, and loose off with the Bren-gun mounted on its bonnet at the tank. Amazingly, the tank fired its cannon once hysterically and reversed sharply out of sight. The jeep came back into the side road. The soldiers in it were splitting their sides with laughter, and clapping one another on the back. Whether the reds lost or held this city, they certainly did not look like beaten men.

Perhaps it was that jeep, not the presence of the mortar-team, or of the heavy machine-gun post which was dug in by the river where the road in front of Short's house met it, that was drawing so much white fire on this quarter. The evening before the whites' 105's had hit the warehouse behind them down by the river. It was about thirty metres from the end of Short's garden. It had burned for hours until the walls were down to the ground and the trees were flaming steadily about it.

The firing was getting heavier. Short was at the end of the trench nearest the river. From where he sat he could see a stretch of the yard. For the first time in his life, he then saw a grenade actually bursting. It was small, perhaps from a rifle. It exploded four metres from the lip of the trench. His mind retained the image of the flash like film, a fan upwards and outwards at thirty degrees. The burst had cut the laundry-wire strung above it. The two ends swung now idly from the corrugated-iron shelter that covered the concrete walk from the servants' quarters to the house.

"Joe," said his wife.

"Pat."

"I'll bet that one had the clasped hands on it too."

"Clasped hands?"

"You know," said Patricia, "that famous symbol of America's aid to underdeveloped countries."

"Bloody South African," said Short.

"No," said Patricia, "it's very edifying. It's such fun to see what our aid really looks like in the field."

"*Our* aid? You're being very loyal."

"God knows why," said Patricia. "*Your* aid. I'm still on your side, Joe. Just. But put a full stop after that."

"Pat," said Short.

"Joe?"

"Ask that underdeveloped character over there for the bottle, will you?"

And the C.I.A. were not the only ones in on this act, he thought grimly, serving himself a second healthy shot of Martell. They had a very ready ally. Short had watched the gun flashes during the night. He had distinctly seen seven or eight very heavy flashes from directly across the river. There had not been the remotest possibility of error about where they came from.

The artillery seemed to have lifted a little. It was still coming down as heavily, but it seemed to be concentrating now near the edge of the airport at Wattai. He wondered what his airport depot looked like. On the first day of the fighting he had sent word to his staff there to lock up and get out. That might not look heroic, but it was good sense. The depot stood right on its own. If it burned it could not hurt anything else. Moreover, he knew that it was much harder than was commonly supposed to set fire to gasoline in underground tanks, even aviation gasoline. It would anyway hardly be an utter tragedy if they did burn. Short was all for loyalty to his company, but he felt that there was a limit to how far you could reasonably get emotional about a stock of gasoline at a time like this.

But it sounded as though the white shells were falling short of his depot, much nearer to the *Mission Militaire Française*. That was the base where the Geneva-approved French instructors to the Lao Army lived in their fragile wooden houses. Short thought it curious that the white shelling should concentrate there. The men and their wives and children were hardly combatants.

Thursday, December 15, 1960; 10 a.m.

"There goes your house," said Dumergue.

"Hit?" said the French captain.

"Direct," said Dumergue. "A 105, I'd say. What a mess."

"Is it burning?" said the captain.

Dumergue pulled his head back quickly into the trench. It sounded like a full-blooded regimental shoot coming down on them.

"Not that I could see," he said, "not yet, anyway."

Dumergue counted about twenty-four shells come down around them. The noise and dust was shocking. He wondered what on earth the white guns were up to. They were supposed to have high-class American advisers, weren't they? If this was an error in ranging, it was certainly some error. Wattai airfield, where Konglé was reputed to have his artillery, started hundreds of metres away. Or was it just a salutary little lesson to let the French know who were really going to run the country now?

He heard the screams during a lull in the firing. They were from about fifty metres off. His bowels twisted. He knew at once where the screams came from. For days about sixty Vietnamese men and women and children had been sheltering in the M.M.F., just where the houses started. Physically the shelters were scanty, no more than the drains at the sides of the dirt roads that led in to the houses. The Vietnamese had not come there for that, but for the moral security of being on French soil. The Geneva agreements had left this and the base at Seno as French territory. The Vietnamese had apparently naïvely thought that such things still mattered.

"*Canaille d'amerigos,*" said the French captain. "Murderers."

"Stop it, Paul," said his wife. "That won't help us."

She was sitting behind him in the dark of the covered trench with the children.

Dumergue put his head out again. The shelling had stopped. He could see about fifteen bodies across the dirt road where the houses began. They had the final broken look of the violently dead. There were some women, a few children. Other Vietnamese were standing by them, apparently oblivious of the danger of further shelling. They were simply standing and looking down passively at the bodies. Between them and the gates of the camp a parked Peugeot saloon burned furiously. Many of the M.M.F. houses had been hit.

An ambulance came through the gates. It was not from the French hospital; Dumergue was sure of that. Perhaps it was from the small British medical mission. It stopped and two Europeans got out of it. They went to the bodies in the road. They looked down at them and wasted no more time on them. They went on to the shallow drains at the sides. Two of the Vietnamese men went back to the ambulance with them for stretchers, and they began to load the wounded into it. The shooting started again suddenly, machine-guns and mortars and artillery, down by the river a kilometre away.

Wednesday, December 21, 1960.

There was a quick burst of machine-gun fire some distance away outside the Embassy and Jean-Philippe saw the Secretary look fretfully up from behind his wide sleek paperless desk. It was nothing, Jean-Philippe thought impatiently. It was some poor bastard of a soldier or student getting shot. Or it was just somebody cleaning his gun. Anyway, it was a long way off.

231

"Could you be a little more explicit?" said Jean-Philippe.

The Secretary glanced back. He looked slightly insulted.

"Explicit about what?" he said.

"Precisely what force does your recommendation carry?" said Jean-Philippe. "It's your government, the French Government, or Nosavan's, which requires my expulsion?"

"Expulsion is your word," said the Secretary. "Expulsion is an unnecessarily aggressive way of putting it."

It was evident that he did not like aggressive words. He had built his hands into a chapel on the desk in front of him and he frowned down at them. It was one of his favourite postures. He looked as though he thought Jean-Philippe's direct question in singularly poor taste. Elegant, inbred, pallid, the Secretary was himself a curiously glancing and elusive character, slipping so discreetly through life as to leave no mark at all on it. At forty, he already looked as he would probably look when he died. It was a face that you could not remember five minutes after you had left him.

"What if I refused?" said Jean-Philippe.

The Secretary looked at him quickly. He seemed genuinely shocked. After a minute he relaxed and smiled.

"There wouldn't be much point to that, you know. They have only to cancel your visa."

"And you'd give me no protection against that?" said Jean-Philippe. "You'd not contest that? Isn't that your job? I'm a French citizen, remember? You'd like to see my passport?"

"My dear fellow, on what grounds would we contest that, for example?"

"On what grounds am I *non grata*?"

The Secretary raised his eyebrows and inclined his head slightly to one side.

"If you must have me state the obvious, what you yourself already certainly know. Prejudiced reporting, hostile to the present government. Pro, shall we say, the left wing."

Jean-Philippe reflected that the other had probably always had that gift of being able to sound righteous whenever he expressed the views of those currently in power. He wondered what the Secretary had done in France in 1941.

"My paper?" he said.

"Has been advised, of course," said the Secretary.

"I see. When am I to be rusticated? Tomorrow?"

Again the Secretary contrived to look shocked. He was not to be pinned down to mere exact detail that easily, even about dates.

"I can't see that a few days would matter," said the Secretary.

"Say by the end of this month. Or say the first week or so next month."

"It's generous of you."

But the Secretary could afford to ignore the irony. He replied with the deeper irony of taking Jean-Philippe literally.

"Well, it's that one understands that you have affairs to arrange, of course. People to see. It's natural. One must remain civilized."

Or was that a quick deft twist of the knife on the subject of Jeanette? Jean-Philippe knew that the Secretary must know about that. People did. But the Secretary's face was expressionless.

CHAPTER XXIV

WHEN Jean-Philippe left the French Embassy he drove down to the river, out of a kind of nostalgia. He stopped by the bank opposite the American Ambassador's house and got out. The U.S. Embassy in the city's centre had been badly damaged, but the ambassador's house seemed to have escaped unharmed.

He looked up the river to the west. The evening was tranquil. *Pirogues* and sampans were plying across from the Thai village of Sichiengmai to sell food at high prices to Vientiane's survivors. Rice was also coming across busily in the motor-ferries from Nongkhye, and medicine. The medicine was vital, for cholera had broken out in the city. Sarit had lifted the economic blockade the moment that Nosavan's troops had taken Vientiane.

Here by the river the calm was striking after the panic which had beset the city during the previous five days. Evacuation had become all the fashion immediately after the last of Konglé's men had been driven out on the sixteenth. French men and women and children from the M.M.F. or the economic mission or from private businesses, French women teachers from the schools, Americans, and other *farangs* had fled by car and station-wagon and pick-up to Thadua, abandoning their vehicles to cross the river in small boats to Thailand.

The exodus of the Thai and Thai Dam and Meo and Lao, and of the Chinese who remained, had been as heavy. They took their belongings in carts, or loaded on bicycles, or in bundles at each end of long bamboo carrying-poles which sprang gently up and down as they walked. They moved in long, serious, antlike columns past the shot-up houses and the burnt shells of the *pilotis*, and past the Nosavan troops who flooded into the city in their G.M.C. trucks and jeeps from the opposite direction. They did not look anything like as surprised or shocked as did the *farangs*. They were traditionally more used to such cataclysms. The flight from home before the advancing conqueror was an old cyclic fact of Indo-China, like the monsoon. Yet here there was a variation. They fled this time towards the official conqueror, and through him, away from the side that was supposed to be beaten. In this sense the direction of their flight did not argue the greatest of confidence in the permanence of this victory. Its timing too seemed strange. The fighting in the city had after all already stopped. It was as if the profound images of history had just jumped slightly out of sequence. Behind them, in the city, the looting had begun, the executions, a little indiscriminate killing.

Now, as Jean-Philippe watched it, the face of the river was as masked as those of the city's people when they had fled. The river thrust down past him, from its source three thousand kilometres north-west in the snows of Tibet. It had not changed. It was thick with silt, and there were curious whorls and steps in its surface from the currents. It carried the world's eternal flotsam carelessly with it, a dead dog or pig, empty bottles, a broken packing-case, a few uptorn and shattered trees, which floated deep in it, their stripped branches projecting up from it like the naked broken arms of bodies. Brown froth marked the edges of its most powerful currents like contour lines.

He could see two *pirogues* out in the river some way off the Lao bank, opposite the customs office, which Konglé's men had defended stubbornly until its walls were pierced by shells. The two *pirogues* sat static at the edge of the main stream. They pointed up the river, hanging delicately in it from their thin steel invisible wires. They were thin and black and fragile in the molten silver of the water, and the fishers who squatted in them were still against the evening sun.

A man was walking towards him in the long empty silver road which ran along the river. Jean-Philippe had not noticed him before. Perhaps he had come out of the *Salle des Fêtes*, where Nosavan was exhibiting the arms captured from Konglé (many of them obviously and embarrassingly American.) At that distance Jean-Philippe could see only that the man was quite tall, with a shock of black hair, and wearing a white open-necked shirt and dark slacks. He looked European, perhaps an employee from the bank, or a counsellor from one of the ministries.

Jean-Philippe drove back to the Constellation and parked his car and went in. With a true trader's realism, Calvastan had kept his bar and the hotel above it open all the time, in spite of the

234

mortar holes in the roof. Foreign correspondents and news photographers choked the bar. Some of the Americans among them were flushed and talking loudly. Jean-Philippe leant against the counter and ordered a Martell.

As he turned his back to the bar with the glass in his hand he saw Pridie get up from a table of journalists and wave cheerfully to them and come out past him. He said:

"Get a good lion, Pridie?"

Pridie stopped and looked at him. He was wearing his Kenya white hunter's disguise again, the khaki bush jacket and slacks, and the leather mosquito-boots, no doubt out of deference to the civil war. Only the Hollywood bush-hat with the regulation leopard-skin band round it was missing.

"Evening," said Pridie coldly.

But again there was that shadow of fear in his eyes, behind the wafer glasses. It had been there the two times that he had seen Pridie since he had taken Jeanette from him. It was as if he had beaten Pridie too cruelly on that ground, or as if he must now know too much about him. Pridie need not have worried on this last score; Jeanette had scrupulously not mentioned him since she and Jean-Philippe had become lovers.

"Have a nice war?" said Jean-Philippe.

"Passable," said Pridie. "Excuse me, I must get home. I've lots to do."

Pridie nodded and went straight on out to his Jeep station-wagon across the road and got into it and drove off. He had done it all, as it were, in one breath. It had taken Jean-Philippe completely by surprise. He had wanted to have the subject of his expulsion out with Pridie there and then. He had no doubt that Pridie and his friends had had a hand in it, as Laclos had warned.

"The Viets wouldn't dare invade in force," said a man at one of the tables in front of him. "Think of the Sixth Fleet."

"It wouldn't be anything much anyway," said the man next to him. "Hell, what happened in this city was nothing."

The first man looked aggrieved. The importance of his story was being deflated. He was not going to give up that easily. He said:

"What d'you want? There were a couple of hundred killed, four or five hundred wounded. The French hospital's stiff with them."

The first man looked at him pityingly.

"And how many of them were Army, tell me that," he said. "You've got no sense of proportion. Hell, think of Normandy."

The first man appeared embarrassed. Perhaps he had not been at Normandy. He said defensively:

"All right, so most of them were civilians—"

"Sure," said the other in an experienced manner. "It was nothing. Why, in the Ardennes—"

He was starting to re-live his national heroisms. Several white officers, carrying their sidearms, were leaning against the bar. The first man was looking at them like an old comrade. They, with the mortar holes in the roof, lent welcome weight to the spurious militancy of the atmosphere.

"The Saar was pretty rough too," said the first man broodingly.

Jean-Philippe wondered how long it would take him to get back to Valley Forge.

"Anyway, that Embassy character's no fairy," said the second man, changing the subject, and virtually admitting that he had no war medals to trade with his companion.

"Not bad for a cultural attaché," said the first man magnanimously. "Why, generally, when I hear the word culture—"

The second man roared with appropriately masculine laughter. Even if he had not fought in France and Germany, he had at least read about Goering.

"They say he even had a mortar bomb in his front garden," said the first man. "Cool as hell, he goes right up to it. He finds they haven't even taken the fuse-cap off it. So he just picks it up and walks down to the river and dumps it in."

The second man looked duly impressed. He said seriously:

"The kind of American we need in joints like this. And no slouch on filling you in on the political stuff either."

Their two companions at the table were watching them dispassionately and without comment. They looked slightly appalled. The first of these silent men was a *New York Times* correspondent the second the Indo-Chinese representative of a major agency. Both had spent time in Saigon and the areas as a whole. They were evidently not impressed either by this mock heroics, or, possibly, even by Pridie.

Not that Jean-Philippe doubted the little story about Pridie and the mortar bomb. That was right in character. It was just the kind of flamboyant and highly dangerous action that Pridie would like. Jean-Philippe did not think that Pridie would have any particular fears of death; rather, certain cold affinities with it.

Lots to do at home, Pridie had said.

Jean-Philippe finished his drink and paid for it and went out to his car and drove down towards the river. There were lights on in Pridie's house, and his Jeep station-wagon was in the short drive.

Jean-Philippe stopped his car a little past the gate. There was a Wat next to Pridie's house, and, after it, thirty metres away, the river. They had been digging another Buddha out at the side of the Wat's grounds. They were always finding them. This one had been lurking in an old disused house, richly overgrown with creepers. He was a big fellow in stone, twelve metres high, facing east along the river. They had stripped away most of his covering, and he stood now in grave and splendid isolation, a dense green burst of vegetation growing up behind his ears like a modish coiffure.

A shaven-headed monk in his saffron robes went into the Wat's grounds from the side road and glanced at Jean-Philippe indifferently. The monk carried something in his hands, a block of wood, or of stone. He walked slowly across the open yard to the entrance to the Wat, his face old and calm as water.

Pridie opened his door the moment after Jean-Philippe had knocked on it. Pridie had had time to change. He stood now in a clean white silk shirt, linked with gold at the cuffs. He wore a neat pale-blue Thai-silk butterfly tie. The tropical weight cream gabardine slacks were knife-edged. If he was pleased to see Jean-Philippe he hid it admirably.

"Yes?" he said.

"Evening, Pridie."

"What, again?" said Pridie. "Look, I'm sorry. I'm awfully busy."

He could have been some senior Oxford student indicating with delicate ferocity to a late night intruder that the outer door to his rooms had been closed for a purpose.

"What, going out again, Pridie?" said Jean-Philippe.

"As a matter of fact, yes. Boun Oum's giving a reception. But perhaps you haven't been invited?"

"Perhaps I haven't," said Jean-Philippe.

"Well," said Pridie. "So nice to have seen you again. Good night."

"Thanks," said Jean-Philippe, pushing in gently. "Just a very few words, Pridie."

Pridie tightened his lips, then shrugged elaborately and let him in. It was clear that Pridie was thinking that there was no adequate answer to really dedicated rudeness like this, except to cap it as inflexibly with politeness. He said icily:

"A whisky-soda?"

"What a nice idea," said Jean-Philippe.

Pridie had gone at once to the jacket of his gabardine suit. It was hanging neatly over the back of an armchair. As Pridie picked it up Jean-Philippe heard something bang dully against the chair. Well, well, he thought. Pridie turned his back to him and put on the coat. Jean-Philippe saw that the fall of the pockets was elegantly smooth. Pridie, he thought, must then have the holster built in under his arm. He wondered if Pridie considered a gun standard equipment for diplomatic cocktail-parties.

Pridie walked over to the little bar in the hall at the back.

"No boy this evening?" said Jean-Philippe.

"No," said Pridie. "He's gone to fetch his sister. She evacuated."

"You really feel it's safe for him to bring her back?" said Jean-Philippe innocently.

Pridie looked round at him sharply from the bar.

"Yes, I do."

Jean-Philippe wondered how long it would take Pridie and his friends to find out how wrong they were. Nosavan had not really beaten anyone. Nobody had beaten Konglé. Jean-Philippe knew from an Air Laos executive who had been up at Wattai airport during the fighting that when Konglé had pulled his men and his guns out on the sixteenth it had been in very good order, almost parade-ground stuff. Konglé and his men had that odd gift of looking as though they believed in what they were fighting for. That was still the thing that won wars in the end in this region. Nobody else had it, except the Pathet. Konglé and Pathet would be back.

Abramov, the Russian Ambassador, had certainly seemed to think so. He was probably feeling rather smug now. He could afford to. Nobody loved Nosavan much, except for Sarit and the C.I.A. The Russians had simply backed the right horse again. They would arm and train him heartily now to make sure that he won next time.

There was an amusing little story about Abramov. He had stayed in the Settha Palace Hotel, near the Boulevard Circulaire, where there had been some brisk fighting. The story had it that he had stayed in his rooms with his two aides drinking vodka and eating caviar, presumably to madden the Americans staying in the hotel. After the city fell, a white lieutenant and two soldiers had come into the hotel, which had correctly been flying the Russian flag with those of all other accredited countries whose representatives were staying there. A soldier had pulled down and untied the Russian flag and hurled it into the air, and the lieutenant had riddled it dramatically with his sub-machine-gun. Abramov had come out to watch him sympathetically. Poor fellow, he had said audibly in French to his aides at the end of the

238

performance, of course they must really think that they've won the war.

Jean-Philippe thought that he must remember to tell Pridie this story during his whisky. He sat down in one of the rattan chairs and lit a cigarette. He put the dead match into the bakelite cavity in the obscene white tiger's skull on the small table to his right. Pridie came back with the whisky and soda and put it down next to the tiger and sat down at the chair on the other side. Pointedly, he had not brought himself a drink.

"Well, Raymond?" said Pridie.

He sounded even more like an old don than before.

"Curiosity, mainly," said Jean-Philippe. "Why did you bother? Are you people really so tragically insecure that you can't stand any kind of criticism at all?"

Pridie did not look at him. He seemed rather bored. He said:

"It's normally considered civilized to explain what one's talking about."

"Come off it, Pridie," said Jean-Philippe. "Why was I expelled?"

Pridie lit a cigarette and looked down at it and tapped its first ash unnecessarily into the receptive tiger. He said:

"I'm no great admirer of fools, Raymond. Of some enemies, perhaps. Of fools, no."

"It does you credit," said Jean-Philippe. "You're quite sure you know who the fool is in this particular game? Not the side that's committed to this amateur-dramatic team of young fanatics and old-time war-lords?"

Pridie observed the glowing coal of his cigarette without comment. Jean-Philippe said:

"Have you ever seen Gilbert and Sullivan, Pridie?"

Pridie controlled himself with a visible effort. He said:

"You're entitled to your opinion."

"Balls," said Jean-Philippe. "It's only too clear that I'm not. At least be consistent."

"All right," said Pridie savagely. "Your last despatch put you right into our hands. The one you tried to smuggle out with that M.M.F. wife via Nongkhye. That was incredibly stupid. The Nongkhye telegraph office just checked it with us.'

"I thought I was rather fair in that one," said Jean-Philippe. "I even mentioned that the Russians had certainly sent some arms in with the Ilyushins, possibly also gunlayers."

"You also highlighted that regrettable mistake of shelling the M.M.F." said Pridie. "In fact, that happened because Nosavan's

Forward Observation spotted some Konglé men going into the M.M.F. grounds."

"Or thought they did," said Jean-Philippe. "That's a nice theory, Pridie."

Pridie took no notice of him.

"You alleged that at one o'clock on the mornings of the ninth tenth, and eleventh the Thai sent five hundred commandos from the Udorn Infantry Division across by the motor ferries from Nongkhye, four tanks over at the same time on the ninth and eleventh, and four 105's over on the night of the fifteenth. And senior American military advisers were present when Boun Oum and Nosavan were flown across in an American helicopter to talk things over with Sarit in Nongkhye on the morning of the sixteenth, before Boun Oum and Nosavan went on in to the captured city. And that once again there was no evidence whatsoever of any regular Viet Minh units in the fighting."

"Our facts seem to check," said Jean-Philippe. "I must have been right after all."

"God Almighty," said Pridie. "What does that matter? What the hell sort of game do you think this is? What the hell do you think that your fellow-travelling world liberal press would have done with a report like that?"

Jean-Philippe could see the charcoal drawing of Pridie's mother above Pridie's shoulder on the wall to the right. The cold patrician face looked down on him. It was pure and perfect and inflexible. Jean-Philippe reflected that the good lady ought to be very proud of Pridie.

"Or was it simply sexual jealousy, Pridie?" he said. "Again, time and the facts are against you. Jeanette won't come back."

Jean-Philippe thought with satisfaction that that was probably irrelevant and certainly unfair. Pridie's mouth had gone white, and the light grey eyes behind their discreet thin rimless wafer lenses were stricken. Pridie's scarred left hand was on the table; he had been tapping the tips of his fingers on it in irritation. But he did not snatch his hand away this time when he felt Jean-Philippe's eyes on it. Instead, by an effort of will that Jean-Philippe could sense, he looked down deliberately at it and stilled it. The hand lay there static, next to the obscene and gleaming tiger's skull. It looked like a small white broken animal, crouching, paralysed with fear, or pinned cruelly by pain, and Pridie considered it deeply. What was this, thought Jean-Philippe, his badge of courage, or suffering, his justification for everything that he did?

The knock on the door was suddenly a relief. Pridie relaxed and looked up at it and sighed. He seemed reconciled to the thought

that his evening was bound to be spoiled now anyway. He said:
"Come in."

Jean-Philippe saw Pridie's eyes narrow again. Pridie began to
get up slowly, his eyes on the door. Automatically, Jean-Philippe
got up too, and turned towards it.

He knew the man at once. It was the Vietnamese who had
picked up the copies of his cables from the pavement in Samsènethai Road, a few days before the fighting had started, and whom
he had somehow thought that he had known somewhere even
before that. The Vietnamese had a heavy pistol in his right hand
now. There was a silencer mounted on it.

The man's eyes flicked briefly to him, and surprise glazed them.
The gun hand wavered slightly. The man said:

"Please. Get out of the way, *mon lieutenant*."

Mon lieutenant? Jean-Philippe understood suddenly that Pridie
must be half behind him from the line of the door. He turned
towards Pridie and saw him go fast for the gun under his arm,
and he threw himself violently backwards as Pridie fired. From the
wreckage of the rattan chair on the floor he saw the Vietnamese
fall back against the door and drop his pistol and turn and run.
Pridie was already across the room when Jean-Philippe got up,
and he ran after him.

Jean-Philippe was five paces behind Pridie when he got out of
the door and he swung hard left across him. The Vietnamese had
broken through the hedge and was running fast across the empty
grounds of the Wat, past the back of the great stone coiffured
Buddha, towards the river. Pridie stopped and shot again, and
Jean-Philippe saw the man hesitate and arch his back abruptly
and throw his arms straight out to his sides, as if in some vast and
eternal and silent speech; as if he appealed thus suddenly in the
agony of his wound to the world, to humanity, to the river. For
he stood already right on its bank now, and he fell then slowly
forward into it.

Jean-Philippe had caught up with Pridie as he shot and passed
him, and he reached the bank and slid down it. The Vietnamese
lay below him half in the water, face down. His bush-jacket had
wrenched open and lapped quietly in the water on either side of
him. His right shoulder was stained black; blood from Pridie's
second shot. As Jean-Philippe bent down to pull him out he knew
that Pridie was beside him again.

"Get him by the other shoulder," he told him. "Carefully."

Jean-Philippe could not at first register the vicious hot blast
of the gun beside him. Amazed, he saw the sudden liquid black
spring out in the centre of the man's back under his hands.

When he had understood, he turned and half rose and chopped with all his force with the edge of his hand against Pridie's wrist. Pridie grunted and clapped his left hand to his wrist, and the pistol flew up and out in a slow arc into the water.

Jean-Philippe bent and pulled the man out of the water and began to haul him back up the steep bank. About half way up Pridie began to help him. They put the man down on the bank. People had gathered, with that brisk infallible certainty with which people of all races in any country will always gather to gaze when death has struck violently in a way that cannot possibly endanger them personally, as though this sight were an inalienable basic human privilege like the right to eat and drink and copulate. Jean-Philippe shouldered them aside and bent and turned the man over on to his back. The man's eyes came open a moment and he looked up at him, puzzled, and he died. His face looked unmarked and very young.

Kneeling, Jean-Philippe continued to look down at him for some time. After a while he realized that the tears were streaming shamelessly down his cheeks. There was no sense to that. Technically the man was an enemy; besides, he did not even know him. But the man had known him. If it was as if, because of that, the man had had some deep claim on him, which he had in some manner betrayed. Perhaps it was even excusable to think in these simple ageless terms of the blood here, for it was difficult indeed to read the imperatives of great warring ideologies into this quiet face.

Jean-Philippe looked up at Pridie, and said:

"Why did you shoot again, you murdering bastard? You had no need to shoot again."

Pridie did not say anything. He stood and looked down at Jean-Philippe with the most complete hatred. He swung suddenly on his heel and walked away.

Jean-Philippe got up slowly. He took his handkerchief from his pocket with the tips of his fingers and began to wipe the man's blood off his hands. The Lao about him were talking incessantly now, in high chattering tones, looking down at the dead man as though he were some great strange white fish hauled up out of the black waters. Jean-Philippe walked to the edge of the bank and looked out across the river. A boat of some kind was going slowly downstream, far out, near the Thai bank. It was already almost invisible in the dusk, behind the brave faint yellow light in its bows.

CHAPTER XXV

THE white D.C.3 with the yellow nose and the royal emblem on the fuselage, three superimposed white elephants, one head facing outwards, one to each side, on a deep red background, taxied slowly to a stop in front of the military hangars at Wattai. Five Beaver aircraft and three Harvards were lined proudly up behind it at the edge of the hard standing, pointing out across the airfield. Their Royal Army markings were freshly painted. A gift from the U.S., they had been fitted with rockets for use against Konglé's men holed up in their mountains. The Americans would find within three weeks that the Royal Army had no pilots left who would fly them; Konglé's men would be shooting them out of the sky like ducks with light quick-firing Russian anti-aircraft guns.

There was a Royal Army colour company drawn up smartly at the right end of the hard standing, towards which the King's D.C.3 pointed. A clutch of senior bonzes faced inwards from the far edge of the rectangle, the light air gently rippling their saffron robes. The ambassadors of the countries which had recognized the new government (Abramov was not there; he had left Vientiane just after the fighting had ended) faced in on the D.C.3 from the near side. The Japanese Ambassador, elderly and bespectacled and gentle-faced, stood at their head with the American Ambassador. Next in this near line were the heads of Boun Oum's and Nosavan's new administration, in white linen suits. Finally, there was a welcoming band, with *khènes* and xylophones and gongs and drums, and, to its left, a line of the senior Lao women of the community, half-sitting, half-kneeling.

The women were in full dress too. They wore their long ceremonial Lao skirts, the hems heavily woven with gold, and gold or silver Lao belts, and wide gold-embroidered Lao scarves over their left shoulders. Their lustrous black hair swept straight up and back from their smooth foreheads.

There were wide silver bowls in front of them. These were chased with the motifs of their culture, the gods and goddesses and heroes and heroines of their mythology, always incredibly slim and thin-waisted, some many-armed, the goddesses and heroines wearing those concentric narrowing needle-pointed crowns which echoed the upward-sweeping curves of the eaves of their

243

temples. On the bowls, these ideal graceful figures spurned eternally under their feet the demons and the magic beasts, the lions with the heads of eagles, the tigers whose curling tails ended in flame, the half-men half-beasts, and the ageless carnal snake. Whirls and spirals and arabesques bound all these figures indiscriminately, the good and the evil, like the lianas of the lush unchanging jungles, locked in their perpetual exuberant re-creation. In these silver bowls the Lao women had placed their offerings of fruits and sweetmeats and great crimson-petalled flowers, in their traditional welcome to their King.

Jean-Philippe stood behind the women, against a hangar door, and their soft high lilting voices lapped him. He knew that he would miss that sound.

He looked across at the heads of the Western missions. They, with a few others interested *farangs*, were standing appropriately a little back from their ambassadors, and craning forward now as the screws of the halted D.C.3 slowed and stopped, and two men went to its side with a short white gangway. Almost all of the watchers were Americans. They had the pleased air of schoolboys about to receive a deserved treat. There were few French present. The new administration had already started to get rid of the French counsellors at the ministries and departments, no doubt because of the dangerously liberal tendencies inherent in their culture, and to replace them by Americans. For the moment, the Americans were certainly the favoured child of history here.

Jean-Philippe wondered what image they would finally leave of themselves in this small country. He knew that you had to be a little careful of history. It could sometimes fix you in the most ludicrous of postures, arbitrarily and for all time. The Dutch merchants and soldiers of fortune who had come to the King of Siam's court in the eighteenth century, for example, were now historically immortalized in porous and discoloured stone as the guardians at the gates of the Bangkok wats, prosperously paunched and splendid in frock coats and tall top hats.

He could see Rolfe, the disguised general in charge of the P.E.O., among the watching Westerners, and, inevitably, Pridie. Jean-Philippe had seen Rolfe just after he had parked his *Deux Chevaux* (it was the last day that he would have it; that night he had to give it over to its buyer) and walked up to the reception area. Rolfe had greeted him with his usual friendliness. He had seemed blithely ignorant of Jean-Philippe's imminent expulsion, or of the fact that this would be the last official function that he would cover for his paper in Laos. Rolfe was a tall muscular man, transparently likeable, dedicated and efficient. He had close-cropped hair, absolutely white, and a boyish face. He had been one of the youngest American infantry-division generals in Germany. Jean-Philippe had said to him:

"How's your friend Konglé?"

Rolfe had smiled at him.

"Elusive," he said. "Still up in his mountains. And fighting like a cat."

"Well, well."

"But we'll get the little bastard yet," said Rolfe.

He sounded like a determined football-coach.

"When, John?" said Jean-Philippe.

Rolfe glanced about him cautiously.

"Christ," he said. "Just give me a couple of companies. Say two Marine companies. I could fix it. I can't get these goddamned local generals off their fat asses, you see."

"It's the climate," said Jean-Philippe.

"Maybe," said Rolfe. "You see, they have this goddamned obsession about victory parades."

The D.C.3's door had opened now and the King came down the short white gangway. The senior members of the new administration had broken across the hollow square to stand in a line at right angles to the aircraft. Sommith was the first of them. He knelt and bowed over the King's hand. The King was wearing a white uniform, with medals on his left breast, and a white-topped cap with a dark peak heavily braided with gold. Boun Oum and Nosavan followed him out of the D.C.3 similarly attired. They looked like a trio of visiting admirals.

The King went slowly past his new heads of administration and they bowed over his hand and prayed at him. The Lao band in front and to Jean-Philippe's right had struck up a high wailing tune as the King stepped on to the gangway. This gave way to the loud gusto of the small military brass band as Boun Oum and Nosavan conducted the King to the colour company. Their colonel saluted and about turned and barked his orders and the three ranks presented arms. The King and Boun Oum and Nosavan went diligently through the ranks in inspection and arrived at the diplomatic corps. The King smiled and shook hands with each of the ambassadors. Boun Oum followed him chubbily. He had swept off his braided cap, revealing his theatrical thick iron-grey hair. Nosavan came correctly behind him, shorter, barrel-bodied, apparently neckless.

The King moved past the remaining heads of his new administration and the Lao band and came to the first of the kneeling women. He had a wide, placid face. He looked regal, gracious, and pleased.

Jean-Philippe supposed that he could afford to. The old order and traditions had been re-established, anyway for the moment. For there was certainly not going to be anything violently revolutionary about this heavily bemedalled assembly of acute right wing gentlemen. A hoary old tribal chieftain like Boun Oum was not going to tolerate any nonsense about the volatile demands of a developing world. Laos could go on being its own static bubble-universe, hermetically sealed. All this explosive modern stuff could go back decently out of sight again, under the old familiar and beloved surface of customs and legend and divine right and langour and rich colour and grace. It would have been hard to blame the King for this result. He had not had the really decisive hand in shaping it. Constitutionally that was not his job. But, being as he was, it was hardly surprising that he looked rather pleased about it.

The little old ladies knelt very low before him, proffering him their gifts. Occasionally he stopped and picked one up and admired it and returned it graciously to its silver bowl. One he held for some time. It was an exquisite forest orchard, with wide reaching petals of a deep and savage crimson that was almost black. As he put back this blood-black flower, and reached the end of the line, and turned, the King's eyes flicked idly over Jean-Philippe, standing back against his hangar door, on his own.

Jean-Philippe had not really noticed it. He had thought suddenly that he would not see Jeanette again, or only once, before he left Laos finally the next day. The shock of the thought surprised him, and he was conscious of a great sense of waste. You did not really have so much time in life. In all your life, you could perhaps know five or six people deeply. Each time, even if the thing started lightly, or for another motive, the investment was great.

It was not the only loss. That of the man whom Pridie had killed seemed more grave and permanent. It was not a loss which in time the emotions would cover naturally, as blood regenerates itself. He could not ever see that man again, at another time, in a far country. And it still concerned him profoundly that he could not place him. The man had had the advantage of him, for he had certainly known him, Jean-Philippe. It must have been somewhere in France, for he had called him *mon lieutenant*, and Jean-Philippe had already been a captain when he came to Indo-China in 1946. It must have been somewhere in that other war, in those far days which by comparison had been (or so at least now it

246

seemed) strong and young and confident, when the enemy had been as simply and irrevocably defined as one in an epic poem. He must have been one of the Vietnamese who had fought for France. Afterwards he had been sucked back into the mainstream of his own people, loyal as he saw it to the dictates of his blood and of his people's developing history. He had been lost to France and the West, and so much of this city's youth had now been lost, who had followed Konglé in the fighting, and into the mountains after that fighting.

Why had it been he who died? Practically, perhaps, because he had not been ruthless enough, or consistent enough. He could easily have killed Pridie at once in the house, and got away, though then he would certainly have wounded or killed Jean-Philippe in the process. Was that the moral, that to survive you simply needed to be ruthless and consistent enough? Jean-Philippe knew that you always sought a moral. You had to impose something on the flooding welter of experience, if only to defend yourself from the final nihilism of absurdity. But was that the moral? That, as ineluctably as the application of any law of pure mathematics, these two towering anxious giants, the Americans and the communists, must always now define themselves with increasing rigidity into that deadly final posture of attack, so that they could not possibly, even with the best will in the world, leave any middle ground? So that there could be no room left for the purely human reaction, for the errors of identity? So that it was always the poor inconsistent human bastard in the middle whom the system had inevitably to single out and destroy?

Boun Oum and Nosavan were conducting the King slowly across to the entrance road now. When they passed the groups of heads of Western missions, they stopped, and Nosavan murmured introductions. Pridie was standing next to Rolfe. Pridie was wearing an elegant pearl-grey suit. There was a red carnation in his left buttonhole and the white silk handkerchief was precise in his breast pocket. Nosavan said something to the King, and the King nodded and turned to the two men and smiled and bowed very slightly. Rolfe and Pridie bowed at once in return, and the King walked on towards his beflagged limousine.

Jean-Philippe could see the two men looking after the King and talking. He thought that ten to one Pridie would be remarking on how you could always tell true aristocracy the moment you saw it. Rolfe was looking definitely impressed. No doubt Pridie was also implying to him (probably quite truthfully) that this was not quite the first time that a crowned head had nodded to him.

Jean-Philippe began to walk towards the entrance road. His obsolete Deux Chevaux was parked discreetly out of sight behind the hangar, overwhelmed by the black Mercedes-Benz and the big gleaming American saloons. As he passed them he saw that Pridie was still busy delivering his line to the general. Jean-Philippe smiled to himself as he walked on. He supposed that that was fair enough. After all, it was Pridie's day.

HISTORICAL NOTE

LAOS has been described as a large country with few people and fewer Lao. About as big as the U.K., it has a million Lao and a million from thirty other racial groups. It is a frontier country, a thousand kilometres long, totally enclosed by Burma, China, North and South Viet Nam, Cambodia, and Thailand. Its characteristics are mountains, savage in the north, gradual in the south, and plateaux, and jungle, and the great Mekong River which runs through it like the spine of a leaf. This river is the true signature of the Lao, almost all of whom live on its fertile banks, or on those of its many west-flowing tributaries, their lives governed by its waters' rhythms. In Laos, you do not locate a racial group by area, but by altitude; the Lao in the river valleys and plains, the Khâ above eight hundred metres, and the Meo on the mountain tops. Laos produces rice, lacquer, teak, a little tin and silver, and a dark red gold.

It has always been a cockpit of wars and cultures. The bronze instruments and burial urns in its Plain of Jars, about Xieng Khouang, suggest a developed Bronze Age civilization. Its first peoples were probably Indonesian. Through time, Cham, Khmer, Thai, and Yunnanese lapped over them. By 1358, as Lang Xang, the land of a million elephants, it included the Shan States of Burma and Siam east of Korat, beyond its present area. It was securely Buddhist, of the Celanese kind, gentler than that which had reached into China and what is now Viet Nam, but with strong residues of primitive animism.

Despite its violent history, its people remained gay and gracious, quite innocent of grey Western notions of identity and guilt. In 1642 the Jesuit de Marini, though he had no luck in converting them, found the Lao docile and sincere and hospitable. The West's commercial interest in Laos just prefaced its spiritual. In 1641 van Wusthoff of the Dutch East India Company, seeking a permanent supply of Benzoin and Musk and Stick-lac, reached the capital, Vientiane, with a nicely calculated set of gifts for King Souligna Vongsa. The King suggested tactfully that he improve his calculations. He did. He was rewarded by a full-dress court ceremony; the panoply of the King's army, splendidly mounted on horses and elephants, reminded him of the Prince of Orange's. That night two hundred sampans, entirely filled with lighted candles, were left to drift past the capital; van Wusthoff says, with a rare burst of poetry, that it was as if the whole great Mekong were afire. Only one custom of this people depressed this sober Dutchman. He also records how hard it was to take his usual evening stroll after another feast "due to the horrible fornications which were being committed on all sides."

From its heights under this King the power of the land declined, riven by wars of succession. By 1713 it was three kingdoms, Luang Prabang in the north, answering to China, Vientiane in the centre, vassal of Annam, and Champassac in the south, linked with Siam. When the French intervened in 1893 all that remained of Laos was the small state of Luang Prabang, its capital city of that name constantly pillaged by Ho *Pavillon Noir* pirates from the Yunnan. Burma, Siam, and Cambodia had eaten up the rest, emptying the cities like a plague, leaving their pagodas crumbling, strangled by the prompt returning jungle.

France's interest at that time was to halt the eastward march of British power from Siam. A French treaty with Siam in 1893 recognized French authority east of the Mekong. A convention with the British the next year entrenched it. The French set Resident Governors in Laos' provinces, admitting Sisavang Vong of Luang Prabang alone as King. Remote, land-locked, with far fewer obvious natural resources than Annam or Cochin-China, Laos changed hardly at all.

Even the Japanese invasion of 1940 changed little, except that the Vichy French administration, whom the Japanese left in place, ceded the right-bank Lao provinces of Sayaboury and Bassac to Siam under Siamese and Japanese pressure. On March 9, 1945, the war's issue in Europe already decided, and Vichy France no longer existing, the Japanese imprisoned or killed all French in Indo-China. The Lao then sided generally with the French, some fighting bravely as guerrillas against the Japanese, until Japan capitulated in September.

But by then Prince Petsarath, Vice-Regent to Sisavang Vong, had already formed a strong independence movement, the Lao Issara, or Free Laos, rigidly opposed to any return to colonial rule. When the French came back to Laos in force in April 1946 the Lao Issara leaders fled to Bangkok. There, under Petsarath, they broke into two wings. One was led by Prince Souvanna Phouma, Petsarath's younger brother, liberal and sophisticated, and a brilliant engineering and architectural graduate of Paris and Grenoble. The other was led by Prince Souvannouvong, Souvanna Phouma's half-brother, also a French engineering graduate, by nature colder, more drastic in his political thinking.

France seemed more alert to the winds of change in Laos than she was in her other Indochinese colonies. She unified it under King Sisavang Vong in August 1946, negotiated Thailand's return of the two right-bank provinces in December, proclaimed a liberal constitution in May 1947, and gave Laos independence within the French Union in July 1949. In October that year Souvanna Phouma and the other moderates dissolved the Lao Issara, considering that it had now lost its reason for existing, and returned to Laos.

Petsarath and Souvannouvong remained in exile; Petsarath because, now old, he saw that history had passed him and his movement by. Souvannouvong's split with Souvanna Phouma and the other moderates was already decisive. In 1946 Souvannouvong had visited Ho Chi Minh in Hanoi. It was the start of his ideological identification with the left wing revolution. When the moderates returned to Laos in 1950 Souvannouvong went to Burma and North Laos. He formed his Pathet Lao Resistance Movement that year, and directed its guerrilla units against the French and the Royal Lao Army until 1957.

Save for Souvannouvong and his Pathet Lao insurgents Laos was almost untouched by France's bitter war with the Viet Minh from 1946 to the final Viet Minh victory at Dien Bien Phu in 1954, though Viet Minh units twice invaded North Laos in 1953. They left a strong Pathet Lao organization behind them, particularly in the two north-eastern provinces of Sam Neua and Phong Saly. The 1954 Geneva Agreements still left Pathet Lao power strong there. It grew farther and fast, aided by a certain governmental reputation for mismanagement during Laos's first few years of complete independence. In 1957 Souvanna Phouma, then Lao Premier, made a great bid to unify the country by including his half-brother in his cabinet and integrating the two north-eastern provinces and their Pathet Lao administration and forces into the nation. Right wing pressure broke Souvanna Phouma's coalition government a year later.

New actors had appeared in Laos, as they had in Cambodia and South Viet Nam, after the French eclipse at Dien Bien Phu. They had already helped rebuild Western Europe. They believed that their continued mission was to preserve these remoter lands as a bulwark against communism. These new actors were the Americans.

Caracas, September 1963.